The Theatre of the Silver Dragon

The Theatre of the Silver Dragon

Founded by Tamela Glenn

1996-2003

INTRODUCTION

Tamela Glenn founded the *Theatre of the Silver Dragon* in 1996. It operated until 2003 in Orono, ME at the Keith Anderson Community Center. The theatre was unique: the plays performed were written by Tamela for children. The goal was to provide children with parts that challenged them but also allowed them to shine. Tamela would ask the children what character they would like to play and then go home and write a play around the characters. While definite limits were set on allowable behavior, the atmosphere in rehearsal was supportive and encouraging. What mattered most was that the children tried their best and that they respected their fellow actors. Each play was about ensemble acting and not a "star system." When children were given the freedom to experiment with their roles in such an environment the results were remarkable – and entertaining.

Not only did Tamela found the theatre, she wrote all the plays, was the artistic director, the set designer and costumer. It was a one-woman endeavor with the emotional support of her husband, Jim Wohlgemuth, who did the lightning. It was low budget. Costumes came from thrift stores and from Tam's sewing machine. The whole emphasis was children and helping them grow. Tamela loved them and they loved her. It was a place where children felt save. The parents were very supportive. Many contributed to the endeavor.

In writing the plays, Tamela drew on her studies and background experiences in art, philosophy, music and theater. The plays were written quickly and revised during rehearsals. Tamela's untimely death prevented her from publishing the plays during her lifetime, so I am putting them in the public domain because that is what I believe Tamela would have wanted. The *Theatre of the Silver Dragon* was a Work of Heart.

The plays are published in two volumes. Book One, *Tamela Glenn: Thirteen Original Plays*, contains the earlier plays written for young children. As the children matured and their interests changed, Tamela changed with them. Book Two, *Tamela Glenn: Nine Original Plays*, contains plays written for teenagers.

.. Betty Glenn

Tamela Glenn, director of *Theatre of the Silver Dragon*, worked with teen actors in the play Borderline. The play addresses the difficult issues surrounding mental illness, the people involved and the doctors who treat them.

Table of Contents and Synopsis

Mother Nature, unhappy with the direction civilization is trending, and with the help of Father Time, sends Time Travelers on a journey into the Past. At each destination they are to find some symbol that might help save civilization from destruction.

While plots abound in the kingdom of Spam, this play with any other name would be a farce.

A mysterious package. The wife of the President of the United States & missing government documents. Her daughter's missing toy poodle. Does mutt + paper = 2?

At the School for Sorcery, things get out of hand when the new sorceress enters; but Zanzibar has a plan to help his students resolve their own problems ...

A look at the tragedy and dilemma surrounding a coma patient, the helplessness of the attending doctor who cannot answer the unknowable questions and the despair of the loved ones who can only wait and hope. Does the coma patient have dreamlike visions in her journey back to reality?

THE TRUTH WILL OUT ... Shakespeare

Welcome to Cliqueville, what price will you pay to fit in?

At the end of 1999 computers all over the world had to be reset. This turn of the century crisis had programming experts scrambling, while another hysterical group prepared for an end of time apocalypse. And the clock was ticking down ...

"I created these characters as disorders,' says Glenn. "And they have grown into people." Then, with a gentle wave of humor: "Now I'd like to re-diagnose some of them."

Photographs, note about Tamela

THE THEATRE OF THE SILVER DRAGON

presents

IT'S ALL ABOUT BEING IN THE RIGHT TIME AND PLACE

by
Tamela Glenn

Mother Nature, unhappy with the direction civilization is trending-and with the help of Father Time- sends Time Travelers on a journey into the Past. At each destination they are to find some symbol that might help save civilization from destruction.

THE THEATRE OF THE SILVER DRAGON presents:

IT'S ALL ABOUT BEING IN THE RIGHT TIME AND PLACE

CAST

MOTHER NATURE..........
JULIET.................
TONY...................
DOC MARTIN.............
BEATRICE...............
DELILAH LAROCHE........

FATHER TIME.......special guest:

The PRESENT

MABEL..................
HENRY..................
VERA...................
THUG...................
ALICE..................
TANYA..................
REP #1.................
REP #2.................

ICE STORM

SUSAN..................
JEFF...................
MOM....................
DAD....................
CALLER.................
D.J....................
FRED...................

THE GOLD RUSH

BETTY..................
ANNIE..................
FATHER DAN.............
MEG....................
JANE...................
MARY JO................
"GOLD".................
MICHELLE...............
SARAH..................

WORLD WAR II

FATHER.................
MOTHER.................
ELIOT..................
CINDY..................
RADIO ANNOUNCER........
WOMAN with the BROOM...

THE GREAT AMERICAN POETRY WAR OF 1968

MARCIA.................
CAT....................
SONNY BONO.............
CHER...................
FLOWER.................
SKY....................
FAYE...................
TRIGGER................
RAIN...................
DOVE...................
LIBRA..................
FELICIA................
ROVER..................
COYOTE.................
GUITAR PLAYER..........
MARCIA'S FRIEND........
GIRL with SIGN.........
Guy Afraid of BOMB.....

SIRENIA

TREE DANCERS...........

" A PLAGUE ON BOTH YOUR HOUSES "

KENNETH................
ELIZABETH..............
MARGARET...............
DR. SAMUEL.............
Wm. SHAKESPEARE........
★ the Patient

THE LABYRINTH

THE ATTENDANT..........
WOMAN with HOURGLASS...
FLIP...................
FLOP...................
MONA LISA..............
Voice of ALBERT EINSTEIN...
SNAKE VOICE............
SNAKE BODY.............

"It's All About Being in the Right Time and Place: Written
Directed, & Costumed by : Tamela Glenn: 1998.

THE SIREN SONG

MOTHER NATURE: Come lay down your head
Fall down in sleep
I see you are weary.
Time passes so slow
Oh, now, I know
I know you need sleep

Sleep, sleep down so deep
Sink down so far
That you are falling
Down, but never a ground
Freely fall on
On until morning

Come lay down your head
Lay down your fears
I know you are weary
Times passes so fast
Oh, now at last
Let go and sleep

Sleep, sleep down so deep
Sink down so far
That you are falling
Down, but never a ground
Freely fall on
Until the dawning

(Keep Repeating)

@1998: Tamela Glenn

ACT I SC i
(Enter Mother Nature. She looks out over the audience.)

M.N: My, my, I do look radiant today! I'm all blue skies and sunshine. 78 degrees fahrenheit. All systems go. No storms on the horizon.

(Enter Mabel and Henry.)

MABEL: Wait up Henry! My varicose veins are killing me! Hey! Hey! (She whistles. Henry who is nearly deaf, finally stops trudging along and turns to her.)

HENRY: What is it Maybell?

MABEL: (loud, so he'll hear) MY VEINS!

HENRY: YOUR PAINS?

MABEL: VEINS! They're killing me!

HENRY: What else is new?

MABEL: We are going to sit down now.

HENRY: HUH?

MABEL: SIDDOWN!

HENRY: I'm going to my Bingo game.

MABEL: I have the money. WE ARE SITTING DOWN!

HENRY: (sigh) We are sitting down. As usual. (They sit)

MABEL: (Takes out a bag of chips.) Here, Hen, have a snack-a-roonie.

HENRY: WHAT?

MABEL: EAT!!

HENRY: All right. I heard you the first time, you old bat.

MABEL: Whadidyou just say?

HENRY: LOOK AT THAT!

(Enter Juliet with her friends Alice and Tanya followed by Tony)

(Tony sees a flower and picks it. M.N. **gasps**)

M.N. Barbarian!

TONY: Hey, Jules, wait up!

JULIET: Terrific.

ALICE: Here comes your Romeo.

TANYA: Every girl should have one.

JULIET: You're welcome to him, my so-called friends.

TONY: Hey, Juliet I got this flower for you. What do you think?

Juliet: As if. (She tosses the flower)

M.N. Ingrate!

ALICE: Loser.

TONY: But, Jules!

JULIET: Scram.

TONY: Hey, come on give a guy a--

TANYA: She said beat it. (Tony walks off. Girls go off and talk. They all exit.)

(Enter Scientist and Doctor. They are talking as they walk on)

SCIENTIST: My latest research proves that in another ten years, we'll be able to extend the human lifespan by 40 percent!

M.N.: Terrific. The forecast is for storms.

DOCTOR: 40 percent? What will the <u>quality</u> of life be like.[7]

SCIENTIST: 115 year old men will be out playing tennis.

M.N.: What about women?

DOCTOR: So you will be able to slow bone lose and--

SCIENTIST: The whole enchilada. No more clogged arteries. No more heart attacks. Or at least not until a hundred.

DOCTOR: So no more dropping dead at forty?

SCIENTIST: In all probability.

DOCTOR: What about people who smoke, eat a high fat diet, etc.?

1998
James glenn

2

SCIENTIST: I think we need to make all of that illegal.

M.N.: Forecast is for a monsoon.

(A woman who has been listening walks up)

VERA: But that's taking away freedom of choice.

DOCTOR: She's got a point.

SCIENTIST: Some people don't have the sense to make the right choices.

VERA: Nazi! Fascist!

SCIENTIST: Now hold on there. (Enter a thug. He runs up to the Scientist.)

THUG: Give me all your money. Now!

SCIENTIST: Why on earth would I do that?

THUG: Because I told you to, and if you don't I'm gonna plug ya.

SCIENTIST: Good reason. (Starts to give him the money)

VERA: You're just going to give in to terrorist demands?

THUG: Shut up, whoever you are!

VERA: My name is Vera. And you can bloody well shut up, punk.

THUG: I don't have time for this. (He shoots her in the foot.)

VERA: (howling) Someone call an ambulance!

SCIENTIST: Here, take this money. Now beat it!

THUG: (to Vera) Sorry.

VERA: You insectoid lifeform!

SCIENTIST: You're a doctor. Help this woman.

DOCTOR: I'd like to, I really would, but she's a high strung nut case. She's likely to sue. I can't afford to help her.

M.N.: Heartless beast!

SCIENTIST: Can't afford to ?

DOCTOR: You do lab research. Population studies. Get all

those forms signed saying; In the event of X, I will not sue you. Do you have the slightest idea how much malpractice insurance costs? Do you know what they will and will not cover?

SCIENTIST: No.

DOCTOR: Well, they won't cover <u>her</u>.

VERA: Listen you rats, while you're chatting about the pros and cons, I'm in serious pain here. Can't you do anything for me, man?

DOCTOR: I can get you a cab. My friend here will have to help you into it. <u>I'm</u> a Doctor.

VERA: So, I've heard.

DOCTOR: You could sue me because I put you into the cab wrong. But, my friend is not a doctor. You can't touch him.

VERA: Fine, fine. Let's go. (They exit)

MABEL: Gee. That was betta than the T.V.

HENRY: WHAT?

MABEL: BETTA THAN TELEVISION!

HENRY: The only way you'll get better vision is if you get your cataracts removed.

(Enter Delila Laroche with reporters)

REPORTER #1: Is it true, Ms. Laroche, that you plan to turn a substantial amount of the rainforest into a Fun Park?

DELILA: Well-

REPORTER #2: I heard it was going to be a casino.

DELILA: Well, actually, it's both!

MOTHER NATURE: The forecast is for gobal meltdown!

REP. #1: Give us the scoop Delila!

DELILA: Well. . .

REP. #2: Pretty please with sugar on top!

M.N.: I'm going to be sick.

DELILA: It's all about Fun, really.

c. 1998

REP. #1: What about global warming?

DELILA: What about it?

REP. #2: What do you have to say to the people that think your idea is a real stinker and will destroy the ecological balance of the entire Earth.

DELILA: What do I, Delila Laroche have to say to them?

REPS: Yes!

DELILA: Fiddle-dee-dee.

REP. #1: Can I quote you on that?

DELILA: By all means.

REP. #2: (writing) "Fiddle. Dee. Dee"

DELILA: I mean, really, that's just a fairy tale. None of it's been proven.

MABEL: What about skin cancer? My Henry had ta have one of them Melanomas removed last year.

DELILA: I don't know anything about that, but I **am** sure that I had nothing to do with it.

M.N. Yet.

DELILA: Now, if you will all excuse me, I have to return to the set of my new movie: Total Burnout. (She exits the reporters run after her)

HENRY: Maybell?! Who was that woman? I'm leaving. I'm going to my bingo party! (He gets up and she follows)

MABEL: What an attractive, yet totally rude young woman.

(they exit)

M.N.: (coming center stage) That's it! I've had it! I'm going to teach them a lesson they will **never** forget.

FATHER TIME: (clears throat) Excuse me, dear, but before you run off in a frenzy, don't you think you should discuss this with me?

M.N.: Did you hear all that? The world is full of no good punks and creeps!

F. T: You think so?

M.N.: Everyone of them is hideous! And that last one— That

5

©1998 Tom SC

actress! What Slime!

F.T.: What do you have on your mind?

M.N.: It's Schooltime, and I have a few lessons to teach!

F.T.: A global flood?

M.N.: Nope.

F.T.: Fire and plague?

M.N.: We're way past all that now.

F.T.: So?

M.N.: I'm going to send them back!

F.T: To the factory?

M.N.: What a swell idea. No, in time.

F.T.: Then you need my help. And my permission.

M.N.: True.

F.T. Are you going to try to send all of them back? I'm not
sure I can spare the-uh-time for that.

M.N.: No. I'll send some of these people--the ones who were
here today being hideous.

F.T.: And the point of the journey?

M.N.: To give them a healthy respect for Mother Nature. And
Father Time, of course.

F.T.: Of course. Can I quote you on that?

M.N.: I always keep my word.

F.T.: True.

M.N. But I'd like to send a few sideways, just to spice up
the mix. Can you manage that?

F.T.: Of course. The ninth dimension awaits them.

M.N.: You really are a sweetheart.

F.T.: As long as there's a point. A direction.

M.N.: I'll call them back now. (THUNDER)

(Everyone from the scene rushes back on.)

M.N.: All right, you bums, listen up and listen good.

DOCTOR MARTIN: Just who are you and why should I listen to you? I have a plane to catch.

M.N.: Shut up. (THUNDER) I am a global terrorist! If you (points) and you and you and you and you don't come here and prepare to be sent back in time--I will annihilate every human life form on this planet!

SCIENTIST: So we have a choice?

M.N.: No.

DOCTOR: Then why ask?

M.NATURE: (THUNDER) Now, you (pointing at the chosen time travellers) are going back in time. In each age you have to get a symbol and bring it back. Otherwise, it's megadeath---for you and the rest of the human race.

JULIET: She's pretty intense. Listen, you don't have to keep threatening us.

M.N.: Oh, yes, I do. That's all you understand.

MABEL: What a thing to say!

M.N.: Oh, really? Tell me, Mabel--

HENRY: She knows your name!

M.N: I know everthing. Except the end. So Mabel. Would you watch the fat in your diet if a possible heart attack didn't threaten you? I doubt it! You'd all be chain smoking, TV head, couch potatoes if death wasn't threatening to take your life away from you.

SCIENTIST: Who are you anyway?

M.N.: I'm the one in control.

DOCTOR: Fine. Now, you were talking about bringing back symbols. What kind of symbols?

M.N.: You'll be briefed in the cube.

MABEL: In the what?

M.N.: The cube. (THUNDER. Everyone looks uncertain, frightened, etc. Mother Nature smiles.)

CURTAIN CLOSE

7

(Mother Nature comes out curtain center. We hear rumbling.)

CURTAIN OPEN

(T.T.'s are getting in The Cube.)

DOC: This is ridiculous. I have a baboon heart to transplant!

SCI: What does she mean: "I am a global terrorist?" She looks like a hippie/pagan lady to me.

TONY: Looks like you'll have to give me the **time** of day after all, Jules.

JULIET: Very funny, Tony. The idea of being blasted into Time in this tin can gives me the creeps. Did you put your friends up to this?

TONY: What friends?

DELILA: Listen, whoever you are. I'll be glad to pay you good money to just let me go. I am a Very Important Person. "Delilah Laroche"? Surely you've heard of me! Can't we cut a deal?

M.N.: Into the cube.(She gets in)

MABEL: This ought to be good, Henry.

HENRY: Huh?

MABEL: GONNA BE GOOD!

HENRY: Beats the heck outta bingo.

M.N.: Around, around, around they go. Where they'll stop ? Only Father Time and I know!

CURTAIN CLOSE

ACT II THE GREAT ICE STORM OF 1998: MAINE

CURTAIN OPEN

(We see a family huddled around a kerosene heater. Juliet & Scientist come out the door and watch)

SUSAN: I am so bored. Three days without power! My friend Donna across town has power. Why don't we have power?

JEFF: Because we live on **this** side of town.

SUSAN: So?

JEFF: So that's how it goes. Electricity is a strange, magical thing.

SUSAN: Get real, you dweeb.

JEFF: I am real. That's why **I'm** not bored. I embrace this situation. The now of it. It's a cosmic moment in time.

M.N.: A boy after my own heart!

SUSAN: Are you on drugs? Mom, Jeff is on drugs!

MOM: Probably just the fumes from the kerosene heater, Susy.

SUSAN: I hate it when she calls me that.

JEFF: Loosen up, Suze. Get now!

SUSAN: I **am** NOW, and now is irritatingly boring. I can't wash my hair, play my CD's. Hey, I can't even do **my homework** it's so dark all the time.

JEFF: Be the darkness.

SUSAN: Listen, you moron, this flashback Sixties, Cosmic Zen phase you're going through is driving me nuts.

JEFF: That's your trip, Suze.

SUSAN: Stop calling me "Suze"!

MOM: Will you two quit fighting? I can't hear the radio. Listen to this one. She sounds really steamed!

VOICE: I have been calling the power company for three days four times a day telling them we don't have no powah. Now how do I know they're gittin' my messages?

D.J.: They're getting your messages, Mam.

VOICE: How do you **know**? They give powah to the mall and the people in the rich part a town and to them farmers. Maybe I should get me a cow! Then they might turn my powah back on!

D.J.: Mam, it's obvious that you are very upset.

VOICE: No kidding!

D.J.: This might cheer you up.

VOICE: I doubt that. Light! Light would "cheer me up".

D.J. Well, this is like a little bit of light at the end of the tunnel. The local Chevrolet dealer is going to give a Chevy Blazer to the last customer to get power back on.

VOICE: A Blazer?

D.J.: That's right. Now, how do you feel?

VOICE: Excuse me a minute. (talking sotto voce to someone) Fred!

FRED: What is it Martha?

VOICE: Go take the "No Power" sign at the end of the drive way down.

FRED: Why?

VOICE: They're given' a Blazer to the last customer to get their power back on.

FRED: Hot diggity dog! (We hear a door slam)

D.J.: Caller, are you still there?

VOICE: Yes, and I'm feeling much better now. Thank you for listening.

D.J.: That's what we're here for. (click) She hung up. This ice storm certainly has us all on edge. Next caller. You're on the air. (Mom turn the radio off.)

MOM: If that don't beat all. Joe! How's that generator coming?

DAD: I got it almost finished. Be right in with her.

JULIET: Where are we? This is like a weird rerun of "The Beverly Hillbillies".

SCIENTIST: Well...It has to be a fairly recent time--

JULIE: Yeah, that guy's wearing Nikes.

SCIENTIST: This must be that big ice storm that hit New England and Montreal two years ago.

JULIET: Two years ago? Oh, I remember hearing about that on the news.

SCIENTIST: But is it Upstate New York, Maine or Montreal?

(Enter Dad, a "true Mainer" with homemade generator)

DAD: Her she is!

SCIENTIST: It's Maine. Absolutely. Down East, probably.

MOM: Think she'll work, Joe?

DAD: I built her just like that fella on the radio said to. Let's fire her up!

SUSAN: I'm going to my room. I'd rather freeze than be blown to smithereens. (She exits)

MOM: Have a little faith in your father, Susy.

DAD: Here she goes!

JEFF: Don't you think we should turn off the heater?

(An EXPLOSION)

DAD: Well. It's back to the drawing board.

MOM: You'll get it right this time, dear. Three times the charm!

CURTAIN CLOSE

JULIET: That was like an episode of the "Red Green Show".

SCIENTIST: The what?

JULIET: You don't get around much do you?

SCIENTIST: Around the TV? No.

JULIET: What was the point of coming here anyway? We weren't told to bring back any symbol from this time/place.

M.N.: This was just a little test. Something close to home to warm you up. Now Back to the cube.

T.T.'S: Yes, Mother. (They exit through door.)

THE GOLD RUSH/Late 1800's. U.S.A.

(Doc. Martin & Delila Laroche get out of The Cube, which exits. People come out door and "pan for gold")

Doc: I wonder where the others are.

Delila: I think this whole thing is some weird, completely tasteless bad joke, and when I find out who thought it up and put it into motion I will personally rip out their vital--

DOC: You talk a lot don't you?

DEL: Yes. If you must know, I really love the sound of my own voice.

DOC: I **didn't** need to know.

DEL: Really!

DOC: Where are we?

DEL: I am supposed to be shooting a movie! Hundreds of people are depending on me!

DOC: We are supposed to find a symbol of Charity. I'm going to start looking around.

DEL: I am supposed to be shooting a movie!

(Gunshots)

DOC: Take cover--Quick, or you'll **get** shot.

(They duck to one side. Enter two gunpersons)

BETTY: Listen, Annie, I told you to stay away from my Appaloosa stallion. You tried to steal him again last night.

ANNIE: I did no such thing.

BETTY: Did!

ANNIE: Did not!

BETTY: Annie get your gun and put some lead where your big lyin' mouth is. I'll count off. Then we'll see who's quick and who's dead.

(Enter Father Daniel)

12

FATHER DAN: Ladies! There must be some other, peaceful, way to end your quarrel.

ANNIE: She called me a liar!

FATHER DAN: Well are you?

ANNIE: Sure, but I don't need her to tell me that!

FATHER: I see.

BETTY: With all due respect, Father Dan, beat it.

FATHER: I know you're angry child, but--

BETTY: Don't call me child. Now get the lead out and leave before I have to shoot you. We've got a duel to fight here.

(He scurries off)

ANNIE: So where were we?

BETTY: I count off and then--

MEG: GOLD!!!!!

ANN & BETT: What?!

(MEG runs onstage with pan.)

MEG: I found gold!

ANNIE: Where?

MEG: In the river! Come see! (They run off and appear on floor/"in river". Doc & Delila come out of hiding.)

DELILA: Those people are insane!

DOCTOR: This is the Gold Rush.

DELILA: What?

DOC: We're in the Wild West. America. Late 1800's.

DEL: So?

DOC: Let's follow them.

DEL: (loud sigh)   (They exit. The gold panners sit onstage)

MEG: It's a miracle! All these months of work. Our supplies just about to run out and here it is--Gold!

John: Gold! Look at it shimmer and shine!

BETTY: (looking at a piece) It's the real thing all right. We should gather it all together, and put it under guard.

FATHER DAN: But first, a word of thanks.

ANNIE: Not so fast. Who made you boss of this town, Betty?

DEL: What "town"?

DOC: Shh. You'll blow our cover.

BETTY: What's the problem Annie?

MEG: She's a lying thief!

JOHN: She tried to steal your stallion. Stole some of our food. Probably try to steal the gold!

BETTY: You got thievin' on your mind, Annie?

FATHER DAN: Let's not start a gunfight, people. Annie, what's on your mind.

ANNIE: Well. I saw Mary Jo running off a few minutes ago.

MEG: Mary Jo from up the river?

ANNIE: That's the one.

BETTY: Then the word is out!

JOHN: We're in for a showdown, that's for sure.

FATHER: Surely, they will stay and keep trying where they are.

DEL: Boy are you naive.

DOC: Great.

BETTY: Who are those people?

JOHN: Spies!

ANNIE: Who in blazes are you two?

MEG: Look at their clothes!

FATHER: You must be up to sin dressing like that, young woman.

DEL: I'll have you know that this is an Adolpho Romeo creation! It cost--

DOC: Will you just shut your mouth before they shoot us. Please. (She glares at him) We aren't interested in your gold, I assure you. In fact, we were just passing through. Actually, we're lost. Sorry to bother you. We'll be leaving Now.

BETTY: Oh, no you won't! I say we hang 'em high!

DEL: Hang? (Shriek)

(Suddenly the clammor of approaching people)

ANNIE: We'll have to deal with them later. Here comes Mary Jo and her gang!

MEG: Everybody guard your gold and get ready to fight.

       (A gunfight starts. Doc & Del. duck to one side)

DEL: What's wrong with you? Why didn't you tell them who we are and what we need so we can get out of here?

DOC: Somehow, I don't think they would understand, and anyway I don't like to get involved in other people's disagreements. It leads to lawsuits and other kinds of trouble. Complications.

DEL: Well, I don't see that we have a choice.

MARY JO: Give us that gold!

MIKE: We need it! We're out of food!

MEG: Liar!

MARY JO: Give me that gold!

EVERYONE: Give us gold! Gold! Gold! Gold!

(Annie is sneaking around collecting the gold. She starts to run off)

JOHN: Annie's got the gold!

MIKE: Shoot her! Thief!

BETTY: Annie! I never thought you'd **really** sell us out!

(Betty runs after Annie)

FATHER: Stop this madness!

(He gets shot. Annie gets away.)

BETTY: After her!

MEG: But Father Dan (She runs to him) He's dead!

Mary Jo: Let's get her!

(They all run off. Except Meg and John)

MEG: (crying) They shot Father Dan. He was only trying to make peace.

JOHN: We've all lost our wits.

DOC: It's gold fever.

MEG: What?

DOC: A psychological state--a frenzy.

John: Psycho-co logic? What are you talking about, mister?

DEL: He's a Doctor.

MEG: You must be a foreigner.

DOC: Yes. That's it. We are both foreigners.

JOHN: Well, could you take a look at Father Daniel?

DOC: You said he was dead.

MEG: It's always best to have a doctor make it official.

DOC: I suppose the idea of suing hasn't occurred to them yet.

MEG: What?

DEL: He's afraid that you'll try to blame the death on him and charge him a lot of money.

JOHN: What an idea! We just shoot people when they do something really bad, and anyways, we know the Doc didn't shoot Father Dan. Why you don't even have a gun!

MEG: Please take a look at him.

DOC: Very well.

DEL: About time you got your hands dirty.

MEG: Are you saying we ain't clean?

DEL: No. I was--uh. I should just be quiet now.

DOC: Good idea. (Examines Father.) I'm sorry, but he is dead.

MEG: God rest his soul.

JOHN: Thank you, Doc.

DOC: Tell me, how come you didn't run after the others?

DEL: Yes, don't you need that gold?

MEG: I'm starting to wonder what we **really** need!

JOHN: It was exciting at first. Go West. Get rich. Now it's a fight for survival.

MEG: A fight for everything! All we all do **is** fight. And pan for gold. And then we find gold, and does it make things better?

JOHN: Nope. (he wanders off. Sees something.) Gold! A piece of gold! I got to get back to the river! To my pan! To the gold! (He runs off)

DEL: Gold fever strikes again.

MEG: Oh, dear. What I am to do? Someone has to bury Father Dan. Will you help me? I'll just get a shovel and then--

JOHN: GOLD!

(MEG hesitates and then runs off)

DOC: I'm not a psychiatrist, but I'd say these people all seem in the grip of mania. We've got to get out of here.

DEL: What about the symbol? What can we take back as a symbol of charity?

DOC: This place is full of the opposite: greed.

DEL: **He** gave his life trying to stop the fighting.

DOC: And that one woman. I thought she was different.

(They hear someone coming and duck out of sight.)

(Enter BETTY)

BETTY: You know Father. I caught up to them and I got the gold. Annie had already gotten shot. I got a graze on my arm. But that'll heal. They're all back in the river panning for more. I'd be dead if it weren't for you Father. I can't go on like this. I'm heading back East. I'll give this gold to people that really need it. I'll try to warn people not to come here, though I'm not sure it will stop them. Now, let me give you a hand. (She drags Father off)

DEL: I wonder if they will stop coming?

DOC: Not until the rivers are panned out and all the people are starving. Then, most of the cities will become "ghost towns".

WORLD WAR II : ENGLAND & JAPAN : @1945

CURTAIN OPEN

(A British family. The sound of bombs. They duck and cover)

FATHER: All right troops. We must brace ourselves for the
next volley! Remember! Stiff upper lip, but keep your head
down. (bomb) That was a close one.

CINDY: Mother, it's bad enough being bombed. Does Daddy have
to run about acting like an idiot?

ELIOT: I think his brain pan is fried.

MOTHER: Have patience with him dears. He hasn't been the
same since they sent him home. The doctors said he's
shell-shocked.

ELIOT: That must be why he runs around with that pot on his
head. Makes him look like a bloody tortoise.

MOTHER: Don't say "bloody", dear.

FATHER: There's a war on! It's a bloody time. Bloody
awful! (bomb)

CINDY: I don't know how much more of this I can take, quite
frankly.

MOTHER: Patience dearest. "This too shall pass". (All clear
signal) Ah, there it is now: The all clear.

ELIOT: Thank heavens.

FATHER: All right troops, we have to regroup. Plan our
counterattack! I'll call headquarters. (He turns on the
radio. Tony and the Scientist come out door and watch.)

RADIO: The bombing has stopped over England. News of a cease
fire is coming in. The Germans have surrendered.

FATHER: Roger! Well, troops the word is we've licked
them. With the help of the yanks, we've brought Mr. Adolph
Hitler to his knees--that beast!

THE FAMILY CHEERS

TONY: Did it happen that fast. One minute a bomb, then the
war was over?

18

SCIENTIST: No, but it probably felt that way.

TONY: Why's that guy got a pan on his head.

SCI: Shell-shocked. People did a lot of strange things during the war. It's practical, when you think about it.

TONY: What?

SCI: The pot. It may not be a helmet, but it will protect his head. They should all be wearing one.

(RADIO STATIC)

FATHER: Troops! Gather round. A message from the front!

MOTHER: Calm down Robert, the war's over.

ELIOT: Not until the Japanese surrender, Mother.

FATHER: Smart boy. Now listen up.

RADIO: The Americans have detonated an atomic weapon. It has destroyed the city of Hiroshima. We are standing by to see if the Japanese will surrender.

CINDY: What's an atomic bomb?

MOTHER: I don't know, dear.

FATHER: Atomic bomb! They've gone and split the atom!. Must have been a tremendous blast and a lot of radiation. We're just lucky Mr. Adolph Hitler didn't get it up and running first. Hurrah for Yankee ingenuity! But why didn't we do it first?! They yanks will probably get to the moon before we do!

ELIOT: It sounds bloody awful. A bomb big enough to bring Japan to its knees?

SCI: Unfortunately not. They will hold out a few more days until they get nuked again in Nagasaki.

TONY: I guess nobody could believe it.

M.N.: Please report to the cube.

CURTAIN CLOSE

(RUMBLING)

CURTAIN OPEN

(The stage is bare except for a charred tree)

19

TONY: Where are we now? On the set of "Waiting for Godot"? This place is a wasteland.

SCI: We're in Japan. Hiroshima or Nagasaki. I say near ground zero, since there is zero here.

TONY: Here's the target. (on ground)

SCI: You're joking!

TONY: No, here. Look. (points)

SCI: This "person in charge" has a bizarre sense of humor.

TONY: What about radiation? Hey, we're toast!

SCI: No. We won't be affected.

TONY: How do you know?

SCI: We'd already be getting sick. Besides, what would be the point of sending us back just to kill us. That wasn't the agreement.

TONY: Well, maybe she's a lunatic. She said she was a "terrorist". They're not known for being very reliasle.

SCI: I don't think so. Anyway there's method to the madness. Now the big question.

TONY: The symbol.

SCI: Right.

TONY: We're supposed to bring back a symbol of life.

SCI: That makes sense. World War II was a time of so much death. Millions of Jews in concentration camps. Soldiers and civilians killed in battles. But there sure doesn't seem to be any **Life** here. We'd better look around.

TONY: Right. Hey, what's your name?

SCI: Beatrice. (They start looking around.) There's this tree. It's standing, but it's also dead.

(Tony sees a flower. He runs over to it.) Hey! Look! It's a miracle. (He almost picks it, but stops.)

SCI: What is it?

TONY: A flower.

SCI: You're hallucinating. (She walks over)

TONY: No, I'm not. See for yourself.

SCI: This is remarkable.

20

TONY: I was gonna pick it, but ...

SCI: But what?

TONY: I picked a flower for a girl once and she threw it away. And then it was just left to die, you know.

SCI: Yes, once you pick something it begins to die.

TONY: So if we pick it, then it's not a symbol of life anymore.

SCI: That's good logical thinking.

TONY: So, we're up the creek without a paddle.

SCI: But we've seen it. We know that it exists. It's in our minds. Logged into our memories.

TONY: (Bends to touch flower) "A rose by any other name"

SCI: What?

TONY: Nothing. That's supposed to be her line anyway.

SCI: Are you going balmy on me?

TONY: No, I'm just thinking about that girl.

SCI: Oh. I wonder, is memory enough?

(THUNDER)

M.N.: Yes! Be a witness.

CURTAIN CLOSE

M.N. That was the beginning of a lot of trouble. You humans
     Grew up and took the power of Nature into your own
      hands. Death and destruction has been the result.
     I have witnessed!

THE GREAT AMERICAN POETRY WAR OF 1968

M.N.: It was the best of times. It was the worst of times. It was the Summer of Love...and hate.

ALL: Heck no we won't go! Heck no we won't go! (keep chanting)

CURTAIN OPEN

(A large gathering of Sixties types. One group is chanting a protest against the Vietnam War. Marcia is getting signatures on a petition. Tony wanders on.)

TONY: Wow! The Sixites--it's gotta be. We're supposed to get a symbol of peace from this time/place. This'll be a breeze. There are peace symbols everywhere! (He goes and sits down.)

MARCIA: Sign to stop the war. (He tries to sign the petition, but the pen won't write.) Pen's outta ink. You're nowhere man.

TONY: Thanks. (Enter Sonny & Cher)

FLOWER: Ohmygoodness! It's Sonny & Cher!

SKY: This is too trippy, man! Is it really them?

ROVER: In the flesh. I am feelin' groovy!

FLOWER: Can I have your autographs?

CHER: Sure. (They sign)

MARCIA: How bourgeois!

SKY: You're one to talk. You're the signature **queen**.

MARCIA: I'm collecting signatures to stop the war, man.

ROVER: Peace, babe. (She stalks off.) What an uptight chick.

FLOWER: Would you please sing a song for everyone?

SONNY: Well.

SKY: Please!

ALL: Please!

SONNY: Gee, what nice kids.

CHER: Looks like we're singing.

(THEY LIP-SYNCH : "I got you babe".)

SKY: Thank you Sonny!

FLOWER: Thank you Cher!

ROVER: Thank you Sonny & Cher.

CHER: We gotta split now.

SONNY: Be cool. (They exit)

FLOWER: That was **so** groovy.

MARCIA: They aren't real hippies. They're just pop stars making a buck of the movement.

ROVER: What movement?

MARCIA: You burn me, man.

SKY: She's a total bringdown.

FLOWER: You said it.

(Enter CAT)

CAT: Now is the time! The time is now!

MARCIA: For what?

CAT: Peace, babe. It's time for our big battle. The Great American Poetry War of 1968. Put your mouth where your beliefs are and may the best poet win. We'll settle our differences with poems not sticks or stones. Who'd like to be in the first slam?

(Two people get up)

FAYE: All right Marcia, I've been waiting to slam your butt for many moons.

MARCIA: I could slam your hide while having my tonsils removed!

CAT: Order! Now. Faye, you're up first. Then Marcia. The crowd chooses the winner and no picking on Marcia just because you all hate her. Be objective.

FAYE: All day. Today.
      I sat with my friends.
      The park
      Got dark
      And here the tale bends
      We went home with flowers
      In our hair.
      I ate sprouts and tie-dyed the air. (applause)

CAT: Okay, Marcia. You're up.

MARCIA: Your eyes
        Two green lotus
        Wilted petal child
        My heart cries
        Napalm
        Be calm
        Grow
        Wild.

(Louder Applause)

ROVER: Man that was profound.

CAT: Marcia wins. (EVERYONE BOOS)
Okay now it's Trigger versus Rain. You're up Trig.

FLOWER: Go Trigger! I think he's a stone groove.

TRIG: Don't break my concentration, babe.

FLOWER: Sorry.

TRIG: It's cool.

      Your hair's so long you step on it
      It follows you night and day
      Hurray!
      Cut it off and I won't know ya'
      Say you will but come tomorrow
      You won't know what hit you
      A ton of chicks
      Models from the U.K. who love
      Mick Jagger.
      The streets hot

      I'm cool and you're not. (applause)

CAT
~~MAGIC~~: Okay, Rain. You're up.

          Roses are red
          Violence is blue
          Sugar makes me sick
          And so do you! (louder applause)

CAT: And the match goes to Rain.

(Applause. Enter Delila. She sees Tony.)

DELILA: What's going on here?

TONY: Some kind of poetry competition. They call it a war.

DELILA: How very Sixties of them.

TONY: This **is** the Sixties.

CAT: Now. How about you (pointing to Tony. What's your name, man?

TONY: Tony.

CAT: Great. Tony against Sky. Sky, you're up first.

SKY: You smiled
     Who cares
     I do I do
     A wedding chant
     In a graveyard
     But it ain't Halloween yet.

     Hallowed ground
     No sound
     A bomb!
     Run away.

     I stayed too late
     Stayed too late and strayed too far.

(applause)

CAT: That was deep, Sky. You're up Tone, man.

DELILA: Give it your best.

TONY: Thanks. (Juliet has entered and watches.)

    Yes, there is magic in the air!
    I wash my hair and the sun shines
    So brightly
    I am a happy bum
    And you can't bring me down, man

    So get lost
    Beat it
    Hit the road

    I'm on a groove
    I'm on the move

    You're a bringdown
    Get out of town

    I'll buy you a ticket for the next bus.

    Don't fuss.
    Just Hush.

    Now hustle your butt to the depot!

(wild applause)

CAT: That was shakin', Ton', man.
Next up Felix-- and hey, man, who's the groovy chick over
there? (He points to Delila.)

DEL: I am Delila Laroche.

CAT: All right then. We got Delila versus Felix. Felix
you're up.

FELIX: Boom Boom Baby
    It's tomb time.
    There's a war going on
    Inside my head.
    I won't sleep
    Until November
    Or until I catch my death
    of lead. (applause)

26

DEL: You call that poetry? Hah!

       Night beats
       Heart beats
       Street beats
       Dead beats
       Bums

       The bowery's finest few
       Walk the dirty concrete

       Hungry!
       I say feed us!
       Tired!
       Let us sleep!

       Deeply
       Completely
       It will all melt away

       You say you got nothing
       And nowhere to go

       Sunk so low
       Down so low
       I can't follow you
       there. (Louder applause)

CAT: Trippy. And the winner is Delila-baby.

TONY: Frankly, I'm surprised. That doesn't seem like your style.

DEL: It's from one of my movies. I played a drugged-out hippie-poet. Of course that's the future, so they'll never know!

CAT: Now for our final rounds. Nose to nose. We'll have Marcia against Tony. Rain versus Delila-baby.

DEL: I wish he would stop calling me that. How does this work anyway?

TONY: They say a line and then you try to top it. The one who can't think of a next line loses.

DEL: Terrif.

CAT: Ladies, get your motors runnin'

DEL: You have a real way with words.

CAT: Thanks babe.

27

DEL: Don't mention it.

RAIN: Stop chatting up the judge and let's get down to it!

DEL: After you, sweetie.

RAIN: Outcry

DEL: Overpopulation

RAIN: The Newspaper

DEL: Loves me

RAIN: What?

DEL: I said loves me!

RAIN: The newspaper says it loves you? What kind a poem is
that!

DEL: Rat-a-tat-tat go the guns in 'Nam

RAIN: I asked you a question!

DEL: But I will not answer.

RAIN: That's it for me, Cat. I'm out.

CAT: The match goes to Delilah-baby! (applause)
Marica and Tone-man, you're up.

MARCIA: I hate you!

TONY: Who cares?

MARCIA: No evasions

TONY: Take a hike

MARICA: In the monsoon of information

TONY: Surf the storm in your head

MARCIA: A Miracle on Haight-Ashbury Street

TONY: But nobody noticed

MARCIA: A child was born

TONY: They gave her a name

MARCIA: This is her story

TONY: Her name, "Morning glory"

MARCIA: Her fame spread like fire

28

TONY: Flies on a screen door

MARCIA: Marshmallow donuts

TONY: Event horizons

MARCIA: Dawn comes like lighting

TONY: French fries for breakfast

MARCIA: A Malibu picnic

TONY: Air-sickness hair net

MARCIA: You bum

TONY: Full of dharma

Marcia: uh, uh uh...

TONY: Nests of snake charmers
         Call glittering stars
         Down from the skies
         You despise yourself
         So you hate us all

         Go look in a mirror
         Then make that call.

(WILD APPLAUSE)

MARCIA: He cheated!

CAT: The winner is Tone-man!

MARICA: He cut me off.

FLOWER: You had dead air-space, honey.

ROVER: Yeah, fair is fair.

MARICA: I protest!

SKY: What else is new?

CAT: Quiet down, Marcia.

(JULIET goes over to Tony)

Juliet: That was really cool, Tony. I didn't know you had so
much passion inside you, dweebo.

TONY: Dweebo? You sure know how to kill a compliment.

MARCIA: Heck no we won't go! (everyone starts chanting)

DELILA: Listen you two. We need to move on. We need a peace
symbol.

29

TONY: They're all over the place. Just grab one.

JULIET: Yeah, but what do they really stand for? The people wearing them sure aren't very peaceful.

Deiliah: She's got a point.

TONY: Then what?

JULIET: I'm not sure.

(The chanting gets really LOUD)

CAT: OHMMMMMMMMMMMM!!!!!!!!! (Gradually the chanting stops.) Everyone OHMs for a while.) Thank you. Peace be with you. How about we have a little Bob Dylan sing-a-long. "Blowin in the Wind"

ALL: (Sing like Bob Dylan.)

(Clapping, and then people are talking quietly in groups.)

JULIET: What do you make of that?

DELILAH: Music soothing the savage beasts?

TONY: What is OM anyway?

JULIET: It's supposed to be the sound of the instant of the creation of the universe.

TONY: Wow! Well, it worked. Too bad we can't take it back with us.

JULIET: Why can't we? "OHMMMMM"

DELILAH: Of course. We can remember it.

M.N. Yes. Be a witness.

CURTAIN CLOSE

THE SIREN SONG

(CURTAIN OPENS on M.N. sitting on a chair. She is
singing. Trees, which are women, are in the background.
Their branches sway to the song. Tne Doctor and Tony enter
during her song. Soon followed by Delilah)

M.N.: SONG

DOC: What a haunting melody.

TONY: It's witchy.

DOC: I feel quite drawn by it.

TREE: It's the Unicorn song.

DOC: Who said that?

TONY: Said what?

DOC: Didn't you hear anything?

TONY: Nope.

DOC: I feel so sleepy. I've got to lie down. (He goes and
falls asleep at M.N.'s feet)

TONY: Hey, Doc! Are you sure it's safe to-- (He falls and
sleeps. Enter Delilah.)

DELILAH: Hey, you lazy bums! No falling asleep on the job!

(The trees move in and surround her)

Help! Get away from me!

TREES: You hurt us. We hurt you.

DELILAH: What? Hurt you? How?

TREES: The rainforest!

F.T.: All right. Cut!

(Everyone freezes)

M.N.: Is there a problem?

F.T.: I think you're getting a little carried away. You are
getting a little too into the villianess trip.

M.N.: What's a girl got to do to have a little fun these days?

F.T.: This isn't productive. You said you wanted to teach a lesson.

M.N.: I am.

F.T.: But they're alseep.

M.N.: **She** isn't. And she needs learning! She needs to gain a healthy respect for trees. As in no rainforest fun park!

F.T.: All right, but wrap this up quickly okay?.

M.N.: of course. I have their rescue all planned out.

F.T.: Good. By the way, your song is lovely.

M.N.: Thank you, dear.

(Unfreeze)

DELILAH: Help! Get off me you--you--you TREES!

TREES: ooh!!!

(ENTER JULIET)

JULIET: Hey! What's going on here? Hey lady, stop singing and back those trees off of her!

M.N.: The magic word?

JULIET: Please?

M.N.: Try again.

JULIET: NOW!

M.N.: Good girl. (She exits. The trees fade back and freeze. The men wake up)

DOC: What on earth?

JULIET: Wake up Antonio!

TONY: Huh?

DOC: The Siren song.

TONY: Hey, Jules, you saved me. That means you like me. At least a little.

JULIET: Don't get your hopes up too high, dweebo.

DELILAH: Let's get out of here! Those trees have a life of their own!

TONY: What's her problem.

JULIET: You had to be there. (They exit)

CURTAIN CLOSE

33

A PLAGUE ON BOTH YOUR HOUSES

(A Shakespearean Actor is rehearsing the part of Juliet. A sick person lies on a cot attended by a doctor. A woman is helping him.)

KENNETH: "O Romeo, Romeo! Wherefore art thou Romeo? Deny thy father and refuse thy name; or if thou wilt not, be but sworn my love, and I'll no longer be a Capulet."

(During this speech. Rumbling is heard.) Rain again I'll wager. This dreary weather! This blasted plague! I would be onstage right now doing Willy's new play if it weren't for the plague closing the theatres. Who gave that stupid decree anyway?

Elizabeth: The King.

(During the following speech. The Doctor, Scientist & Juliet enter. They speak during his pauses)

Juliet: He's reciting Shakespeare. But why's he doing the part of Juliet?

DOC: Because this is Shakespeare's day. Back then the guys did all the roles.

JULIET: Really? You know, it's dark as a dungeon in here.

DOC: They've closed the houses against the plague.

JULIET: The plague! Can we catch it?

SCI: I doubt it. The radiation didn't bother us in Japan, so I figure we are observers and somehow shielded from harm.

JULIET: I sure hope you're right.

KENNETH: Oh well, back to work. 'Tis but thy name that is my enemy. Thou art thyself, though not a Montague. What's Montague? It is nor hand, nor foot, Nor arm, nor face..." Blast! I've forgotten the next. Oh, yes: "What's in a name? That which we call a rose By any other word would smell as sweet. So Romeo would, were he not Romeo called, ..." And then what. Oh yes: " Romeo doff they name--ahh!

Who are you? Elizabeth! Look at these people. Who let them into the house? What odd apparel they have on. Are those our new costumes. I don't like them one straw.

JULIET: What's wrong with that guy on the bed?

KENNETH: "Guy"? How oddly she speaks.

ELIZABETH: He has the plague, dear. The doctor is bleeding him. We've said our prayers. All we can do is wait now.

JULIET: Bleeding him! Somebody stop him! Why one earth?

DOC: People once believed that there were substances inside sick people that needed to be bled out before they would or could recover.

JULIET: What a dweebo notion!

SCI: True, but they thought it helped.

DOC: Usually just drained the life out of them.

JULIET: That is so gross! Somebody stop that!

SCI: Juliet, we can't interfere.

KENNETH: Juliet? Did I hear you say Juliet?

JULIET: I'm Juliet.

KENNETH: Oh, no you are not! I am Juliet. I have been waiting two seasons for a leading role.

JULIET: You don't understand.

KENNETH: The very notion! Placing women on the stage.

ELIZABETH: 'Tis shameful.

JULIET: But--

KENNETH: Do they think that I am not man enough to play the part!
Will! Willy! (He storms out)

SCI: Uh oh.

JULIET: Do you think we will actually get to meet Shakespeare?

DOC: I have no idea. Let's just try to get out of here. What do we need?

SCI: A symbol of hope.

JULIET: Why are they all shut up like this? I thought you got the plague from rats.

DOC: To be precise, you get it from flea bites. The rats carry the fleas.

SCI: It was a definite mistake closing people up like this. The last thing they needed.

JULIET: How did they get rid of the plague?

SCI: A huge fire, I believe. It was an accident, but it burnt up all the rats.

DOC: Really cleaned up the town.

JULIET: Then why don't we just torch the place and give them a push towards health.

SCI: We can't interfere.

DOC: We aren't allowed to alter history. Don't you remember that hours-long briefing in the cube.

JULIET: Oh, yeah.

(Kenneth enters with Will)

WILLIAM: I have told you already; we are not putting women on stage.

KENNETH: Ask her!

WILLIAM: He says you are Juliet.

JULIET: I am.

DOC: It's her name.

WILLIAM: And it is lovely. Now, Kenneth, I am going back to work. (exits)

ELIZABETH: Can I help you?

(The Doc and Sci are looking at the sick person. SAMUEL has exited with a pan of blood.)

SCI: Oh, we were just examining your patient.

KENNETH: I personally think she was witched.

DOC: Witched?

ELIZABETH: Oh, everyone knows that two out of four cases of the plague are due to witchery.

JULIET: They're joking, right?

SAMUEL: (who has reentered the room) Not at all. Tis the most likely cause. What else would do it?

SCI: Rats.

SAMUEL: Ah, yes. The witches' familiars.

JULIET: Their what?

KENNETH: Do not pretend to be so ignorant of these matters.

SAMUEL: (to Elizabeth) These people are very queer.

ELIZABETH: Do you think they could be witches?

KENNETH: Of course!They are witches! Especially the one who calls herself Juliet. She is trying to witch me!

ELIZABETH: Sound an alarm!

DOC: Madame, please calm down. We are not witches. We are...(thinking fast)--from Norway!

SAMUEL: (sniffs them) Could be. Could be.

JULIET: Why'd he smell us?

SCI: I have no idea.

DOC: Physicians relied a lot on their noses in those days.

KENNETH: Well, what can we do for you?

JULIET: Nothing I guess.

KENNETH: Well then, I'm going back to my rehearsal. Sooner or later the theatres will open back up and I am going to be ready! (recites speeches from above.)

SAMUEL: I had better bleed her again, Elizabeth.

DOC: That's sure to finish her off.

SCI: We should do something!

DOC: Finally up close and personal for you, Beatrice? A little bit different than a lab rat isn't it?

SCI: (going to bed) Please don't.

SAMUEL: Tis all we have. Our only hope.

JULIET: Hope!

SCI: I think, perhaps, some rest may help. Please just let her alone. Please.

ELIZABETH: Do you want her death on your hands, dear?

SCI: No, I don't. So please stop bleeding her.

SAMUEL: Well, I could use a nap. Wake me if there is any change.

ELIZABETH: Of course. (She sits on bed and does needlework)

DOC: We'll never find a symbol of hope here!

JULIET: There's got to be some reason we were sent here.

SCI: (looking at Kenneth) What about that?

DOC: What?

SCI: Shakespeare. The desire to create in the face of death. That's hope.

M.N.: Yes. Be a witness!

JULIET: "Parting is such sweet sorrow"

(WILL has wandered on.)

WILL: What a good line! I must write that down at once!

(The PATIENT WAKES UP AND LOOKS AROUND)

CURTAIN CLOSE

38

THE LABYRINTH

(Rumbling. CURTAIN OPENS)

ATTENDANT: I'm sorry, but you cannot enter until all of your party has arrived. It says right here: party of five. I only count 1,2,3,4. You will have to wait. Have a seat, please. (She exits)

DELILAH: Where? There aren't any chairs.

SCI: Where could Martin be? One minute he was with us and then, gone!

TONY: Beats me.

(LOUD RUMBLE. The Doc stumbles in dressed in Sixties clothes.)

JULIET: What happened to you? We left the Sixties ages ago.

DOC: I must have flashed back. Some obnoxious woman named Marcia kept ranting wretched poetry at me. It was a nightmare. I must have been gone for hours.

SCI: Just a few minutes, actually.

DOC: Where are we now?

DELILAH: We have no idea.

JULIET: They wouldn't let us in.

ATTENDANT: (appearing) Party of five? Right this way please.

CURTAIN OPENS

FLIP: Goodbye. It was nice to have met you.

JULIET: What's his problem? (Flip walks backwards and sits in a chair.)

TONY: Now **that** is weird.

FLOP: I feel like I've known you all of my life. I will miss you so much. (Walks backwards and leans against a wall.)

DELILAH: I've had it up to here with this funhouse monkey biz. I want to go home. First a bunch of grabby trees, Now a comedy routine. You belong in a circus!

FLIP: How's the weather?

SCI: You tell me.

FLOP: My name is Flop. That is Flip (points to Flip first and self last). What's yours?

DOC: My name is Doc Martin.

FLIP: Hello. You have a dear old soul.

DOC: Hello.

FLOP: Goodbye.

SCI: We're back where we started.

(Flip and Flop start walking around backwards and doing other backward things.)

TONY: I say we split. This is a sand trap.

JULIET: Tony's right.

DOC: But which way is out?

(ENTER the Mona Lisa)

MONA: Hi!

DELILAH: I don't believe it. Actually I do. I'd believe almost anything at this point.

MONA: I'm Mona. Lisa. **The** Mona Lisa. Maybe you've heard of me. I'm famous.

TONY: You're a painting.

MONA: So? You're a person.

SCI: Do you know how we can get out of here?

MONA: No, but Albert might.

DELILAH: Well, go ask him.

JULIET: Hey, why do you smile so funny in the painting.

MONA: I'd just swallowed Leonardo's gold fish. (She exits)

(We hear an argument.)

ALBERT: (Offstage) What do you mean they want out?

MONA: They want out.

ALBERT: God does not play dice with the Universe!

40

MONA: No one is demanding that you accept that Albert.

ALBERT: Yes, they all want me to accept it!

MONA: Well, I don't. And I don't think they do. They just want out.

(MONA ENTERS)

MONA: Albert says the password is E=mc2. But watch out for the snake on your way out.

DELILAH: What snake?

TONY: That one. (The snake has entered, Flip & Flop have backed off)

(The snake is made up of people.)

SNAKE VOICE: Charm me and I'll let you pass.

DOC: My, you are a lovely snake.

SNAKE: HISSSSSSSSS!

SCI: Wrong charm. Anyone got a flute?

TONY: Charm me?

JULIET: You got a theory?

DELILAH: I've got a headache.

DOC: Three times the Charm. Prince Charming. Charmed to meet you. A charmed life.

Snake: HSSSSS.

SNAKE VOICE: Your time is almost up.

JULIET: Time! A charmed hour! Free us!

SNAKE VOICE: Very good. (Snake hisses away)

SCI: Now what?

M.N.: Back to the cube!

ALL: Yes, Mother.

CURTAIN CLOSE

41

BRINGING IT ALL BACK HOME

(RUMBLING. M.N. IS WAITING TO GREET THE T.T.'S. MABEL and
HENRY are sitting on their bench. The T.T.'s exit The Cube)

DOC: (To Mabel) Hey, what time is it?

MABEL: Two-thirty.

DOC: What day?

MABEL: Friday.

SCI: But what Friday? We can't have only been gone an hour
and a half!

M.N.: Yes, and hour and a half. Exactly.

TONY: But--

M.N.: No buts. Now, what have you learned, humans?

JULIET: People are strange.

M.N.: True. I sent you back in time to teach you a lesson. I
expect you to pass the word on to others. The human race is
out of control. You are destroying this planet. Your
home. I note progress and I am pleased.

F.T.: So do I.

DELILAH: Who was that?

M.N.: Father Time.

DELILAH: Then who are you?

M.N.: Yo' mama! and stop messing around with my
neighborhood! (She exits)

F.T.: It's not nice to fool with Mother Nature.

(THUNDER)

DOC: Well, that's that. I guess.

SCI: Are you going to do your transplant, Martin?

DOC: I missed the plane.

SCI: There's always another plane.

DOC: True. Nevertheless, the baboon heart will have to
wait. I need some time off. I've got to reassess my
priorities. You want to go to a movie, Beatrice?

42

SCI: Sure. Let's just see something modern, okay?

DOC: And funny! (They exit. Enter reporters)

REP #1: There she is!

REP #2: Tell us, Ms. Laroche about that Fun park!

DELILAH: There isn't going to be any fun park.

REPS: What? No fun?

DELILAH: No fun park and casino. I'm setting the land into trust as a Wildlife refuge. In fact, I think I'll go take refuge there for a few months right now. (She exits followed by Reps.)

JULIET: That just leaves us Tony.

TONY: You know Jules, we're destiny.

JULIET: How so?

TONY: You're "Romeo & Juliet". I'm "West Side Story". It just took us a few hundred years to get together.

CURTAIN CLOSES

MABEL: Now there's a happy ending.

HENRY: WHAT?

MABEL: HAPPY ENDING!

HENRY: As along as it's over we might as well go home.

MABEL: NO PLACE LIKE IT!

M.N. : BE A WITNESS!

(End)

THE THEATRE OF THE SILVER DRAGON

PRESENTS

"TO BE!"
THE ANTI-HAMLET PLAY

by
Tamela Glenn
1999

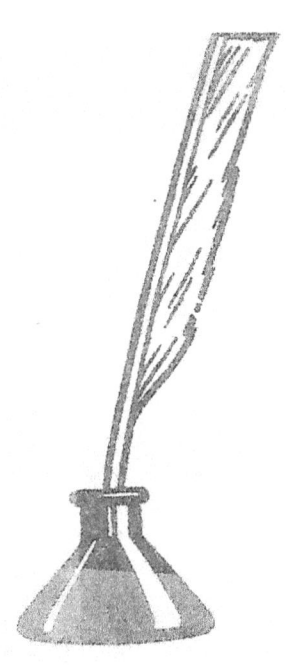

WHILE PLOTS ABOUND IN THE KINGDOM OF SPAM, THIS PLAY WITH ANY OTHER NAME WOULD BE A FARCE.

CAST

[Somewhat in the order of appearance]

KING ARTHUR BIGELOWBES
SIR REGINALD BANDICOOT
BRIAN the JESTER
LADY LAUREL
PRINCESS ARGENTINA
LORD IVAN, DUKE OF NORWHALE
KATE, the Great GRACE
ROSE, A GRACE
DAISY, A GRACE
GREMLY the SORCERER
THIMBEL the APPRENTICE
SIR ADAM WHYTE the KNIGHT

[& Malcolm his Evil Twin]

ACT I

PROLOGUE

(Enter Brian the jester from curtain center)

BRIAN:

Welcome ladies and gentle men
Welcome all from far to near
Welcome all who've come to hear
Our play today. Be full of cheer!

Welcome all: old and young
Let the strungs pluck the song
With your goodwill we'll do no harm
Listen now to the tale we'll tell

Welcome to our fairytale!

SPUDS ! I've blown it. "Tale" and "tell" and "tale" again! How will I make ends meet?

KING: Brian? BRIAN! Where is my fool?

BRIAN: Jester.

(Enter Laurel from door)

LAUREL: What's the matter Brian?

BRIAN: I've ruined the prologue. Rhymed off on the same word.

LAUREL: What?

BRIAN: "Tale" and "Tell".

LAUREL: Well, Brian, all life is a tale.

KING : Told by an idiot! Signifying nothing!

BRIAN: Who's he calling an idiot? First he calls me a fool and now this.

LAUREL: The King is just reading his Shakespeare.

BRIAN: Oh. Well, what about the prologue?

LAUREL: I'm sure it was fine.

REGGIE: Brian! *(entering)* Oh, there you are. The King is in a royal stew. Come along, now. He needs amusing.

BRIAN: Oh, very well. But I'm telling you, Sir Reginald, I don't know how much more of that "fool" business I can take. I'm a professional jester.

REGGIE: Yes. Yes, of course you are. Now come along. *(They exit)*

LAUREL: Welcome friends to our play
      Listen as our plot we lay
      Follow as it twists and bends
      The winner's the one still awake
      When the final curtain brings
            The End.

(She exits out door)

(Enter Thimbel from back of House. Walks to stage, looking all around. Goes up on stage. Looks at paper in his hand.)

THIMBLE: I guess this is the place. Or rather, the Palace. I hope my new master is better than that last foul, old weezing lout I studied with. *(sounds gong)*

(Grembly appears)

GREMBLY: On time and having good manners. Rang at the servants' entrance. Good. Good. Well, come along lad.

THIMBEL: Who are you?

GREMBLY: I'm Master Sorcerer Grembly. You are my new apprentice Thimbel, aren't you?

THIMBEL: That I am, sir.

GREMBLE: Well then. Come along then. I've got a brew on the stove to tend to. *(They exit)*

CURTAIN OPEN

SCENE 1

(The King is reading on his throne. Enter Brian and Sir Reginald Bandicoot)

BRIAN: You bellowed for me, your majesty.

KING: At last! Brain, my fool!

BRIAN: That's Brian, majesty, the jester.

KING: I much prefer Brain. Couldn't you change it? For your King.

BRIAN: Sorry, majesty. Brian's the name my mum gave me.

KING: Couldn't we try to lift the mummy's curse?

BRIAN: What?

REGGIE: The King's just making a little joke, Brian.

BRIAN: I thought that was my job.

REGGIE: Well, yes, but it does a King good to have a sense of humor.

BRIAN: Well, tell him to stop calling me a fool.

KING: What is this whispering?

REGGIE: Brian would prefer you didn't call him a fool, your majesty.

KING: Why? What's a King without his fool? Just look at King Lear.

BRIAN: Look at him! Look at what a mess he turned out to be.

KING: Sacrilege!

REGGIE: Let's all calm ourselves.

BRIAN: It's not PC.

KING: What? What is he talking about?

REGGIE: Personal computers. But they haven't been invented yet.

BRIAN: No, "politically correct".

REGGIE: We haven't invented that either.

BRIAN: Well, we will and for a reason!

KING: What is wrong with you today, Brian? Reggie, take him off to Gremly and have him bled.

BRIAN: No, thank you very much!

REGGIE: You are aware, your majesty, that the Princess Argentina, your bride-to-be arrives this afternoon.

KING: Of course I'm aware. I'm so bloody aware I could vomit.

BRIAN: I'd advise you to do it before she arrives. Don't think the bodily functions impress the maidens very much.

KING: I don't want to impress her. From what I hear all that girl-- princess or not--cares about is parties and dancing.

BRIAN: Not a big reader, eh?

KING: It will be a wonder if she can even write her own name.

REGGIE: I'm sure that your majesty will be an excellent influence on the princess.

KING: Words, words, words.

REGGIE: Brian! Have you no jokes, no rhymes or riddles for the King?

BRIAN: Fresh out. I think I'll go and get bled. *(exits)*

REGGIE: While we have this moment alone.

KING: Yes?

REGGIE: I don't have to stress how important this marriage is...do I?

KING: I know my duty.

REGGIE: Good. The Kingdom of Spam needs an heir. As do you, to keep that dreadful cousin of yours, Lord Ivan, from stealing the throne right out from under you.

KING: He's been banished from the court.

REGGIE: He is very resourceful and he **is** next in line for the throne. If you do not marry and produce and heir, well--

KING: Stop harping!

REGGIE: All right. It's just that it is my job as the royal advisor to make sure that you are informed and aware of all your positions in regards to all and every thing that goes on within, and sometimes without, the Kingdom of Spam..

KING: ENOUGH! I think you have just defined long-winded!

REGGIE: So, what is the King reading?

KING: Don't refer to me in the third person, Reggie. It riles me..

REGGIE: Sorry, your majesty..

KING: I'm reading "Hamlet".

REGGIE: Has the King--I mean, have **you** considered putting on a little play? It might be fun. Might even impress the Princess.

KING: A play! What an idea! Based on "Hamlet". Onty my hero won't hesitate to take action.

REGGIE: He'll take arms against his sea of troubles.

KING: Yes! And end them. He'll butcher everyone. Maybe even Ophelia that whiner. Who can respect a girl who goes mad because some man rejects her?

REGGIE: I fear the King is, while wise in matters of the book, a bit at sea when it comes to the mysteries of the female heart.

KING: What are you muttering about?

REGGIE: It is a good thing that Sir Adam Whyte is staying at court, Majesty.

KING: He's a nice enough fellow. Top notch knight.

REGIE: I'm glad to hear you say so. Perhaps you'd like to bend his ear for some tips on chivalry?

KING: I'd rather have my teeth pulled out.

REGGIE: I see. What a pity. So, who will be your actors?

KING: Oh, yes. The actors. Hmmmm. Ha! I have a novel thought. Let's have The Three Graces play the female roles. Give them something to do to earn their keep.

REGGIE: Women on the stage?

KING: A scandal! I love it. The graceless graces appearing soon at a theater near you!

REGGIE: I'll approach them about the project.

KING: They either do it, or they find a new castle to live in. Now, you may go, Sir Reginald. I have work to do. A play!

REGGIE: The play's the thing to distract the conscious of our King. (exits)

(The King gets paper and a pen.)

KING: Let's see. Aha! The Anti-Hamlet! An Anti-tragedy. I'll call my hero Letham. That has all the letters of Hamlet and is somewhat sort of backwards. Letham will act. None of that "to be or not to be". Just being!

CURTAIN CLOSE

SCENE ii

(The Three Graces: Rose, Daisy & Kate are eating a huge feast, very messily)

DAISY: Pass me the creampuffs, Rose!

ROSE: Hold on. I'm not finished with them yet.

KATE: You should have some of this fudge. De-lish!

REGGIE: *(off)* Your Graces! Hello? YOUR GRACES!!!!

ROSE: Stop. Do you hear something?

KATE: Shhh! Someone's at the door.

DAISY: A spy!

KATE: A spy. I seriously doubt that. *(she goes and peeks)* It's Sir Reggie! A moment, Sir Bandicoot. We were just getting ready for our beauty rest.

REGGIE: *(off)* I'm here on the King's business.

ROSE: Of course you are. Just a moment, and we'll be decent.

KATE: Hide the food. Quick. And wipe off your faces!

DAISY: What's all the bother? Just let the bloke in and see what he wants.

KATE: How you ever came to be a Grace, I'll never know.

DAISY: I cheated on the exam.

ROSE: Figures.

DAISY: What's the big deal?

KATE: **We** are the Three Graces. **We** represent the female ideal of beauty, refinement, manners, etc.

DIASY: Then what is this? *(gesturing to the mess)*

KATE: Reality. *(They sit down and pose)* You may come in now, Sir Reginald.

(Reggie enters)

REGGIE: Your Graces! *(bows)* How are you?

KATE: Divine as always.

ROSE: Most excellent.

DAISY: I'm famished.

REGGIE: Well, I won't keep you long. The King is putting on a little play, and he desires that you participate--as actors.

KATE: Go on!

REGGIE: No, really. Something he's writing based on Shakespeare's, "Hamlet".

ROSE: Do we get costumes?

REGGIE: Oh. I don't know. Probably.

ROSE: I want a lovely flouncy costume.

DAISY: Women on the stage. It's shocking. I love it.

REGGIE: So you'll all do it?

KATE: The King's wish is our command.

REGGIE: How gracious of you.

KATE: Has The Argentina arrived yet.

REGGIE: Her ship docked an hour ago. She's on her way to the palace as we speak.

KATE: Well, we hope her trip was pleasant.

REGGIE: Yes. Well, I'll leave you ladies now. Good Night. *(bows)*

GRACES: Bon Nuit! *(he exits)*

ROSE: I can't wait to get a look at her.

DAISY: Princess Argentina! Sounds like a cruise ship.

KATE: Let's just hope she has what it takes to be our Queen.

ROSE: I heard she's a real party girl.

DAISY: This palace could use a little revelry.

KATE: Nevertheless, a queen has to have a certain something.

ROSE: What thing?

KATE: Substance. I mean, of all the maidens in the world, why her? Is she the best candidate to be Queen of Spam?

(They sit thinking and finally shrug)

DAISY: I'll get the chocolate!

CURTAIN CLOSE

SCENE iii

(Enter Princess Argentina from door.)

PRINCESS: What a gloomy old castle! I hate it here, and I am sure I will hate the king. I've heard that he is a dried up bookhead. I am too young to be walled up in a library. Buried in the Kingdom of Spam. I want parties! Balls! And many, many flouncy gowns! Ah me! Oh my!

ADAM: Hark! Did I hear the cry of a maiden!

PRINCESS: I'm so alone!

ADAM: Fair maiden, what is troubling you? But Wait! You are the Princess Argentina.

PRINCESS: So I am. Sadly.

ADAM: Why sadly?

PRINCESS: Because I must marry a bookhead.

ADAM: You mean the King?

PRINCESS: King Arthur Bigelowbes the bookhead!

ADAM: But the King is a very intelligent young man. You haven't even met him-- have you?

PRINCESS: Nope.

ADAM: Then why rush to judgement?

PRINCESS: I just know I won't like him.

ADAM: Well, I like him.

PRINCESS: So you marry him!

ADAM: Not that way! I am a white knight. Protector of damsels and general all around nice guy.

PRINCESS: Then rescue me! For I am in distress!

ADAM: Allow me to escort you back to your chamber, Princess. I'm sure that a good night's sleep will make your future seem brighter.

PRINCESS: I doubt it. *(They exit)*

CURTAIN OPEN

SCENE iv

(The King is sleeping on his throne. Enter Ivan with the pen of Destiny)

IVAN: Dream away Arthur. And while you dream, dream of this! The pen of destiny! Once the quill of William Shakespeare. You could have it. But lose your throne. Then I will be king!

(Enter Laurel)

LAUREL: Give that back, Lord Ivan! That pen is mine to guard. And mine to pass on. I am the muse of the pen of destiny.

IVAN: I know who you are Lady Laurel. You are a pain in my behind!

LAUREL: How dare you speak to me that way! Now, hush, or you'll wake the King!

IVAN: And then he will see this. And he will surely want it. And gone will be the marriage plans.

LAUREL: You scoundrel!

IVAN: True. But don't you think the King would make a better writer than a ruler. Hah! A joke! Tell me, how do you measure this King?

LAUREL: As having an excess of all the qualities you lack.

IVAN: This bellowing tryant?

LAUREL: He is bored.

IVAN: She's fond of the loudmouth crank.

LAUREL: How dare you speak of the King that way. You could be hanged for it!

KING: Alas! (snort) poor (snort) Alas, poor, Porridge! I knew him well--(snorts and wakes) What is going on here? Ivan! Is that you, my most miserable coz? Wha? What's that? A quill most beautiful. Feathered and Divine. I must be dreaming!

(Ivan teases the pen before the King. Laurel grabs it and runs off)

IVAN: Spuds! (dashes after her)

KING: What a magnificent pen. A pen of dreams. That surely was the most vivid dream I have ever had. (Falls back asleep soundly)

(Enter Thimbel)

THIMBEL: Look at all pages of writing. And books! (picks one up) Hey, this is "Hamlet" by Mr. William Shakespeare. I've read this one! Now where's that speech? (flips through book) Here it is. "To be, or not to be, that is the question:"

KING: (snorts in sleep) No! No, "Not to be"! JUST BEING!

THIMBEL: (screams) Help!

KING: (Waking) Who in blazes are you? An assassin? Sent from my vile cousin Ivan no doubt!

THIMBEL: Me? Oh, no, Mr. King, sir. I'm.... I'm a dream, sir. Yes, a figment of your most royal imagination. Impressive, huh?

KING: Most impressive. Genuis that I am. (falls back asleep)

THIMBEL: That was frightful. I best go back to Master Gremly! (exits)

(Enter Laurel with the Pen of Destiny)

LAUREL: Sleep good King; and while you sleep, dream of this pen and of all the lovely words, sentences, sonnets and plays both tragic and comical it--you--could write. A Sweet Good Night!

CURTAIN CLOSE

SCENE V

(Enter Princess from door)

PRINCESS: And still I cannot sleep! Oh, spuds! Why can't I marry someone like Sir Adam, the white knight? I a so lonely. And bored. Perhaps if I sigh a bit, he'll return. *(sighs loudly)*

ADAM: What! Did I hear a maiden sigh? I'm exhausted, but duty bids me ferret her out. Oh, it is you again.

PRINCESS: Such a cold greeting. Are you not the least bit happy to see me?

ADAM: That happiness is not mine to wish for or to enjoy. You are the King's.

PRINCESS: That makes me sound like a thing!

ADAM: You are. You are a princess.

PRINCESS: Don't you like me at all?

ADAM: Well, of course, but-- Please, dear maiden, just allow me to escort you back to your chamber.

(Enter Ivan)

IVAN: What's this? An intrigue? How charming. The King's favorite knight parading about in the wee hours with the queen to be.

ADAM: We are not parading about. And you are not supposed to enter these castle walls. I should slay you on this spot.

IVAN: Then why don't you?

ADAM: It might give the fair maiden bad dreams. Leave the palace, Lord Ivan. Say nothing of seeing me with the Princess...and I did not see you tonight. Come Princess Argentina, let us go.

(They exit slowly)

PRINCESS: Who is that man?

ADAM: Lord Ivan, Duke of NorWhale. Cousin to the King.

PRINCESS: He is rather dashing.

ADAM: What is it with you?   *(they are off)*

IVAN: Not bad at all. Perhaps I'll make her my queen when I am king. Which I shall be. And soon! *(exits)*

SCENE Vi

CURTAIN OPEN

(Gremly is making a potion)

GREMBLY: Now, Thimbel. You stay very quiet and fetch me what I call out.

THIMBEL: Right, Sir.

GREMBLY: But be sure to join in for the chorus.

THIMBEL: The chorus?

GREMBLY: Right. I wrote it down. here. *(hands him a card)* You'll recognize it when we get there.

THIMBEL: If you say so, sir.

(Thimbel runs and gets bottles as Gremly recites. Gremly puts the ingredients into a pot and stirs.)

GREMLY: Here goes!

GREMLY: Bark from a willow tree struck by lightening at
                             midnight
            Hair from a black graveyard cat
            Toenail clippings from a rabid llama
            Spit from the mouth of an killer whale!

And last but not least, my special ingredients:

            Dandruff from a fat man's jacket &
            Boogers from the nose of a whiney lad who
            got a sound thrashing for taking cookies from the
            pantry without asking his mum.

            THERE! and--this bit is the chorus lad--

BOTH: Hocus pocus, Hullaballoo, RAZZMATAZZ, All that Jazz,
Jumping Jack Flash hit the gas, PIZAZZ!

GREMBLY: It's through!!!!

(Tastes)

Not bad. Now, where's the bread and the butter?

(Enter Ivan. Thimbel fades back and watches.)

IVAN: Gremly! Thank the stars you're in.

GREMLY: Where else would I be? Let me guess, you're here about
the pen. She wouldn't let you have it. I told you she wouldn't.

IVAN: But I see a way to get it. Into the King's hands at least. She's
soft on him. I can tell. She won't give it to me, but she'll give it to him.
All I need is the Right moment. The Right touch. the Right push.

GREMLY; All RIGHT! I catch your drift.

IVAN: So are you going to help me?

GREMLY: That all depends.

IVAN: On what?

GREMLY: I hear the King is putting on a little play. I want a part. Not
a big one necessarily, but something crowd pleasing.

IVAN: Done!

GREMLY: I won't even ask how you're going to manage it. Anyway, you get me a role and I'll help you out with the pen.

IVAN: A most excellent exchange! Hey! Who's that lurking about in the shadows? An assassin sent by my most vile cousin the King?

GREMLY: What? Him?

IVAN: Yes. That one. Him!

GREMLY: Just my new apprentice. Thimble's his name. Come on out lad and let me make a proper introduction. This is Lord Ivan, Duke of NorWhale and cousin to the King.

THIMBEL: How do you do, sir?

IVAN: I could be better. I will be better. When I am King.

THIMBEL: You are going to be King, sir?

IVAN: Yes. But keep your trap shut about it. I wasn't here tonight.

THIMBEL: But...

GREMBLY: He wasn't here tonight. Get it, lad? Quickly if you value your life.

THIMBEL: He wasn't here tonight. Of course he wasn't. In fact you aren't here now.

GREMLY: Hah! Good one, laddie. Now, you best be gone, Ivan. I was just sitting down to my supper anyway.

IVAN: I do apologize for intruding.

GREMLY: "I do apologize"! Spare me your antics. You're just happy because you think you're going to get what you want.

IVAN: Well, yeah. But! You'll have a script in the morning.

GREMLY: Dandy. *(Ivan exits)* Now, what did I do with the bread?

CURTAIN CLOSE

ACT II

CURTAIN OPEN

(Everyone is assembled except, Princess Argentina, Ivan, and Laurel and the Graces.)

KING: Now here are the scripts. Sir Reggie, you shall play Claude. Sir Adam, you get Horace. Gremly you take a stab at the ghost of Letham's Dad and-- Well, where in blazes are those women! Sir Adam! Go and fetch the Graces!

ADAM: Right away, your majesty. *(exits)*

GREMLY: Now is the winter of the discontented!

KING: What? That's not Hamlet. That's Richard the Third and that's not correct. It's: "Now is the winter of our discontent".

GREMLY: Just warming up my vocal cords, majesty.

KING: I see. Where's Brain? Where's my fool!

BRIAN: That's Brian, majesty. The jester.

REGGIE: Don't argue with him Brian.

BRIAN: Well, it's really beginning to stick in my craw, sir.

REGGIE: I sense trouble afoot in the palace. We must get the royal wedding off as planned. The King needs this distraction. So grin and bear it like a good fool.

BRIAN: Arrrrr.

REGGIE: My apologies.

KING: BRIAN!

BRIAN: What can I do for you, majesty? A joke, a riddle a tall tale?

KING: No. Come get a script. You will be playing the Polonius character--now called Polo, idiot father to Opra.

BRIAN: Let's see *(reads)* Hmm. I get killed off early on. Good.

KING: Gremly!

GREMLY: Yes, majesty?

KING: Who is that hiding behind you? An Assassin? Sent by my coz, the wicked Duke of NorWhale? Wooh! Déjà vu!

GREMLY: This lad?

KING: WHO IS HE?

GREMLY: My new apprentice. Real keen to get in on this play. Says he's read "Hamlet".

KING: Come here then, lad.

THIMBEL: Yes, your majesty. *(goes to King)*

KING: Got a name, lad?

GREMLY: Call him what you like. He'll answer, I'm sure.

THIMBEL: *(angry)* My name is Thimbel! Majesty.

KING: He's got spunk. I like him. Well, lad. Read "Hamlet", have you?

THIMBEL: Yes, majesty. I've read most of Mr. William Shakespeare's plays. Some of the sonnets, too.

KING: Quite a find, Grembly! Well then, you will play a part in my little play.

THIMBEL: Oh, thank you sir!

KING: Let's see... you will play Sir Rosey Guild.

THIMBEL: Rosencrantz and Guildenstern?

KING: Yes.

BRIAN: Whom of course will soon be dead.

KING: Right. You're all starting to catch on. Most excellent!

REGGIE: Majesty, why don't I go and fetch the Princess Argentina? I'm sure she would enjoy watching your rehearsal.

KING: I'm not so sure about that. Party girl type if you ask me.

REGGIE: It's too soon to make judgements, Majesty.

KING: Oh, all right. Go get her, then. By the way, you play Lariot, Opra's brother.

REGGIE: The Laerte's character?

KING: Correct.

REGGIE: Then, I get to kill you in a sword fight, correct?

KING: Not in my version.

REGGIE: Of course. I shall return shortly. *(exits)*

ADAM: *(entering)* The Graces, majesty.

KING: It's about time. Finishing off your morning's toilette, I suppose.

ROSE: You can't rush beauty. *(wipes sugar from a pastry off her mouth.)*

KING: No, we wouldn't want to do that.

BRIAN: Bad for the-uh-digestion.

KING: A good one, old boy!

KATE: So, we're doing a variation on "Hamlet", I hear.

KING: YES! And you shall play the Queen Gerturde character.

KATE: I've never liked that name. Couldn't we change it?

KING: I already have. To Gertie. Now, Rose.

ROSE: Can I see my costume?

KING: No. You shall serve as prompter.

ROSE: But!

KING: Sorry. There aren't many ladies in this play. You read well, so there it is.

ROSE: Then I won't have a costume!

KING: Correct. Now, Daisy, you get the role of the Ophelia character. I call her Opra. Here's a script. Look it over.

DAISY: (reading) What? Wait one bloody moment. I'm not playing some dithering whiner who goes cuckoo when some stuck up gumby rejects her, and--Listen to this: While she's gathering up flowers and weeds to makes these hippy necklaces--can you believe it--she climbs on a tree branch and CRACK! falls into a bleedin' creek and drowns.

BRIAN: Carried under by her weight.

DAISY: (glares at him) By the weight of her clothes, moron.

KING: No, he is a fool. He's playing a moron.

BRIAN: I'm playing your Dad.

DAISY: I won't do it!

ROSE: I will.

KING: Oh, well fine then. Daisy, you prompt.

DAISY: Much more to my liking.

GREMLY: Can we get the show on the road, majesty. I've got a brew cooking that I must get off the stove by twelve.

BRIAN: Better yet, call it done and let us get on with our lives.

GREMLY: What? My brew or this little pageant?

KING: I CANNOT STOMACH A GRUMBLING FOOL!

REGGIE: (Off) Please come along Princess Argentina. This will be most entertaining.

PRINCESS: (off) I'd rather stay in my room. Unless...

REGGIE: (off) What?

PRINCESS: (off) Well, will Sir Adam be there?

REGGIE: *(off)* Certainly.

ADAM: This cannot end well.

PRINCESS: *(off)* Let's give this play a look then.

(Enter Reggie with Princess Argentina)

REGGIE: The Princess Argentina.

(People bow. Not the King or the Graces)

PRINCESS: I could hear you all the way down the hall King Bigelowbes. Your projection is excellent.

KING: Yes, my projection is excellent. However, the rehearsal has not yet started.

PRINCESS: Oh. I see. Hello, Sir Adam!

ADAM: Good morning, Princess. Oh, this will not end well.

GREMLY: What's going on between those two?

BRIAN: You tell me. Reggie won't like it, that's for sure.

GREMLY: The King hasn't a clue.

BRIAN: Well, he wouldn't would he.

KATE: What do you think of her?

ROSE: She is lovely.

KATE: Definitely shallow.

DAISY: Why?

KATE: Because I want her to be.

KING: Let us begin. But first, a speech from the director and star.

GREMLY: If you think it's necessary.

KING: What?

GREMLY: I didn't know I was directing. But the ghost is always the people's favorite, so I figure I'm the star.

BRIAN: We'll all be dead before nightfall.

KING: I am the star and the director. **And** the writer, come to think of it. And you are all beginning to pain me! *(starts to stalk off)*

REGGIE: And marvelous you will be, majesty.

GREMLY: Suck up.

BRIAN: He's worried about the wedding.

GREMLY: He should be.

THIMBEL: Why?

GREMBLY: Hush lad, I'll tell you later.

REGGIE: Please don't leave, your majesty. Everyone is just nervous. Stage fright, you know.

KING: No, I don't know. Anyway, this isn't a performance.

PRINCESS: What a nasty temper he has! I cannot imagine marrying him.

REGGIE: I'm sure he'll show a softer side to his wife and queen.

PRINCESS: What do you base that conjecture upon?

REGGIE: Hope.

PRINCESS: Hmmpf. Now, Sir Adam, **he** would make a most excellent husband. Perfection! *(sigh)*

REGGIE: Oh, no. It can't be. But look at her! It's Lancelot all over again. Excuse me, Princess.

PRINCESS: With pleasure.

THIMBEL: I do wish we'd get on with the rehearsal. This play the King's written is very exciting. Quite novel.

GREMBY: "Quite novel". Would you listen to this lad babble on.

BRIAN: I think you missed your calling, Thimbel. You'd make a good jester.

THIMBEL: I'd like to be a writer.

GREMBLY: Seems everyone's always wanting to be whatever they aren't.

BRIAN: Good one!

REGGIE: Sir Adam, what have you been saying or, heaven forbid, doing with Princess Argentina?

ADAM: I never touched her!

REGGIE: Good. Don't. It seems that she favors you over the King.

ADAM: I was just nice to her. She was wanderng the halls last night. Sort of depressed. I just tried to cheer her up.

REGGIE: You expressed caring concerning her **feelings!**

ADAM: I suppose I did, Sir Reginald.

REGGIE: We're sunk.

ADAM: Why?

REGGIE: That's what they want, those princesses.

ADAM: What?

REGGIE: For someone to notice and heed their sighs.

ADAM: Sorry. But I **am** a white knight. It's my nature.

REGGIE: Yeah, yeah. Just stay away from her.

ADAM: I'll do my best.

GREMLY: CAN WE BEGIN, majesty? What's the hold up?

KING: What indeed? Now! I have cut out all the unimportant characters and stripped the plot to the barest of bones. I call my play THE ANTI-HAMLET. We shall call our hero Letham. And he shall be a man of action! None of that "to be or not to be" baloney! He will BE! No doubts about it. And he will kill off everyone!

GREMLY: He won't kill **me**, I'm already a ghost.

KING: NO, no, no. He kills off everyone, **because** Claude his uncle killed off his dad, whom you are playing, and married his mum Gertie.

KATE: That name!

ROSE: Do I have to go bonkers and drown myself? Can't Letham marry Opra and live happily ever after?

KING: Read the script. He saves her from the icy drink and then kills her for being a whiner. And then Letham, as you put it so eloquently, lives. Happily? I hope so. But that's another play.

DAISY: The taming of the shrewd.

KATE: Shrew.

DAISY: Well, you would know.

KING: I cannot stand this bickering! I'm going to my private chamber. Reggie, if you can get this crew to class up their act, maybe--just maybe--I'll return after luncheon. (stalks out)

ROSE: I don't know what he expects. We aren't trained actors.

REGGIE: You are the Three Graces, however. Try to remember what that means.

KATE: Ladies, we have just been insulted.

DAISY: We are going to our room! (They stalk out)

GREMLY: I'm going back to my brew.

THIMBEL: But sir, the play!

GREMBLY: It will all come out in the wash. Now come along, lad!

THIMBEL: Yes, Master Grembley. (They exit)

REGGIE: Brian! It is your duty as court jester to go cheer up the King.

BRIAN: Could I just go throw myself out of the north tower instead?

REGGIE: NO! Go to the King and--and--cheer him up!

BRIAN: If it is humanly possible to do so. (exits)

REGGIE: Well, that just leaves... (Notices the Princess making eyes at Sir Adam) Oh, dear.

PRINCESS: Sir Adam, would you escort me to my chamber? I'm quite marooned.

ADAM: Help!

PRINCESS: What?

ADAM: Of course, Princess Argentina. Duty compels me.

REGGIE: NO!

PRINCESS: Is something wrong, Sir?

REGGIE: Yes! I mean, No! What could be wrong? The King is totally peeved at the entire kingdom and his bride to be is---

PRINCESS: Do you mean me?

REGGIE: Yes. Of course. You are to wed the King.

PRINCESS: I will never marry that man! *(stalks off)*

(Adam starts after her)

REGGIE: Where are you going?

ADAM: I cannot let a maiden roam the castle unescorted! *(exits)*

REGGIE: Of course you can't you goody two shoes. What is a knight, but a fancy escort service for princessess. I am having a really bad day! I am the royal advisor! And nobody! Nobody! Is listening to me! ARRRRRRRRRRRR! *(exits)*

IVAN: *(who has been watching)* Now this is going well.

LAUREL: *(who has been watching)* If only they could channel all of this passion into the work. I rather like King Bigelowbes' "Anti-Hamlet".

(Enter Gremly. Ivan spies and listens.)

GREMLY: Greetings Lady Laurel. I've been looking for you.

LAUREL: That can't be good. What do you want? Something to do with the pen I'm sure. And Ivan.

GREMLY: Don't paint me out the bad guy. You see how things stand. The King would sooner have his hair pulled out than marry. Perhaps Ivan should be King.

LAUREL: That power-crazed viper? The King does not want to marry, true. But is it marriage, or is it the lady he is being asked to marry?

GREMLY: Why not let the King have the pen?

LAUREL: Several reasons, but mainly that he has yet to prove that he deserves it. Time will tell. Hmm. Do smell something burning, Gremly?

GREMLY: My brew! *(exits)*

LAUREL: So much ado about nothing. *(exits)*

IVAN: For too long I have had to hide in the shadows. Waiting. I will be King! I should be king. I shall be king! *(The Curtain starts to close. He fights his way through it.)* You can't shut me up! I've waited long enough. And I'm not that patient. I shall be king. Just try to stop me!!! *(turns. Runs into curtain. Fights his way through it. pokes head back out.)* Just you all wait and see!

CURTAIN CLOSE

ACT III

SCENE I

(Enter MALCOLM front of curtain)

MALCOLM: At last I've lost her. At least she's gone. Don't get me wrong. I have nothing against the princess. Nice enough girl. But I can't get anything done with all this pretending to be Mr. Goody Two Shoes. I hope I won't have to kill her. That would be a pity. However, Ivan is actually making progress. I can't have that. The throne is to be mine. Oh, I see you're puzzled. Fooled you! I'm a bad guy. Worse than Ivan. Sorry. I'm not really Sir Adam Whyte. I'm his evil twin, Sir Malcolm the Blackhearted. My brother left the knighthood to become a monk. He coudn't deal with the Princess Argentina thing. He was madly in love with her. But he didn't want to be another Lancelot. Nice guy, huh? Left no forwarding address. I took his identity. And soon I shall steal the throne!

CURTAIN OPEN

SCENE ii

(The Three Graces)

DAISY: Rose, I don't know why you bother with that?

ROSE: What?

KATE: Leave her alone, Daisy. If she wants to learn her lines what's it to you?

DAISY: It's pointless. The King's fed up. He said so.

KATE: He'll get over it.

DAISY: How do you know?

KATE: I know the King. Once he gets a thing into his mind. It stays there.

DAISY: Too bad for Sir Reggie that the King doesn't have Argentina on his mind.

ROSE: Maybe he'll get around to her after we finish his play.

KATE: I hope not. That girl is not fit to be Queen of Spam. Let her go back and be queen of Argentina. Or Mozambique.

DAISY: Since when are you so concerned about Spam?

KATE: We live here, remember.

ROSE: I think Kate has a crush on the King.

KATE: I do not! What a notion.

DAISY: I bet you're right, Rose. Hah! So **you** want to be Queen of Spam!

KATE: Shut up all of you. I just don't think that the Princess Argentina is a good pick to be our queen.

DAISY: Face it Kate. You don't want be queened over by anyone.

KATE: Do you?

ROSE: What choice do we have?

KATE: We are The Three Graces. We have our wiles. We have imagination. Also, in case you haven't noticed, Lord Ivan is lurking around. He's sure to muck up the royal wedding.

ROSE: That vile lout!

DAISY: Personally, I think he's a bit dashing.

KATE: He's a good distraction.

DAISY: And?

KATE: All great battles begin with a good distraction.

ROSE: Really?

KATE: It's a theory.

(Knock)

27

DAISY: Now what?

GREMLY *(off)*: Your Graces!

KATE: What?

GREMBLY: I have that beauty potion you ordered.

ROSE: Oh! It's Germly! Come right in!

GREMLY: Here you go. I even wrapped it up with a pretty bow.

DAISY: Thank you ever so much, Gremly.

GREMLY: Yes, well, I hate to have to be the one to bring it up, but how's about my payment.

KATE: Did we really agree to this?

GREMLY: Yes.

DAISY: I don't see what the big deal is. A few toenail clippings. A few locks of hair.

KATE: It just creeps me out. Remember Gremly, we're sealed against hexes.

GREMLY: As if! What an insult! I'm not into that kind of thing. I am the King's sorcerer!

DAISY: Calm down Gremly. You can't blame a gal wanting to know where her toenails are going.

KATE: Right.

GREMLY: Of course. Well thanks.

ROSE: Oh, Gremly, before you go. Any news of the play?

GREMLY: It's still on. Reggie is cooling down the King.

ROSE: Excellent.

DAISY: Oooh. I smell somethig burning!

GREMLY: My brew! Thimbel! *(exits)* Thimbel! Now where is that boy?!

DAISY: What a cut up!

ROSE: What does that mean?

DAISY: I have no idea. I must've heard it somewhere.

(KNOCK)

KATE: Now whom?

ROSE: Who is it?

PRINCESS: I hope I'm not bothering you.

DAISY: Who are you?

KATE: It's her!

DAISY: Who?

KATE: The Argentina!

DAISY: What should we do?

ROSE: Why don't we let her in?

KATE: I guess we'll have to. Come in Princess Argentina.

(Enter Princess)

PRINCESS: How did you know it was me?

KATE: Process of elimination.

DAISY: What?

KATE: There are only so many women in this palace. Right?

ROSE: True.

KATE: What can we do with you--I mean, for you?

PRINCESS: Well, I hate it here. Except for Sir Adam. Who seems to be avoiding me. Why do you think that is?

DAISY: He values his neck.

PRINCESS: Oh. Well, I thought I'd seek out women friends. For advice.

KATE: You want my advice?

PRINCESS: I'm desperate for a clue what to do. I cannot marry that-- that--

KATE: King?

PRINCESS: I know he's King. He's just....

ROSE: Not your type.

PRINCESS: Exactly. We are all wrong for each other!

KATE: I quite agree.

PRINCESS: You do?

KATE: It's obvious. You need fun and frolic.

PRINCESS: I do!

ROSE: So do I. I'm sick of being a Grace. I want to be an actress.

KATE: Sacrilege! Anyway women aren't allowed on the stage. Except in this little play of the King. In Spam. I can assure you this is a one time travesty.

ROSE: Then I'll go to France.

DAISY: Why?

ROSE: They're progressive. Aren't they?

DAISY: How would I know.

KATE: QUIET! We are trying to guideThe Princess.

DAISY: We are?

KATE: Yes

PRINCESS: Please. I have to marry someone. Or my father will disown me.

KATE: I have a thought!

DAISY: When don't you? Her mind is always hatching plans.

KATE: Do shut up, Daisy. Now. Princess Argentina, have you ever considered becoming a Grace?

PRINCESS: Good gracious, no! I mean there already are Three Graces.

KATE: I sense an impending vacancy.

PRINCESS: I don't know. It's a rather drastic step.

KATE: Desperate times call for desperate measures.

PRINCESS: I was hoping to marry Sir Adam.

KATE: That won't happen, though please don't ask me to tell you why. That gets revealed later in the play.

ROSE: What play?

KATE: This one. All the world's a stage, my dear.

ROSE: I see.

DAISY: I don't.

KATE: That hardly matters. Now Princess, you must have a name.

PRINCESS: Grace.

DAISY: You gotta be joking!

PRINCESS: No, I assure you My name is Grace. I am the Princess Grace Angelina Madonna Angelica of Argentina

DAISY: What a mouthful.

ROSE: It's fate!

KATE: Tell me, Grace, do you like chocolate?

PRINCESS: I adore it!

DAISY: And pastries?

PRINCESS: De-lish!

ROSE: She'll fit right in. But then, who's out?

DAISY: I thought you wanted to go to France.

ROSE: Well, that was just talk. I don't know. I have to consider all this very carefully.

KATE: Rose, don't fret. The details will sort themselves out. Now girls, let's eat!

CURTAIN CLOSE

SCENE iiiii

(Enter Brian with paper and quill)

BRIAN: "Dear King". No. "Dear Majesty". Awful! "To whom it may concern." To vague! I'm a speaker, not a writer. Oh well, here goes. "Your majesty the King. I, Brian the jester, do hereby give my two weeks notice. I quit! Due to unwarranted cruelty. Such as insults, namecalling, and..." Oh, now what!

(Enter Reggie)

REGGIE: Brian! What on earth. Why aren't you with the King?

BRIAN: I'm writing my resignation.

REGGIE: Oh, this is just ridiculous.

BRIAN: He keeps calling me Brain!

REGGIE: A compliment!

BRIAN: It riles me!

REGGIE: You know how the King loves words.

BRIAN: It still riles me.

REGGIE: I'll have a word with him.

BRIAN: I'm sure you will. But nothing will change.

REGGIE: Well, this is pitiful. There's nothing worse than a sad fool.

BRIAN: And that's the other thing! I'm not a fool! And I'm not sad. I'm angry!

REGGIE: Of course you are. Angry. About the "fool" business. You really need to see what the King means by the word.

BRIAN: Words again!

REGGIE: Yes. The King loves words. He doesn't mean that you are an idiot. He means it in a affectionate way. Like a man speaking of his dog.

BRIAN: Oh, that's just lovely! Now I'm the King's spaniel!

REGGIE; What? No. I just mean that the King really likes you Brain. I mean Brian! He appreciates you. You're his buddy. His fool. His friend. The most excellent jester, Brian.

BRIAN: Hmpf.

REGGIE: At least sleep on this idea of quiting. Eh?

BRIAN: Very well. *(exits)*

REGGIE: This kingdom is coming unglued! And who will history blame for the demise of the kingdom of Spam? The distracted King? The offended jester? Nooooo. The Royal Advisor. Me! *(Exits)*

CURTAIN OPEN

SCENE iv

(The King's room. Thimbel is reading a book. Enter the King. Laurel follows and observes)

KING: What are you up to young fellow?

THIMBEL: Oh! Sorry, your majesty! I was just reading.

KING: **My** book.

THIMBEL: Yes. It's very good.

KING: What have you got there?

THIMBEL: "Henry the Fifth"

KING: Good one.

THIMBEL: Yes, majesty..

GREMLY: *(off)* Thimbel! Thimbel! Where in blazes are you?

KING: You've run off then?

THIMBEL: No sir. I just wanted to read a little while. I guess I lost track of the time.

(Enter Gremly)

GREMLY: And there he is! Thimbel, my brew! Two cheetah's whiskers away from ruination.

THIMBEL: Sorry, sir.

GREMLY: And well you should be! Sorry to barge in your majesty, but the lad was AWOL.

KING: He's been reading my books.

GREMLY: Reading the King's books! Reading the King's books! Without permission!

THIMBEL: Sorry!

KING: Calm yourself, Gremly. Take the book you have, lad. Return it when you've finished.

GREMLY: You'll spoil him, majesty.

THIMBEL; Oh, thank you. And what about your play?

KING: We'll resume rehearsals in the morning.

GREMLY: So we should learn the lines?

KING: By all means.

GREMLY: Come Thimbel. The night is old though you be young.

THIMBEL: What?

GERMLY: I'm tired. It was the best I could think of at the moment.

KING: Good night, Gremly, Thimbel.

GREMLY: Majesty. *(bows and makes Thimbel bow)*

THIMBEL: Bye, sir. *(They exit)*

KING: "Bye"! What a fresh lad! I should have him thrashed! "Bye." To a king. Ah! Spuds! What of it? I like the lad. Now, to work on the gravedigger scene!

LAUREL: How much happier the King seems working on his play. And that lad, Thimbel. He should be a apprentice writer. To give or not to give--the quill! That is the question.

KING: No questions! Just action!

LAUREL: Perhaps he's right. But I can't have Lord Ivan on the throne. And of late, I've sensed another even more wicked presence in the palace. I must ferret it out! *(exits)*

ACT IV

SCENE i

(Rehearsal for the "Anti-Hamlet")

KING: Now. Put down your scripts and let's walk through the action. We don't want anyone--me!--to get hurt now do we?

REGGIE: Of course not, your majesty.

KING: Lariot and Letham are dueling. Well, come on Reggie!

REGGIE: Of, yes, that's me. Lariot.

KING: If nothing else, people, remember who you are.

KATE: How could I forget with a name like Gertie.

ROSE: What I want to know is when do we get our costumes?

35

DAISY: What I want to know is how did I end up a gravedigger?

KATE: You wouldn't play a lovestruck girl.

DAISY: Oh, yeah. This is better.

ROSE: Just keep telling yourself that. Where's the Princess?

KATE: Last I remember, she had passed out in the crumbcake.

DAISY: Right. Sugar overload.

KING: Flummox me again fair maidens!

DAISY: What?

ROSE: Is he accusing us of something? Sounds vile. Flummox?

DAISY: Perverted.

KATE: Probably just a line from the play.

KING: NO! I was just puzzled at what might be so interesting that you would blabber so loudly as your KING is trying to conduct this rehearsal!

GRACES: Oh. Nothing.

KING: Then sHUT UP!

KATE: Sorry, your majesty.

KING: Now, we're dueling Reggie. (they do so) I win a round and I'm thirsty. I go to Gertie, and she gives me the goblet that Claude has dropped a poison bauble into. I say: " You must be nuts. Drink it yourself. I brought my water bottle. All I need is wine to disorient me from my annointed task!"

REGGIE: Excuse me, majesty, but shouldn't that be "appointed"?

KING: I'm doing wordplay here Reggie to go with the swordplay.

BRIAN: It doesn't make any sense.

KING: What?

BRIAN: It doesn't make sense!

KING: *(Thinks)* The fool is right. "Appointed" it shall be then. It's so hard to know when you're writing how a thing will sound up in the air.

REGGIE: But!

BRIAN: He obviously values the opinion of a fool over an advisor.

REGGIE: Apparently.

DAISY: I never think about how what I say is going to sound "up in the air". I speak fully confident of the impression I'm gonna make.

KING: No doubt you do, Daisy.

DAISY: Thank you, your majesty.

ROSE: He's insulting you.

KATE: Let sheep graze in their little pastures, Rose.

ROSE: What?

KING: Rose!

ROSE: Yes, majesty?

KING: Rose, be any other name you'd **still be Rose!**

ROSE: What else should I be?

KING: Quiet!

REGGIE: Your majesty, may we continue? I must attend to the Princess shortly.

KING: Pack her off. Short and sweet.

REGGIE: Now, that's no way to talk.

KING: So then Lariot. You say, "Good madame, allow me a sip of that drink" Claude shakes his head no and makes gestures *(King demonstrates)*--all trying to stop you from drinking. But you drink away. We fight some more. *(they do)* And you fall down dead from the poison. *(He does)* You'll have to work on that Reggie.

BRIAN. A bit stiff.

37

KING: Good one! Then, I tell Gertie all the bad things Claude has done and he gets upset and I kill him. Enter Horace. Where's Adam!

KATE: Probably with Princess Argentina.

KING: Why?

DIASY: He seems to be her appointed escort.

KING: What? Can't she get around by herself. The castle isn't exactly a labyrinth.

ROSE: I think it's a question of love.

REGGIE: Your Graces!

KATE: The King asked a question. We only want to help.

REGGIE: Now why don't I believe that?

KING: Is something going on here I don't know about?

BRIAN: Of course.

KING: What?

BRIAN: You've been so busy with this play, majesty, that you've ignored the termites.

KING: Well, call an exterminator.

BRIAN: Already too many of them squeaking about.

KING: What are you babbling about Brian?

REGGIE: You **have** let the Princess drift, majesty.

KING: I've been busy. King's have a lot to do. She should know that. It's no excuse to go running off with another guy.

IVAN: (like a Grace) It's Lancelot all over again.

KING: AHHH! Don't mention that Spud's name. I swore after the Lancelot incident I'd never look at another princess.

REGGIE: What? You never told me that. Here I've been breaking my back trying to get you married and all the while--

KING: Quiet! Even a King has a right to a private life.

BRIAN: I don't think so, majesty.

IVAN: *(as a Grace)* The Kingdom of Spam is in peril!

GRACES: AHHHHHh!

REGGIE: What is going on here? Something is off.

(Enter Gremly and Thimbel. Germly notices everyone is upset)

GREMLY: Sorry we're late. We didn't think it would matter. We weren't in the first scene.

KING: *(sword in hand)* I'll kill them all! I am Letham and I will not hesitate to act! *(exits)*

GREMLY: So this is going to be one of those multiple location plays?

REGGIE: No! The King has lost his marbles. *(exits)*

THIMBEL: What can we do to help?

BRIAN: Stay out of his way, lad, if you value your life. I'm going to my room. And locking the door until this is over. I'm a jester. I do the comedy. This is the tragedy. Not my field at all.

DAISY: Let's go watch.

KATE: Right.

ROSE: I do enjoy a good fight! *(They exit)*

GREMLY: Well, Thimbel, I better go see what I can do to help get things back under control. You go work on that brew I was teaching you!

THIMBEL: Yes, Master Gremly. *(Gremly exits. Thimbel goes and looks at a book.*

IVAN: *(Stepping out of shadows)* Hey kid, Beat it! This is the King's chamber.

THIMBEL: Who are you?

IVAN: The King's cousin.

THIMBEL: You're the evil Duke of NorWhale! I'm going to have to report you to the King! *(runs out)*

IVAN: That little imp! Oh, what am I worried about. By the time he gets to the King, Sir Adam, aka Malcom the madman, should have finished him off. Which I don't want to miss! *(exits)*

LAUREL: If only this pen were a sword that I could wield to save the King! Such treachery as this I have seldom--outside of Shakespeare-- seen!   *(sits on throne)* Oh, how to rewrite history!

CURTAIN CLOSE

SCENE ii

(Thimbel is working on a brew)

THIMBEL: One pinch of crushed rhino horn. *(puts it in)*
Add to that Two sprinkle's of butterfly wing dust. *(sprinkles)*

Now, let's see, oh yes: one drop of bear fur. And lastly, one pinch of boogers. *(looks at jars.)* We're out. No boogers. Why do all his brews have boogers? Must be his special ingredient. Doesn't say if they are supposed to be dried or fresh. I can't say I didn't try! *(blows his nose into brew)* There! *(tastes)* Yuck! I've done something wrong. Again. I'm failing as a sorcerer's apprentice. When in doubt, read! *(sits down and reads. Enter Gremly, panting)*

TIMBEL: Master Gremly!

GREMLY: It was HORRIBLE. Bloody AWFUL! AWFUL bloody! What's cooking? *(tastes)* Needs some dandruff, lad.

THIMBEL: Of course!

GREMLY: It's a **secret** ingredient, Timbel. I don't write it down. You have to remember.

THIMBEL: But what happened? Is the King all right?

GREMLY: The King! Oh, the King!

THIMBEL: What, sir?

REGGIE: There you are, Gremly! Bring your leeches and come quickly.

GREMLY: Sorry, Sir, Reginald. I got distracted. Time to praactice medicine lad. *(They all run out)*

CURTAIN OPEN

SCENE iii

(The Graces are huddled watching. The Princess is with them. Laurel also watches. The King is at a standoff with Ivan and Adam.)

KING: Two vipers slithering through my palace! Prepare to be butchered.

(Enter Reggie, with Gremly and Thimbel)

REGGIE: All right. I've brought a medical team. Now let's have this out like civilized people. Which we are. Don't forget that! One duel at a time please!

MALCOLM: Let me fight Ivan, first! I'm sure I can kill him. I have doubts don't about the bookhead besting him.

KING: I'll slay you for that remark! I'm fully trained at swordplay!

PRINCESS: I don't understand what's come over Sir Adam. To fight his King. Over me?

KATE: I don't want to burst your bubble, but it's not over you.

PRINCESS: *(disappointed)* Oh.

ROSE: Don't feel bad. That's not Sir Adam.

PRINCESS: What?

DAISY: They found his body in a closet. That's Malcom, his evil twin.

PRINCESS: So my dear Adam is dead?

KATE: Sorry, love.

41

PRINCESS: Get me to a nunnery!

DAISY: How about just becoming a Grace?

ROSE: What about Ivan the terrible?

KATE: Malcom is much worse.

DAISY: They're both rodents.

KING: QUIET! I will fight you both. One at a time or all at a time. I care not! I've had it. I will take action! For too long cousin I have suffered your slings and arrows and now outrageous fortune has blown Malcom up on my shores like so much flotsam. But enough of words. To sword!

IVAN: After you. *(shoves Malcom)*

(They fight. Enter Brian.)

BRIAN: This is still going on?

REGGIE: In many ways it just started.

BRIAN: Timing is everything.

(They fight offstage. A SCREAM)

REGGIE: Your majesty! Was that you? That was! That was the King's scream. Is all lost?

GREMLY: Things aren't looking good, kid.

THIMBEL: I don't want the King to be dead!

(ENTER THE KING)

KING: He isn't. Gremly go see what you can do for Malcom, that idiot.

(Exit Gremly with Thimbel)

REGGIE: You're alive! But wait, there's no blood on your sword.

KING: It was amazing. You know that statue down the hall.

REGGIE: The one of Hercules?

42

KING: That's the one. Malcom backed right into the blade. He's still attached.

BRIAN: I don't believe it. So. One down!

IVAN: And one to go! And I'm not backing into any statues.

KING: They're all taken at the moment. En Garde!

(They fight)

IVAN: You know I should be King, Arthur. Give up the throne and I will spare your life!

KING: Oh, shut up. You've been bugging me for years you power hungry naive.

(Enter Gremly and Thimbel dragging Malcom who is moaning)

GREMLY: He'll live.

REGGIE; Don't distract the King!

GREMLY: Oh! Still at it. Sorry.

THIIMBEL: Can't you put a spell on Ivan to stop this, master?

GREMLY: The King wouldn't want that, lad.

THIMBEL: I can't stand this. (grabs a book and starts whacking Ivan with it in the butt)

IVAN: What? A gnat? Begone little gnat or I'll slay **you**!

KING: Out of this Thimbel! I can handle it!

REGGIE: I can't. I'm going to have a breakdown.

BRIAN: Think of it all as a play, Sir Reggie.

REGGIE: I'm not capable of that kind of detachment.

KING: LETHAM!

IVAN: What?

43

KING: I am taking action! I will survive. I won't be carted around at the end of this play, dead, but somehow admirable. Die my most viperous coz! *(Ivan stumbles and falls)* And now the death thrust!

GRACES: AHHH!

DAISY: This ought to be good!

REGGIE: Is this necessary, sir? What about compassion? You've won the fight and frankly I can't stand the sight of blood.

KING: He'll always be at my heels!

REGGIE: Not if you wed. How about today?

BRIAN: Ivan could be best man.

GREMLY: Good one.

KING: WED? TODAY? Who am I supposed to marry? I don't want to marry her and she doesn't want to marry me! So who then? Prepare to die!

LAUREL: How about me?

KING: Who in the name of Spam are you?

REGGIE: Identify yourself, madame.

LAUREL: I am the guardian of the Pen of Destiny, once the quill of Sir William Shakespeare. *(shows the pen)*

KING: I dreamt of that pen.

IVAN: No, I showed it to you in your dreams.

LAUREL: He wanted you to fall so in love with your books that you would never marry.

REGGIE: Is this true?

IVAN: Yep. *(getting up)* Take that pen and the throne is mine. You'll fall under its spell!

DAISY: She's a witch!

ROSE: She doesn't look like one.

44

LAUREL: I am Lady Laurel, muse of the pen. But I have this one moment in time to become mortal. Marry me and take the pen and keep your kingdom.

KING: Are you lying, madame? Perhaps you have been conjured up by one of my enemies.

IVAN: I conjured her!

LAUREL: A lie!

IVAN: Marry her and the throne is mine!

KING: All right. I 'll do it.

REGGIE: What!?

KING: Well, if Ivan says it's a trick, it can't be. So there it is. Come Lady Laurel the chapel is down the hall. Reggie, wake up the priest.

REGGIE: A royal wedding! At last!

EVERONE ELSE: But what about me????????

KING: We'll sort out the problems of the masses later.

(Exit Reggie, King and Laurel)

CURTAIN CLOSE

EPILOGUE

(Curtain Open. The King's chamber. The King and Laurel are on thrones.)

KING: Princess Argentina, what can I do for you?

PRINCESS: I have decided to become a Grace.

KATE: And we accept her as having all the qualities required to be one.

ROSE: Yes, we do.

LAUREL: But there are already Three Graces.

DAISY: I'm quitting.

KING: Why?

DAISY: To marry Ivan.

IVAN: What?!

REGGIE: We think it is a fitting royal punishment. Marriage to a Grace and exile from the Kingdom of Spam.

IVAN: But I like Spam!

BRIAN: Might I suggest you try Ham? Charming little kingdom, and I Ithink you're very distantly related to the King there.

IVAN: Ah! Possibilities!

BRIAN: Exactly. That's all one needs to have hope.

DAISY: So you'll marry me?

IVAN: Sure. It will help my image.

ROSE: I wouldn't count on that.

KATE: Let him discover that on his own and over time.

KING: Thimbel!

THIMBEL: Yes, majesty?

KING: Gremly tells me that you are not working out as an apprentice.

GREMLY: Sorry. lad.

THIMBEL: I know.

KING: Thimbel, you are to study writing and reading with Laurel and I. You shall be court scribe. Perhaps one day, the Pen of Destiny will be yours.

LAUREL: Your true calling.

THIMBEL: Oh, thank you, majesty! You won't regret it!

KING: Last but never least, Malcolm.

MALCOLM: Go on an hang me. See if I care!

KING: I've decided to let Brain--I mean Brian--see what he can do with you. He says you have comic timing. You shall be court jester. Brian shall always, of course, be my fool.

BRIAN: I'm sure that was meant to be a compliment, majesty.

REGGIE: Of course. Of the highest order.

MALCOM: I've always fancied the entertainment field. I never even really wanted to be King. That was Ivan's idea. Hey! You used me!

IVAN: What can I say?

IVAN: How about sorry! And I did not kill my brother. He's a monk now. You can check that out!

KING: We did.

KATE: But what about the body in the closet?

REGGIE: A dummy. Planted by Ivan to frame Malcom.

BRIAN: Good one!

KING: SO! All's well that ends!

LAUREL: Do you smell something burning?

GREMLY: Spuds!!! My brew! *(runs out)*

KING: All right everyone: Places for LETHAM: ACT I, SCENE i

(Reactions of shock, some happiness, some dread

KING: GREMLY! Get back here! We need The Ghost!

CURTAIN CLOSE

48

Theatre of the Silver Dragon

Presents:

THE PEKING DRAGON
by
Tamela Glenn

A mysterious package. The Wife of the President of the United States &
missing government documents. Her daughter's missing toy poodle.
Does mutt + paper= 2?
In a town full of dangerous villains, thugs and double-crossing dollies-where
everyone wants a piece of the action- Tom Toronto and Samantha Angel
sleuth it out in this comic salute to all things Bogart.

THE PEKING DRAGON

CAST
In order of appearance:

Nico, Ninja
Jazz, Ninja
Samantha Angel
Tom Toronto
Abigail Cross
Alice Cross
Woman
Dixie Delight
Lucy Bazooka
Mickey Melody, undercover agent
Boots Walker
Madame Olaya
The Black Lotus
Euripides, "the ripper" Wire
Zelda Wire

PROLOGUE

(ENTER NICO from stage center. She is waiting. She hears a
noise and hides in the shadows. ENTER JAZZ moving
carefully. NICO springs on her)

NICO: One + One ='s ?

JAZZ: One more song and dance.

NICO: I thought you'd never get here!

JAZZ: I got held up at The Hot Spot.

NICO: Is everything in place?

JAZZ: As far as I can tell. You know the new plan?

NICO: Sub plan 45 Z?

JAZZ: That's it.

NICO: I'm ready.

JAZZ: Now, all we have to do is wait.

NICO: Until then--

BOTH: It's showtime!

CURTAIN OPEN

0.

ACT I SCENE i

(Samantha Angel is in a really bad mood. Tom is late.
Again.)

(Enter Tom Toronto)

TOM: Well, it's about time! I know. You don't have to say it.

SAM: Well, it is, and I do have to say it. Where have you--
No, I can guess. Checking out that singer Dixie Bell.

TOM: (dreamily) Dixie Delight.

SAM: Sounds like a race horse.

TOM: Do I detect a note of jealousy in your voice, Sam?

SAM: No you do not. If I have a "type", you sure aren't it.

TOM: Well, taste doesn't always go with brains.

SAM: Watch it, Tom.

TOM: OKay. Okay. I'm sorry I was late.

SAM: Again.

TOM: Again. Can we?

SAM: What?

TOM: Start again.

SAM: Sure.

TOM: So. Do we have a new case yet?

SAM: Nope.

TOM: Then why does it matter if I'm late?

SAM: It's the principle of the thing.

TOM: Oh, good gravy!

(SUDDEN SHARP **KNOCK**)

SAM: Get the door.

TOM: Got it.

1997:

(ENTER ABIGAIL CROSS)

SAM: "Ching-ching"

TOM: What's up?

SAM: Who knows, but she's loaded.

TOM: Can we help you, miss...

ABIGAIL: "Mrs.". Cross. I certainly hope so. You are Tom Toronto aren't you?

TOM: Sure. And this is my girl friday and right hand gal, Samantha Angel.

ABIGAIL: Hello to all. Now, everything I say is confidential. In fact, I was never here tonight.

TOM: Never here? Huh?

SAM: Of course, Mrs. Cross. Let me tell you up front though that time is money and the meter is running, whether we end up being able to help you or not. And fuel keeps that meter running.

ABIGAIL: Of course. (She takes out money) How's this?

SAM: Premium.

TOM: Now that that little song and dance is over, spill the story.

ABIGAIL: (looking him up and down) Yes, well, manners don't always come with brains.

TOM: Listen, lady, do you want a detective or a gentleman escort for the evening?

SAM: Think of him as a bloodhound. Good on the trail. Best kept out of the house.

TOM: Hey!

SAM: What can we do for you Mrs. Cross?

TOM: I think I asked that five minutes ago.

ABIGAIL: Well, it concerns my husband.

SAM: The President?

TOM: The president of what?

ABIGAIL: Excuse me? You mean you don't know--

2.

SAM: Excuse us. (hauls Tom off) Her husband is Arnold
Cross.

TOM: Should I know who that is?

SAM: He's the President of the United States, you idiot.

TOM: All right! You don't have to insult me.

SAM: Yes, Tom, sometimes I do.

(crossing back to Cross)

TOM: So, Mrs. Cross, do you think your husband, our
president, is playing hanky-panky with some juke joint
bimbo?

ABIGAIL: Really!

SAM: I think what Tom is trying to say is why have you come
to us and not, say, the FBI?

TOM: Right.

ABIGAIL: This concerns national security!

TOM: They're usually pretty good with that.

ABIGAIL: My daughter Alice is waiting in the hall. This all
involves her dog, so could we bring her in now?

TOM: A mutt?

ABIGAIL: Alfredo is a champion Toy Poodle!

SAM: I'll get the girl.

(ENTER ALICE CROSS)

ALICE: Have you told them, mother?

TOM: She ain't told us nothin' yet, kid.

SAM: Tom.

TOM: Well, if someone doesn't spill the beans soon, I'm
gonna call this night a night.

ABIGAIL: Well. This concerns my daughter's prize Poodle
Alfredo and some very important government documents.

TOM: What did he do? Chew 'em up?

ALICE: Of course not! Alfredo isn't that type of dog.

SAM: What happened Mrs. Cross?

ALICE: First of all, Alfredo just hasn't been himself lately!

TOM: What the heck does that mean? Off the Alpo?

ALICE: Alfredo does not eat Alpo!

TOM: Sorry, kid.

SAM: What's been different about your dog, Miss Cross?

ALICE: Well, he hasn't been eating his food. Turns his nose up at it.

TOM: Probably rather have Alpo--or a burger.

ALICE: And he just seems like a different dog.

SAM: How so?

ALICE: He pees different?

TOM: He **pees** different. Of all the--

SAM: Could you be specific?

ABIGIAL: Must she?

ALICE: He prefers mother's prize rose bushes to the stone walls. Alfredo never used to pee on the rose bushes!

ABIGAIL: He certainly didn't. I'd have had him put down as a pup if he had.

ALICE: Mother!

ABIGAIL: Sorry dear.

TOM: So he don't eat and he pees different. So what?

ALICE: He's disappeared.

TOM: Sounds like a lucky break for both of you.

ABIGAIL: The last time anyone saw him- Alice's maid to be precise--he was carrying a file marked "Top Secret".

ALICE: And that night, Daddy was very--

ABIGAIL: And we mean very.

ALICE: Upset.

ABIGIAL: I overheard him talking to a man about some missing documents.

TOM: So mutt plus paper equals number two.

SAM: Tom!

TOM: What? I just said--(realizing) Oh, sorry ladies. Guess I should keep my deductions to myself.

SAM: You'll get a deduction if you don't shut up.

ABIGAIL: Is something wrong?

TOM: It certainly is for you, Mam.

ABIGAIL: True. What do you make of all this Mr. Toronto?

TOM: Well...

SAM: Tom has to mull these things over. It's not good to draw hasty assumptions. Do you have any idea what these documents were about?

ABIGAIL: No, I don't. Sorry.

ALICE: Well, I do. They had something to do with China.

ABIGAIL: And how do you know that dear?

ALICE: Dad keeps muttering about it when he thinks he's alone. Which is a laugh since the whole house is bugged. He keeps grumbling about those blasted China documents. I think it was a list of the names of U.S. spies in China or maybe Chinese spies is the U.S. (shrugs)

SAM: Well, that's something. So basically you need us to get back the documents and the poodle.

ABIGAIL: Precisely

SAM: We'll be in touch.

TOM: Feel free to give us a clue if you get one.

ABIGAIL: Of course.

(ALICE and ABIGAIL exit)

TOM: Well, Angel, I don't get it. Most dogs just chew up papers. Why run away from home with them? Unless of course he ate the papers, then got afraid he'd get punished and split.

SAM: Good grief.

TOM: Well, you got a better theory, Sherlock?

SAM: Yes. What if it was a different dog?

TOM: Huh?

SAM: She said he was acting different. What if someone dognapped Alfredo and put in another poodle, and that poodle stole the documents!

TOM: You think? Wow! That's pretty wild. A spy poodle.

SAM: Maybe.

TOM: How not?

SAM: Maybe it wasn't a poodle. I'm going to call Mrs. Cross. I want a look at the dog bed.

TOM: Why?

SAM: Hair samples.

TOM: Oh, brother. You're getting forensic on me again.

(SUDDEN KNOCK ON THE DOOR)

SAM: Tom, get the door. (He opens the door and a woman clutching a bundle staggers in)

TOM: She looks pretty messed up, Angel.

SAM: Who are you? Can we help you?

WOMAN: Take this. Hide it.

TOM: What is it?

WOMAN: Don't open it!

TOM: But--

WOMAN: Don't ask why. Hide it. Someone will come. You'll know.....

SAM: How will we know?

WOMAN: D---- (She dies)

TOM: "D" as in dead.

SAM: We better call the cops.

TOM: Yeah, let them sort this one out. We got the dog caper to deal with.

SAM: No. We keep the package. The cops take care of her.

TOM: But?

SAM: She came here for some reason. Someone must have sent her. We never got a package, okay?

TOM: But it's right here, Sam!

SAM: Tom, repeat after me, "We never got a package."

TOM: All right. All right. We never got a package.

(SAM takes package and hides it. Tom dials the phone.)

CURTAIN CLOSE

ACT I SCENE ii

CURTAIN OPEN

(The Hot Spot nightclub. Dixie & Lucy are talking at a table. Mickey is at the piano. Nico & Jazz are milling about. Boots is at a table with Madame Olaya, the club owner.)

LUCY: Gee, Dix, do you think Tommy Toronto will come in tonight? I think he's awful swell. A real looker.

DIXIE: You make him sound like a racehorse.

LUCY: But do you? Will he be here?

DIXIE: Oh, he'll be here. He's always here.

LUCY: (pouting) Yeah, but he comes to see **you.**

DIXIE: Tell me something I don't know. Luce.

LUCY: What have you got that I don't got anyway, is what I'd like to know!

DIXIE: Style?

LUCY: What?

DIXIE: Beats me. Does Madame Olya look different to you, Luce?

LUCY: Different?

DIXIE: I can't quite put my finger on it.

LUCY: She looks like she lost some weight. Other than that, I don't see big diff.

7.

DIXIE: Probably just my imagination. Always running wild. I keep thinking some big talent scout will walk in and I'll end up in the movies. (sigh)

LUCY: I think the very same thing! Isn't that weird?

DIXIE: Creepy. Well, excuse me, Luce, I need to talk to Mickey about my new song. (She gets up and crosses to Mickey)

LUCY: Hmmphff. New song? I haven't gotten a new song in six months!

(ENTER TOM. LUCY immediately goes up to him)

LUCY: Howdy-doo Tommy!

TOM: Evening, Luce. Seen Dixie?

LUCY: She's at the piano talking to Mickey. Anyway, you're not her type.

TOM: I'll let **her** be the judge of that Lucy.

LUCY: Suit yourself. I see rejection in the crystal ball of your future, pal.

TOM: Take a hike, Luce.

LUCY: Whatever you say, big boy. Just stick around for the show. (She walks off)

(Madame Olaya gets up)

OLAYA: Welcome to the Hot Spot old friends and newcomers! Our first songbird of the evening is Miss Lucy Bazooki!

(LUCY DOES HER NUMBER--**SONG and DANCE**)

OLAYA: Thank you Lucy, dear. And now, that moment all men are always waiting for! The Hot Spot's Dixie Delight! (Dixie gets up and sings)

SONG

(During the song LOTUS joins OLAYA and they disappear. Olaya returns as the song ends.)

OLAYA: Marvelous as always Dixie, darling! And now, The Hot Spot Girls will kick up their heels for all!

DANCE

TOM: (goes to Dixie) Gee, kid, that was awful swell.

DIXIE: (cooly) Thanks Tom.

TOM: How about you and I go out and get a steak and some fries?

DIXIE: Tom, you're a nice guy I guess, but you're not my type.

TOM: Well, I've heard **that** once this week already.

DIXIE: Huh?

TOM: Nothing. Well, what **is** your type.

DIXIE: I'm drawn to mysterious men who treat me like dirt.

TOM: Why?

DIXIE: How about you tell me, Mr. Detective?

TOM: I haven't a clue.

DIXIE: I didn't think so. Maybe I'll ask Sam.

TOM: Sam who? You seeing some guy, Dix?

DIXIE: Uh, hello, Joe. I'm talking about your assistant, Samantha Angel. Hey, why don't you go out with her?

TOM: I'm not her type either.

DIXIE: How sad for you. (ENTER SAM)

SAM: Just where I thought I'd find you, Tom.

DIXIE: See you, Tom-Tom. (She waves and walks off)

TOM: Gee, Sam, I think I was just starting to make a little time with Dix.

SAM: I seriously doubt it.

TOM: Well, what is it?

SAM: I got the dog bed.

TOM: What?

SAM: Alfredo, the document thieving poodle's, dog bed. It's in this bag.

TOM: Oh, please. Don't take that out in here. I'm almost a laughing stock already!

SAM: I wasn't going to take it out. Someone might recognize it.

SAM: Let's go.

(CURTAIN SHUTS)

They come from door onto stage.)

TOM: I should be in the pictures by now. If someone had told me, "Tom in five years, you'll be standing in an alley inspecting a dog bed for hairs", I'd have said--

SAM: Pipe down and hold the light steady. You see this? It's not a Poodle hair at all!

TOM: So some of the girl's hair got in the basket and--

SAM: The Chinese link grows stronger! It's Chow!

TOM: You mean the mutt threw it up?

SAM: Not chow, bozo, a Chow Chow. It's a Chinese dog. They were bred to hunt bear.

TOM: Listen, Angel, I did not appreciate the bozo bit. I appreciate you hiring me for this job, but I will not stand for verbal abuse.

SAM: Sorry.

TOM: Okay. So there's this Chinese dog hair in the Poodle's bed. You sure it wasn't a doggie girlfriend?

SAM: You would come up with that angle.

TOM: Well?

SAM: No, it is not a girlfriend. No one is allowed into Alfredo's room.

TOM: Room?

SAM: Yes. Alfredo has his own room.

TOM: Lucky dog!

SAM: He might have been once, but he could be in great danger or worse now.

10.

TOM: So what's hypothetically up?

SAM: I think this is a case of an imposter Poodle.

TOM: A plant?

SAM: Exactly. I can think of only one person capable of training a dog to do this kind of stunt--Zelda Wire. I'll put a call out to her right away.

TOM: And me?

SAM: Feel free to go back into the club and moon over Miss Dixie Delight.

TOM: Thanks! (He exits)

SAM: Oh, brother.

(She exits)

CURTAIN OPEN

ACT I Scene iii

(LOTUS is seated in her chair. She is surrounded by Jazz, Nico, and Boots Walker, her bodyguard.)

LOTUS: Boots, did you check the room?

BOOTS: It's clean. No bugs. What's up, Lotus?

LOTUS: I've called you all here to tell you that step one of my plan is working. Toronto and Angel have taken the bait and are running with it.

JAZZ: The fake Poodle bit was brilliant.

LOTUS: Thank you.

BOOTS: So do you have the documents?

LOTUS: What documents?

NICO: I thought we were stealing secret government documents.

JAZZ: I see plans within plans.

LOTUS: Exactly. I let Mrs. Cross believe that her daughter's poodle had stolen some of her husband's-- President Arnold Cross's--secret papers.

BOOTS: Why? A pratical joke?

LOTUS: Hardly. I had Nico, who has been posing as a maid, suggest they take the case to Toronto.

JAZZ: But why?

LOTUS: Because I need them good and distracted.

BOOTS: And again, Lotus, we ask why.

LOTUS: First of all, I talked to Madame Olaya, and she says the package arrived from Shanghai this morning. Second, Tom Toronto had a visitor, tonight, bearing a very important--and very valuable--package.

JAZZ: And it's the same package?

LOTUS: Of course.

BOOTS: Well, what is it?

LOTUS: That I am not prepared to say.

BOOTS: Why the heck not? Why should we work to help you if all the cards aren't on the table?

LOTUS: You might live longer if you don't know.

NICO: That's good enough for me.

JAZZ: Me too.

BOOTS: Well, it's not good enough for me. Spill or I'm splitting.

LOTUS: Sit down, Boots. Relax. Think. Would you rather know everything now or have ten grand later?

BOOTS: I'll take the dough.

LOTUS: I thought you might. Now, Nico, did you pay off Zelda Wire?

NICO: Yeah. She was a little suspicious, so--

BOOTS: Who's Zelda Wire?

JAZZ: The dog trainer.

NICO: The best in the City.

BOOTS: You know that for a fact, doll? She train you?

NICO: Listen you bum, I'm not a dog!

JAZZ: He said doll, not dog.

NICO: Yeah, maybe, but he was insinuating something.

LOTUS: Boy and girls, may we continue?

BOOTS: By all means.

LOTUS: Jazz, tell us what you saw tonight.

JAZZ: This woman crawled up three flights of stairs with a package in her arms. She never came out until the cops came and took her out on a stretcher.

NICO: Yuck!

LOTUS: So what does this mean?

BOOTS: The package is at Toronto's office.

LOTUS: Exactly. And what else?

BOOTS: You want us to get it.

LOTUS: Clever man.

BOOTS: I'll ransack the dump.

LOTUS: Oh, goody. Take Nico along for the ride. Jazz and I need to talk a little business.

BOOTS: Let's hit the road, dolls.

(They leave. Lotus and Jazz start to talk)

CURTAIN CLOSE

(Tom comes out stage door. He's waiting for Dixie. Lucy comes out)

TOM: Dix! Oh. Hello, Lucy.

LUCY: Don't sound so disappointed Tom.

TOM: Sorry. I'm just crazy for that girl.

LUCY: Well, don't rub it in.

TOM: Gee, Luce, you must have some guys after you.

LUCY: They all look like they took one too many punches in the ring. Besides Tom, your the man of my dreams.

TOM: Sorry, doll, you aren't my type.

13.

LUCY: Well, I'll leave you to pine away for Miss Dix.
(She walks off in a huff) (Tom wanders off the other way.
Lucy turns to come back) Tom! Tom! Shoot. I just wanted to
say I was sorry.

EURIPPIDES: Miss Dixie?

LUCY: Huh?

(She sees a knife, **screams**, and runs with "The Ripper"
trailing her)

ACT II SCENE i

(Dixie is leaving the club. Out door. She walks humming to
herself. Mickey Melody comes after her.)

MIC: Hey, Dix, wait up!

DIXIE: (turning sharply) Oh, it's you Mickey. What's up?

MIC: Allow me to walk you home. The streets aren't safe
this time of the night.

DIXIE: Thanks Mickey, but I'm a big girl. I can take care of
myself.

MIC: Then see **me** home!

DIXIE: You'll try anything won't you, Mickey?

MIC: To spend a little time with you doll, you betcha.
Dixie, those few hours I get to play the piano and listen to
you sing are the best part of my day.

DIXIE: You're joking, right?

MIC: Nope. You've got the voice of an angel, doll face.

TOM: Evening, Dixie. You want me to tell this guy to bug
off?

MIC: Dix and I are friends, chump.

TOM: Who are you calling a chump?

DIXIE: Stop it the both of you. Hey, why don't you see each
other home.

MIC: I play piano for Dixie, pal.

TOM: Yeah, I know. Now scram.

MIC: Why don't you scram, loser.

TOM: Who are you calling a loser, gorilla boy!

MIC: Where do you get off calling me a gorilla, knucklehead?

TOM: Knucklehead? Well try out this knuckle sandwich!

(They start a fist fight. Dixie finally shouts)

DIXIE: Stop it! Stop it! Stop it, you clowns. (They fall apart panting.) You trying to ruin your hands, Mickey? You trying to ruin my show, Tom? Now both of you scram before I call the cops. I said beat it. (They get up and exit) Can I walk you home, Dixie? Oh brother! With escorts like that who needs--(Jazz jumps out and grabs her)

JAZZ: Kidnappers? At your service. Don't scream or you're one dead songbird, sweetie-pie. (She pulls her offstage)

CURTAIN OPEN

(SAM in ransacked office.)

SAM: Look at this dump? Now who and what?

(Enter Tom)

What are you doing back tonight? Struck out again huh?

TOM: Yep. Hey, Angel, you redecorating?

SAM: Someone was looking for something.

TOM: Did they find it?

SAM: Nope.

TOM: The package?

SAM: What else?

TOM: Where'd you hide it, anyway?

SAM: Don't ask. You'll probably live longer.

TOM: But since everyone thinks I run this show, they'll expect me to know.

SAM: True.

TOM: So?

SAM: Forget it. You'd manage to botch it all up.

TOM: Thanks for the vote of confidence.

SAM: Don't mention it. (Sudden **KNOCK** on the door) Be a dear and get that, Tom.

TOM: At your service.

(Enter Zelda Wire)

SAM: Evening Zelda. Thanks for stopping by on such short notice.

ZELDA: The price sounded right. What do you want to know?

TOM: Yeah, what do we want to know?

SAM: Who hired you to train a Chow to impersonate--

TOM: Don't you mean in-dog-i-nate?

ZELDA: You're talking about the Poodle scam.

SAM: Right.

ZELDA: I got paid a lot of dough to keep my mouth shut about that.

TOM: Well, we'll pay you more to open up about it.

SAM: Right.

ZELDA: How much? Cash--no checks please.

SAM: Two hundred smackers.

ZELDA: Okay, but you didn't hear it from me.

TOM: No, we heard it from the mutt.

ZELDA: Whatever.

SAM: So?

ZELDA: Some weird Chinese dame--

TOM: Got a name?

ZELDA: Let's see... Laura? No, Lola. No. Uh...

SAM: Lotus?

ZELDA: Bingo! She wanted me to train a Chow to wear this Poodle rig and snatch some papers. You know, Chow's are pretty vicious. Forget Doberman's! A Chow may look like a teddy-bear, but it would just as soon eat one than be one. You know, they are on the top ten most likely to bite a human list.

TOM: We get the picture.

SAM: But you were able to train the dog.

ZELDA: Of course.

SAM: What happened to the real Poodle?

ZELDA: I don't know. Maybe that Lotus dame has him. Now, can I have the dough? Please.

SAM: Sure. Thanks, Zelda. (Gives her money) You hear anything, you come back, okay?

ZELDA: Wherever the grass is greener.

(She exits)

TOM: So who's Lotus?

SAM: "The Black Lotus": Also known as Death Lilly. A.k.A. Jill Thrill Kill.

TOM: And then?

SAM: And then what?

TOM: And then what else is she known as?

SAM: That's as far as it goes. She's really American, obviously, but she tarts herself up like a China doll.

TOM: Personally, I think The Black Lotus sounds a lot classier than Jill Thrill Kill.

SAM: Obviously. The exotic Far East versus the wild L.A. West. But don't let the upgrade name fool you. She's still a thrill killer.

TOM: Anything else?

SAM: Yeah. She's got a pack of ninja gals backing her up. In fact, I bet half the show girls down at The Hot Spot are working for her!

TOM: They **are** in pretty good shape.

SAM: You noticed that huh?

TOM: It's hard to miss, Angel.

SAM: I see.

TOM: I sure have.

SAM: Enough already!

TOM: Sorry. Anything else on this Lotus dame.

SAM: I heard Boots Walker's been working for her.

TOM: That thug? This is getting heavy.

SAM: It was heavy the minute the wife of the President of the United States walked in our door.

TOM: True, but Boots Walker. He'd just as soon blow a hole through your heart as tell you the time of day.

SAM: Goes with the territory, Tom.

TOM: Maybe I should think about going back to my old line of work.

SAM: What line is that? The unemployment line?

TOM: Acting!

SAM: But I'm paying you to act right now.

TOM: I'm talking about the stage or silver screen, Angel.

SAM: Three months ago you were an unemployed second rate actor. Now you are a fairly well-dressed, fairly well-fed employed actor.

TOM: What do you mean second rate?

SAM: This part fits you perfectly. Aside from the occasional major gaff, your doing an Oscar caliber job.

TOM: You think so?

SAM: Would a girl like Dixie Delight have given you the time of day three months ago?

TOM: She still won't go out with me.

SAM: But she talks to you. You're just not her type.

TOM: I know. She likes mysterious guys who treat her like dirt.

SAM: She does?

TOM: That's what she said.

SAM: That sounds like--(KNOCK) Now who on earth? (ENTER ABIGAIL) Mrs. Cross, whatever brought you out this late?

ABIGAIL: My daughter. She's disappeared. She left this note. "Dear Mother, I simply must find poor dear Alfredo. Love, Alice".

SAM: Do you have any idea where she'd go looking for the dog?

ABIGAIL: None whatsoever.

TOM: Your husband notice the missing documents?

ABIGAIL: No, and here's a twist. I'm not sure there ever were any.

TOM: Huh?

ABIGAIL: Well, all of this is Alice's story. Of course Alfredo certainly hasn't been himself lately, but--

TOM: But what?

ABIGAIL: I asked my husband flat out tonight if anything was wrong. He said no and asked me why I thought something might be. I told him about what Alice said about him muttering about Chinese spies, and he said he never muttered about Chinese spies!

TOM: Whaddaya know.

ABIGAIL: He said she must have an active imagination! I don't know what to think!

SAM: I do. I'm sorry Mrs. Cross, but it sounds like your daughter is mixed up in all this somehow.

ABIGAIL: Great Scott! Well, I certainly can't tell her father. This could ruin his career! What do you think she's up to?

SAM: I'm not sure. Go home. Don't talk about this to anyone. Don't report your daughter missing until I contact you, all right?

ABIGAIL: No FBI?

SAM: Definitely, no FBI.

ABIGAIL: All right. But don't expect me to be calm about this.

TOM: No, one expects you to be calm, just keep your trap shut until we contact you.

ABIGAIL: Really!

SAM: (Showing her to the door) You know men. Tactless beasts.

ABIGAIL: You said it. Call me.

SAM: As soon as we know anything. (Cross exits) Really Tom, that was rude.

TOM: Sorry. This whole case is really beginning to get on my nerves.

SAM: Why don't you crash on the sofa? I'm going to go out and explore what few leads we have.

TOM: You sure you don't need help, kid?

SAM: You'd just--

TOM: Botch things up? Thanks.

SAM: I just don't want both of us to stick our necks out too far. That wasn't part of our deal. You're the actor. I'm the detective. Night. (She exits)

TOM: Now that certainly doesn't sound hopeful.

CURTAIN SHUT

(**SCREAM** from Lucy offstage)

ACT II SCENE ii

(ENTER JAZZ with DIXIE. BOOTS meets them.)

JAZZ: Did you hear that scream?

BOOTS: That wasn't Dixie?

JAZZ: No. She hasn't made a peep since I grabbed her. Kicked the heck out of me though. Here, you take her. She's a real fighter for a dolly.

BOOTS: We better get the lead out. Lotus is waiting. You were supposed to be back an hour ago.

JAZZ: I had to wait until two guys got tired of fighting over Miss Dixie Cup.

BOOTS: Cut the chatter. We got work to do. Let's hit the road.

(They exit with Dixie)

(ENTER MICKEY)

MIC: Dixie! Now where'd she go? I can still smell her perfume in the air. What a girl! (he sniffs) She went that-a-way! (He follows)

(**SCREAM** from offstage. Then Enter Lucy followed by the knife weilding "ripper")

LUCY: Beat it you creep!

EURIPPEDES: Not until I kill you, you double-crossing dolly!

LUCY: Kill me? Double what? Help! (**Scream)**

EURIPPEDES: Shut up, you banshee! Stand still and let me kill you!

LUCY: You've gotta be nuts! (She flees screaming. The Ripper trails after her.)

CURTAIN OPEN

(LOTUS is pacing. Nico is trying to stay out of her way.)

LOTUS: Where in blazes are they! Jazz should've been back here an hour ago. Boots a half hour ago.

NICO: I think I hear them coming!

LOTUS: Good. (She sits. Boots enters first with Dixie. Jazz is right behind them.)

JAZZ: Sorry we're late. Miss Dixie Cup had fighting boyfriends handing all over her.

LOTUS: Were you followed?

JAZZ: No.

BOOTS: I don't think so. Who can tell in this town?

LOTUS: Miss Delight, have a seat. Girls, sit her down. (Nico and Jazz do so) Cat got your tongue? Well, you better start talking if you value it, or this big mam cat is going to cut it out. Then it'll be bye bye songbirdie!

NICO: That's disgusting!

JAZZ: She's crude, but she pays well.

BOOTS: Shut up you two.

LOTUS: Where is the package? We know your friend took it to Toronto's office. But we can't find it. I can't find it. And I want it! Now!!!

DIXIE: Go suck and egg, Jill.

LOTUS: I am the Black Lotus and--

DIXIE: You are Jill Thrill Kill. Or should I say Jill Willikers.

LOTUS: You'll pay for that Doris!

NICO: Doris?

BOOTS: Can we get off the name calling. Everyone in this joint's using an alias. What's the diff?

LOTUS: I am the Black Lotus! Boots, take her out into the alley and work on her!

BOOTS: With pleasure!

(Boots and Dixie exit. The girls comfort Lotus)

CURTAIN SHUT

BOOTS: How you holding up kid?

DIXIE: I though Jill was going blow a gasket!

BOOTS: Well, be careful or she'll blow one of yours.

DIXIE: Oh, Bootsy, I'm counting the days until we can be together!

BOOTS: Right. Now, where is the package?

DIXIE: I don't know. The gal from Shanghai left it with Toronto and Angel.

BOOTS: Then your going to have to work on him.

DIXIE: Work on him?

BOOTS: Use your feminine wiles. He's crazy in love with you already.

DIXIE: Even if it means....

BOOTS: Whatever it takes.

DIXIE: Oh, Bootsy, you treat me like dirt, but I love it!

BOOTS: Yeah, right. Now, here's the plan. I rough you up a bit, to make things look believable for Lotus and then I'll convince her to send you after Toronto. Got it?

DIXIE: Whatever you say, honey bunny.

BOOTS: One more thing, doll. I think Eurippedes is in town.

DIXIE: The ripper!

BOOTS: I heard this scream a while ago that made my hair stand on end. And Madame Olaya at the club tonight. She just didn't look right.

DIXIE: That's what I thought. So you think he followed me from Shanghai and disguised himself as Olaya?

BOOTS: I'm afraid so. Well, let's go around the corner. (We hear punching sounds.)

CURTAIN OPEN

(ENTER DIXIE and BOOTS)

NICO: Look who got hit with the ugly stick!

LOTUS: You call that roughing up, Boots? her hair is a little messed up, but where's a good black eye, a broken nose?

23.

BOOTS: We need her pretty face as is, Lotus.

JAZZ: You going soft on us?

NICO: He probably has a crush on her.

BOOTS: Listen up! She doesn't know where Toronto hid the package, but he's crazy in love with her, so I figure she can weasel its whereabouts out of him. Got it?

LOTUS: Good work, Boots. Escort Miss Delight to Toronto's office. And Dixie, the package or I will personally rearrange your face.

DIXIE: Whatever you say, Jill.

LOTUS: (growls) Get her out of here! (Boots exits with Dixie) Nico, Jazz Follow them! (They exit)

CURTAIN CLOSE

(SCREAM from offstage. Lucy runs through pursued by "The Ripper")

(ENTER ALICE CROSS)

ALICE: Alfredo! Alfredo! Now where is he? I told him to meet me tonight. I said lay low until Friday and then meet me on the corner of ---(collar jingle) That must be him. (She runs off)

SAM: Now that's what I call a well trained dog. I wonder what Miss Alice and her wonder Poodle are up to? (She exits)

(Enter Mickey)

MICKEY: Good old Sam. They wouldn't let her join the force, so she struck out on her own. Got more brains than half the joes I know. I'd hate to see her take a bullet though. (Exits following her)

CURTAIN OPEN

(Tom is sleeping. KNOCK.)

TOM: Huh? Who? (KNOCK louder) Coming!

DIXIE: It's me, Dixie! Open up! Hurry!

TOM: Dix! What's the matter, doll?

DIXIE: Oh, Tom like everything else, this is so complicated.

TOM: Huh? **I'm** a pretty uncomplicated guy.

DIXIE: My life!

TOM: Oh.

DIXIE: Listen, Tom, I'm in a real jam. I....

TOM: Go ahead, doll, just spit it out. You'll feel better.

DIXIE: Will you still respect me?

TOM: I thought I wasn't your type.

DIXIE: You're starting to grow on me.

TOM: Really? Swell! So what's the trouble?

DIXIE: Someone came in here and died, right?

TOM: Word's out the street already?

DIXIE: I sent her here with a package.

TOM: **You** did?

DIXIE: Yes. Do you have it?

TOM: What is it?

DIXIE: Do you have it?

TOM: "We never got a package".

DIXIE: You sound like you're reciting a speech.

TOM: How can I help you, Dix?

DIXIE: I need that package!

TOM: What is it? And how did you get mixed up in this murder and mayhem?

DIXIE: Oh, Tom, it's a long story.

TOM: The night is still fairly young.

DIXIE: Well, I met this man in Shanghai. He had this statue. It's priceless. It's the Peking Dragon. Ever heard of it?

(Sam has entered)

SAM: No, he hasn't, but I have.

TOM: Sam!

DIXIE: How'd she get in here?

TOM: She works here.

SAM: Right. Now finish your story.

DIXIE: I've suddenly lost my desire to talk.

SAM: An unfortunate choice. Maybe you'd like to go back empty-handed to your friend Lotus.

TOM: Huh?

DIXIE: You know about the Black Lotus?

SAM: You betcha. You tried to double-cross her didn't you?

TOM: Hey, what's going on? Information please.

SAM: You and your friend Boots Walker.

TOM: That thug? Say it isn't so, Dix.

DIXIE: Sorry, Tom.

TOM: But why?

DIXIE: Money. And besides, he's my type. Mysterious and--

TOM: He treats you like dirt. I'm going to step out for some fresh air.

DIXIE: Oh, Tom, I wouldn't do that if--

SAM: Why not?

DIXIE: No reason.

(Tom leaves)

SAM: Now, Dixie, why don't you finish that story.

DIXIE: Why should I?

SAM: Because I have the package.

DIXIE: You?

SAM: So?

DIXIE: Well, I was singing in this rat hole of a club in Shanghai. This man came to me about the statue.

SAM: Eurippedes "the ripper" Wire.

DIXIE: You know him?

SAM: He's the father of Zelda Wire the dog trainer.

DIXIE: Who?

SAM: Skip it. So Eurippedes contacted you about the statue.

DIXIE. Right. He said that he had a buyer in the U.S. I was supposed to bring it over. He was going to give me twenty grand.

SAM: And then Lotus offered you more.

DIXIE: Right.

SAM: And then you fell in love with Boots and he convinced you to double-cross Lotus.

DIXIE: A perfect score.

SAM: So who was the gal that got killed and why'd you send her here?

DIXIE: I had to convince Lotus and Boots that someone stole the dragon from me.

SAM: Why Boots?

DIXIE: I started wondering if he was using me. I thought I'd make him marry me before I gave him the dragon.

SAM: You thought that would keep him from rubbing you out?

DIXIE: Bad idea?

SAM: Not very effective. So who was the woman?

DIXIE: Just a dancer from the club. Mabel. Mabel Smart.

(Gunshots)

SAM: Uh oh. Your friend Boots escort you tonight?

DIXIE: Yep.

SAM: Let's go! (They exit)

CURTAIN CLOSE

(Enter Boots chasing Tom)

BOOTS: Hey fella, stop running or I'm gonna plug ya'.

TOM: (to self) I'm a detective. Why don't I have a gun?
All right. All right. What do you want?

BOOTS: The statue, dumbo.

TOM: Hey, watch your mouth, you low-life thug.

BOOTS: Why don't you make me?

 TOM: Put the gun away and I will. Fists against fists.

BOOTS: You got it! (They start fighting.)

(ENTER LOTUS and her Ninja girls)

LOTUS: Break them up! (The girls start fighting the guys and
eventually subdue them.)

BOOTS: What do you think your doing Lotus? I was trying to
sack this guy.

LOTUS: Shut up!

NICO: Yeah, shut up, you double-crosser!

LOTUS: Bootsy, I'll deal with your lying hide later.

BOOTS: Then you know?

LOTUS: About your little plan with Miss Dixie? Yeah.

(

BOOTS: (pulling out gun) Sorry, Lotus. You're a swell gal. We've been through a lot of wild hard times together, but that's the past and I've got my future to think about. You just lost yours. (He goes to fire gun, but Jazz kicks it out of his hand. Nico and Jazz grab him and Toronto. Boots struggles, breaks free and runs off.)

JAZZ: Sorry, Lotus.

LOTUS: We'll deal with him later. I don't know why people have to make speeches before they shoot someone. I'd be dead now if he didn't think his little monologue was so important. Now, Mr. Toronto, I'm going to let my girls rip you apart if you don't tell me where that package is!

TOM: The dragon?

SALOME: You've seen it?

TOM: No. Dixie was just telling me--

LOTUS: Where is it?

TOM: I have no idea.

JASMINE: Wrong answer.

LOTUS: Get him!

(ENTER SAM with DIXIE)

SAM: Not so fast, or I'll blow you all to palookaville.

TOM: (to self) Now she gets a gun. She's the girl friday/secretary and **she** gets the gun. Of course, as things have turned out, that's probably for the best. Watch out Sam, they're foxy with their feet.

SAM: My bullet is trained on your heart Lotus. I've got reflexes you wouldn't believe. I see any--and I mean **any!**--movement and this gun goes bang!

LOTUS: At ease girls. So what's the point, Angel?

SAM: You're going to jail, Jill.

LOTUS: You've got to be joking.

(Mickey steps out of the shadows)

MIC: The jokes on you Jill. I'm taking you in.

DIXIE: Mickey? What are you doing with a gun?

SAM: He's a cop.

29

TOM: Then how come you let me rough it up with you over Dix?

MIC: I've been undercover.

LOTUS: Get them girls!

JAZZ: All of them?

NICO: They've got guns!

JAZZ: Sorry. Lotus, I don't feel like taking a bullet for you tonight.

NICO: Run!!!! (The ninja girls split)

SAM: Guess that just goes to show, Jill, you can't buy loyalty.

LOTUS: Oh, please.

MIC: Let's go, Jill. (He cuffs her)

LOTUS: Are these really necessary?

MIC: Oh, yeah, honey, I think so. I trust you about as far as I could throw you if both my arms were broken.

LOTUS: Well, I **am** a force to be reckoned with.

MIC: That you are.

DIXIE: What about me, Mickey?

MIC: You mean, am I gonna arrest you too?

DIXIE: Right. Are you?

MIC: Have you learned your lesson?

DIXIE: Almost. Maybe you could come by the club sometimes and rehabilitate me.

MIC: I thought I wasn't your type.

TOM: You're starting to grow on her.

DIXIE: Right.

MIC: Here's looking at you kid. Let's go, Jill. I still gotta round up Boots before the night is through.

SAM: And Eurippides Wire.

MIC: The Ripper's in town?

SAM: He's the one who was trying to sell the statue in the first place.

MIC: The fun just never stops, Angel. (He exits with Jill)

LOTUS: None of you have heard the last of The Black Lotus!

SAM: Why don't you see Dixie home, Tom.

TOM: You sure you'll be all right, Angel?

SAM: Yeah, I got some loose ends to tie up.

TOM: It's your call. Come on doll face, let's hit the road.

(They exit)

DIXIE: "Hit the road Black and don't you come back no more, no more, no more, no more..."

SAM: I better go get that package! (She exits.)

CURTAIN OPENS

(ALICE and ZELDA are in Sam's office)

ALICE: You sure Alfredo can find it?

ZELDA: Of course, I trained him! (yapping) He's got it!

ALICE: This is so much more exciting than being the daughter of the President of the United States!

(They run offstage and enter carrying the "dog' and the package.)

ALICE: Open it quickly, Zelda. My heart is pounding!

(Zelda tears the package open. It is cans of Alpo)

ZELDA: It's Alpo!

ALICE: I don't believe it. My dog fetched Alpo?

ZELDA: He's been out on the street too long. I warned you that there were risks associated with putting such a well-bred dog out on the street!

ALICE: Are you sure this is the right package?

ZELDA: I'm sure. It's got blood all over it.

ALICE: Spare me the gory details!

ZELDA: This was all your idea in the first place.

ALICE: Actually it was Bootsy's.

ZELDA: I was a respectable show dog trainer until you came along. I'm going home. I'm out of the criminal mischief business as of now! (She stalks out)

31

ALICE: Looks like it's just you and me, Alfredo.

(Enter Boots)

BOOTS: Not so fast! Hand over that package.

ALICE: You're welcome to it, you two-timing jerk. Thanks for nothing! (She stalks out with her poodle. Boots goes to package)

BOOTS: What? Alpo? I don't believe this!

(ENTER MIC)

MICKEY: You lie down with dogs, you get up with fleas. Let's go, Boots. I'm taking you in. (Cuffs him)

BOOTS: Listen, Mickey, just keep me as far away from Jill as possible okay?

MICKEY: I'll see what I can do. (They exit meeting Sam who is coming in)

SAM: Still cleaning up the streets, Mickey?

MICKEY: I think I'm done for the night. You take care, Angel.

SAM: You too, Mickey. (She crosses to package) Alpo? Now how did--

(Enter Tom)

TOM: You didn't think I knew where you hid it, did you?

SAM: Quite frankly, no.

TOM: Wait right there, Angel. (He runs off and comes back with Dragon.)

SAM: Good Grief, Tom! What are we going to do with that!

TOM: I have no idea. Turn it over to the feds?

SAM: Possibly. Possibly. But first, how'd you like to grab some breakfast?

TOM: I thought I wasn't your type?

SAM: You're staring to grow on me.

TOM: That's a start. Let's go, Angel. (They exit.)

32.

(Jazz and Nico come out of the shadows toward
the dragon as the CURTAIN CLOSES)

CURTAIN CLOSE

(ENTER ABIGAIL in front of curtain)

ABIGAIL: Should I take the fact that I've heard no news as
good news? Or does it simply mean that Toronto hasn't got
any infromation good or bad? Where on earth **is** Alice.

(Enter Alice with Alfredo)

ALICE: Mom?

ABIGAIL: Where have you been, Alice?

ALICE: Looking for Alfredo. Look, I found him.

ABIGAIL: Have you been messing around in criminal
activities, dear?

ALICE: Of course not mother!

ABIGAIL: Good, because your father--If he found out about
any of this--

ALICE: He won't. Shall we go home?

ABIGAIL: Yes, let's. (They exit)

(Enter Lucy still pursued by "The Ripper". They are both
exhausted and panting.)

LUCY: (Tries to scream) I don't have any screams left in
me.

EURIPPEDES: Slow down and let me kill you. Oh, I'm getting
to old for this Dixie.

LUCY: Dixie! I'm Lucy, you thug!

EURIPPEDES: Who?

LUCY: Lucy Bazooki! (Enter Zelda)

ZELDA: Dad? What are you doing back in America? You know the
feds will lock you up if they find out you're on U.S. soil!

LUCY: He's trying to kill me. (**Scream**) and she staggers off)

EURIPPEDES: I thought she was Dixie Delight. I was trying to
fence this dragon statue and I got double-crossed.

ZELDA: Daddy, you never had any head for business. Come on,
I'll see what I can so to smuggle **you** back out of country.

EURIPPEDES: Apologize to that young woman for me, okay.

ZELDA: Sure, Dad. Now let's go. (They start to exit.)

(ENTER Nico and Jazz with the statue)

NICO: Look what we brought you boss.

JAZZ: Special delivery!

EURIPPEDES: So now, I'm back where I started. Only in Amercia. (They all exit)

(ENTER--from door--Tom and Sam)

SAM: Oh, Tom, do you think I should call Mrs. Cross?

TOM: Oh, yeah. We told her we would. But only if we heard something about her kid. Which we didn't.

SAM: True.

TOM: The rest of the country can take care of itself, Angel. Tonight, it's just you and me. Let's hit the road!

(THEY EXIT CURTAIN CENTER)

34.

THE THEATRE OF THE SILVER DRAGON
presents

THE CRYSTAL APPARITION
by
Tamela Glenn
2000

At the School for Sorcery, things get out of hand when the new sorceress enters; but Zanzibar has a plan to help his students resolve their own problems....

THE CRYSTAL APPARITION

@2000;Tamela Glenn

CAST

EMPRESS GINKO

MASTER ZANZIBAR

SOPHIA

DIMITRI

IVY

IVAN

STARINA

GALAXANA

CURTSY

KISMET

MYSTIC

URTHE

WYNDE

PHYRE

RAYNE

CRYSTALLA

SLIVER

SHARD   } THE CRYSTAL APPARITION

SLICE

SHINE

MRS. LACY YAK

0

THE CRYSTAL APPARITION

CURTAIN OPEN

PROLOGUE

THE CRYSTAL DANCE *(The actors who play the "Crystal Appartion" & Crystalla perform a dance)*

BLACKOUT
CURTAIN CLOSE

LIGHTS UP

SCENE i: IN FRONT OF CURTAIN

(Enter Empress Ginko with her big book: *The History of Magic": Part "I*)

GINKO: I am Empress Ginko. I am very powerful! And, I know a lot. So listen and learn!

(gong)

I live in a in a kingdom far too magical for me to tell you its name. Don't even try to ask me! It's a secret! Shhhh! Be patient. I have a fine tale to tell. *(she hold up the book)* This is the History of Magic. Part One. Part two is still being written. As we speak! For today, the story called: "The Crystal Apparition"! *(gong)*

Once upon a time--many, many, years ago. In fact, **several thousands of years ago** in the kingdom of NIMCOBOD, there was a very powerful socerer named Zanzibar. Master Zanzibar ran a school for the most talented apprentices. Everyone wanted to go to his school. Only the best could get in. Zanzibar's best apprentice was Dimitri. Dimitri had moved quickly all the way up to the ninth level of magic, but, alas, he was not a very nice person. He was a real a meanie!A jerk! *(catches herself. To audience again)* Oh! So sorry! *(bows)* To continue. Dimitri never helped anyone. He cared only about himself. Selfish boy! He picked on all the other apprentices and like to play jokes on them. Zanzibar knew that Dimitri was getting too big for his britches--or was it his hat?-- I forget. Anyway, Zanzibar decided it was time to teach Dimitri a lesson. He decided to go and seek the advice of the oracles Starina and Galaxana.

 (GINKO exits to one side. Enter Galaxana & Starina.They stand and study the sky)

GALA: Look at that, Starina!

STAR: My heavens! There are so many shooting stars tonight!

GALA: It is an omen.

STAR: Yes. *(sound of bell)*

I

CURTSY: *(enters)* Someone's at the door, your majesties!

STAR: Somone?

GALA: Who one?

CURTSY: Master Zanibar!

STAR: Well show him in for goodness sakes!

GALA: Yes. By the way, we are not majesties. We are oracles.

CURSTY: Well, if you don't mind me asking-- and I'm only asking because my friend Calico asked me about this at the wishing well last week--what is an oracle, anyway?

STAR: Goodness gracious!

GALA: **You** hired her.

STAR: *(sighs)* So I did. An oracle is a person who is very wise.

GALA: And, who can see into the future.

CURTSY: Wow.

STAR: Now send in Master Zanzibar!

CURSTY: Right away! *(She runs out)*

GALA: Where did you find that girl?

STAR: She's a good cook.

GALA: That much is true.

(Enter Zanzibar with Curtsy)

CURTSY: *(Loudly)* MASTER ZANZIBAR!!!

GALA: There is no need to bellow, Curtsy.

CURTSY: Sorry.

ZANZIBAR: Oh, a little yelling never hurt anyone. As long as she doesn't start throwing things.

CURTSY: What? I would never throw anything at you. What a notion!

ZANZIBAR: Just a little joke.

CURTSY: Hmmff.

STAR: Go finish whatever it is you were doing, Curtsy.

CURTSY: I was just twindling my thumbs.

STAR: Then go on back to the kitchen and twindle them some more.

GALA: Now.

CURTSY: Yes, your oracle-nesses *(she leaves)*

ZAN: She's...um....interesting.

STAR: She's a good cook!

ZAN: I see.

GALA: WELL, how can we help you, Zanzibar?

ZAN: I have come for advice. I am sorry to say that I have a very talented apprentice who is also very vain and well, I just have to say it--hateful.

GALA: Mean?

ZAN: Very mean.

STAR: Oh dear!

ZAN: Oh, dear indeed. I need to try to teach him a lesson. Now, before it's too late. Do you have any ideas?

STAR: We have seen many shooting stars this night.

ZAN: An omen?

GALA: Of course.

ZAN: What does it mean?

STAR: Go to the village of UKIYO. There you will find a match for your unruly apprentice.

GALA: Go at once. I sense trouble.

ZAN: Well then, I am on my way! Thank you, Galaxana. Starina. *(bows and exits)*

STAR: I hope he makes it in time.

GALA: *(looking at sky)* Look! another falling star.

STAR: Some stars must fall to make room for new ones.

GALA: Sad, but true.

(Enter Ginko)

Theatre of
the Silver Dragon
P.O. Box 171
Stillwater, ME 04489-0171

3

GINKO: Master Zanzibar set off for the little village of UKIYO. It took him many days to get there. Don't ask how many! I don't know! It isn't written in the book. But! One day, he got there. And he looked around. What else would he do? He didn't even really know why he was there! (she exits to side)

CURTAIN OPEN

SCENE ii

(Sophia is scrubbing the floor. Kismet and Mystic the cats watch. Enter Mrs. LacyYak)

LACY: You missed a spot!

SOPHIA: Where?

LACY: *(pointing)* There!

SOPHIA: *(looking)* I dont see anything, Mrs. Yak.

LACY: Then I guess you're blind as well as stupid. I wonder why I ever traded my milk cow Daisy for you. Lazy girl.!

SOPHIA: I am not lazy!

LACY: Don't **ever** talk back to me.

SOPHIA: But I'm trying as hard as I can!

CATS: Yeowwwww!

LACY: I told you to stop letting those mangey cats hang around here!

SOPHIA: They aren't mangey!

CATS: Yeowwww!

LACY: All right! That's it. Mr. Grumph offered me two new goats for you, and I'm going to accept his offer.

CATS: Yeowww!

SOPHIA: Mr. Grumph?

LACY: Yes, Mr. Grumph. Maybe you'll enjoy digging in his goldmine more than scrubbing my foors.

SOPHIA: But there's no gold in that mine!

LACY: How do you know?

SOPHIA: I just do.

KISMET: YEOWWWWW!

MYSTIC: HISSSSSSSSS!

LACY: And those cats go with you. Now go get your things! *(Sophia exits)* Good help is so hard--make that impossible--to find!

CATS: HISSSSSSSSS! YEOOWWWW! HISSSSSS!

LACY: Where's my broom? *(She starts chasing the cats. Enter Zanzibar)*

CATS: *(hiding behind him.)* Meowww!

ZAN: Why are you chasing these cats?

LACY: There a couple of mangey pests! And you're a trespasser. All of you just scram!

ZAN: QUIET! *(raises his magic staff. She stops shouting)* I was told to come to this village, and that I would find the answer to my problem here. All signs lead to this house. I am Master Zanzibar. And who might you be?

LACY: Lacy Yak. What are you, some kind of travelling magician?

ZAN: No. Is there anyone else here?

LACY: No!

KISMET: Yeaow!!!

LACY: Quiet!

ZAN: No! **You** be quiet. What is it cat?

KISMET: Mew!

ZAN: Oh, Kismet. Nice name.

MYSTIC: Mew. mew.

ZAN: And you are Mystic. Another good name for a cat. Now tell me the truth for I know **she** never will.

LACY: I don't know who you think you are coming into my house and bossing me all around! Really!

ZAN: QUIET! *(She stops talking.)*

MYSTIC: Meow--ow---ow-- ow---ooooow!

ZAN: Really? Where is Sophia?

LACY: Who?

ZAN: Why do people insist on being so difficult?

SOPHIA: *(enters)* Are you looking for **me**?

ZAN: Yes.

LACY: You're too late. I'm trading her for some goats. Now leave.

ZAN: Perhaps I can change your mind with this. *(takes out a pouch of gold.)*

LACY: *(looking in)* Gold! Take her **and** the cats and hit the road!

MYSTIC: Meowwww!
KISMET: HISSSSS!

ZAN: Are you ready to go?

SOPHIA: Yes! This is one place I won't miss! *(They leave)*

LACY: Gold! Gold! Gold! *(dancing about)*

CURTAIN CLOSE

SCENE iii: in front of curtain

(ENTER GINKO)

GINKO: What a laugh! Of course is was fool's gold! I'm sure you can guess why! As Master Zanzibar, Sophia and the cats Charm and Kismet travelled back to Nimcobod, Zanzibar tested Sophia and found that without any training at all she could pass the seventh level of magic. He unsterstood why the oracles had sent him to find her. She was a natural! One day she would be a very powerful sorceress. Zanzibar also knew that Dimitri would be very jealous of her talent. Zanzibar decided--as he always did--to use opposite forces to create balance. *(She exits)*

CURTAIN OPEN

ACT II- Scene i: The Lectard School

(The apprentices are "practicing magic")

DIMITRI: I am better than all of you! All of you put together! I passed the ninth level yesterday! The rest of you--hah! You're at--what? Levels three and four? You'll never be any more than apprentices! On day I will be a great master and I will laugh at you then as now!

WYNDE: You shouldn't be so vain, Dimitri.

DIMITRI: And you shouldn't be so untalented!

RAYNE: The Master says that vanity can be a sorcerer's downfall.

DIMITRI: It won't be mine.

6

PHYRE: Stuck up jerk!

URTHE: Sometimes the first to go the highest is the first to fall.

DIMITRI: That's really deep, Urthe. Did you read that in a book?

(Enter Zanzibar, Sophia , Kismet & Mystic)

ZANZIBAR: Urthe has a point, Dimitri. you would do well to keep your pride in check. Now, students, Please welcome a new apprentice to our school. Her name is Sophia and she is at level seven.

ALL: WOW!   *(not Dimitri)*

DIMITRI: So what? I am at level nine!

ZAN: There's not much magic between levels seven and nine. Remember how quickly **you** moved between then?

DIMITRI: Well, she's a girl.

WYNDE: So what?

ZAN: So what, indeed!

DIMITRI: Is that a cat? Two cats? I hate cats!

CATS: REOWWWWW!

ZAN: I don't think they like you either. Now, I must go. Resume you studies. Sophia, if you need anything, Ivy and Ivan will help you.   *(they wave. Zanzibar exits)*

DIMITRI: I hate you already!

SOPHIA: Why?

DIMITRI: Why ask why? From now on, think of me as your worst nightmare! *(exits)*

KISMET: Reaoowww!

MYSTIC: HISSSSS!

PHYRE: Don't pay attention to him. He's a jerk.

URTHE: But he is trouble.

RAYNE: He can be very jealous.

PHYRE: And mean!

WYNDE: Try to stay out of his way is my advice.

SOPHIA: I'll do my best. Who are they?

7

URTHE: They are the master's servants. Ivy and Ivan.

SOPHIA: I've never seen anyone like them!

RAYNE: They come from one of the moons of Jupiter. That's why they look that way.

PHYRE: There are a little strange.

URTHE: Don't scare her. You'll get used to them.

WYNDE: To everything! You are living in the realm of magic now.

ALL: Anything is possible!

CATS: Meeeeeow!

(They start "doing magic")

(Enter Ginko from the side)

GINKO: And so the first moon passed. Sophia moved up to level eight. Dimitri was as mad as a bee that cannot sting what it most want to sting! Master Zanzibar knew that the time was ripe to teach everyone a lesson!

(Exit Ginko. Enter Zanzibar)

ZANZIBAR: Good day to you all. I must leave you and go teach for a day at the HUBBLE school. I have just noticed that my prized Plutonian crystal ball is very dusty. Sophia, I would like you to clean it. Ivy! Ivan!

IVAN: Yes, master?

IVY: At your service!

ZAN: I want you to show Sophia the secret crystal ball cleaning method.

DIMITRI: But that has always been **my** job!

ZAN: But you have not done it well, Dimitri. Right now, my crystal ball is so dusty that I cannot see anything in it .

DIMITRI: But!

ZAN: Silence! I have given my orders. Now, I will see you all tomorrow. *(exits)*

PHYRE: You are too proud to get your hands dusty, Dimitri!

RAYNE: You're falling behind.

URTHE :Lazy bonehead!

WYNDE: Sophia will soon pass you by!

ALL: In a cloud of DUST!!!

DIMITRI: I hate you all!   *(storms out)*

SOPHIA: Perhaps you shouldn't have teased him so much.

WYNDE: We weren't teasing.

RAYNE: We hate him.

SOPHIA: But you are making him hate **me** even more!

PHYRE: To tell you the truth, Sophia, we are all a little tired of you.

URTHE: Teacher's pet!

WYNDE: I have **never** gotten to dust the crystal ball.

RAYNE: Neither have I!

SOPHIA: I thought you were my friends.

RAYNE: Times and people often change.

WYNDE: The only thing we like about you now is how mad you make Dimitri. We hate him.   *(They exit)*

URTHE: I'd watch my back if I were you. *(exits)*

SOPHIA: This place is horrible!

KSIMET: Reoww.

SOPHIA: No one likes me.

MYSTIC: Meoow.

SOPHIA: Except you, Mystic and you Kismet. And Master Zanzibar. I feel so alone!

IVY: Don't upset yourself so much dear.

IVAN: Come along and let us show you the crystal ball and how to polish it.

IVY: Those who aren't your friends today may be your friends again tomorrow!

IVAN: There's nothing like work to take you mind off your troubles.

SOPHIA: *(suddenly angry)* How do you know?

IVY: We're just trying to cheer you up.

IVAN: When you've lived as long as we have, you do come to know a thing or two!

SOPHIA: I'm sorry. I'm just confused.

IVY: Well, of course you are.

IVAN: Only natural at this point.

SOPHIA: What?

IVY: You're in training.

IVAN: In the realm of magic!

ALL: Anything can happen!

CATS: Yeoooooow!   *(They all exit)*   *(Enter Dimitri)*

DIMITRI: That wretched girl! Trying to take my place! Well, I am First Apprentice here. She is just Little Miss Nobody. I can deal with her. When the master returns, she's history! *(exits)*

CURTAIN CLOSE

SCENE ii: In front of Curtain (*Starina & Galaxana*)

STARINA: Look! There goes another one!

GALAXANA: Something big is on the way.

CURTSY: Your Oracle-nesses! I present: MASTER ZANZIBAR!

STAR: We ARE going to have to teach her some manners. I don't care how good a cook she is.

GALA: I agree. Well, hello Zanzibar! How are you?

ZAN: I could be better, but then I could be worse. I 've set up an experiment. And I am sure that while this cat's away, Dimitri will play.

STAR: You found the girl!

ZAN: You knew about her?

GALA: of course.

ZAN: Well, why didn't you tell me I was looking for a girl when you sent me to UKIYO?

STAR: We're oracles. We're supposed to point the way.

GALA: Give you signs.

STAR: Not a roadmap.

GALA: It keeps you on your toes.

ZAN: That it does. What now?

STAR: You are on the right course. Continue.

10

GALA: Stay here for the night and return to "pick up the pieces" tomorrow.

ZAN: That doesn't sound good.

STAR: Whatever else, all is well that ends.

GALA: Curtsy, prepare dinner for three!

CURTSY: YES YOUR ORACLE-NESSES!!!

ZAN: She's very good at that.

BOTH: What?

ZAN: Yelling.

CURSTY: Thank you, Sir. *(curtsies)*

CURTAIN OPEN

SCENE iii: Zanzibar's room *(Ivy, Ivan, Sophia , Mystic & Kismet)*

IVY: Here it is! Isn't it lovely?

IVAN: Nine thousand years old if I'm a day!

IVY: Came all the way from Pluto!

MYSTIC: Weooww!

SOPHIA: It's magnificent!

IVAN: Of course it is.

IVY: I just love the way it sparkles.

IVAN: When it's properly cared for. That Dimitri is a lazy one.

IVY: Chores are not one of his gifts.

IVAN: Neither is modesty.

SOPHIA: Enough about Dimitri! I try my best to forget he exists.

IVAN: That's wise. Isn't she a smart girl?

IVY: Shhhh! You'll give her a big head!

IVAN: Really? I didn't kow I had magical powers.

SOPHIA: About this Crystal ball. Do I wash it off with a clean, wet cloth?

BOTH: NO!

SOPHIA: Don't get so upset.

IVY: Well, if you were to do that--oh! dearie, dearie me!

IVAN: It would melt away!

KISMET: Yeowwwww.

SOPHIA: Are you serious?

IVAN: As serious as a bad headache!

SOPHIA: Well how **do** I clean it?

> Ivy gets a bottle of oil and pours a ilttle into Sophia's hand)

IVY: You take this special oil of Minx Tree leaves and Hummingbird Spit.

SOPHIA: Spit?

IVAN: It's full of the most excellant nectar.

MYSTIC: Yeowww.

KISMET: (**purrs**)

SOPHIA: I didn't know hummingbird's spat.

IVY & IVAN: You're in the realm of magic. Anything can happen!

CATS: Weoowww.

SOPHIA: So you keep telling me.

IVAN: So you will soon see!

IVY: Just a teeny, tiny bit in the palm of your hand. Now! concentrate all your happiest-

IVAN: Purest.

IVY: "Purest". Thank you Ivan. Thoughts on the oil in your hand.

IVAN: Feel love and light warming in the palm of your hand.

CATS: (**purrr**)

IVAN: Well?

SOPHIA: I'm trying.

IVY: Now, take the ball in your other hand and begin to rub the oil on the top.

SOPHIA: What if I drop the ball? This oil is very slippery.

12

IVAN: That's why this is a "special" task.

IVY: If your thoughts are pure and focused then you won't drop the ball.

IVAN: That's why Dimitri never cleans it. He's always in such a foul mood.

SOPHIA: Please don't talk about Dimitri. Let's all just be very quiet. All right?

IVY: Dimitri. Well, he certainly would sour your thoughts.

IVAN: Shhhh.

SOPHIA: Concentrate. Love. Light.

(Enter Dimitri)

MYSTIC: Hisssss!

KISMET: REOWWWWW!

SOPHIA: (to herself) Concentrate.

DIMITRI: "CRASH"!

IVY & IVAN: SHHHHHH!

CATS: Reoow!! HISSSSS!

SOPHIA: I must concentrate.

DIMITRI: Stupid, clumsy girl. It's slipping!!!!

IVY: Be quiet!

IVAN: Get out of here!

MAGIC: Hisssssssss! Reoowwww!

SOPHIA: Oh! Concentrate. Please! Just let me set it down.

DIMITRI: KLUTZ!!!!!!!!

(CRASH as the ball falls)

ALL: Ahhh!

DIMITRI: Hah! Stupid girl! The master will send you away for this!

SOPHIA: I tried to keep my thoughts pure, but little by little anger crept in--at you! You mean, horrid boy!

DIMITRI: I can't wait until you're gone.

IVAN: Why should the master send her away? This is all **your** fault!

13

IVY: You made her drop the ball!

DIMITRI: Did I?

BOTH: yes!!!

DIMITRI: Did I touch her? Did I knock the ball out of her hands?

BOTH: No.

IVY: But you distracted her with all that shouting.

IVAN: On purpose.

SOPHIA: It's my fault. I couldn't keep my focus. I allowed myself to get angry.

DIMITRI: There! She just admitted that it is her fault. You heard it with your own ears!

IVY: But it was her first time cleaning the crystal ball. No one came in hollering at you when you first tried to clean it.

IVAN: And even then the master had to step in and help you. You couldn't concentrate. You were too busy thinking about how you were going to brag about getting to clean it before the job was even begun!

DIMITRI: Well, the master isn't here now is he? She dropped the ball. The ball is broken. It is her fault. Don't even think of trying to blame **me**.

IVY: You can believe me when I tell you that the master will get a full report of this!

IVAN: That he will, Mister Smarty Pants!

KISMET: Reooowwww!

MYSTIC: Hissss!

DIMITRI: You won't say a word.

BOTH: Of course we will!

DIMITRI: NO.......YOU.......WILL........NOT.   *(They cannot speak)*

BOTH: *(They try to talk, but can only make **sounds**)*

SOPHIA: How could you? That is so mean and cruel! Give them back their power to speak. I told you already that I will take the blame for this.

DIMITRI: Who trusts you? Not me! *(exits)*

CATS: HISSSSSSSSS.

SOPHIA: What are we going to do?

IVAN: *(making **sounds** indicating they should clean up the glass)*

14

SOPHIA: What? Oh! You think I should clean up the broken crystal ball.

IVY: (*Sounds* like "yes")

SOPHIA: Of course. Show me where to get a broom! (*they exit*)

CURTAIN CLOSE

SCENE iv : IN FRONT OF CURTAIN

(*Ginko goes to center stage*)

GINKO: NOW! There are two things you should know. Because I doubt if you've figured them out already. First: Master Zanzibar was no dummy. Even from far away he knew both what would and what did happen. And, of course, he had the oracles Starina and Galaxana to make sure he knew. Second: Master Zanzibar hadn't left out his prized Plutonian Crystal Ball to get broken. What a notion! (*laughs*) Only the master himself cleaned **that** crystal ball! "Cleaning the Crystal" was just an exercise to teach concentration. But if the apprentices didn't think that the crystal ball was **special**, they never tried very hard. So you see, The Big Tragedy that seemed to have happened when Sophia dropped that crystal ball, had only happened in their minds. The Truth be told, Zanzibar would rather have had a thousand broken **priceless**, Plutonian Crystal Balls than to have so much hatred among his apprentices.

As the night wore on, everyone waited for the master's return. Dimitri waited with his heart full of hateful glee. Sophia waited sadly knowing that she would be sent away. Mystic and Kismet tried to comfort her, but she kept dreaming about digging in Mr. Gumphs mine-- which she knew has no gold for her or anyone to find. Hey! You! I can see you are wondering: How did she know? Magic, of course! What else? Oh! Now I've lost my place! (*looks at book*) Oh, yes! As the night passed on into the wee hours of the new morning, Ivy and Ivan discovered that Dimitri's magic spell had weakened. They could talk again about anything **except** the crystal ball. They hoped that by the time the master returned the spell would be completely broken so they could tell him what had really happened the night before. (*She exits*)

ACT III

Scene i: LECTARD SCHOOL

CURTAIN OPEN

(*The Apprentices are gathered "practicing magic".*)

PHYRE: Dimitri said you dropped the master's crystal ball!

URTHE: Is it really true?

SOPHIA: I do not wish to speak about the things that Dimitri says.

WYNDE: It must be true!

RAYNE: Sophia will be kicked out of here for sure!

15

SOPHIA: And then you will all be back where you started!

URTHE: What?

SOPHIA: With Dimitri spending all his time picking on all of **you**!

PHYRE: She's right. If she leaves, he'll start back in on us!

WYNDE: Well, it can't be helped. She broke the master's pricelss crystal ball. She can't stay. What might she do next?

RAYNE: Someone else will come along that Dimitri will hate more than us.

APPS: Right!

SOPHIA: I don't understand why they hate me so. I haven't done anything to hurt them!

URTHE: Wait a minute. I think I could take Dimitri.

WYNDE: You? Urthe, you are only at level four.

URTHE: So? I still think I could take him. Let me at him!

CATS: EEOOOOW!

PHYRE: Be careful what you ask for, Urthe.

URTHE: Why?

RAYNE: You just might get it!

   (Enter Ivy and Ivan)

IVY: How are you doing this morning, dearie?

SOPHIA: You can talk again!

IVAN: As long as we don't try to talk about the *(sounds)*.

SOPHIA: What?

IVAN: The *(sounds)*.

SOPHIA: Oh.

IVY: We're hoping that **all** of Dimitri's spell will wear off before Master Zanzibar returns.

SOPHIA: It doesn't matter. I did drop the crystal ball.

IVAN: *(sounds Like: But he made you)*

IVY: Give it a rest, Ivan.

   (Enter Dimitri)

DIMITRI: The master is home! I hope you've packed your bags, Sophia.

URTHE: The master is home!

WYNDE: Been interesting knowing you, Sophia.

PHYRE: So long!

RAYNE: Don't remember to write!

   (Enter Zanzibar)

ZANZIBAR: Greetings all! It certainly is nice to be home. What a long journey! My ears are still ringing. I think I will retire at once to my study. i want to do some "seeing" with my Plutonian crystal ball.

APPs: *(Giggle)*

ZAN: That's funny to you?

URTHE: No, sir.

ZAN: Many of you do not take you magic seriously enough. And some of you take it far too seriously!

PHYRE: What?

ZAN: Puzzle upon it, Phyre. Think!

PHYRE: Yes, sir.

ZAN: Now, Sophia, come along with me.

CATS: eeeooowwww.

SOPHIA: Exactly.   *(They exit)*

DIMITRI: She's history!

CURTAIN CLOSE

SCENE ii: IN FRONT OF CURTAIN: (Starina and Galaxana with Curtsy)

CURTSY: *(Humming loudly)*

STAR: Why is she doing that?

GALA: How should I know? Why don't you just ask her?

STAR: Curtsy!

CURTSY: Yes?

17

STAR: Why are you humming?

GALA: So **loudly**.

CURTSY: Because I'm trying to keep my mouth shut.

GALA: Why?

CURTSY: Because, with all due respect to your oracle-nesses great magical powers, I think we're lost!

STAR: Lost! How dare you even **think** that **we** could get lost!

CURTSY: I knew you wouldn't handle criticism well. That's why I was humming!

GALA: Well, thinking about it Starina, where **do** you think we are?

STAR: Hmmmmmffff.

GINKO: *(walking over)* "HMMMMFFF" never solved anything or got anyone anywhere.

GALA: Who are you?

CURTSEY: I'd say she was the narrator. The narrator is always the one left holding the book.

GALA: Empress Ginko? Is that really you?

GINKO: In the flesh and bones.

STAR: I think you're doing a great job. I just love your work!

GINKO: Thanks. Now we gotta keep this story moving along. The Lectard School is thataway! *(points)*

STAR: Thank you.

GALA: Can we grant you a favor?

GINKO: Yes. Get moving.

BOTH: Oh!

CURTSEY: I'll lead the way. *(marches off)*

GINKO: Goodbye ladies. *(Watches then leave)* This job is a lot harder than it seems. *(exits)*

CURTAIN OPEN

SCENE iii: ZANZIBAR's ROOM

(Zanzibar enters with Sophia, Ivy, Ivan , Kismet & Mystic.. Dimitri slips in)

ZAN: *(looks around, making a "big show" of looking)* What? Now, where is my crystal ball? I don't see it anywhere. Isn't that strange? Sophia, why didn't you put it back on the table when you finished cleaning it?

SOPHIA: I---

DIMITRI: BECAUSE SHE BROKE IT!

ZAN: I do not remember asking you to come with us, Dimitri.

DIMITRI: One does not always have to be called to know when to come....sir.

ZAN: What are you a puppy dog?

MYSTIC: Reoooooow.

KISMET: Yeoooow

DIMITRI: (Barks at the Cats)

CATS: HISSSSSSSSS!

ZAN: SILENCE! Sophia, **did** you break my crystal ball?

SOPHIA: Yes, Master Zanzibar. I am sorry to say that I dropped it while I was trying to clean it.

IVY & IVAN: But she *(sounds)*.

ZAN: What is the matter with you two? Cats got your tongues?

CATS: Meoooow.

SOPHIA: No, Dimitri has.

ZAN: How do you explain this, Dimitri?

DIMITRI: I was practicing the "muting spell". I just can't remember how to remove it.

ZAN: Perhaps I should show you.

IVY: *(sound like "Yes"!)*

DIMITRI: But how will I get any better if you do my work for me?

ZAN: Very clever answer. Now, everyone, except Sophia, please go about your business.

DIMITRI: BUT!

ZAN: Leave us! *(Dimitri storms off)* Ivy, Ivan! Back to work. And take the cats with you.

CATS: REEOOOOW!

IVY & IVAN: (*Noises* of protest)

ZAN: Everything will be all right.

IVY: Promise?

ZAN: Give me a night's magic to set things right.

IVAN: The master is such a good master! (*They exit*)

ZAN: Sophia.

SOPHIA: Yes?

ZAN: I admire your truthfulness. You make no excuses for what has happened.

SOPHIA: I didn't concentrate enough.

ZAN: But you are still in training. Concentration is very difficult. It has to be developed over a long period of time.

SOPHIA: Yes, sir.

ZAN: Are you too proud to admit you weaknesses?

SOPHIA: No. I have just admitted that I cannot concentrate enough!

ZAN: Sometimes the **whole** story is important, Sophia. For everyone. Even Dimitri.

SOPHIA: What?

ZAN: Puzzle upon it. And after you have puzzled that out, think of how you can get the peacock to sing.

SOPHIA: Peacocks don't sing. Do they?

ZAN: Puzzle upon it. Now go. (*she starts to leave*) Sophia.

SOPHIA: Yes?

ZAN: Where are the pieces of my crystal ball?

SOPHIA: In this box, sir. (*She gets the box*)

ZAN: Take them. Use them. They are your future.

(*Sophia looks very puzzled and then she walks out*)

ZAN: It's so hard for them until they understand.

CURTAIN CLOSE

SCENE iv: IN FRONT OF CURTAIN-- SOPHIA enters with the box.

20

SOPHIA: What am I going to do with a box of broken crystal? My future is a box of broken crystal? My future is broken?   And getting peacocks to sing? I don't understand. "Puzzle upon it," he says. Well, I AM puzzled!

(Enter CRYSTALLA)

CRYSTALLA: You are in the realm of magic. **Anything** can happen!

SOPHIA: *(turning)* Ivy? Ahhhhh!

CRYSTALLA: Don't be frightened, Sophia. I am Crystalla. The spirit of purest crystal. I have come to help you.

SOPHIA: Why?

CRYSTALLA: Because you need me. And because your heart is pure.

SOPHIA: But I get so angry at Dimitri!

CRYSTALLA: Moods come and go. You will learn to control them. Tell me, do you really hate Dimitri?

SOPHIA: No. I just wish he didn't hate me.

CRYSTALLA: We can only control our own feelings.

SOPHIA: Even that is hard.

CRYSTALLA: Yes, it is. But it is also possible.

SOPHIA: *(Thinks about that and then asks)* Tell me, if you can: Do peacocks sing?

CRYSTALLA: Was your master really speaking of birds?

SOPHIA: He said I needed to get the peacock to sing.

CRYSTALLA: Puzzle upon it. Think!

SOPHIA: I'll try. Lets see......peacocks. Peacocks are beautiful birds. They have shiny blue and green feathers. They like to show them off by holding them in a wide fan.

CRYSTALLA: More!

SOPHIA: More what?

CRYSTALLA: What is a peacock, really?

SOPHIA: A bird!

CRYSTALLA: Concentrate. Now. What if a peacock **was** a person? How would that person feel about having such beautiful feathers?

SOPHIA: Proud?

21

CRYSTALLA: Puzzle upon it!

SOPHIA: Why?

CRYSTALLA: Why not? What else have you got to do?

SOPHIA: Pack?

CRYSTALLA: Then pack.

SOPHIA: No! I want to stay here!

CRYSTALLA: Then puzzle upon Zanzibar's words. Find the meaning!

SOPHIA: Get the peacock to sing. **The** peacock. If a peacock was a person it would be...who? Dimitri! Of course! To sing is to speak! To get proud, arrogant Dimitri to speak the Truth!

CRYSTALLA: Yesssssss.

SOPHIA: But how?

CRYSTALLA: You are in the realm of magic.

BOTH: Anything is possible.

CRYSTALLA: Use the broken crystals.

SOPHIA: How?

CRYSTALLA: You will have to solve **that** mystery on your own. So sorry. I must go. You already know the answer. *(She exits)*

SOPHIA: I do? *(getting the box)* What am i going to do with these? Jab Dimitri with the pieces until he confesses? Surely that is **not** what the master had in mind. Magic. Anything is possible. Wat did Dimitri say to me when I first came here? *(thinks)* Oh yes! "I'm your worst nightmare!" *(She starts to "do magic")*

BLACKOUT

CURTAIN OPEN

SCENE V-- Dimitri's Room

(Dimitri is sleeping on his mat. Strange lights and sounds. Enter the Crystal Apparition)

SLIVER: AWAKE!

SHARD: AWAKE!

SLICE: AWAKE!

SHINE: AWAKE!

22

SLIVER: We command you!

SHARD: Liar!

SLICE: We have come for you!

SHINE: Proud, arrogant Dimitri!

DIMITRI: Urthe, is that you? Go away! I'm trying to sleep!

ALL: AWAKE DIMITRI!

DIMITRI: This is really too much! *(sits up)* AHHH! What are you?

SLIVER: I am Sliver!

SHARD: I am Shard!

SLICE: I am Slice!

SHINE: I am Shine!

ALL: We are the spirits of the shattered crystal ball!

DIMITRI: Well, go haunt Sophia. She broke you!

SLIVER: I am the sliver that will get under your skin.

OTHERS: Until you tell the Truth!

SHARD: I am the shard that will mark you.

OTHERS: Until you tell the Truth!

SLICE: I am the slice that pricks your heart.

OTHERS: Until you tell the Truth!

SHINE: I am the light that will shine.

OTHERS: If you tell the Truth!

DIMITRI: Leave me!

SLIVER: The fault is yours!

SHARD: You might as well have pushed her!

SLICE: Proud, arrogant Dimitri!

SHINE: Your time has come!

DIMITRI: I said leave me!

SLIVER: This is our promise to you.

(They walk around him)

If the truth you do not tell
Walk your days-but never well!
Both your feet will rack and swell
From glass stuck deep as a rusty nail!   (3Xs)

DIMITRI: STOP! Away from me!

SHARD: We will go for now.

SLICE: But if you do not do tell the Truth.

SHINE: What we have said will come to pass.

ALL: Look to the glasssssssssssssssssss! *(They whirl away. Dimitri looks frightened)*

BLACKOUT

CURTAIN CLOSE

SCENE Vi -- IN FRONT OF CURTAIN--*(Galaxana, Starina & Curtsy)*

GALA: This is the place.

STAR: At last. And we're right on time

CURTSY: What?

GALA: Life always gives you little detours. It is still possible to end up at the right place at the right time.

STAR: Announce our arrival, Curtsy.

CURTSY: HELLO LECTARD SCHOOL PEOPLE! Open up! I AM PLEASED TO ANNOUNCE THAT YOU HAVE THE PLEASURE OF BEING VISITED BY THE GREAT ORACLE-NESSES STARINA AND GALAXANA!

GALA: I though you told her not to call us oracle-nesses?

GINKO: When some people get a notion in their head there's just no going back.

STAR: You are right as usual, Empress Ginko.

(The apprentices come out)

PHYRE: Can I help you?

CURSTY: We hope so!

WYNDE: It's Starina!

24

RAYNE: And Galaxana!

URTHE: Please come in. Welcome to the Lectard School!

BLACKOUT

SCENE Vii : ZANZIBAR"S ROOM.

(Zanzibar is reading. The cats are grooming themselves. Dimitri rushes in)

MYSTIC: HIssssssssss!

KISMET: Reooowwww!

ZAN: Good morning Dimitri! Did you sleep well last night?

DIMITRI: Master! I have a confession to make.

ZAN: Well then, let's call the others.

DIMITRI: No!

ZAN: Then go.

DIMITRI: I can't.

ZAN: Then you must accept my terms. (***rings a bell. EVERYONE** enters)* Oh, hello there Starina, Galaxana and of course Curtsy. You're just in time. Dimitri says he has a confession to make.

WYNDE: This ought to be good!

ZAN: Silence.

WYNDE: Sorry.

ZAN: I said silence.

RAYNE: She just wants you to know she's sorry.

ZAN: SILENCE! *(pause)* Thank you. Now, Dimitri, what would you like to confess?

DIMITRI: I distracted Sophia when she was trying to clean your crystal ball.

ZAN: Hmmm. Well, Dimitri, just **how** did you distract her?

DIMITRI: I spoke to her.

ZAN: Is this the truth, Sophia?

SOPHIA: Yes,

ZAN: The whole of the truth?

25

IVY: Putting it nicely.

IVAN: Hey! You can talk about it!

IVY: I can! Good! Master, Dimitri ran about the room bellowing at the poor girl!

ZAN: Enough!

IVAN: She's just trying to help.

ZAN: I know that. But people must learn to speak for themselves. Sophia, it is right to take responsibility for your actions, but you can't be too hard on yourself. How would you tell a friend about what Dimitri did?

SOPHIA: I would say that he acted like a jerk! That he distracted me on purpose. That he wanted me to drop the crystal ball!

ZAN: Thank you. Is there anything you want to add, Dimitri?

DIMITRI: I was forced into this confession by a bunch of glass!

SOPHIA: The Crystal Appartion.

DIMITRI: What?

SOPHIA: **My** magic.

DIMITRI: A trick! Did you hear that!

ZAN: You are in the realm of magic!

ALL: Anything can happen!

CATS: WEOOOOW!!!

CURTAIN CLOSE

EPILOGUE--in front of Curtain--Empress Ginko

GINKO: On that day, Zanzibar felt that everyone had learned a valuable lesson.

In time, the apprentices passed all their magic levels. URTHE, PHYRE, WYNDE and RAYNE went to to four corners of the world and became teachers at their own schools. At the Lectard School, MASTER ZANZIBAR continued to teach the most gifted apprentices the proper ways of pure magic, with IVAN and IVY always there to help him. SOPHIA's talents were so great that she became an oracle. With the cats KISMET & MYSTIC she went to live with STARINA & GALAXANA--and of course--CURTSY. SO! Everyone was on the way to living happily ever after. *(She starts to walk away)*

What? Ohhhhh.... I know what you want to know. Should I tell you? I could make you beg, but I'm not that kind of gal. So! What about Dimitri? Well, you can't change everyone. Proud, arrogant Dimitri finally had to be kicked out of the Lectard School. He had a lot of trouble finding work at first, but eventually he met Mrs. Lacy Yak and became a goat herder.

DIMITRI: *(off)* Wait a minute!

GINKO: THE END. *(She bows)*

Blackout

CURTAIN OPEN

BOWS

© 2000

Theatre of
the Silver Dragon
P.O. Box 171

27

THE THEATRE OF THE SILVER DRAGON

presents

BERMUDA

by

Tamela Glenn

A look at the tragedy and dilemma surrounding a coma patient, the helplessness of the attending doctor who cannot answer the unknowable questions and the despair of the loved ones who can only wait and hope. Does the coma patient have dreamlike visions in her journey back to reality?

BERMUDA

CAST
(in Order of Appearance/speaking)

GIRL 1

MOM 1: Mrs. Suddon
DAD: Mr. Suddon
DR. BELLS

BRENDA
HORTENSE
LAURA
GERTRUDE

GIRL 2

CLARISSE
MARY
DAWN

STEWARDESS
AMOC
TIAW

AMY
JANE
WREN

ECHO
SKYE

ALICE/ALISON

GINGER
BUNNY
CINDY

WITCH

ECHO
SKYE

CLEO
LUCRETIA

MOM 2
MOM 3

VANNA
GIGI
MS. BLANK
MS. NOIR

BLACKOUT

(Radio is playing. Car sounds. Then: Voices.)

VOICE 1: Oh, dear God!

VOICE 2: Alison!

VOICE 3: Ahhhh! (scream)
(LOUD CRASH NOISE)

(A horse whinnies. Sirens. Flashing Red lights. A flashbulb. Back to BLACK

Steel Drum music up, growing LOUDER. Then, out.)

(Girl 1 sits up. Gets up and comes downstage)

VISION 1

GIRL1: I was born in Bermuda. I wasn't supposed to be. I was a premie. Mom was eight months pregnant and Dad had a computer software conference he had to--had to--- had to-- go to and they were holding it in Bermuda. Mom said there was no way she was going to let him have all the fun in the sun without **her**--eight months pregnant or not. She ignored all medical advice. They told her not to fly. And just getting around was hard. The discomfort of month eight. But Mom wanted, probably needed, a holiday. I was glad. I wanted to be born in Bermuda. I wanted my life to be "special" from Day One. *(sound of Ocean)*

I used to walk on the beach and collect shells with my mother. I loved the smell of the ocean. The feel of the sand under my feet, squishing between my toes. The bright, white light of the Bermuda sun. One day we found a huge conch shell. I blew it and it summoned a white dolphin. *(stands staring out at her vision)*

We never left Bermuda. We never have. *(Sound of horn. fade to black. Girl 1 goes back and lies down)*

I

(SPOT ON figure lying on white "bed". Figure is GIRL 1 in white gown. She looks like she's floating. Light fades up on Doctor with parents, who are downstage left and right of figure.)

MOM: Well? Well?

DOCTOR: I'm sorry, but not very.

DAD: We've been waiting all night.

MOM: Waiting.

DR: They're waiting.

DAD: For some word.

MOM: I wish someone would....

DR.: What?

MOM: Tell us...

DR: What?

(They cross to center stage and meet on their next lines)

MOM: Doctor Bells! How is she?

DR: Well, Mrs. Suddon, not Well.

DAD: Not well?

DR.: Not well at all.

DAD: Meaning?

MOM: Signifying?

DAD: All adding up to?

DR.: COMA.

M & D: *(gasp)*

DR.: *(sighs and crosses away)* And so it goes. This is my twentieth coma in as many years. Hi! I'm Dr. Bells. Coma specialist. Whatever that is. I mean, how do I know: Why. When they'll come out of it. What they're doing while they're in it. What exactly it is? And, don't let

2

me forget, the most important: Will she or will he, your little Jessica or Billy ever be the same....again.... How do I know? Of course I have theories, ideas, hunches, feelings, data, research, educated-at-a-"big-bucks"-med school and years-of-experienced GUESSES. *(pause & a shrug)* Or you can toss a coin.   *(crosses back)*

MOM: A COMA!

DR: Mr. and Mrs. Suddon, I know this is a shock to you--

DAD: A coma.

DR.: She could wake at any time and--

DAD: When?

MOM: At any time? Will she...

DR.: Be the same?

DAD: Or--

DR.: Will she have brain damage?

MOM: Brain damage? Our little girl! She's only sixteen! Sweet sixteen.

DAD: Well?

DR.: Not well.

MOM: But not dead.

DAD: There's still hope.

MOM: Isn't there?

DR.: Of course.

DAD: The odds?

DR.: This isn't a crap shoot! Well, maybe it is.

M & D: WHAT!

DR.: Nothing. Excuse me. I'm sorry. A Coma. Very hard to predict the outcome.

DAD: Why?

DR.: It's the nature of the beast.

MOM: What beast?

DR.: Coma.

MOM: But she **could** wake at any time.

DR.: She **could** regain consciousness. Yes. But...

DAD: What?

DR.: The other injuries are rather severe.

MOM: What? What?

DR.: Broken nose, jaw, collar bone, ribs, shattered---need I say more?

DAD: I've heard enough.

MOM: I want to hear everything.

DR.: Impossible.

MOM: Why?

DR.: Because she's in a coma.

MOM: A coma.

DAD: A coma.

(Lights fades down on them)

WOMAN'S VOICE: AL-I-SON!

VISION

(Spot up on Girl 2)

GIRL 2: I heard someone calling. My mother? I flew to her. She was on this beach collecting beautiful shells. I asked where we were. She laughed and said, "We're in Bermuda of course". That seemed good. I put my feet down. The sand was warm. I looked down, my feet were so small. I asked my mother how old I was. She said I was five. That seemed good. I felt safe. I started looking for shells.

VISION

BRENDA: Hortense! You simply have to get a new mare--that's just good horse sense!

HORTENSE: Well, the old gray mare **ain't** what she used to be!

BRENDA: I saw the most exquisite Warmblood last weekend. The way she snapped her legs up into a tuck as she went over the jumps gave me such a thrill! You have to have her. If you don't get her, I will!

(Enter Laura and Gertrude)

HORTENSE: Well, I'll talk to mother.

LAURA: Still into horses? How passé!

GERTIE: Real women ride boars.

BRENDA: I told you already: Don't talk to me about that!

LAURA: Brenda, you're such a wimp.

BRENDA: Polo is a stupid game. And it's abusive to animals!

GERTIE: The boars don't seem to mind it.

HORTENSE: They have no grace, no beauty, no refinement.

GERTIE: Beauty is in the eye of the beholder.

LAURA: You haven't lived until you've played polo from the back of a wild boar!

HORTENSE: They are not wild!

BRENDA: Touché.

GERTIE: But they were. We've tamed the savage beasts. We're like the cowboys of the Old West.

HORTENSE: Yee HAH!

LAURA: I **did** get this nasty gash on my leg this morning, though.

GERTIE: Sorry, Laura, it's hard to control Tusky when he gets riled.

6

BRENDA: I think you should have the tusks removed!

GERTIE: Where would the danger be then?

HORTENSE: What's so special about danger?

BRENDA: Anyway, there's plenty of danger riding a horse that's rocketing over a six foot rock wall.

LAURA: Horses are so predictable.

BRENDA: No they aren't!

HORTENSE: Dogs are predictable. A horse is like a 1200 pound cat.

GERTIE: Horses are so insecure. Little pea brains.

BRENDA: Shut up!

HORTENSE: And go take a bath. Frankly, you both **smell** like pigs.

*(**sounds** of boars and horses starts low and builds)*

LAURA: How would you know, Miss Lilly White?

BRENDA: Come Hortense, to horse!

GERTIE: Real women ride boars!

HORTENSE: You **are** a bore.

GERTIE: The goal is to be one with your mount.

BRENDA: "Woman who run with boars and the people who run from them."

LAURA: I count only the strong of heart among **my** friends.

HORTENSE: And the strong of stomach.

(Sound is LOUD)

BRENDA: Our horses are running away!

LAURA: Well, **hold** your horses!

HORTENSE: WHAT is the meaning of this?

GERTIE: Meaning? There is no "meaning"!

(LIGHTS UP. Doctor is stage center. Mom & Dad. Stage left and right)

DR.: There's no significant improvement as far as the coma goes.. Do I tell them that? Of course, she's healing. I tell them that.

MOM: Is she awake? I had a dream she woke up.

DAD: She isn't sleeping.

DR.: She's still in a coma, Mrs. Suddon.

MOM: Oh.

DAD: Any improvement?

DR.: Well, as far as her injuries are concerned, yes.

MOM: Maybe she's decided to not to wake up until she's all better.

DAD: She isn't sleeping.

DR.: She's unconscious.

MOM: I read that coma victims can hear people.

DR.: Perhaps.

DAD: I hate the word "victim".

MOM: Why do you have to be so negative?

DAD: Our daughter is in a coma.

MOM: But not dead. There's still hope.

DAD: She may be a vegetable when she--

MOM: Don't say that awful word! So negative!

DR.: We're doing all we can. *(exits)*

DAD: I'm sorry.

MOM: I know.

BLACKOUT

VISION

(MOM, DAD, STEWARDESS & ALIENS)

(PING)

STEWARDESS: As you can see, the pilot has put on the seatbelt sign, so everyone buckle up.

MOM: Miss, are we going to have turbulence?

STEW: I have no idea.

MOM: I hate turbulence. I knew we shouldn't have flown today.

DAD: We had to fly today. I have my conference.

STEW: We are now flying over the Bermuda Triangle region.

MOM: The what?

DAD: Just some mumbo jumbo. Don't worry. Just sit back and close your eyes. Do you need a Xanax?

MOM: I already took four.

STEW: And she's still wired!

DAD: Shh!

STEW: The Bermuda Triangle is a legendary area where a number of planes and boats have disappeared without a trace. There are many theories as to---

(Bump)

MOM: Ah!

STEW: Just think of it as a pothole in the road, Mam.

DAD: In a road 20,000 or so feet above the ground.

MOM: Ah!

STEW: Shh!

DAD: Sorry!

STEW: I'm just trying to calm her.

DAD: I know.

(Bump)

MOM: I have a bad feeling about this.

STEW: I have a bad feeling about this.

DAD: Why?

STEW: Sorry, but I do.

(Bump. They fall out of their seats)

STEW: You should have fastened your seat belts.

DAD: We don't have seat belts. I think we have grounds to sue.

STEW: If we all live through this.

MOM: What? Are we going to crash?

STEW: Being honest? I think there's a good chance of it.

DAD: Why?

STEW: Call it a gut feeling.

(Green lights sweeping and an eerie sound)

DAD: What are those lights?

MOM: And that sound?

STEW: The song of the Bermuda Triangle.

DAD: Just can the Bermuda Triangle crap all right? Go to Disney World and work on a theme ride if you want to scare people, okay?

STEW: That's a good idea. If we get out of here, alive.

MOM: Who are they?

STEW: Who are who?
(ENTER TWO ALIENS)

MOM: Them.

DAD: Is this a joke? Are we on some TV show?

AMOC: Vee-bo blebcobob. Dip widick.

STEW: I beg your pardon?

TIAW: Deem-bo locobob.

MOM: What are they?

DAD: Somebody's idea of a bad joke.

AMOC: Wadda wadda wooger.

TIAW: Woggie kokka do.

STEW: Hey! You two! You have boarded this plane illegally.
Therefore, you are illegal aliens. Speak English or get off this plane at
once.

AMOC: Welcome to the Bermuda Triangle!

TIAW: We hope your stay will be enjoyable!

STEW: Great. A tourist trap.

TIAW: Ricky ticky twotoo!

DAD: I demand a logical explanation.

AMOC: Go fish.

MOM: But what about our lives? What about Alison?

BLACKOUT

(Sound of plane in a nosedive into steel drum music)

11

VISION

(Spot up on Girl)

GIRL: The next time I blew the shell, the dolphin didn't come. Instead, a white stallion appeared on the beach. I wasn't little anymore and mother was gone. I was alone on the hot beach with the white horse. There was a breeze. I put down the shell. I held out my hand. And the horse began to walk toward me. Slowly.
Finally, the stallion's velvet muzzle touched my outstretched hand. I blew into the soft, flaring nostrils. When he breathed out I breathed his breath in, and then, we began to know one another.

An hour passed, and when I felt I could, I dug my hands into the stallion's thick mane. He backed up one step. I walked with him that one step back. And then we stood. The sun shining down. I buried my face against the stallion's neck. The smell was sweet. Sea salt air and sweat and something I cannot name.

(Spot closes down to black)

12

VISION

(*Ballroom Music. Girls are dancing with imaginary partners. Other girls are standing to one side talking*)

CLARISSE: Sean promised me the next dance.

MARY: I don't understand why you stand around waiting to dance with Sean, when every other guy in here wants to dance with you.

CLARISSE: Every other guy isn't Sean.

DAWN: You should play harder to get.

CLARISSE: Why?

DAWN: Look at it this way. Why isn't he dancing with you **now**?

CLARISSE: Because he's dancing with her.

MARY: But if he liked you as much as you like him, then he'd be dancing with you **now**.

CLARISSE: Would he?

MARY: Yes.

CLARISSE: Why?

DAWN: Clarisse only sees what she wants to see.

MARY: She's got hearts in her eyes.

CLARISSE: I am doing what I will. I want to dance with Sean. He is dancing with her. Then he will dance with me. I am waiting. For what I want, which I will get at the proper time.

(*The dancing continues as the lights fade to black*)

13

(SHRIEK that turns into a siren)

VISION

GIRL 2: One day, I wandered too far away from my mother and got lost. I sat down under a palm tree and fell asleep. I had a terrible dream. I was a horse. I was grazing in my safe pasture on sweet green grass. Suddenly I heard a strange loud noise. My head shot up. My nostrils quivered. What was happening? A car roared down on me and slammed into my side. I staggered out through the broken white rail fence into the road and collapsed. Alone. I lay in the road trying to get up, but I could not.

I fled from that dream, waking up with a start, gasping. I heard my mother calling. I got up and ran towards the sound of her voice.

14

VISION

(Girls are playing "Light as a feather. Stiff as a board")

AMY: This is so lame. I'm board stiff.

WREN: Well, it won't work now.

JANE: Don't stop! Come on guys. I felt...

WREN: What?

JANE: Tingling in my toes and back.

AMY: It's just the workings of your overactive imagination.

JANE: No. I really felt something. I want to try again. I bet we can do achieve lift off.

AMY: You bet? All right! Put your money where your mouth is!

WREN: Don't bet.

JANE: Why not?

WREN: I don't know. Seems creepy. What would you bet, anyway? A pizza? Five bucks?

AMY: Bet your life.

JANE: What?

AMY: Bet you life. The stakes should be pretty high. I mean, we are talking about breaking the laws of physics here. Right?

WREN: No! This is too creepy.

JANE: Calm down, Wren. What's your problem anyway, Amy? Why does everything always have to be such high drama for you to get your kicks.

AMY: Life on the edge, or no life at all!

WREN: Why don't **you** bet **your** life then?

AMY: It isn't my turn.

JANE: What?   BLACKOUT

(LIGHTS UP on DOCTOR & MOM stage right and DAD stage left.)

DOCTOR: There's been no change. No lightening.

DAD: "Lightening"?

DOCTOR: No sign that she is emerging from deep unconsciousness.

MOM: This isn't fair. She's only sixteen! She's too young to be in a coma. To be gone.

DOCTOR: Perhaps you should speak with the hospital Chaplain, Mrs. Suddon.

MOM: No! I want to speak with you! Tell me something!

DR: What? What do you want to know?

MOM: Everything! What's going to happen?

DR. I don't know.

MOM: That's not acceptable.

DR.: I'm sorry.

MOM: Are you?

DR.: Yes. *(exits)*

DAD: Are you coming home tonight?

MOM: Of course not. I have to stay in--

DAD: In case she wakes up.

MOM: Yes.

DAD: She's not sleeping.

MOM: It's a figure of speech.

DAD: You haven't been home one night in two months.

MOM: She might wake up.

DAD: I'm leaving. *(Does not exit)*

BLACKOUT

16

(Ephemera with her sisters who are weeping)

EPHEMERA: *(singing)*

SONG

ALICE: I followed your singing. It's quite lovely.

EPHEMERA: That is kind of you to say.

ALICE: It is such a sweet song: why are they crying?

EPHEMERA: They are weeping. There is a subtle difference.

ALICE: There is?

EPHEMERA: Oh, yes.

ALICE: Could I sit down a moment here?

EPHE: You could if you would.

ALICE: Then I can?

EPHE: Yes. *(sighs)* That is what everyone always want to do. And then...they never leave.

ALICE: But there is no one here, except... *(she gestures at sisters)*

EPHE: My sisters.

ALICE: There is no one else but you and me.

EPHE: And the hungry ghosts.

ALICE: Hungry?

EPHE: Oh, yes. Starved out of time and existence. But floating. Look there.

ALICE: I don't see anything there.

EPHE: Try harder.

ALICE: Dust motes? Pollen?

EPHE: Oh, no.

ALICE: I'm sorry, i can't see what you say you are seeing.

EPHE: Perhaps it is better that you do not.

ALICE: And if I stay?

EPHE: I wouldn't recommend it. It's not your time. Or rather, it doesn't have to be. You're hanging in the balance.

ALICE: *(rubbing her neck)* Hanging.

EPHE: Floating.

ALICE: But there's still hope?

EPHE: Oh, yes. There is almost always is that.

ALICE: My head aches.

EPHE: That does not surprise me. And you are confused?

ALICE: Tremendously!

EPHE: No idea which way goes up?

ALICE: Or down or around this...

EPHE: Island. Bermuda.

ALICE: The Triangle.

EPHE: The mother and the father and the child.

ALICE: What?

EPHE: The human trinity.

ALICE: Sing to me some more. Please.

EPHE: Then, you will never leave me.

ALICE: Would that be so bad?

SISTERS: Ask the ghosts!

18

VISION

GIRL 2: Mother? Mother? Where did she go? I only turned away a moment to watch the white dolphin playing in the ocean.

WITCH: T'only takes one moment for de entire Universe ta change completely aynd forever.

GIRL 2: What?

WITCH: Ya heard what I said.

GIRL 2: I don't understand it.

WITCH: Ya understand. Ya just don't like it.

GIRL 2: I cannot say I truly understand, but no I **don't** like it.

WITCH: Dat's better. Put yar question ta me, den.

GIRL 2: I challenge the statement that the "entire Universe" changes "completely". Don't you mean parts of it?

WITCH: Like yar part? *(chuckles to herself)*

GIRL 2: Or **your** part!

WITCH: *(laughs)* I see I'm gittin' under yar skin, missy.

GIRL 2: What? No! No. Just answer the question.

WITCH: Aynd who are ya ta be bossin' me around?

GIRL 2: I was here first!

WITCH: Oh, ya think so?

GIRL 2: Wasn't I?

WITCH: No, child. I have always lived on dis island. Both before ya and after ya.

GIRL 2: After me? Oh! You mean when we leave and go home.

WITCH: We?

19

GIRL 2: Me and my mother and my father.

WITCH: I don't see nobody here but you, girl.

GIRL 2: But if you've been watching me, then you've seen my mother. We collect shells together everyday!

WITCH: Do ya now?

GIRL 2: Stop it!

WITCH: I ain't seen yar mother, child. Aynd I don't lie.

GIRL 2: Then maybe you've mistaken me for another girl.

WITCH: If dat makes ya feel better.

GIRL 2 What? (pause) You didn't answer my question. About the Universe.

WITCH: As if dere was one!

GIRL 2: (angry) You said--

WITCH: I know what I said. It's de words "whole" and "completely" dat's puzzlin' ya. It would seem, as ya say, that dis bit and dat piece might change aynd not de complete picture, but dis Universe ya're living in is alive, child. Ya poke at dis aynd de whole rest of it feels dat pokin'--at some place. I blow out my breath (she does so) aynd I've moved da whole Universe. Not because I'm special. Because I'm part. Ya can do it, too. Try. (GIRL 2 blows out) Ya feel dat ripple moving out a ya? (GIRL 2 nods) Now. Concentrate. Ya feel de ripples coming in at ya?

GIRL 2: Yes.

WITCH: Aynd ya think ya can control all of de ripples all of de time?

GIRL 2: Can the ripples hurt me?

WITCH: Ya know de answer ta dat. Our actions have consequences. Yars. Mines. Ev'rybody's. One day de sun shines down on ya. One day, out of de blue, a car runs ya down.

GIRL 2: Why did you say that!?

WITCH: I thought ya were ready to hear it. Maybe I was wrong.

GIRL 2: Who are you?

WITCH: That don't matter. Why don't ya ask what ya really want ta know.

GIRL 2: What?

WITCH: Ya ain't dead, child. Ya're in Bermuda.

GIRL 2: Bermuda?

WITCH: Jyes. People been waiting for ya on the mainland. Don't ya keep 'em waitin' too long. There's a window open for de bird to fly in aynd de bird to fly out, but de bird wait too long, somebody come along aynd close dat window. Shyut fer good.

GIRL 2: Am I the bird?

WITCH: Puzzle on it. I hear yar mother calling, child. *(She starts to exit across the stage)*

GIRL 2: Mother! But you said--wait! *(the witch keeps walking. Does not look back. Waves her hand.)* Come back! How much more time?

(Fade to black)

21

(Light up on Mother. Alice enters)

MOTHER: I've been doing a lot of reading about Coma.

ALICE: I've been doing a lot of reading about the Bermuda Triangle.

MOTHER: I wonder if you hear me when I talk to you. I wish you could tell me just that, if nothing else. Something! Anything.

ALICE: My parents disappeared in their private jet in the Bermuda Triangle region. Now they're part of its legend.

MOTHER: You have to wake up. You're only sixteen. This can't be your life. Not all, or the end of it.

ALICE: What can I possibly do to top **that** in a lifetime?

MOTHER: This has to end. You have to wake up! I can't deal with this.

ALICE: Why did they leave me?

MOTHER: Why did you leave us? Me? I'm sorry. I'm being selfish. I can't help it.

ALICE: Where are you?

MOTHER: Where are you?

BLACKOUT

DAD: This waiting. No answers. She thinks it's easy for me. She thinks she cares more than I do. She believes she has to. She's the mother. Is she selfish? Am I? For wanting her to come home once in a while? We can't live in a hospital. I have to get away from this place. This prison for sick people and their waiting relations. Does that mean I don't care? I care. But I feel helpless. What can I do? Just wait. And I have to work. I have to. Insurance or not, this is going to cost us. A lot. And rehabilitation. I have to plan. But her whole world has just stopped to spin around and around this moment, like a vulture waiting for--No! I didn't mean that. Didn't mean to sound like I think our daughter will die. But will she? And if she comes up out of this coma and is brain-damaged will the rest of our lives revolve around sick beds. Will I lose a daughter and a wife?

I should have been a doctor instead of going into computers. But I didn't like the idea of blood and guts. And making life and death decisions. And looking into a patient's or a family member or a friend's eyes and saying "terminal". Whatever they're ultimately used for, computers are clean. No slip of a scalpel during surgery. Ruining a life. Just pushing keys. Maybe blowing up a city. Usually just transferring funds from company to company. And you know when a program is obsolete. And the viruses are controllable. No, If I'd become a doctor I'd be just as helpless now. No certainty. That's what Dr. Bells said. Nothing for sure. Just waiting.

"Coma". It's like some strange, wild animal. The great white coma that swallowed my daughter.

Maybe I should go talk to the hospital Chaplain. Maybe it's time I started believing in...something. I mean, is this "Fate"? One of those New Age obstacles that are supposed to make us stronger--We have a choice in how we deal with this? But what about Alison? What if she never comes out of the coma? What if she dies there. Wherever there is. What then? And what did she learn?

VISION

(Girls are assembled. They are wearing party hats.)

ALICE: Thank you all for coming to my celebration! And now, a Coca Cola toast to Father & Mother and the Bermuda Triangle!

(GIRLS toast and exchange looks)

ALICE: I'll be right back! *(runs off)*

GINGER: Am I the only one who thinks this is strange?

BUNNY: It's a free party. I say, whatever. Think of it as a kind of Wake.

GINGER: I think of it as kind of in bad taste.

BUNNY: Okay, maybe if one of us invited Alice to a "Gee and Wow, your parents disappeared over the Bermuda Triangle: Let's party!" shindig, I'd agree. But it's her party, right?

CINDY: Do you think her parents really did disappear over the Bermuda Triangle?

GINGER: Well, yeah. I mean, it was on the local and the national news.

BUNNY: Day in and out for months. The disappearance. The search. We all got interviewed for CNN, though, and that was cool.

CINDY: Cool? It all grossed me out. "Poor little rich girl!" "Girl inherits millions when her parents' private jet disappears over the Bermuda Triangle."

BUNNY: The last radar mark was over the triangle. You can't make that up.

(ENTER ALICE with presents)

ALICE: Of course you can. Of course they could have.

BUNNY: Sorry, if we're bumming you out, Alice.

ALICE: You think I haven't wondered about this? How many people can say their parents disappeared over--or into--the Bermuda

24

Triangle?

GINGER: It would be a pretty select club.

ALICE: Exactly. And here's another thing. A lot of people don't believe the whole "Bermuda Triangle" Mystery anyway.

BUNNY: It's like the Loch Ness Monster.

ALICE: Right.

BUNNY: But, all those ships and planes have disappeared in the Triangle.

ALICE: Yeah. I still can't decide which theory I like best: sudden strange weather phenomena or space-time warp.

CINDY: So, do you think your parents did disappear in the Bermuda Triangle?

ALICE: I'm still making up my mind. On the one hand, yeah. I mean, like, hello!, why would my parents get involved in a weirdo hoax.

GINGER: And on the other hand?

ALICE: Yeah, that other hand.

BUNNY: What about that other hand?

ALICE: Well, they could afford to.

BUNNY: To what?

ALICE: To disappear. To do, whatever, basically. I mean, they might have been puting money into Swiss bank accounts for years just for that moment.

GINGER: But why? And why wouldn't they take you with them?

CINDY: Yeah, I mean, your Mom went to all the trouble giving birth to you. I'd think she'd want to hang onto you.

ALICE: You'd think so, of course. But I'm adopted.

BUNNY: Since when?

ALICE: Since I was about two months old.

.25

GINGER: Wow.

ALICE: Yeah. I found out when the lawyer read the will. It was quite a good read, that will. Very well written.

GINGER: That's creepy.

ALICE: Creepy? I think it's interesting. And, I think it's evidence.

BUNNY: Evidence of what? A plan?

ALICE: Yeah. I mean, my parents had it all. My mom was an actress. Okay, she wasn't that good. No Oscars on the mantle, but it helped her catch the attention of my dad the mega-rich businessman. Say they decided after twenty years of parties and being invited to every major function we could possibly think of from the ribbon cutting ceremony of Euro Disneyland to the launch of the first space shuttle, that they'd had enough of the social whirl to last their two lifetimes.

GINGER: And?

ALICE: And so they buy an island somewhere or have plastic surgery to look like other people--I mean, they could be living right here in town.

CINDY: Keeping an eye on you?

ALICE: Possibly.

BUNNY: Why?

ALICE: Why not, is a more interesting question.

CINDY: This is whacko...with all due respect, Alice. Everything your saying flies in the face of....of...

ALICE: What?

CINDY: Parental instincts.

BUNNY: She said they weren't her real parents.

GINGER: Define "real"! There's more to being a parent than flesh and blood, isn't there?

BUNNY: But that is an important bond.

CINDY: Shut up, Bunny!

26

ALICE: She's got a point. One I've considered thoroughly.

BUNNY: Do you wonder who your real parents are?

ALICE: No.

BUNNY: Why not?

ALICE: I just don't. Why bother?

GINGER: If your wild theories are true, then why? Why would they something so kooky?

ALICE: Well, it's certainly one thing they didn't have.

CINDY: What thing are you--I don't get this.

ALICE: The oddity factor. It leads to the strangest and sometimes most lasting kind of fame. Like Amelia Earhart. People still are trying to find her.

CINDY: I thought they found her.

ALICE: Really? Well, if they did, she'll probably soon be forgotten. It's the mystery that keeps people hooked.

GINGER: And seeing Elvis at gas stations across America.

ALICE: It's a spectacular retirement for my parents whether or not they faked it, or the Triangle swallowed them up.

GINGER: "Retirement?"

ALICE: That's the way I like to look at it. And, of course, I have to be left behind.

CINDY: Why?

ALICE: You read the headlines. I keep the story alive and I make it more interesting. Now, open your gifts!

BLACKOUT

27

VISION

(Sound of a horn and the ocean. Spot up on Girl 1)

GIRL: At the edge of the End, the White Stallion stopped. I knew it was time for Time to resume its course. I only had so much left after all. I slipped off the horse's broad smooth back. My feet touched wet sand. A cloud passed over the sun. I heard a sound like wind through tall grass. I knew, the horse was gone. And I was alone. At the edge. And I knew I had a choice.

(GIRL goes and lies down on bed. Spot bright, then closes to black)

28

VISION

(The Raven is on a chair. Enter Girl 2. The Raven ignores her.)

GIRL 2: Are you the bird? Are you the bird the Witch told me about? I thought she meant me. That I was the bird. But then here you are. Can you speak? *(pause)* Of course you can't speak. You're a bird. *(she runs off)*

(Enter Alison)

ALISON: Now what?

RAVEN: I am the bird.

ALISON: What bird?

RAVEN: How do you like it here... in Bermuda?

ALISON: *(looking around)* It's beautiful. Bright blue sky. White light. Clean ocean air.

RAVEN: Decaying roses.

ALISON: What?

RAVEN: In every thing is its opposite.

ALSION: I suppose. So what?

RAVEN: I wouldn't trust my eyes here if I was you. If I was eye.

ALISON: "I" like me, or "eye" like eye ball.

DR. BELLS: SRRRIKE! TWO!

WITCH: Three strikes and you're OUT.
RAVEN: OUT.

RAVEN: Do you see the window?

ALISON: I thought I wasn't supposed to trust my eyes.

RAVEN: Do you see the window?

29

WITCH: Closing.

ALISON: I think I'm lost.

RAVEN: Up in the sky. Look! The window.

ALISON: I can't see anything.

RAVEN: You're blind.

ALISON: I am not. I just don't see your window.

RAVEN: **Your** window. You have to leave this place.

ALISON: I'm not going without my mom and dad.

RAVEN: They are waiting for you.

ALISON: At the hotel? On the beach?

RAVEN: Go back. Go back. Go back. Go back. *(circles her and exits)*

ALISON: I don't understand.

WITCH: OPEN YOUR EYES!

ALISON: They're open. Mother! *(runs off)*

(Witch exits. Girl 2 enters)

GIRL 2: I think I'm lost.

(Enter Raven)

RAVEN: Look! The window.

GIRL 2: Where?

RAVEN: Up there! In the sky.

GIRL 2: I see it!

RAVEN: Take these wings. *(Girl 2 takes wings off the Raven)*

GIRL 2: Now what?

RAVEN: Learn to fly.

BLACKOUT

30

VISION

ECHO: The weather never changes here. Have you noticed?

SKYE: No.

ECHO: No, what? No, it never changes or no you haven't noticed?

SKYE: Did you just say the same thing twice backwards?

ECHO: No!

SKYE: Oh. Good. What was the question?

ECHO: Does the weather here ever change?

SKYE: Not that I've noticed.

ECHO: Not that I've noticed.

(Skye looks at Echo)

ECHO: What?

SKYE: You're odd.

ECHO: **You're** odd.

SKYE: And there it is again.

ECHO: What?

SKYE: Nothing.

ECHO: Nothing.

SKYE: *(getting angry)* Stop it!

ECHO: Stop it?

SKYE: That!

ECHO: That?

SKYE: That "that" that.

31

ECHO: What!?

SKYE: If we stay here much longer, you'll ruin me.

ECHO: You'll ruin me.

SKYE: Here comes someone. Thank God!

(Enter ALICE)

ECHO: Can I help you?

SKYE: Don't talk to her, she'll ruin you.

ALICE: Ruin me?

SKYE: Don't tell me. Another one.

ECHO: Another one?

ALICE: Excuse me?

SKYE: If I must.

ALICE: Is this Bermuda?

SKYE: Be specific.

ALICE: I thought I was.

SKYE: Do you mean Bermuda or the Triangle?

ALICE: Is there any difference?

ECHO: Is there any difference!

SKYE: A great deal. One is a tourist trap and the other is trapped tourists.

ECHO: But which is which?

ALICE: I want to know about the Triangle.

SKYE: There are three points to the Triangle.

ECHO: Three points of the Triangle.

ALICE: Really?

32

SKYE: Of course. That's why it's called a triangle, stupid.

ALICE: You don't have to be rude.

SKYE: I'm sorry.

ECHO: I'm sorry.

ALICE: What are the three points?

SKYE: Bermuda, Puerto Rico and Miami.

ALICE: And this is?

SKYE: Somewhere in the middle. Left of center.

ECHO: Left of center.

ALICE: Left of center.

(PAUSE)

SKYE: Who sent you?

ALICE: I don't know.

ECHO: You don't know?

SKYE: How tragic.

ALICE: It doesn't feel tragic.

SKYE: It will.

ALICE: When?

SKYE: When you wake up.

BLACKOUT

33

(Enter Girl 1)

GIRL 1: I have walked to the edge of the ocean. I have walked to the center of the triangle. I stand now on a high cliff over the ocean. I cannot find the horse. And I cannot go back. *(She freezes with her arm stretched out)*

(Enter Girl 2)

GIRL: Mother! She's gone. Where did she go?

(ENTER WITCH)

WITCH: She's right behind ya.

GIRL 2: *(looks)* No, she isn't.

WITCH: She's right there before ya!

GIRL 2: What? Ah! A cliff. It must be a hundred feet straight down. And then the sharp rocks.

WITCH: I don't see no rocks.

GIRL 2: Just look!

WITCH: My eyes are wide open. It's just an easy step down.

GIRL 2: Are you trying to help me or kill me?

WITCH: You're lookin' fer good aynd bad. Things aren't so black aynd white here--in Bermuda. Just blue. Bright blue. Unfiltered sun. It can blind ya ta certain things if ya stay too long.

GIRL 2: What things? What kinds of things?

WITCH: Puzzle on it, child.

GIRL 2: Are you some kind of witch?

WITCH: Or maybe I'm your fairy godmother.

GIRL 2: What?

WITCH: Call me whatever ya like. It's just two sides o' the same coin. Two sides o' da same coin. Spinning.

(Girl 2 sinks to her knees.)

GIRL 2: I want to go home!

WITCH: And where might home be? Have ya forgotten?

(Witch walks past Girl 1)

WITCH: Wake up, child.

GIRL 1: *(seeing drop of cliff)* Ah!

GIRL 2: Who are you?

GIRL 1: Who are **you**?

WITCH: Two sides o' da same coin. Spinning.

(Witch exits. Girl 1 & 2 walk toward each other and form a "mirror" Image)

35

VISION

(White plaster statues. Girls 1 & 2 are nearby. Enter Alison.)

ALISON: A garden of stone! I didn't know they had ruins in Bermuda.

CLEO: Look, Lucretia. A new girl.

LUCR: Look? I can't turn my head. Why can't you remember that?

CLEO: Hello! Just visiting the Garden or have you come to stay?

LUCR: Of course she hasn't come to stay. We'd have seen her before if she was coming to stay.

CLEO: **You** might not have.

LUCR: That's nice, Cleo. Do I make fun of you?

CLEO: There's nothing fun about me.

LUCR: Now there you're right. Girl, whoever you are, come over here where I can see you.

ALISON: *(going over)* Can't you move?

LUCR: "Can't you move?" Of course I can't move. We're statues. Isn't that obvious? Or did you think you'd walked into a figure drawing class?

CLEO: You don't have to be rude.

LUCR: Yes, I do. I have a pain in my neck no one would believe.

CLEO: You'll scare her away.

LUCR: Like that would be a bad thing.

CLEO: Shh.

LUCR: RUN! While you still can.

ALISON: Why? Is it dangerous here?

CLEO: Shhh!

36

LUCR: Just open your eyes!

MOM: Al-i-son! You have to wake up!

DAD: She's not sleeping.

ALISON: What was that?

CLEO: Radio static. Here in the Triangle we pick up just about everyone.

LUCR: Literally.

ALSION: It scunded like my--

CLEO: Favorite TV show?

LUCR: Run! While you still can.

CLEO: Lucretia, I will have to report this to Ms. Noir.

ALISON: Who?

LUCR: Go ahead. If they hadn't locked my head like this then maybe I'd play ball. How long have I been standing here? Ten days? Ten years?

CLEO: Just be glad you aren't like the others. (Indicating with her eyes a pile of broken sculpture)

ALISON: Who?

CLEO: This is a private matter between Lucretia and myself.

ALISON: But I'm standing here and you're talking so--

LUCR: (To Alison) We can't move. You can. So scram! (To Cleo) At least they're resting peacefully.

CLEO: Well, they **are** resting. In pieces. But what are they?

LUCR: What are **we**?

CLEO: When you've been here longer, Lucretia, you'll understand.

LUCR: What about my neck?

CLEO: Just stop fighting this. It will all work out in the end.

ALISON: What end?

CLEO: The End.

ALISON: Is there ever a final END?

LUCR: Now that's redundant.

ALISON: I just meant--

CLEO: Haven't you read a book? It says "The End".

LUCR: Most modern books don't say "The End" at the end. That's pretty old-fashioned.

ALISON: And you can always read another book.

LUCR: She's clever.

CLEO: She's a troublemaker.

ALISON: I'm lost. I want to get back to the beach. To my mother.

CLEO: They're are no mothers here.

LUCR: Or fathers.

ALISON: No! My father is at a conference. My mother is on the beach. Collecting shells.

CLEO: Wild dreaming.

ALISON: Can you help me?

WITCH: Dere's a window open fer da bird to come in aynd da bird ta go out. Ya wait too long. Dat window gonna shyut fer good.

GIRL 2: Am I the bird?

GIRL 1: Am I the horse?

ALISON: I have a choice?

CLEO: What's to decide?

LUCR: Don't confuse her.

CLEO: I'm trying to guide her.

38

LUCR: She's already here.

CLEO: But undecided.

WITCH: You've lost track a' time, child. Beware it don't lose track a' you.

ALISON: I'm confused.

CLEO: That goes with the territory. Don't fight it.

ALISON: *(to Lucretia)* I have a choice?

CLEO: I'm in charge here. If you want a definite answer to anything ask me.

ALISON: I don't trust **you**. *(To Lucretia)* I have a choice?

LUCR: Yes.
[
WITCH: Dere's a window open fer da bird ta fly in aynd da bird ta fly out. Ya wait too long...

GIRL 1& 2: The window gonna shut for good.

WITCH: Maybe it be time fer ya ta fly.

WOMAN'S VOICE: Al-i-son!

(Alison walks nervously around the statues. And then flees.)

CLEO: Ms. Noir will not be impressed, Lucretia.

LUCR: *(Razz)* To her.

CLEO: We'll see what you say when **you've** been here a thousand years.

BLACKOUT

39

(Lights up on Moms sitting stage left and right)

MOM 1: My daughter is in a coma.

MOM 2: She is? Mine is too.

MOM 1: How long?

MOM 2: A year. And yours?

MOM 1: Six months.

MOM 3: Three weeks. Maybe it's for the best. So many injuries. Maybe this is better for her. But it's hell for me.

Mom 1: Yes.

MOM 2: Yes.

MOM 3: The not knowing. When?

MOM 1: If.

MOM 2: What will remain.

MOM 3: This waiting.

MOM 1: Yes.

MOM 2: Limbo.

MOM 1: I try to pretend that my daughter's on vacation. Some place wonderful where she's healing. And soon, one day soon, she'll come back.

MOM 3: Wake up.

MOM 2: Come home.

MOMS: Yes.

MOM 1: My daughter was--is--an excellent horsewoman. The day before the accident, she won the junior state championship in stadium jumping. Now I don't know if she'll ever ride again.

MOM 3: Was she wearing a helmet?

MOM 2: No.

MOM 1: What?

MOM 2: I'm sorry. I thought you meant me. My girl. She was in a motorcycle crash. No helmet. Now coma.

MOM 3: I'm sorry.

MOM 1: I'm sorry. My daughter didn't fall off her horse. She was in a car accident on the way back from the championship. With her coach. Head on. The other driver was drunk.

MOM 2: I'm sorry.

MOM 1: Her coach and horse survived. I wish she knew that. Maybe she'd come back.

MOM 3: Where do you think they've gone?

MOM 1: I think of her in a special protected place. I wait for her to come home.

MOM 2: I think of her as sleeping. I wait for her to awake.

DAD: She's not asleep.

DOCTOR: I'm Dr. Bells. Coma specialist. I specialize in educated guesses. No definitive answers. I can't say when, if, how. I can say maybe and maybe even soon. So sorry.

BLACKOUT.

41

VISION

WOMAN'S VOICE: AL-I-SON!

(Spot up on Girl 2)

GIRL 2: I remember waking up. My ears roaring. An explosion of metal slamming into metal. Everything grinding to a halt. Except me. I was flying forward. My head hit something so hard, I felt my brain keep going and crash into my skull. My neck snapped back.

WITCH: Like banging your head into a brick wall.

GIRL 2: It was this dull thud. It was this internal shriek. I felt a cold logical panic: this is not going to be all right. And this is not a dream. My bruised mind made a decision to go on holiday. At that moment, some part of me left myself. I was flying. It was warm. Most important, there was no pain. It was a clean break.

(Spot closes to black)

42

(Enter ALISON walking, disoriented. GIRLS 1 & 2 watch)

ALISON: *(out)* I keep meeting the same people twice. Don't I? Or do I? Well, they're not the **same** person. The same type of person. They're not really even people. Are they? More like...what? Parts of this... and that. Emotions. Voices. Maybe I'm going crazy. I feel like I'm walking in a big circle...waiting to land. *(she sits and falls asleep)*

(Enter Urthe, Phyre, Rayne & Wynde. They form a circle around her.)

URTHE: I claim this girl.

PHYRE: On what grounds?

URTHE: Precisely that. She's sitting on the ground. And I am Urthe.

WYNDE: I claim her.

URTHE: How can you top my claim, Wynde?

WYNDE: Her spirit is adrift. Therefore, it is mine.

RAYNE: But she is unhappy. Full of water. Therefore, she belongs to me.

PYHRE: But something still burns within her heart, so she belongs to me as well.

ALL: *(Walking clockwise)* What to do? What do do?

ALISON: *(Standing)* Who are you?

URTHE: Urthe.

WYNDE: Wynde.

PHYRE: Phyre.

RAYNE: Rayne.

ALISON: The four elements?

ALL: Yes.

ALISON: This is just ridiculous.

WYNDE: Is it?

43

ALISON: You can't be real!

PHYRE: That is ridiculous.

URTHE: We are trying to decide who may claim you.

ALISON: What? How dare you!

RAYNE: It is our right.

URTHE: As you stand on this earth and shall return to it: I claim you!

WYNDE: As you are a spirit drifting through this material world: I claim you!

RAYNE: As you are filled with sadness, your body full of water: I claim you!

PHYRE: As your heart still burns with hope: I claim you!

(They begin walking around her again)

ALL: As she is (urthe, phyre, rayne or wynde) I claim her!

ALISON: I've fallen down the rabbit hole.

WITCH: Hah!

ALL: The Witch!

ALISON: Please, make them go away.

WITCH: She's more dan a sum a ya. It isn't Time.

RAYNE: Yet.

URTHE: Her time is running out. I feel it in her bones.

WITCH: Ladies, don't ya be vultures! Now is not your now. It still be hers. Git yourselves gone!

(They exit)

ALISON: This place makes no sense.

WITCH: Of course it doesn't.

ALISON: Won't you help me? I want to go home.

44

WITCH: Ya can go home at any time. As long as the window is open.

ALISON: Where is the window?

WITCH: ya best keep walkin', child.

ALISON: Which way?

WITCH: Dat's up ta ya.

(Alison looks at her a long time. Then exits. The Witch watches and then follows her off)

45

VISION

*(Spot on Girl. **Sound** of wind and ocean)*
GIRL: The breeze grew stronger. I could smell rain. I saw lightning on the horizon. I heard my mother's voice, calling. The white stallion snorted and tossed his mane. I knew I had one moment. To go. I swung up onto the broad back, landing softly. I wrapped long strands of the mane around my fingers. The horse began to walk.

I rode the white stallion all day into the night. The breeze had turned to wind and the wind to a hard rain. For the first time ever in Bermuda, I felt cold. We galloped on into the waking day. The rising sun set the ocean dancing with light. Blinding. Bright. Shattering the deep blue. Scattering the dawning day to the three corners of oblivion.

(Spot closes to black)

46

VISION

(Alison is sitting, waiting in a chair with Vanna, who is reading a magazine. Alision is nervous. A Gigi comes out door. Vanna looks up)

VANNA: How'd it go?

GIGI: I get to stay another week.

VANNA: Great! Let's go hit the beach.

GIGI: Fab!

(They exit)

MS. BLANK: Next!

(Alison just stares at her)

MS. BLANK: That means you. Do you have your papers?

ALISON: What papers?

MS. BLANK: I'll take that as a "no." Well, come on. Ms. Noir is waiting.

ALSION: Why am I here?

MS. BLANK: Move it!

ALSION: All right! *(She follows)*

(They enter Ms. Noir's office. She is at desk reading papers.)

MS. BLANK: No papers.

MS. NOIR: Of course. Well, Alison, at least you're on time.

(NOIR goes through Alison's chart)

ALISON: Speaking of time, I don't remember coming here at all.

MS. BLANK: No one ever does.

ALISON: Why not?

MS. BLANK: Don't ask why, how, when or whatever.

47 ·

MS. NOIR: You may go, Ms. Blank. I'll ring when it's time.

MS. BLANK: Of course, Ms. Noir. *(exits)*

MS. NOIR: Now, Alison. You're a classic variation on a theme.

ALISON: A what?

MS. NOIR: Textbook exception to the rule.

ALISON: You're giving me a headache.

MS. NOIR: No, you brought that with you.

ALISON: I, what?

MS. NOIR: According to our records, you've been here--

ALISON: Where? The waiting room?

MS. NOIR: In Bermuda, of course.

ALISON: Bermuda.

NOIR: For two blips and a blop.

ALISON: What?

NOIR: You seem to be having trouble hearing.

ALISON: You seem to be having trouble speaking.

NOIR: This from someone who can't even remember how she got here. Well. You can stay one more week and then, if you want to stay longer, you'll need to get a visa.

ALISON: Have you seen my parents?

NOIR: They're are no parents here.

ALISON: Why not?

NOIR: You really don't have a clue, do you?

ALISON: About what?

NOIR: About anything. That's going on.

48

ALISON: I guess I don't. I just woke up here.

NOIR: She just woke up here! You've been in Bermuda for two weeks. One more week, and you'll need a visa to stay. Now. For now, I'll stamp your passport. You may go.

(RING)

ALISON: Where?

NOIR: Out.

ALISON: Out where?

NOIR: Back out into Bermuda.

ALISON: The Triangle?

NOIR: Is there a difference?

ALISON: Is there?

NOIR: In your case, probably not. Now, I'll see you in one week.

ALISION: How do I leave? If I want to?

NOIR: No one's keeping you here. You may go at any time.

ALISON: But how?

(Enter Ms. BLANK)

BLANK: Don't ask how, why or whatever.

ALISON: Why not?

NOIR: You are a curious girl. Do you have a clue who I am? What kind of operation this is?

ALISON: No.

NOIR: Maybe this will be easier for you to understand. Ms. Blank, give me a hand. *(She ducks under her desk. Comes up with skeleton mask on. Ms. Blank whips out a scythe)*

ALISON: *(screams)*

BLACKOUT

49

VISION 14

(Spot on girl. She stands on "bed". White feathers began to fall down around her)

GIRL: I stood on the beach with outstretched arms ready to go home. Now. To give up that special private retreat. Awake from something more than sleep. I closed my eyes and felt something soft fall down out of the wide blue vault of the Bermuda sky, brushing my cheek.

Horse Feathers! Enough to make a set of wings. Enough to get me out of Bermuda. In that instant, I understood that I **wasn't** home. That I had been gone a long, long time.

(SPOT OUT)

50

VISION

(Girls are sitting down cross-legged. Music is playing. Enter Alice. Girl 1 & 2 Are stage right and left)

(Music out)

ALICE: Can I join you?

LAURA: Of course.

BUNNY: Hi, Alice!

WREN: The more the merrier!

CLARISSE: We've been waiting for you.

(Alice sits)

ALICE: For me? Why?

BRENDA: To become the horse.

ALICE: What horse?

GIRL 1: The White Stallion.

ALICE: I don't think I have much time. I need to get home.

CLARISSE: There's always time.

AMY: No there isn't. You bet you life there isn't.

WREN: Shh!

GIRL 2: I want my mother.

ALICE: Yes. Mother where are you?

BRENDA: There are no mothers here. Not any more.

LAURA: There never were.

GIRLS 1 & 2: But I used to look for shells with my mother.

DAWN: A mirage.

GINGER: A mirage.

DAWN: Sweet dreaming.

WREN: Hallucinations.

LAURA: Elysian Fields

ALL: Yes.

ALICE: I came here to find my mother and father. They disappeared over the Bermuda Triangle.

CLARISSE: Bermuda is a refuge. What are you hiding from?

ALICE: I'm not hiding. I'm looking for my parents.

LAURA: There are no parents here.

WREN: What can't you face?

ALICE: I don't understand.

AMY: This is Bermuda. You need three points of reference to get around.

BRENDA: Triangulation.

GINGER: To find someone.

ALICE: I want to find my parents.

BRENDA: They are looking for **you**.

ALICE: What?

CLARISSE: We have been waiting.

ALICE: For me?

CLARISSE: To become the horse.

ALICE: What horse?

GIRL 1: The white stallion. Where did he go?

GIRL 2: Perhaps he is with the witch. Perhaps it is her horse.

52

ALICE: Why do you want to become a horse?

CLARISSE: THE horse. You need to be more particular. Some things are worth waiting for and some are not.
WREN: Leave her alone.

ALICE: Don't leave me alone!

GINGER: She's confused.

LAURA: You're wasting her time.

ALICE: Doesn't one of you know how to get out of here?

BRENDA: The horse is the way out.

ALICE: That makes no sense.

AMY: You've heard the Time Warp theory?

ALICE: You **know** I have. We were talking about it at my party!

AMY: What party?

CLARISSE: Shhh. I feel the ripples.

WREN: I feel them too.

(Sound of hooves under the scene and music, drumming)

ALICE: What is the horse?

DAWN: Your passion. Your desire.

GINGER: Where are they leading you?

GIRL 1 & 2: To this moment.

(The Witch enters)

WITCH: Everyone stand. It is time. No more waiting!

BRENDA: Alice, you are the key.

ALICE: I don't understand any of this!

WITCH: It's nothing ya **can** understand.

53

GIRL 2: I am the bird.

GIRL 1: I am the horse.

ALICE: Who are they?

WITCH: Ya already know da answer ta dat question. Stop Thinkin' and **feel**.

ALL: The ripples. Moving in.

GIRL 1: *(approaching)* I am your spirit shield.

GIRL 2: *(approaching)* I am your memory.

BRENDA: I am your stubborn doubt..

LAURA: I am your courage to try.

DAWN: I am your sense of grace.

AMY: I am your brush with death.

WREN: I am your fear.

GINGER: I am your hope.

CLARISSE: I am your will.

WITCH: I am your mind.

ALL: Playing tricks!

GIRL 1: Become the horse and vault the sky!

] 3xs

GIRL 2: Become the horse and fly

WITCH: De window is closing, child! You're heart is de horse's legs. Yar mind its eye. De window is closing, child.

ALL: Fly, girl, Fly! High and home! *(spin)* High and home! *(spin)* High and home! *(spin)*

WITCH: Or stay aynd perish, alone.

(The girls swirl away and off. Girl 1 & 2 stand left and right. Alison vaults over the Witch's back. She lands on her feet)

54

WITCH: It's time ya were back on yar feet, girl.

(GIRL 1 & 2 come and take her to bed. They help her lie down. They stand on each end of the bed for a moment. Then they step back.)

(Steel Drum music which soon goes backwards into Sound of crashing, sirens. Red lights flashing. A horse whinnying. Shouts. and a horn)

(SPOT on ALICE sitting up on "bed". Her mother is slumped down. Her father stands nearby.)

ALICE: Mom? Dad? Are you here?   *(Her parents turn slowly to her)*

MOM: Alison?

ALICE: Mom.

DAD: She woke up.

ALICE: Where did you go? Where have you been? I was looking for you. In Bermuda.

(SLOW fade to Black)

55

THE THEATRE OF THE SILVER DRAGON

PRESENTS

ART ISN'T EASY

by
Tamela Glenn

THE TRUTH WILL OUT
—Shakespeare

CAST

MIRA MINUET

FRANZ FRILK, the elder & the 14th

MARGOT

LISETTE

PROFESSOR STENK

JUDGE MINT

PHIL ITTEN

MISS SALLY WALLOOP /the COURIER

DECTIVE JANE JUNEJULI

WILLIAM WILLIAMS/BOB

MR. THYME/JOE/FUNERAL DIRECTOR

GLORY FRILK

PHYLLIS the MUSE

ART ISN'T EASY

ACT I, Scene 1

(The park. People are gathered. Mira is drawing Franz.)

Mar: I simply do not believe it! Lisette come quickly! (She does)

Lis: What is it, Margot?

MAR: Look!

LIS: Oh, my! Oh, dear! Oh me!

MAR: Can you believe it?

LIS: I guess I will have to.

MAR: A woman drawing a man? How ludicrous!

LIS: Ridiculous!

MAR: It is absurd.

LIS: Immoral!

MAR: It should be against the law.

LIS: Your right. (pause) Why?

MAR: My dear, it just is not done.

LIS: Right. Of course. I wonder if she is any good?

MAR: Why?

LIS: Just curious.

MAR: Hmmmm. Perhaps it is, in a way, our-uh-**duty** to see if she is.

LIS: If you think so! (They start sneaking over to look)

MIRA: Those two ladies are coming over. They think it is wrong for me to try to be an artist, but they cannot resist taking a peek at my work.

FRANZ: I have never understood why artists are so fascinating to other people. All you do is scribble marks on paper. So what?

MIRA: It is a skill. A way of seeing.

FRANZ: Seeing what?

MIRA: A kind of truth. A you-er you!

FRANZ: A me-er me? So what. I know who I am.

MIRA: I am making you immortal. You will be gone one day, but this drawing and the painting I am going to create from it will live one. Well, at least as long as the materials hold together.

FRANZ: Why not just hang my skeleton in the museum?

MIRA: Right now? Stay still please!

FRANZ: No, silly, when I am dead. My bones will last longer than your painting.

LIS: How morbid!

MAR: What do you expect from peasants?

MIRA: It does not matter if you understand. I am not even sure you want to understand, Franz. Just stop moving. I am almost finished.

FRANZ: Good. I do get paid today, right?

MIRA: Yes. Yes.

MAR: Who ever heard of a man posing for a woman.

LIS: We have. Today.

MAR: Well, it is not proper!

2

(They can see the drawing)

LIS: Oh, my!

MAR: I do not believe it!

LIS: She is very good!

MAR: But she cannot be good.

LIS: Why cannot she be?

MAR: She is a woman. Women are not allowed to be good!

LIS: They--We-- are not?

MAR: Not as artists. Not **that** good.

LIS: But she **is** an artist. Look at her drawing.

MAR: It is the principle of the matter. It is the way of the world! Come Lisette!

(They exit)

FRANZ: Did you hear that? It is the Way of the World, Mira. You are pretty brave to fly in the face of the whole world.

MIRA: Stubborn is what I am. I have a gift. It would be criminal not to use it.

FRANZ: And I have a hunger. It would be criminal not to feed it. Money please. You are finished, right?

MIRA: (Looking at drawing) Yes. I guess. (pause) As if anything is ever really **done**.

(She gives him money. He runs off. She works on her drawing. Enter Margot & Lisette.)

LIS: I thought we were going home, Margot.

MAR: I just had to have one last look.

LIS: Now can we go? It's getting rather cold.

MAR: Just look at her! Who does she think she is?

LIS: We could ask her.

MAR: Maybe she is a witch!

LIS: Oh! How frightening!

MAR: I wonder if my Uncle, the Duke of St. Ausberry is still burning them?

LIS: Burning them?

MAR: Yes. That is what you do with witches.

LIS: Oh! How horrible!

MAR: We cannot allow this to go on in our public parks!

(They exit.)

MIRA: I know it is a man's world. I just do not understand why the women in it seem to be so eager to keep it so. (pause, thinking) I wonder if she is as dangerous as she sounds? (exits)

ACT I SC ii

The Present

PROF. STENK: This evening we are gathered for the unveiling of a painting long lost to us. So few of the great works of the painter Franz Frilk, the elder, survived when his studio burned down in 1493. Only those he managed to carry out with him as his art went up in flames all around him. The Painting you are all about to witness--a stunning self-portrait--turned up in the collection of a rich Japanese businessman, who died last year. Thanks to you--our generous patrons, especially Miss Sally Walloop (She stands and waves at the crowd) we were able to buy it at auction last month in London. Tonight we unveil it! (Unveils Mona's painting)

(Everyone gasps)

SALLY: Worth every dime, Professor.

JANE: Magnificent!

WILL: Bravo!

(They all crowd around. Talking quietly--a buzz)

(MIRA, now a ghost, has entered)

MIRA: I do not believe it! How many times do I have to watch that lout, Franz get credit for my work? (Trying to get people's attention) Hey! Hey, you idiots! Can't you see? Don't you realize that those brushstrokes come from the hand of a woman?

JANE: Frilk certainly must have been a sensitive man.

SALLY: Yes, look at those brushstrokes.

MIRA: He was a Clod. All he wanted to do was eat, drink and be merry.

WILL: Quite an acquisition, Professor Stink!

STENK: It's "Stank", Williams.

WILL: I apologize. I've only seen it written down. I'm terrible with names.

JANE: He is. Oh, he is!

MIRA: You are all terrible with names--that is **my** painting. That is "Freeloading Franz" as painted by Mira Minuet.

SALLY: I'll bet he was handsome cad. Romantic! Exciting.

MIRA: You are looking at him right now, woman! He's staring at you with those beady eyes!

WILL: (joking) I think I'd be a little jealous if he wasn't a **dead** painter.

MIRA: He is lucky he is dead, because if he wasn't, I'd----

(Enter Judge Mint)

5

JUDGE: You'd what? Kill him? How?

MIRA: How can this happen? Where is fairness? Where is credit where credit is due? That is my painting. Franz Frilk was a bum! Now he is being called a genuis!

JUDGE: Who ever said life was fair, dear?

MIRA: This is death.

JUDGE: So it is. Tell you what, there may be a way for the truth to come out.

MIRA: How? My studio--the entire building-- burned to the ground. I never made it out. Franz did. With a handful of **my** paintings. People thought they were good. Good enough to buy. He signed his name on them! It's sickening. It's desecration, that's what it is.

JUDGE: People **did** wonder why he never painted again.

MIRA: He never had to. He made enough money from the one's **I'd** painted to eat, drink and be merry the rest of his life. He told them he was sick with grief over "his model's tragic death". Can you believe it! He said I was **his** model! Now, they call **my** self-portraits portraits!

JUDGE: And vice-versa. Yes, I know. It must be quite annoying.

MIRA: Annoying! Why do you think I'm still hanging around this place?

JUDGE: That's what I came to talk to you about. But first, the facts. Did Franz burn the studio down?

MIRA: If you are who I think you are, then you know he didn't.

JUDG: Just testing. I wanted to see if you'd tell me the truth. The fire spread from the building next to yours. Your turpentine and varnishes well, they caused it to move rapidly.

MIRA: Why was the building next door on fire?

JUDGE: That's another story I'm working on. Now, why was Franz at your studio that night, Mira?

MIRA: He wasn't. He ran up to try to save me when he saw the building was on fire. He lived across the street.

JUDGE: So, he was trying to save you.

MIRA: Yes. But that is my painting!

JUDGE: I am getting to that. If it wasn't for Franz, that painting wouldn't still exist, correct?

MIRA: Correct.

JUDGE: What is more important: That you get credit for it or that it is considered to be a masterpiece? That all your paintings are considered to be masterpieces? If that was enough, **you** could rest in peace, Mira.

MIRA: What am I supposed to say to that? Of course I'm glad the paintings were saved.

JUDGE: In your own time, no one would ever have accepted you as an artist, Mira. Maybe this is all for the best.

MIRA: All for the best! All for the best! That is my painting! I painted it. Created it. That is my immortality!

JUDGE: But you told Franz it would be his. And you were right.

MIRA: I had hoped it would be ours. Why did the roof have to fall in me? Why did I have to die!

JUDGE: We all die. Franz did too. Of the plague.

MIRA: Well, you don't.

JUDGE: I do not exist.

MIRA: Oh, really? Then why am I talking to you?

JUDGE: You sure are stubborn. I exist outside time. In this little limbo which you won't leave.

MONA: I'd like to R.I.P. I'd like to R.S.V.P. to the big cake walk in the sky, really, I would. I just can't. I want credit where credit is due. My paintings are my children. They're what I left behind when I passed through. I want them to know who their real Mother was! Franz may have died from the plague, but not before he became a father. And, can you believe this, one of his great, great, great, great, not-so-great grandkids thinks he's a talented sculptor!

JUDGE: I am aware or that. And that may be your way out. But it won't be easy.

MIRA: It never has been. What's the deal?

JUDGE: Come this way. I need to sit down. My feet are killing me.

MIRA: You're joking, right?

JUDGE I never jest. Do you have any idea how old I am? Let's go.

(They exit)

SALLY: Now, Professor, tell everyone about the museum's next big coup!

WILL: Did you hear that? Something new!

JANE: Speech! Speech!

STENK: If I must. Just kidding! I always love to talk about the museum. Well, this is sort of "family" month at the museum. After two years you will all see a new piece of sculpture by Franz Frilk, the younger.

WILL: Frilk the 14th?

SALLY: Yes, and guess who commissioned it!

STENK: Our patron saint of the arts, Miss Sally Walloop, of course.

(applause for Sally)

JANE: There's only one question.

WILL: Will it get stolen before the unveiling again?

JANE: No, what should I wear of course. Oh, Professor Stank, when is the unveiling?

STENK: You should all receive your invitations tomorrow!

JANE: But we want--we **need**-- to know now!

JANE: But we want--we **need** to know now!

SALLY: Tell them Professor. Or I will!

STENK: Oh, very well, the unveiling of the new sculpture by Franz Frilk the 14th is next Friday at 8:00 p.m. Reception to follow. Don't forget your checkbooks!

SALLY: I never forget mine. Do I Professor?

STENK: No, Miss Walloop you do not.

JANE: I've got to get a new dress! and Shoes!

WILL: I have to get a new tie.

STENK: Well, it's time to shut and bar the doors, people--I mean dear patrons--so good night to you all! (They take one last look at the drawing)

JANE: It's sublime!

WILL: I wonder what Art News will say?

(They exit)

SALLY: Goodnight Professor! There's just one thing.

STENK: Sorry, Miss Walloop. THANK YOU! From the bottom of my heart I thank you and the entire staff of the museum thanks you! We love you. The very stones that make up this building thank you. Without you, we'd be nothing.

SALLY: It was nothing! (waves and exits)

STENK: Now I know why it is better to give than to receive.

CURTAIN CLOSE

9

ACT I Scene iii

(Enter Phil with a hammer and a box containing a shattered sculpture. He bangs his head against the wall)

PHIL: It always happens! Just when I am one masterstroke away from creating my first masterpiece the hammer slips on the chisel and crash. De-construction! Wasted time and wasted marble. (Sits down and looks at pieces of the sculpture) This was good. And this. They were better when they were one piece of course. I am an idiot!

MIRA: He certainly seems to be.

JUDGE: An idiot savant.

MIRA: What's "savant" about him?

JUDGE: He's a very talented artist. Or he will be if I can get him to stop the sculptural overkill. Just when he reaches the point of perfection, he loses control and delivers a death blow.

MIRA: Why?

JUDGE: He's a perfectionist. They can never leave well enough alone.

PHIL: Oh, hammer! You are friend and enemy! Tool and Weapon!

MIRA: He's quite dramatic. Maybe he should try acting.

JUDGE: He is only capable of playing himself.

MIRA: That hasn't stopped most of the actors in the world.

JUDGE: True.

PHIL: My work should be in that museum. It will be. My latest work sits on my sculpting table awaiting the next blow of this hammer! I can only FAIL!!!!

MONA: He certainly has a positive outlook.

JUDGE: His time will come.

MONA: You've got to be joking. (He gives her a "look") Sorry, you never jest.

JUDGE: You're beginning to get the hang of this. Good. (exit)

CURTAIN OPEN

ACT I SCENE iv

GLORY: Fawn, I'm really worried about our "dear" brother, Franz.

FAWN: Why? He's not sick. Is he?

GLORY: I'm worried about his work! Have you seen the new sculpture?

FAWN: The pink and yellow thingy?

GLORY: Yes, the pink and yellow "thingy". It's called "Venus in Sunlight".

FAWN: Why?

GLORY: Because it is.

FAWN: Oh. Well, it's not finished, that's all.

GLORY: He says it is.

FAWN: He does?

GLORY: Yes, he does. I asked him if he was experimenting with abstraction, and he wondered why I asked.

FAWN: Why did you?

GLORY: Because if it's done, and if it is supposed to be a piece of realistic sculpture, then it's, well, a disasterpiece.

FAWN: I see what you mean. Do you think he's lost his gift?

GLORY: Did he ever have one?

FAWN: At one point, I thought he was getting so bad he was almost good.

GLORY: I remember that point. (pause as they remember) You know, I even asked him if he'd been working with a blindfold on, hoping it was some kind of performance-art piece. He said no, and he even got mad and accused me of insulting his work!

FAWN: Well, you were, weren't you?

GLORY: No! Well.....I suppose it depends on how you look at it. I was trying to figure out if he has lost his marbles. I was trying to **understand.**

FAWN: And do you?

GLORY: No! All I do know is that if this work is unveiled at the museum next week, he's ruined. I wonder if this has anything to do with his model Roxanne leaving to be on that TV Soap Opera?

FAWN: I keep hoping they'll kill off her character and she'll come back and work for Franz.

GLORY: She's the only person he has liked to sculpt for years.

FAWN: Why doesn't he like to sculpt us?

GLORY: We don't inspire him, remember?

FAWN: I still can't believe he actually said that.

GLORY: I can. He doesn't inspire me either.

FAWN: I heard this guy in the health-food store say that Franz is a "washed up-never was".

GLORY: Well, if he shows that piece of twisted muck there won't be any doubt!

(Enter FRANZ)

FRANZ: What do you think? "Venus in Sunlight"! Is she not exquisite?

FAWN: Does he want an honest answer?

GLORY: Of course not.

FRANZ: Observe how light plays off the surfaces. Making planes of pink and yellow. True eye candy! Ah! I am a genuis! (Sets sculpture on table) Wrap her up. The museum is sending over a courier to pick her up in an hour. I have to dash off now and buy some materials. Chow!

FAWN: I'll get the packing stuff.

GLORY: Wait! We can't let this piece of trash out of the room.

FAWN: It's out of our hands.

GLORY: Oh, no it isn't. It's just gotten in them. (She grabs the statue)

FAWN: What are you going to do, Glo?

GLORY: What we did the last time, Fawn!

FAWN: So then we?

GLORY: YES!

CURTAIN CLOSE

13

ACT I Scene v

(PHIL is sweeping. Enter PROF. STENK)

STENK: Now, Phil, as you should remember, the new sculpture by Franz Frilk the 14th arrives this afternoon. The big unveiling party is set for this Friday. You are to guard the statuette until I return. Don't let it out of your sight! We don't want a repeat of last time or the time before that.

PHIL: You said it.

STENK: If our loyal patrons would give us more money we could hire full time, top notch security. As it is, we have you, Phil.

PHIL: Thank you, Professor.

STENK: Oh, well, after two major thefts of Franz the younger's works, the public is clammoring to see something new--which should mean a good turn out for the unveiling. At least we'll make money off the $25.00 a head opening night admission fee. So, Phil, don't let the statuette out of your sight. Do you understand?

PHIL: Loud and clear as a belly.

STENK: Are you sure?

PHIL: Over and out you go!

STENK: Good. I'm just going to duck out a minute and buy my daily lottery ticket.

PHIL: Good luck, Professor.

STENK: It's not luck, Phil. It's odds. Sooner or later my number is bound to come up, and then I won't have to keep grinning my ears off to get money for this museum from people I don't like! (exits)

PHIL (sweeping) Wonder what Franz Frilk the 14th has come up with this time? I think he is "greatly overrated" to quote Art News.

COURIER: Package for Professor Stink.

JUDGE: You guess or you know? There's nothing worse than whiners.

MAR: The old grump is back.

JUDGE: Do you think I didn't hear that? Shape up, pipe down, in general, LISTEN! That is, if you'd like to move on in death.

BOTH: What?

JUDGE: Oh, well that sure got your attention.

MAR: What do you mean move on? Are you saying we can get out of here?

JUDGE: CRIME?

LIS: I beg your pardon?

JUDGE: What was your crime? Why have you been kept walking the earth?

MAR: You already know that. **You** told **us** centuries ago.

LIS: She is right.

JUDGE: CRIME?

MAR: Oh, very well. I started a fire that killed Mira Minuet.

LIS: But I did not help her. I was just there!

JUDGE: But you did not stop her, now did you?

LIS: No, Judge Mint, I did not. I am sorry to say!

JUDGE: The fire was the action you took, Margot, but your true crime is far more serious.

MAR: What? Why? Is this some game?

JUDGE: No. What was your crime!?

MAR: What are you getting at?

PHIL: That's Stank. I'll take it.

COURIER: You Stink?

PHIL: That's STANK! I'm supposed to take the package. I work here. I'm Phil Itten.

COURIER: Right. (Writes) Now if you'll just sign here, Professor Stenk.

PHIL: I'm not--

COURIER: No signature, no package!

PHIL: Okay! (signs and takes package)

COURIER: Nice. Nice Nice. Have a NICE day. (exits)

PHIL: I wonder what it is this? I wonder if it's good. (He starts to unwrap it. Stops) No, I mustn't spoil the Professor's fun. Mustn't get fired. Again. (Puts it on table. Sweeps and then stops suddenly) Whatever it is, I know my work is better! I am talented. I have a calling--I hear it calling: "Phil Itten, your time has come!" (grabs statue and runs out. Sounds of paper and taping.)

(Enter Margot and Lisette.)

LISETTE: Why have we been doomed to walk through dreary museums forever?

MARGOT: You know why.

LIS: But it was your idea!

MAR: You were still an accomplice to the crime.

LIS: Oh, me! Oh, my! (pause) Well, I still don't think it was fair. It was all your idea!

MAR: But you did go along with it.

LIS: So I did, I guess.

(ENTER JUDGE MINT)

16

JUDGE: Why did you set Mira Minuet's building on fire?

LIS: Well, actually, with all the gunpowder she rounded up she burned down the whole block. (Margot glares at her) You did.

MAR: I know I did! (To him) So, you want to know why, right? (he nods) Well, she had to be stopped! She was flying in the face of decency. She did not know her place. She was dangerous.

JUDGE: What about you, Miss Firefly?

MAR: We are talking about the rules that glue a society together! She was an anarchist.

LIS: You said she was a witch.

JUDGE: Yes, you did. You even tried to get your uncle, the Duke of Ausberry, to burn her as one.

LIS: And he wouldn't.

JUDGE: That's right. What was it he told you?

MAR: That no one would buy her work and just to forget about it. Sooner or later she'd starve or get married or both.

JUDGE: But you couldn't stand that. You took matters into your own hands. Now, there is a debt to be paid.

MAR: All right! Okay! What do we have to do?

JUDGE: You have to get credit where credit is due.

LIS: I would not even know how to begin.

JUDGE: I'll leave you ladies to think about it. (exits)

MAR: Wonderful. I suppose this will involve an apology to Miss Mira Minuet. I hate apologies.

JUDGE: (popping in) At last the word: "HATE". **That's** what you are guilty of!

LIS: I didn't hate her. I just went along!

JUDGE: BAHHHHH!

LIS: Why is he doing that?

JUDGE: You are guilty of being a sheep! Of not thinking for yourself! (exits)

LIS: This repentence thing is really going to be hard, Margot. For you not to hate and for me to think? Oh my! Oh dear!

MAR: Oh, shut up! (They exit)

(Enter Professor)

STENK: Phil! Phil! Where's that boy gone off to! (Phil runs in with a different package.) Oh! There you are, and there it is! Hand 'er over.

PHIL: Here you go, sir! Open 'er up!

STENK: No, Phil. I promised Franz--and it was hard!--that I would wait until Friday. I have to unwrap the statuette before everybody.

PHIL: Good. Do it now.

STENK: What?

PHIL: Open it **before** everybody.

STENK: Oh! Ha! Ha! That's funny, Phil. No, I mean I have to unwrap the statuette on Friday night in front of the crowd.

PHIL: But you need to put the red velvet cloth over it and all that, right?

STENK: I'll put the velvet over the package, Phil.

PHIL: But it'll snag a bit, won't it?

STENK: We'll just have to see now, won't we? Now, into the safe with this. (exits)

PHIL: I'm doomed. (Runs out the other way. CRASH and OUCH! on Stenk's side)

PHIL: What's happening!-- (enter Courier from Stenk's side) I thought you'd left.

COURIER: Oh! Professor Stink--

PHIL: That's Stank and I'm not--

COURIER: I lost my way. This place is a labyrinth. I'll just be going. That's the way out, right?

PHIL: Yes, but--Hey, what's that package you've got there? You didn't have a package. I took it!

COURIER: This old thing? My next delivery! (runs out)

PHIL: Oh.

(Professor Stenk staggers on holding his head)

PHIL: What happened, Professor?

STENK: Some thug dressed as a courier hit me over the head with something and grabbed the statuette.

PHIL: That was the courier that brought it here. He/She was lost. I guess he/she took the statuette back. Maybe Franz wants to work on it some more. OH NO! (realizing the courier has Phil's statuette)

STENK: I wondered when you'd figure it out. We've been burgled! I can't believe it. Another theft of the work of Franz the 14th! I'm ruined. The insurance company refused to cover his work this time. Too high risk, they said.

PHIL: Guess they were right.

STENK: I'll call the police.

PHIL: Professor, I have a confession to make.

STENK: Are you partners with that thug?

PHIL: What? Oh. No. You see, I switched the statuette.

STENK: Why would you do that, Phil?

PHIL: I wanted you to really take a serious look at my work. I thought you were going to look at it right when you came back. I thought you'd be very impressed, and then I'd say, "Gee Professor, thanks! I am the person who created this work of art" and then I'd become famous and could stop sweeping floors and devote myself totally to my work.

STENK: So the criminal took **your** sculpture?

PHIL: Yes.

STENK: I'm saved!   (CRASH-- OUCH!)

PHIL: Oh, no!

STENK: What was that?

COURIER: The door at last!

STENK: That isn't?

PHIL: The Courier. I think he/she just knocked over the real Franz Frilk the 14th.

STENK: NOOOOOOOOO! (Runs out. Enters with a brown paper-wrapped smashed statuette.)

PHIL: Sorry, Professor. I almost saved the day. What now?

STENK: ARGHHHH!!!!!   (He runs out holding his head.)

PHIL: I don't think there is any way this could be good: I'd better clean the windows. It's important for the light to get in to illuminate the works which haven't been stolen. (Starts using Windex)

(Enter Phyllis, the spirit of Phil's broken statuette)

PHYLLIS: Hello, Phil. You look sad.

PHIL: (startled) Ah! (jumps and sprays Mira's painting) Who are you?

PHY: Don't you recognize me? I'm that little voice in your head that always said "stop" right before you dealt the death blow to your sculptures. I am your muse. I'm what you were looking for.

It's too bad that the first time you finally captured me, the piece got stolen.

PHIL: I have a muse?

PHY: I'm what inspires your work.

PHIL: Really? But we've never met.

PHY: I don't exist.

PHIL: Then why am I talking to you?

PHY: I don't know. Let's go make another sculpture.

PHIL: Okay, There's not much else to do except worry. (They exit) Oops! (Runs back on and blots the painting. Runs out. We can see Mira's signature)

VOICE of THYME: Judge Mint! Please report to your superior at once!

JUDGE: This can't be good. I haven't had supervision for two hundred years.

(Enter Mr. Thyme.)

THYME: Well.

JUDGE: Long Time no see.

THYME: Very funny. Do you have any idea how many times I've heard that joke?

JUDGE: I never jest, Mr. Thyme.

THYME: Oh, yes, that's right. That's why you got the job: no sense of humor. Well, Judge Mint, got everything under control?

JUDGE: Well, I thought I did. But if I really did, you wouldn't be here.

THYME: Very good.

JUDGE: So fill me in.

THYME: Are you sure your case load isn't too much for you to handle?

JUDGE: I'm fine. I've almost got two cases closed.

THYME: Do you?

JUDGE: Don't I? What's the problem?

THYME: Too many spooks hanging around.

JUDGE: They scrabble the frequency, don't they?

THYME: Exactly. And, probably as a result of this, Phil Itten's muse had materialized. She's walking around talking to him. I thought you would want to know.

JUDGE: Thank you Mr. Thyme.

THYME: Tidy up the pieces, old boy. I can count on you, right?

JUDGE: Of course, sir.

THYME: Of course. Well, I'll see you in a few centuries .
      (exits quickly)

JUDGE: My, how Thyme flies.

CURTAIN CLOSE

ACT I, SCENE vi

(Fawn and Glory come out to wait. Judge enters with Mira to watch)

MIRA: Who are these people?

JUDGE: Watch, listen and learn.

FAWN: He/She's late. What if he/she couldn't get it? What if--

GLO: What if she/he's gotten hung up. Crimes don't run on time.

FAWN: Right. So while we have this time to talk, there's something I've been wanting to ask you.

GLO: Oh, really? Is it, "What color is puce" by any chance?

FAWN: No, but that's a good question.

GLO: Puce is in the eye of the beholder.

FAWN: I see. Well, what I really wanted to know is why you don't sculpt anymore?

GLO: That's an easy one. Because I don't want Franz to rip me off anymore.

MIRA: What!?

FAWN: What?

GLO: He only got successful by showing my work. He said we had to use the name of Franz Frilk and a female Frilk just wouldn't do. He railroaded me. But, we were making good money, so I kept my mouth shut. I figured that at least my work was getting shown--and I knew who the real artist was. I didn't need to be an egomaniac about it.

JUDGE: You catching all this, Mira? (he gives him a look)

FAWN: But when he decided to do his own work, you stopped doing yours. I never understood that.

GLO: I needed a break. And I was mad. I mean, how was I going to get **my** stuff shown?

FAWN: But what about the joy of creation?

GLO: You're right, but at the time I was jealous, angry, hurt, insulted--you name it. Then, when it turned out that Franz had absolutely no talent, well, it became a matter of principles.

FAWN: So now we have to steal his sculptures.

GLO: Yes.

FAWN: Why? Exactly.

GLO: I can't have my name on those insults to the human eye. I am Franz Frilk the 14th--artistically. I have a reputation. I'm not going to let him trash it!

(Enter Franz)

FRANZ: Protesting something, sisters?

FAWN: You could say that.

FRANZ: Good for you. Well, I can't wait until the unveiling. At last one of **my** pieces will be seen by the world! Then Glory can stop thinking she has all the talent in this family. I am Franz Frilk the 14th, after all. (he exits)

GLO: Jerk!

MIRA: The resemblance is creepy. He looks just like Franz. Acts just like Franz, too!

(Enter Courier)

COURIER: Sorry to keep you waiting. Hit a few snags in the museum.

FAWN: But you got it?

COURIER: Right here.

FAWN: Saved again. You always do such good work.

COURIER: Speaking of work, when are you going to start sculpting again, Glory?

GLORY: This isn't the same package. What is this? (She starts to unwrap it)

ALL: What? (looking at it)

FAWN: That's pretty good.

COURIER: I took it right out of the Professor's hands. You should have heard him freaking out about it being stolen.

GLORY: Could Franz have figured out our scheme and...

ALL: Nooo.

COURIER: He has shown no signs of talent.

FAWN: True.

GLORY: This doesn't have our seal on it. There's another hand in this mix.

COURIER: Come on, we have work to do. (They exit)

JUDGE: A regular three-ring circus.

MIRA: And this is going to help me?

JUDGE: Well, it's going to be a bumpy flight. (They exit)

END OF ACT I

25

"ART ISN'T EASY"

TAMELA GLENN @1998
ACTS II & III

Theatre of
the Silver Dragon
P.O. Box 171
Stillwater, ME 04489-0171

CAST

MIRA MINUET

FRAN FRILK the elder & the 14th

MARGOT

LISETTE

PROFESSOR STENK

JUDGE MINT

PHIL ITTEN

MISS SALY WALLOOP/THE COURIER

DETECTIVE JANE JUNEJULI

WILLIAM WILLIAMS/BOB

MR. THYME/JOE/FUNERAL DIRECTOR

GLORY FRILK

FAWN FRILK

PHYLLIS THE MUSE

ACT II, SCENE i

CURTAIN OPEN

(The Museum. Enter Prof. Stenk.)

STENK: Phil! Phil! Come here immediately!

PHIL: (running in with a hammer in his hand, followed by Phyllis) Yes, sir?

STENK: Good gravy, Phil, you look like a madman. Been sculpting on museum time again, huh?

PHIL: Well, I got this sudden inspiration! (points to Phyllis, whom the Professor cannot see)

STENK: I see.

PHIL: No, over there. (Phyllis waves.)

STENK: Huh?

PHYLLIS: He can't see or hear me, Phil.

PHIL: Really?

PHYLLIS: I'm **your** muse. As far as I know, he doesn't have one.

STENK: Talking to himself again. Thank heavens for Miss Sally Walloop and her checkbook!

PHIL: Why's that, Professor?

STENK: She gave the museum the money to hire two--can you believe it--TWO! security guards. They're coming over any hour now. I have to step out and see Franz about the well, you know.

PHIL: The theft.

STENK: (wincing) Thank you for rubbing it in, Phil!

PHIL: You're welcome, sir. I do my bestest.

STENK: Well, try to hold off the artwork until the security people arrive. We wouldn't want anything else to get stolen would we?

PHIL: To be honest, sir, I wouldn't really care if someone stole that one. (points)

STENK: (looking) Yes, I see what you mean. Well, I'm off. Behave yourself.

PHIL: Yes, Professor. Have a nice day!

STENK: I don't think that's possible at this pointl. (exits)

PHYLLIS: Come on Phil! I'm tired of waiting. We have work to do. (she skips out)

PHIL: I hear my muse calling and I must obey! (exits with raised hammer)

(Enter Bill Bob and Joe Bob, security)

BILL: Well, this is the place.

JOE: No wonder they need security! All this art and nobody home.

BOB: Why if I was a robber I'd just weasel on in the door and take that one and that thing and weasel on out to the pawn shop.

JOE: I wonder what this high class stuff goes for? It's not my taste, I have to say.

BOB: Well, we don't have to like it.

JOE: Just guard it.

BOB: Right.

JOE: That Miss Sally Walloop really knows how to throw her money around. You have to admire that in a person.

BOB: As long as they're throwing it to us!
(They both laugh loudly)

(Enter Stenk)

STENK: Phil! I forgot--

BOTH: Password!

STENK: I beg your pardon?

JOE: This museum is open 10 a.m. to 4 p.m. today. It is 9:30 a.m.

BOB: If you want to come in **now**, you have to be someone who knows the password.

STENK: But I--

JOE: Don't know the password.

STENK: Well, nobody told me!

BOB: But you do know what a password **is**?

STENK: Well, of course, I know what a password is!

JOE: So then, do you know what **our** password is?

STENK: How could I? Listen I'm Professor Stenk. I run this museum.

BOB: I thought Professor Stink ran this museum.

JOE: So did I.

STENK: It's "Stank".

BOB: What do you mean "it's Stank"?

JOE: You are obviously an imposter.

BOB: Right. If you were the real Professor you would know your name. "Stink"

JOE: Right. "Stink"

STENK: Listen, get Phil Itten and--

BOB: Oh, that's what they always say!
STENK: What?

28

JOE: Just fill it all in later.

BOB: Right.

STENK: Listen, you cretins, I am Professor Stenk!

JOE: Well, good for you, but you aren't getting into **this** museum.

BOB: We work for "Stink".

STENK: It's "STANK"!

BOB: Stink, stank, stunk: Hit the road, pal.

JOE: Yeah, before we call the **real** cops!

STENK: Are you threatening me?

BOB: Time to take out the trash, Joe.

JOE: Right, Bob. (They throw Prof. Stenk out. Enter brushing themselves off)

BOB: Nothing like sending an imposter packing!

JOE: Your art is safe with us, Miss Sally Walloop.

BOB: Right.

(phone ringing)

JOE: I'll get that. (Answers the phone) Oh! Hello there Miss Walloop. What? Really? Oh. Well, we're sorry, but how can we help it if the gent doesn't know his own name?

BOB: Right.

CURTAIN CLOSE

STENK: This has **really** been a bad few days. Thrown out of my museum by a pair of Bobby Joe-Joe Bobs! Of course, Sally will get that straightened out. At least they're guarding the place. Too bad they weren't there yesterday. Then I wouldn't be here, today. Then I wouldn't have to do apologize to Franz. That guy! Well, he really can be a jerk sometimes!

29

CURTAIN OPEN

(FRANZ's studio)

(Enter Jane)

JANE: Hello. Oh, hello, Franz. Are you home?

(ENTER Franz, half awake)

FRANZ: Oh, Jane it's you. Why are you here?

JANE: You called me, remember? To pose? Well, here I am!

FRANZ: Yeah. Here you are. Oh, goody.

JANE: Maybe you need a morning wake-up cup of coffee?

FRANZ: That might help. I wanted you to come at 10 tonight, Jane. I work at night. This is the morning. This is early.

(GLORY enters, soon followed by Fawn)

JANE: Ten is early?

FRANZ: It is for me.

GLORY: Think of him as a vampire. (aside) Ready to drain the life blood out of everyone around him.

FAWN: Try to be nice, Franz. Maybe a new schedule would do your work good!

FRANZ: You think so, Fawn? I don't think so. I want to go back to sleep.

GLORY: Franz!

FRANZ: What?

GLORY: I could always just tell the world our little secret at any time.

FAWN: And your big opening is tomorrow night.

30

FRANZ: Hey! Are you threatening me?

FAWN: No, we just think--

GLORY: YES!

FRANZ: I'm not sure which one of us has more to lose, Glory.

JANE: What's everyone talking about?

ALL: Nothing.

JANE: You seem awfull upset about nothing.

FAWN: Sibling rivalry. Pay no attention.

GLORY: Yes, ignore us. Now, Franz, Jane has come all the way downtown to pose for you. Did you take a cab, Jane?

JANE: Yes.

FAWN: Think of the cost, Franz! You'll have to reimburse her!

FRANZ: Okay. All right. Hi! Jane. Thanks for coming over so early.

JANE: You're welcome! I'm really quite excited about this.

FRANZ: But next time, it's ten p.m. All right?

JANE: All right!

FRANZ: You'll know because it will be dark outside.

GLORY: I'll prep the clay.

FAWN: I'll make some coffee.

JANE: What should I do?

FRANZ: Hmmmm. Stand like this. (Shows her. She strikes the pose) Now hold it.

(KNOCK on door. It is STENK)

FRANZ: Seems the whole city's on the move and coming to my home this morning. What's up Stank?

STENK: Well, we have a little bit of a situation.

(GLORY and FAWN come in)

FRANZ: If you expect me to figure out what you're talking about, forget it. So spill.

STENK: I could come back later, when you're not busy. (pointing to Jane who is about to fall over)

FRANZ: Don't worry about her. She's fine. Now, tell me why you came here and then leave. My sculpture didn't get stolen again did it? (laughs like he just told a joke) You aren't laughing Stank.

GLORY: It's not a very funny subject, Franz.

FAWN: I'm a little worried about--(points at Jane)

FRANZ: She's fine. Now what's going on?

STENK: No, not stolen. Well, at first we ,um, well, we, uh, thought that it might have been, but another statue was stolen and--

FAWN: Another statue?

FRANZ: Good. Now, if I can just get on with my work.

GLORY: So you still have Franz's statue?

FRANZ: Of course he does. Locked up safe in his safe. The only big question is **why** you came all the way to tell us this. You do have a phone at the museum.

STENK: Broken.

FRANZ: Broken. Broken what?

GLORY: Broken how?

FAWN: The phone?

STENK: No. The, uh,--

FRANZ: Statuette?

STENK: Beyond all repair.

GLORY: Good!

ALL: What?

GLORY: I mean, Good Gracious! How did it happen?!

STENK: A courier brought your sculpture and stole someone elses and while they were making the big getaway, they kicked over your statuette, and broke it. Sorry, Franz.

FRANZ: Kicked it over? Do I sculpt footballs? Why was it on the floor?

STENK: Well, Phil, the museum custodian, he put it there.

FRANZ: Why? Dusting a table?

STENK: No, he was switching his sculpture for yours.

FRANZ: And again I ask: Why?

STENK: It's a long story. The short of it is that his is the statuette that was stolen.

FAWN: He's good.

STENK & FRANZ: What?

FAWN: He's good and fired! You should have his hide for this!

FRANZ: Broken beyond repair and no insurance. Well, it's out of your pocket, Stenk! You owe me!

STENK: Actually, Franz, you've already been paid by Miss Sally Walloop. I thought you'd be upset about the loss of your work. Again.

FRANZ: Right. And I am! (He storms out, knocking the struggling Jane over)

(Everyone rushes to help her)

CURTAIN CLOSED

33

ACT II, SCENE ii

(ENTER JUDEGE, MARGOT & LISETTE)

JUDGE: So Miss Hate Crime, how's your apology coming?

MARGOT: The more I see of these modern times the more disgusted I am.

LISETTE: Really? I like it now. No corsets.

MARGOT: Yes. No corsets and a lot of loose women!

JUDGE: Now that we've heard your opinions, do you mind answering my question.

LISETTE: What question?

JUDGE: APOLOGY!

MARGOT: Yes, fine. Whatever it takes to get us out of here.

JUDGE: To get **you** out. She just has to think for herself.

LISETTE: So I could move on without her?

JUDGE: Yes.

MARGOT: Traitor.

LISETTE: If that is the case, then what do I have to do to make things right with Mira Minuet?

JUDGE: Excuse me, ladies. (exits)

LISETTE: Well, that certainly is rude! How dare he walk out when I am in the middle of a question.

MARGOT: Apologize? Why should I apologize!?

LISETTE: Let us think about it.

MARGOT: I have been. I was upholding the rules of society!

34

LISETTE: Maybe they were wrong.

MARGOT: Pah.

LISETTE: Well, whatever you say, Margot, you set yourself up as judge and jury. This country was founded on religious freedom!

MARGOT: We are talking about the rules of society not religion.

LISETTE: I think it was founded on that too!

MARGOT: We are French!

LISETTE: Oh, yes.

JUDGE: (entering with Mira behind him) Actually, you are dead. When you die all nationality ends.

LISETTE: Really?

MARGOT: Be quiet, Lisette. **She** is here.

MIRA: I suppose you are referring to me. Hey! You're the sour-puss from the ParK!

JUDGE: Correct. Sourpuss plus lambchop, her friend.

MARGOT: You enjoy insulting us I think.

JUDGE: I thought I was just stating facts.

MIRA: More dead people.

LISETTE: Can we all agree to use the word "ghosts"?

MIRA: Why are they here?

JUDGE: They have been condemned to walk museums for eternity or until they make amends for their CRIMES!

MIRA: No need to shout.

MARGOT: He always does that.

MIRA: So?

35

JUDGE: It's their move at this point.

LISETTE: Mira Minuet, I have a confession to make. I (looks at Margot) allowed someone to set fire to your building. By not stopping them or reporting them I helped to cause your tragic death.

MIRA: Yeck! Why would you do that?

JUDGE: BAAAHHHHH!

LISETTE: I was a little sheep who couldn't think for herself, I am ashamed to say.

MIRA: But why did someone want to kill me?

LISETTE: Because---

JUDGE: QUIET! You've done your part. You will be allowed to move on.

LISETTE: (jumping for joy) Oh, my! Oh goody

MIRA: So I was Murdered?

JUDGE: Basically.

MIRA: Why?

MARGOT: You did not know your place! Out in the park **drawing** a man! You brazen girl!

MIRA: You set my building on fire because I was an artist.

MARGOT: Yes, I did! It was not the way of our world. And this place. What a nest of impropriety. 'Tis shameful, if not sinful. It is probably both!

JUDGE: Margot, what am I going to do with you?

MARGOT: I will not say I am sorry!!!!!!!

MIRA: You **were** as dangerous as you looked.

JUDGE: Well, Lisette, time to move on. Mira, Margot, you'll have to stay together from now on.

MARGOT: You have got to be joking!

MIRA: He never jests.

LISETTE: Can I please stay until Margot apologizes? I really do not want to miss that!

JUDGE: Well, I can't make you leave. But, have you ever heard the expression, "when hell freezes over"?

LISETTE: Maybe Mira will wear her down.

JUDGE: Let's hope so. All right, spooks, let's break this little party up. My feet are killing me!   (They exit)

CURTAIN OPEN

ACT II SCENE iii

(BOB & JOE are guarding the museum)

BOB: So, do you think, "Stink" will give us a hard time about kicking him out of the museum?

JOE: It's "Stank" and we gotta remember it's "Stank". Anyway, we weren't properly informed at the time.

BOB: Everyone makes mistakes.

JOE: Right!

(ENTER STENK)

STENK: (seeing them) Don't either one or both of you come near me. PHIL!

BOB: Calm down Professor.

JOE: It was all a mistake.

STENK: So what's my name?

BOTH: STANK!

STENK: Good. And the password?

BOB: It's better if you don't know.

JOE: But what if someone disguises themself as him?

BOB: Unlikely.

JOE: True.

STENK: Why?

JOE: Who'd want to disguise themself as someone with the name Stink.

BOB: STANK.

JOE: Right!

STENK: I'll be in my office.

BOB: Would you be careful? It's "stank"! Now get that straight Joe.

JOE: Sorry. Bob. Should we do the drill again?

BOB: Right!

BOTH: STINK, STANK, STUNK, A SKUNK! IT's STANK. STANK! (Xs)

(Enter Jane. She walks right behind them and sees the name on the painting. She runs to the Professor's office)

(ENTER FRANZ)

BOTH: PASSWORD!

FRANZ: What?

BOTH: Right!

FRANZ: That's the password?

BOB: No.

JOE: We just remembered that the museum is open to visitors right now.

FRANK: Seen Stenk?

BOB: He's in his office. That way.

FRANZ: I know where it is.

JOE: Just trying to be helpful.

FRANZ: Well, do you know a guy named, "Phil"?

BOTH: Hmmmmmmm? Oh!

BOB: The custodian.

JOE: That way. (points)

FRANZ: Thanks. (exits)

CLOSE CURTAIN

(PHIL is sculpting PHYLLIS. ENTER FRANZ)

FRANZ: The guy's got a muse. No wonder he's good. Now all he needs is a break.

PHYLLIS: You can see me?

FRANZ: Apparently.

PHIL: AH! (Holds up hammer) Sorry, you startled me. You're Franz Frilk the 14th.

FRANZ: And you're Phil the first, the guy who got my sculpture smashed.

PHYLLIS: If it hadn't been smashed, it would have been stolen! Lost either way.

PHIL: It's worth money stolen or in pieces, because I made it.

PHYLLIS: But it was awful. And not even awful enough to be good.

FRANZ: She's pretty sassy. How do you put up with her?

PHYLLIS: I don't talk to him that way, I'm his muse. Actually, Franz, you and I are a lot alike.

FRANZ: In what way?

PHYLLIS: Think about it.

FRANZ: We both say what we think.

PHYLLIS: For starters.

VOICE OF STENK: Well, call me "stink"!

JOE & BOB's VOICES: STINK!

VOICE OF STENK: PHIL!!!!!

PHIL: I better go. (exits with Phyllis following. Franz looks at sculpture)

FRANZ: I have to admit, he's good. This gives me an idea. (exits)

40

ACT III

CURTAIN OPEN

(Stenk and Jane are looking at the painting. Phil, Phyllis, Franz, Glory & Fawn, Judge, Margot, Mira & Lisette and Miss Sally Walloop are gathered. Joe and Bob are on duty.)

STENK: I still can't believe I didn't notice this.

WALLOOP: Well, come on, Professor. Share the news! You called. We came. Now tell all!

STENK: I leave that to Detective Jane Junejuli.

FRANZ: Who?

JANE: It just so happens that I have been working undercover.

GLORY: Why? (gives a worried look to Fawn)

JANE: Suspected Insurance Fraud.

ALL: Oh!

MIRA: My name! They uncovered it!

MARGOT: I noticed.

JUDGE: I had a little help from a friend on that. The muse over there--Phyllis. She was your muse once, Mira. Her name was Miracle then.

LISETTE: How exciting!

MARGOT: Quiet.

FAWN: Have you noticed the painting?

GLORY: Yes. The walls are starting to crumble.

FRANZ: Just flow with it, Glory.

GLORY: You aren't worried? The noose Is tightening on all of us, Franz.

41

FRANK: KKKKKK------(Makes a strangled sound.)

PHYLLIS: Hi, Mira! It's nice to actually be able to talk to you. I used to be that voice in your ear!

MIRA: The one that told me not to strangle Franz?

PHYLLIS: Yes!

MIRA: What do you think now?

PHYLLIS: Well, maybe you should have strangled him. His not-so-great many-a-times grandson is up to no good.

LISETTE: What do you mean?

JUDGE: Quiet! We don't exist, remember? (Phyllis sticks her tongue out at him)

WALLOOP: So Jane, what is going on?

JANE: You are under arrest Miss Sally Walloop!

WALL: You've got to be joking! Professor, talk some sense into this woman.

JANE: You've been buying and commissioning sculptures and then stealing them!

ALL: OH!

WALL: She's nuts. That is the nuttiest thing I have ever heard. I am insulted and offended and--

JANE: Going to jail! With your friends, Glory and Fawn Frilk.

ALL: Oh!

PHIL: What about Franz?

JANE: As far as I can make out, he's only guilty of being a jerk. And a phony!

ALL: Oh!

42

FRANZ: Who are you calling a phony, baby jane?

JANE: Can we all turn our attention to this painting, please?

WALL: What about it?

JANE: Let's start with the signature.

STENK: "Mira Minuet".

JANE: Who is responsible for uncovering this?

BOB: Wasn't me, I haven't touched it.

JOE: Wasn't me, I haven't even taken a real look at it until now.

PHYLLIS: You did it Phil.

PHIL: I did?

STENK: Well, did you or didn't you?

PHYLLIS: When I appeared and startled you, you sprayed the painting with cleaning fluid. Remember?

PHIL: I did?

STENK: Hello, Phil.

JANE: Is there something wrong with him?

STENK: Yes, but that has nothing to do with this.

(FRANZ slowly sneaks out)

PHYLLIS: And then you ran back and blotted off the paint that was covering her name with a rag. Don't you remember? Try hard, Phil!

PHIL: Oh, yeah. I did, Detective!

JANE: Why? How did you know about the signature?

PHIL: I didn't. It was an accident. I was cleaning and--

JANE: Don't try to con me kid.

STENK: I'm sure he isn't.

JANE: How can you be sure?

STENK: Just trust me, I **know** him.

PHIL: I did it, but I didn't see it until now. I promise. You Betcha.

JANE: I can spot a lie a mile off, AND, he's not lying.

PHIL: Thanks. But what does all this mean?

GLORY: That someone else painted this picture.

ALL: Oh!

GLORY: That Franz Frilk the 14th was no more a painter than my brother is a sculptor!

ALL: What?

FAWN: Where is Franz?

JANE: He snuck out. We'll get to him later.

STENK: So who is Mira Minuet?

MIRA: I am. Hey! Look over here. At me! Why can't they see me, just once?

JUDGE: They'll see you more than that. Have a little patience.

LISETTE: What's a few more minutes after all these centuries?

MARGOT: This really has a stink to it.

STENK: Stank!

WALL: What's wrong with you?

JANE: Too much excitment. Now, Glory Frilk why don't you spill the beans? (goes and gets self-portrait of Mira)

ALL: AH!

GLORY: Mira Minuet. I see you've done your homework.

JANE: So you **do** know?

FAWN: We all know. It's an ages-old family secret.

GLORY: Passed down from Frilk to Frilk.

WALL: This stinks Stenk! After all the money I've put into this museum. To be treated like a criminal.

STENK: You are a criminal.

WALL: Not really. I took what I bought. Franz's sisters asked me to steal his sculptures.

JANE: Well, you've defrauded the insurance company. They didn't ask you to steal the sculptures!

WALL: I **own** the company. It was my money. To give and take and give again.

JANE: Well, you are guilty of something! Let me see. Aha! Lying!

WALL: I have never lied. No one ever asked me!

JANE: She has to be guilty of something!

STENK: Assault and Battery on my head. But I don't want to file charges.

JANE: Why not?

WALL: I think the answer to that is obvious. I keep this museum going!

JANE: But you knew about the Frilk fraud!

WALL: Well, yes, I knew about the Frilk the younger part, but not the elder.

JANE: And you expect me to believe that?

GLORY: She's telling the truth.

FAWN: We told you, it's a **family** secret.

JANE: Not any more!

F & G: Right.

PHIL: So Franz Frilk the 14th is a fake? But his early works are great.

GLORY: That's because I did them.

ALL: You!

FAWN: Our dear brother said that no one would want them unless they were by a male Frilk.

JANE: Chauvinist!

STENK: The art world **is** still more a man's world than a woman's. And people like traditions, mysteries, legends. Come to think of it, this whole incident is going to increase the value of the works. A big scandal equals big money! You can't buy this kind of publicity!

PHIL: But who was Mira Minuet?

GLORY: If life was fair, you'd be asking: Who was Franz Frilk? Answer, he was Mira Minuet's model.

FAWN: Everyone has things backwards. The self-portrait is a portrait and the portrait is a self-portrait.

GLORY: That is Mira Minuet. (pointing)

ALL: Ah!

WALL: What happened to her?

JANE: As best I can determined, she was killed in that fire. Frilk must have just come to her studio, otherwise he'd have died too.

GLORY: Frilk the elder lived next door. He tried to save her and failed. He was able to grab a few paintings.

FAWN: Then things got out of control before he really understood what he was doing.

GLORY: He knew exactly what he was doing! Don't try to paint a prettier picture of things, Fawn!

FAWN: I'm just hoping for a happy ending.

JANE: Dream on.

GLORY: He signed his name to her paintings, after painting over her name! After that he never had to work another day in his life.

STENK: The interesting thing here is that at that time women artists just weren't taken seriously. She'd be totally unknown if Franz hadn't, well, become her.

MARGOT: Now that's telling them!

GLORY: But it stinks, Stenk, and I should know.

MIRA: I guess I owe Franz a favor after all.

JUDGE: You have the fame you wanted. Now everyone knows your name. How does it feel?

MIRA: Like this big knot in my insides is loosening.

JUDGE: Do you forgive Franz Frilk the elder?

MIRA: Yes, I do.

JUDGE: Well, that's a relief.

MIRA: So I can move on?

JUDGE: Yes, Please do.

(CRASH)

JOE: GOLLY!

BOB: Better check it out Joe! (They exit)

JANE: Nobody move!

WALL: You're a cop, shouldn't you help them?

JANE: Somebody has to keep an eye on all of you!

STENK: I could do that. I'm not suspected of anything am I?

JANE: Everyone is a suspect in the Frilk fraud.

STENK: I knew nothing about it!

(GUNSHOT)

JANE: Nobody move!

GLORY: You already said that.

PHIL: Please go check that out. Those two Joe-bobs--I don't know?

STENK: He has a point.

JANE: So he does. (exits)

JOE's VOICE: He's DEAD!

ALL: Who's Dead!!!!!?????

JUDGE: Just what I need: Another dead person. Hopefully they don't have any issues that'll make them want to hang around here.

MIRA: If it's one of the Joe-Bobs, I think you're safe.

LISETTE: A murder? Oh, my! Oh, dear!

MARGOT: You are always free to move on. He said so.

LISETTE: Not until you apologize.

MARGOT: Forget it!

MIRA: Why do you hate me so much? I never did anything to you.

JUDGE: You didn't have to. Hate comes from not understanding.

JANE's VOICE: It's Franz Frilk!

ALL: What?

48

FAWN: Oh no!

GLORY: I don't believe it.

JANE: (enters) Bring him in boys.

(Enter Bob & Joe with Franz's body)

ALL: Oh!

BOB: I'm telling you I didn't shoot him!

JOE: But he's got a bullet hole in him, he's dead and I didn't shoot him!

BOB: Yes, you did!

JOE: No, you did!

BOB: Didn't!

JOE: Ditto!

BOB: Are you calling me a liar, Joe?

JOE: I guess I am, Bob.

(They start to wrestle)

GLORY: He's stiff as a board. Does rigor mortis set in this quickly?

JANE: Every body's different. (she examines the body) Shot in the heart. He didn't have a chance. What's this? (Takes papers out of pocket) Funny. He's got a will on him. And a note. It says he wants to be cremated.

GLORY: Let me see that!

JANE: Later. Right now it's part of the crime scene, and only I can mess with it.

FAWN: I can't believe that Franz is dead!

STENK: Money in the bank!

49

JANE: What?

STENK: I can't believe my name is Stenk!

JANE: So change it.

WALL: Hey, you two knuckleheads. Break it up!

JANE: Yes, there's a murderer loose!

(They pry them apart)

JOE: Sorry, Bob, I don't know what came over me.

BOB: The thrill of the crime. Did you see anyone?

JOE: No, did you?

BOB: No.

JANE: Both of you give me your guns. (examines them) They haven't been fired. I'm calling downtown. We've got to dust this place for fingerprints. Everyone into Professor Stenk's office to await questioning.

STENK: When this is all over, I just want everyone to know that I'm going to have a special exhibit of sculpture by Phil Itten and Glory Frilk. It'll be the Art event of the century!

PHIL: Wow-golly-gee-thanks, Professor. This is like a dream come true! And you'll help? (to Phyllis)

PHYLLIS & STENK: Of course!

GLORY: This is unbelievable!

FAWN: Our brother is dead.

GLORY: Also, somehow unbelievable.

JANE: Enough chatter. Into the office!

CURTAIN CLOSED

ACT III, SCENE ii

(JUDGE , MIRA, LISETTE, MARGOT enter)

JUDGE: No one's shown up yet.

MIRA: Do you think the young Frilk will stick around?

JUDGE: Depends on how he was killed, and how he feels about it.

LISETTE: He was shot.

JUDGE: But why, and by who?

MARGOT: As far as I can see, he was a vain lout who got what he deserved. That so rarely happens that we should all just enjoy it.

MIRA: What's wrong with you?

MARGOT: Nothing.

JUDGE: I am getting nowhere with these spooks. My feet are killing me, but I'm not allowed to sit down on the job. Do you think that's fair? (to audience)

MIRA: Here they come!

(Enter Stenk, Glory, Fawn, Phil, Phyllis, Jane, Miss Walloop, Williams & The Funeral Director with an urn.)

GLORY: At last, the reading of the will.

WILLIAMS: Hello, everyone. I am William Williams attorney at law, and I will be reading you the will.

WALL: Well, Will, get on with it.

WILLIAMS: Hmmmm. Seems he left everything to a numbered Swiss bank account.

FAWN: How do you leave money to a bank account? Banks already have all the money!

WALL: It means the money has already left the country.

51

GLORY: What?

JANE: Yes, it's more like a note saying what he did than what he wanted done.

GLORY: Let me see that. (grabs the urn) What? This is light as a feather! Ashes weigh more than this.

FAWN: What's going on?

FUNERAL DIRECTOR: Well, I am sorry to say....

GLORY: What? What are you sorry to say?

FUN. DIR.: You said to cremate him. When we were done there was nothing left.

STENK: What do you mean, nothing?

GLORY: (opens urn. Pours out glitter) Glitter!

JANE: What's going on here? I want some answers!

FUN. DIR.: I told you **nothing** was left. So I had to think fast. I didn't want to put someone else's ashes in.

ALL: YECK.

FUN. DIR.: Exactly. So I thought--glitter--shiny, like angels' wings.

STENK: Phil, is this guy related to you?

PHIL: Why?

JANE: This makes no sense. Could someone have stolen the body?

FUN, DIR.: Oh, no, mam.

GLORY: Fawn you're distraught.

FAWN: I am?

GLORY (stepping on her foot) You are.

FAWN: OWWWW!

52

GLORY: I'd better get her home. (they exit.)
WILLIAMS: Funeral adjorned! (everyone leaves)

MARGOT: Now what, Mr. Death?

JUDGE: I am Judge Mint. And now we wait and watch. This is getting good.

(Re-enter Glory and Fawn and Walloop)

WALL: Good. They're gone.

FAWN: That hurt.

GLORY: Sorry. I had to improvise.

WALL: You're good at thinking on your feet.

FAWN: My feet! Foot!

WALL: Girls, this whole thing stinks.

GLORY: He's still alive I know it.

FAWN: But we saw the body!

GLORY: All his--all **our** money--gone into a Swiss bank account. If he wasn't dead, I'd kill him.

FAWN: Glory, really, he was our brother.

WALLOOP: Is there anyway he could not be dead?

GLORY: We **did** see the body. It was stiff as a board. Rigor-city.

PHYLLIS: (who has snuck in) Which doesn't make sense!

GLORY: No, it doesn't.

WALL: Huh?

PHYLLIS: Maybe he faked his death!

GLORY: I've been wondering about that, but how?

PHYLLIS: What about all those materials he was buying lately.

GLORY: That's it! Pay dirt! WHOOWEEE!

FAWN: Glory, you're scaring me. What's the matter with you?

WALL: Stress. It's a killer.

GLORY;. It wasn't a body!

ALL: It wasn't?!

GLORY: Franz turned out to be a sculptor after all. He cast himself in plaster and latex and then painted the whole thing. He should have been a Special Effects designer! It was brilliant!

FAWN: So he's not dead?

GLORY: No. He's just run off to some tropical paradise with all our money!

WALL: You'll make tons more with your show. And this just adds to the hype. The mysterious disappearance of Franz Frilk. They'll make it into a movie!

FAWN: I wonder who will play me?

GLORY: I wonder if they'll change Stank's name.

ALL: You betcha!

WALL: I'll call the media!

GLORY: I'll prep some clay!

FAWN: I'll make some coffee!

GLORY: Skip the coffee. We don't need the caffeine.

ALL: Right!

(They exit)

54

CURTAIN OPEN

ACT III, SCENE iii

(The Museum. Enter Judge, Mira, Margot & Lisette.)

MIRA: I just want one more look at my paintings before I go. Hello, babies. I'm your mother, Mira Minuet, and never forget it. I loved making you.

MARGOT: Blah.

LISETTE: You could try to be nice, Margot.

MARGOT: Why?

LISETTE: You must be very patient. (to Judge)

JUDGE: Well, yes, I am, but she is really beginning to bug me.

MARGOT: (looking at a painting of flowers) Now this is nice. This is really quite lovely.

MIRA: (going over) I did that. The summer before I died.

MARGOT: No!

MIRA: Yes. Sorry.

MARGOT: NO, no, no,no no no no! I like that one.

MIRA: I'm glad.

MARGOT: But now I don't want to like it.

MIRA: Just because I painted it? That's really stupid!

MARGOT: Are you saying I am stupid?

JUDGE: You **are** being ignorant.

MIRA: Stubborn. But then so was I. I did what I felt called to do. To draw and to paint. That's what my life was about. Creating art.

55

MARGOT: You really put that well.

MIRA: Thank you.

LISETTE: (to Judge) Do you think?

JUDGE: Shhhh. We've reached critical mass. Do not disturb.

Margot: (looking at painting) You really were good. I'm sorry I cut your time short. Just think how many more lovely paintings you might have created.

MIRA: That's the past.

MARGOT: You forgive me?

MIRA: Why not?

MARGOT: WAHHHHHH! (starts crying)

JUDGE: When it rains, it pours.

MARGOT: I am sooooooo sorry!

LISETTE: Oh, me! Oh you!

JUDGE: At last! Now you can all rest in peace.

(Franz enters and goes to painting of Franz Frilk the elder)

FRANZ: Just had to see it one last time. The resemblance is uncanny. It could be a picture of me. Maybe I should just take it along with me.

(Enter Phyllis)

PHYLLIS: Franz!

FRANZ: Who's there? (Turns, Bumps table. A sculpture falls on him)

JUDGE: You couldn't resist could you?

PHYLLIS: Nope!

MIRA: So what was that?

JUDGE: The hand of fate.

CURTAIN CLOSE

JUDGE: So all the spooks moved on and are resting in peace. And Phil and Glory are famous artists. Fawn became a rocket scientist. Jane got a promotion. Bob and Joe are working for the CIA. Miss Sally Walloop just opened an amusement park in Bosnia, Professor Stenk is still at the museum, and let's see--

(Enter Franz)

FRANZ: You must be Judge Mint. I was told to come see you about this ghost thing. I'm Franz Frilk the 14th. Perhaps you've heard of me?

JUDGE: NOoooooo! (runs off)

FRANZ: I seem to have quite an effect on people. (shrugs and then exits)

THE END

57

THEATRE OF THE SILVER DRAGO

presents:

WHO
WE are

WELCOME TO CLIQUEVILLE...

WHAT PRICE WILL YOU PAY TO FIT IN?

WHO WE ARE

by
TAMELA GLENN

THEATRE OF THE SILVER DRAGON

presents!

WHO WE ARE

Written, Directed, & Costumed by: TAMELA GLENN

CAST
(in order of appearance)

PANDORA	ANNYA TISHER
TIFFANY	LESLIE SHRADER
EMMA	AMANDA CRINER
CANDY	LUCY GROSS
JO'	RACHEL SMITH
HEATHER	DEBBIE COOK
BARBARA	MONICA RANSON
GINIFIRE	MEREDITH KIRK-LAWLOR
MERLE	JOANNE KILGOUR
DAHLIA	ANNA WIECK
SUE Z	JOANNE KILGOUR
DARBY	ALEXANDRA KELLY
BLANCHE	DEBBIE COOK
STELLA	RACHEL SMITH
MARY WALTERS	MONICA RANSON
GRETA SULINSKI	LUCY GROSS
THE PRINCIPAL	ANNYA TISHER
MRS. WRIGHT	JOANNE KILGOUR
TEACHER 1 & 2	ALEX KELLY
TEACHER 3	AMANDA CRINER

THANKS TO TIM FOR ALL YOUR HELP!!!

PANDORA: *(Centerstage sitting on a chair which is turned backwards)*

If I've learned one thing in my first fifteen years alive on planet earth, it's this: People can be truly cruel. Not just mean. Cruel. And sometimes, they don't even know it. Or notice it. Even when it's too late. And there is a point when it is too late. Too late to stop what I have come to call the ultimate emotional rollercoaster. You're on the ride. You and your friends and your aquaintances and your enemies and there is no getting off. You can't even remember whose idea it was to take the ride in the first place. Or what day you climbed on. The tickets were free for the taking, but the bill is in the mail. All you know for sure is that you are on the ride for the duration. Which is an unkown. But it is finite. It ends--the ride--and usually in a real spill. Crashing.... Sparks and screeching metal. Fears and tears and untold internal damages. Then, it's time to sort the wreckage.

VOICE: *(off)* Is everything all right, Pandora?

PAND: I'm just working on my monologue for Theatre class, I

BLACK OUT

CLOSE CURTAIN

LIGHTS UP

(Girls are waiting for school bell. They stand in cliques. Ad-lib.)

TIFFANY: I wish Emma was here. Should I go stand with Marty & Zoe? *(pauses. looks around.)* Barbara looked right at me! She hates me, I know it! I hope Emma gets here soon. I feel like I'm going to freak. I shouldn't have worn this. This makes my stomach look big. I tried on five different outfits. I need new clothes. I'm so totally clueless! *(Emma enters)* Emma!

EMMA: Hi, Tiffany.

MARTY: Emma! I see you've gone directly to jail like the rest of us idiots.

ZOE: Welcome back to William Jefferson High crimes and misdemeanors

EMMA: Hi Marty. Zoe.

HEATHER: Figures we'd go to a school named after the first elected president to be impeached.

BARBARA: Well, he wasn't when they named the school. Hello, Emma. I heard you aced the Trig test. Way to go girl.

EMMA: Thanks, Barb. How's it going Heather?

HEATHER: Not bad.

TIFF: Everyone likes Emma. Everyone. She cuts across every clique. It's like magic. She doesn't even try. People just like her. EMMA! *(bolts to Emma)*

EMMA: Tiffany. Hi. *(quieter)* Are you all right?

TIFF: Oh, I was just having one of my stupid "nobody likes me" freak outs. But now you're here!

EMMA: And?

TIFF: And I know you like me and I'm safe. How do I look?

EMMA: Great.

TIFF: You're not just saying that because I look so awful I'm beyond all hope?

EMMA: Of course not. Hey, calm down. You gotta learn to trust yourself a little--a lot--more.

TIFF: I know. I know. Hey, do you think I'd look good with a nose ring?

EMMA: No.

(Enter GINIFIRE, heaphones of walkman blaring)

MARTY: Someone ought to pry those off her before she has a cerebral hemorrhage.

ZOE: Yeah, I mean like "hello" jello head.

2

MARTY: What is that? Marilyn Manson?

ZOE: That guy's a freak.

MARTY: A he/she.

ZOE: It.

MARTY: What a loser.

GINIFIRE: Who? Me or Marilyn Manson? *(pause as girls stare at her. She stares back.)* Anyway this is Nine Inch Nails for all you musical trivia buffs. *(She walks away)*

ZOE: Was that like creepy or what?

MARTY: She must read lips.

(Enter Merle in a hury all excited)

MERLE: Hey guys, guess what?!

Z & M: What?

MERLE: Brad Bancroft called me last night and asked me to the movies!

ZOE: Wow!

MARTY: Way to go, girl. He's **the** hot ticket.

(Barbara & Heather, suddenly go on the alert)

BARB: Brad Bandcroft?

HEATHER: This has to be a joke. He's the fabbest senior in school and she's what? Just some nobody sopho-moron.

BARB: This goes totally against the natural order.

GIN: What order is that, Barbie? The survival of the fattest...heads.

BARB: You know, Ginifire, that I do not like being called "Barbie". My name is BARBARA. You can call me Barb, if Barbara is too long for

3

your junk food, decibel-challenged brain to handle. I mean, I take the trouble to call you "Ginifire", when your name really is Jennifer. So, you know, make an effort.

GIN: Or what? You'll call me Jennifer? So does my mom. You know come to think of it, you sort of remind me of her. Nag, nag, nag. I'm really quaking in terror here....Barbarella.

HEATHER: Oh, bark off, Gin, or we'll call the dog squad.

GIN: Woof. Woof. Wow. Losers.

(Bell rings. Girls start leaving)

BARB: Something has to be done, Heather.

HEATHER: You mean, Gin? She's just a big mouth.

BARBARA: No, Brad Bancroft, my planned boyfriend to be. I broke up with Dylan Spears to go out with Brad. Remember our strategy meeting last semester?

HEATHER: Oh, yeah.

BARBARA: I mean who is Merle McDonald, anyway?

HEATHER: Right.

BOTH: This goes totally against the natural order of things in our universe as we understand it. (They Exit)

CURTAIN OPEN

-

(Girls sit in chairs. There is an empty chair in row one, which represents Brad. Other chairs are empty & other girls who do not have lines are also seated)

VOICE: (distorted) Please take out your pencils and papers people. We will be having a pop quiz on last night's assignment.

TIFFANY: What **was** last night's assignment, anyway?

EMMA: Chapter thirteen. The war in Vietnam.

TIFF: The whole war?

EMMA: Yeah. They actually squeezed it into twenty pages.

TIFF: My Dad fought in that war.

EMMA: Mine was in law school.

TIFF: My Dad lost the lower part of his leg.

MERLE: Wow. Well, you'd never notice. At least I haven't.
Hey, Brad is looking at me! *(she waves to empty chair)*

BARB: Look. Brad is making goo goo eyes with Merle. I could just
spit!

HEATHER: Don't worry about it. Hey! Now he's looking at you.

(Barbara gives him a big smile)

BARB: He's probably just flirting with her to work up the nerve to ask
me out.

HEATHER: Right. Did you hear that? Tiffany just said her Dad is
missing part of his leg.

BARB: So? Tiff is missing part of her brain. So much more tragic.

VOICE: QUIET! *(echoes)* Let's begin. On what year did France first...
(echoes while everyone scribbles answers. BELL RINGS)

TIFF: Free at last. You want to go to The Garden after school?

EMMA: I can't. We're picking up the AFS student this afternoon.

TIFF: You're getting an AFS student? Boy or girl?

EMMA: Her name is Darby. She's from Australia.

TIFF: Hey! No language barrier!

EMMA: Right. See you. *(exits)*

HEATHER: So Tiff, is it true your Dad is missing part of a leg?

TIFF: What? Who told you that?

BARB: She heard you telling Emma.

TIFF: I was just trying to impress her. You know, "My Dad the war hero".

HEATHER: Just trying to pull her leg?

TIFF: Uh, right. I gotta go. *(exits)*

BARB: Run, little rabbit! Hey! Oh, no! Look! Brad's walking out with Merle.

HEATHER: Chill. Only true losers are desperate enough to look desparate.

BARB: Watch your mouth, Heather. Let me remind you just who is the most popular girl in this school.

HEATHER: And I'm second. So, it's my job to keep you on top or step over you.

BOTH: It's the natural order of things.

CLOSE CURTAIN

(Enter Ginifire. She is flipping through a goth magazine. Enter Dahlia)

DAHL: Anything new or different in goth land, Gin?

GIN: Yeah, look at this. *(Dahl looks)* What do you think?

DAHL: B-zarre. I didn't know you could pierce that.

GIN: Me neither. Do you think blue looks good on me?

DAHL: What kind of blue?

GIN: You know, for streaks in my hair.

DAHL: No. It goes against your whole image.

GIN: How so?

DAHL: Think about it. You're Ginifire. You should go with red or even better orange.

GIN: You are so absolutely right. Wanna go to The Death Vault and get some supplies after school.

DAHL: Sure. I wanna get a new choker. (She has on a half dozen already)

GIN: Pretty soon you're gonna be like one of those African women with the long necks.

DAHL: That would be smashin'.

GIN: Hey! You wanna try that new bruise makeup?

DAHL: I'll try anything once.

GIN: Anything?

DAHL: Referring to makeup only. I mean, I'm only fifteen. How do I know if I want a pierced tongue when I'm thirty--ugh!

GIN: They are pretty x-treme.

DAHL: Yeah, but I was thinking about being thirty. Oh, but hey it's all relative, isn't it? When I was nine, I thought like--sixteen--was grown up.

GIN: You're a real philosopher, Dahl.

DAHL: I 'spose. Let's swim. (they start to walk as)

CURTAIN OPEN

(They go and sit in chairs. Zoe, Marty, Tiffany, Barbara, Heater, Pandora, etc. are seated.)

ZOE: Look at her hair. It's like totally nuked.

MARTY: Sucked any good blood lately?

7

DAHLIA: SSSSSS!

GIN: How're you doing puke-face?

ZOE: How dare you!

MARTY: That is just, like, too gross for words.

GIN: "Puke". "Face". Words.

ZOE: What is your problem?

DAHLIA: You started it.

BARB: You know Sarah, you used to be such a nice--normal--person. I remember when we were in third grade together. You were such a sweet little thing. Your mom always dressed you in pink, right?

DAHLIA: *(Yawns)* It's so tragic when people live in the past.

MARTY: Well, what's this "Black Dahlia" thing about anyway?

GIN: It's so hard for little minds when they don't understand.

DAHLIA: The Black Dahlia was a starlet in Hollywood. They found her body cut in half. The head was missing. They only were able to ID her because of a tattoo she had. A black Dahlia. *(Shows tattoo on her shoulder)*

GIN: She was a-head of her time! *(laughs)*

HEATHER: Yuck!

DAHLIA: At least as far as tatts are concerned. Not many women got them back then.

ZOE: You guys are like totally sicko.

GIN: They used to like us, but then we gru-some. *(Dahl & Gin laugh)*

BARB: That is **so** lame.

MARTY: Freaks!

8

GIN: Oooooooooooh!

VOICE: *(distorted)* *(Gavel bang)* This class will come to order. Where is Susan Wright?

ZOE: I haven't seen her today.

MARTY: Neither have I. Maybe she's sick.

GIN: You think **everyone** is sick! *(laughs)*

(Enter SUE Z in full effect)

SUE Z: Everyone can just chill cause I'm here. Better late than never, right homes?

HEATHER: "Homes"?

SUE Z: Home-roomies at least. You sure aren't **my** soul sister, Heather-horsefeathers.

VOICE: Miss Wright please take your seat.

SUE Z: Hey, like why, man?

VOICE: This is a class. We sit in our seats. Those are the rules. And don't call me man, again, or you can have a week of detention.

SUE Z: Younguns weren't meant to sit on their butts all day, Teach.

VOICE: That's a week, Miss Wright.

SUE Z: Stop with the "Miss Wright" jive.

ZOE: What is wrong with her?

MARTY: Don't ask me.

GIN: It's like she got hit by a bus and woke up as a rapper.

SUE Z: I am Sue Z. I have been reborn.

VOICE: Take your seat, Miss Wright. We can talk about your "rebirth" in detention.

SUE Z: Would you stop with the uptight school biz. Stop trying to

9

bust my butt, Teach. We have been oppressed for too long!
DAHLIA: Oppressed?

BARB: What is your prob Suzy Q?

SUE Z: For too long black people have carried the white man's burden.

HEATHER: You are not black.

SUE Z: I am a young black man in America.

ZOE: She thinks she's a boy.

SUE Z: Don't call me "Boy" whitey.

BARB: Are you out of your mind?

SUE Z: No, I'm just getting into it.

DAHLIA: Just stop making sense, okay?

SUE Z: Blackness is more than skin color. It's a state of being. I feel it. I'm flowing through it. Say it loud: I'm black and I'm proud!

VOICE: Report to the office at once Miss Wright.

SUE Z: You see? Busted by The man! When will the oppression cease. (exits. shaking her head)

VOICE: Let us begin. Our French lesson today focuses on male and female words and how to identify & use them.

CURTAIN CLOSE

10

(On A TV. Two mothers talking)

BLANCHE: Stella, I'm really worried about Jennifer.

STELLA: You mean, because of the Goth thing?

BLANCHE: Yes! She looks like a cross between a vampire and a battered woman. Aren't you concerned about Sarah?

STELLA: You mean "The Black Dahlia".

BLANCHE: How can you joke about this?

STELLA: It's just a phase. They're trying to figure out who they are.

BLANCHE: Well, who are they?

STELLA: Two high school kids.

BLANCHE: What about that morbid Black Dahlia story?

STELLA: Sarah's always been one for theatrics.

BLANCHE: Well, what about her tattoo? That's permanent. She won't grow out of that!

STELLA: I think it's pretty.

BLANCHE: It's a tattoo!

STELLA: Calm down, Blanche. Listen, I went with her when she got it.

BLANCHE: No!

STELLA: And I thought she picked out something tasteful. We had a deal. If she picked something I thought she could live with then I'd pay for it.

BLANCHE: *(alarmed)* You paid for it?

STELLA: Yes. And, I got one, too. *(Rolls up her sleeve and shows a tattoo.)*

BLANCHE: Ahhh! *(runs off screen)*

STELLA: Parents! What? Hey, I was a teenager once too!

11

THE MALL

GIN: What did you get?

DAHL: Some old stuff: A Ministry CD, and this. "Christian Death".-- It's got all these photos of people from those early insane asylums.

GIN: Cryptic. Look at this: takes out a spiked collar.

DAHL: Uh-uh. No. Too Sid Vicious. Too bow wow.

GIN: Let's take it back.

DAHL: Okay, but we gotta hurry if we're going to catch the bus back home. *(they exit)*

(Enter Zoe & Candy and Barbara and Heather)

CANDY: Zoe! Over here!

ZOE: Hey, can I bum a ride home?

CANDY: Sure. Did you get anything good? I got a new top. I'm going a wear it tomorrow to school.

ZOE: I'll start holding my breath. *(does so)*

(She finally has to stop. They giggle.)

HEATHER: Look at them. They must be on drugs.

BARB: Too much sugar.

ZOE: *(whispers)* Ooh. The Barbie patrol does not approve. *(They bust into laughter. Tiffany scurries by carrying a bunch of bags.)*

BARB: She's late! She's late!

HEATHER: For a very important date?

BARB: Not!

12

CANDY: Hey, Tiff! That's quite a haul. Whaddya get?

TIFF: Nothing important. Gotta run! *(scurries off)*

ZOE: Is she like really weird or what?

CANDY: Emma says, she's shy.

ZOE: Oh, Candy! I just wanna be liked.

CANDY: Oh, boo! Oh, hooey.

ZOE: She doesn't stand still long enough to be liked.

CANDY: Yeah, I mean like just **who** is she anyway?

ZOE: I haven't a clue.

BARB: That's obvious. Hey, are you ready for tomorrow?

HEATHER: You still want to go through with it?

BARB: Hello. Do I ever change my mind?

HEATHER: Not that I can recall. What if this backfires?

BARBARA: **We** don't make mistakes. We control our universe.

BOTH: It's the natural order of things.

BLACKOUT

DARBY: It's odd being here in America. At first it was shocking. Different colors in the landscape. Different light. Now, it's like home is Dreamland. Kind of unreal. It's nice to be away. Escape. Give Mom and Dad time to figure out if there're going to stay together or bust apart. In a year I'm going to college in Melbourne. I want to be a doctor. I'm not sure about the family thing. *(pause)* Back home in the big Down Under, Life is going on without me. I could be dead. And gone to this as heaven. *(laughs)* No worries.

(TV. Greta Sulinski who owns the Garden of Eden with reporter)

MARY: I'm Mary Walters. Welcome to "Visiting the Local Yokels". Today my guest is shop owner Greta Sulinski. Greta runs the popular Garden of Eden health food store and snack bar. Our focus today is on the Garden's popularity with teens. I hear that some of the older patrons have complained to you about the teens hanging out in the Garden afterschool.

GRETA: Yes, they have.

MARY: Why do you think that is?

GRETA: Well, I think that some of the patrons are bothered by the teens' clothing.

MARY: And what kind of clothes are you referring to?

GRETA: Most of them. I mean, some people don't like the hemp jewelry--

MARY: Which you, in fact, sell in your boutique.

GRETA: Yes.

MARY: So are you pro-marijuana?

GRETA: You can't smoke the jewelry. I'd like to see someone try!

MARY: What else bothers people?

GRETA: Well, I guess I get the most complaints about the Gothic group.

MARY: Also called "Goths" They have a fixation with death and vampires. They wear a lot of black and a lot of corpse-like make up right?

GRETA: Well, yes. It's kind of like every day is Halloween for them.

MARY: What about reports that they have made rude remarks to older Garden patrons?

GRETA: In all fairness, they were provoked.

14

MARY: How?

GRETA: Well, in one particular incident a man in his sixites started in on a table of goth girls. He told them they were a blight on humanity and if they were his kids he'd hose them all down and send them to Florida to bake in the sun. It got quite ridiculous, really. The girls tried to ignore him at first and then one finally lost it.

MARY: What did she do?

GRETA: She accused him of being a fascist and then took his cane and broke it over her leg.

MARY: And then?

GRETA: She gave it back to him.

MARY: What about rumors someone spate on customers?

GRETA: Actually, that was a peer thing. I'd rather not go into that. The parents are handling it.

MARY: Ms. Sulinski, do you really want this kind of activity going on in your establishment? Doesn't it hurt business?

GRETA: Business is fine. And, they really need some place to hang out. Don't they? *(TV out)*

15

CURTAIN OPEN

(Emma & Darby)

DARBY: You want to rent another video tonight, Em?

EMMA: I've--we've--got a major French test tomorrow, remember?

DARBY: Yeah, but I started studying French when I was seven, so I'm set. I'll be happy to quiz you though.

EMMA: Deal. *(knock)* Hello?

TIFF: *(off)* It's me, Tiffany. Can I come in?

DARBY: Enter at your own risk!

(Tiffany enters cautiously. She sees Darby)

TIFF: Oh, hi! You had me a little worried. *(laughs nervously)* You must be Darby.

DARBY: I must be. You've met Emma of course.

TIFF: What? Oh. *(laughs feeling clueless)* How do you like it here?

DARBY: Just fine. Just dandy. And who are you?

TIFF: Oh!

EMMA: This is Tiffany. She's a little shy.

DARBY: Nice to meet you Tiffany.

TIFF: Thanks.

EMMA: What's up Tiff?

TIFF: Did you hear the news?

DARBY: Must be something big if she's calling it news.

EMMA: We had a field trip today. *(to Darby)* Tiffany is a sophomore.

DARBY: I see.

EMMA: So what happened?

TIFF: Barbara and Heather totally humiliated Merle.

DARBY: That's the two snooty seniors?

EMMA: Yeah. What did they do? I know they like to sort of push people around, but I've never seen them, well, "humiliate" anyone. Are you sure you're not exaggerating?

TIFF: No way. Brad Bancroft has taken Merle to the movies a couple of times.

EMMA: Yeah.

TIFF: Well, I guess Barbara was jealous. Yesterday Merle had this really big zit on her nose.

DARBY: I remember that. It was a real wanger.

TIFF: Well, Heather had her camera at school to take pictures for the yearbook and she took a picture of Merle, and they blew it up poster size on a color zerox machine and taped it on Brad's locker.

DARBY: (laughs) That's rare!

EMMA: Darby!

DARBY: I'm sorry. I don't know these people. It's like a video. If it happened to me--I get it. I'm sorry!

TIFF: Merle went home sick. I tried to call her, but her Mom said she's "indisposed".

DARBY: That's being delicate about the situation.

TIFF: I wanted to try to make her feel better.

DARBY: It's very hard to **make** people feel better. They just sort of feel better when they do.

EMMA: I wonder what Brad will do?

DARBY: Probably dump her, right?

17

EMMA: Maybe not. He's a pretty decent guy. Guess we'll have to wait and see.

(Everyone sits bummed out)

DARBY: All right. Ace the doom and gloom. We can't do anything about this. At least right now. Unless of course you want to go and beat up those girls? *(silence)* I didn't think so.

TIFF: Darby, do you have any neat Australian slang you could teach me?

DARBY: Sorry, love, I'm not really into Slanguage.

TIFF: Well, I guess I'll be going. Nice to meet you Darby. I hope I'll see you both around soon. *(Exits)*

EMMA: See ya', Tiff.

DARBY: Now there is a lonely girl.

EMMA: Yeah. She's kind of the nervous type.

DARBY: Seems real attached to you.

EMMA: Yeah. I think I'm her only friend.

DARBY: And now I'm here.

EMMA: Right.

DARBY: Well, I'm settled in. You don't have to spend all your time squiring me around town.

EMMA: I know. I like hanging out with you.

DARBY: So we'll include Miss Tiff from time to time.

EMMA: Right. Now, back to the books.

DARBY: Oui!

CLOSE CURTAIN

18

(Dahlia is working on a dress.)

DAHLIA: And a little of this there and ....not bad! *(Holds dress up in front of her "modeling" it. Then tosses it down)* Sometimes when I'm chained to a desk in study hall, I think about just getting up and running out of the room. Full tilt down the hallway, out the door and jump into the next bus headed for New York City. I'm on the edge of my seat and then...something--fear--stops me. Why don't I just do it? Plunge. Dive off the board without looking to see if there's any water down in the drowning pool. I'm such a coward! *(pause)* I've got $500 saved up. One day, who knows? I wish I did. *(she sits and freezes)*

GIN: *(Enter Gin)* School is so claustrophobic. The air is really weird. I can't breath it. I get a migraine every Monday--no joke! I have to go home and sleep it off. My head pounds like the big bad bass drummer from hell is jamming. Our family doc said I have "schoolitis". Moron. I'm the one chained to my bed. Sick. In the dark. Alone. *(She stands and freezes next to Dahlia.)*

(Music up. Unfreeze)

GIN: That's really good, Dahlia.

DAHLIA: Thanks. Did you read that article in the paper?

GIN: What article?

DAHLIA: The one about that bunch of people that got arrested out in Texas. A cult of vampires.

GIN: Real vampires?

DAHLIA: Define "real". *(they give each other a look)* I mean, I don't suppose they're immortal or any of that, but they **were** drinking each others' blood.

GIN: No joke?

DAHLIA: Said so. Said they were like biting and sucking blood out of each others' wrists. Apparently, if you actually bite the neck you could hit this major artery and--

GIN: Bang! You're dead.

DAHLIA: Exactly. They got busted for drugs though.

18 B

GIN: I couldn't get into that. No way.

DAHLIA: The story said that a bunch of them had their teeth filed by a dentist to be like fangs.

GIN: The better to suck your blood with, my dear.

DAHLIA: Right. Drugs and blood though--two easy ways to get the big A.

GIN: I wonder if vampires can get it?

DAHLIA: There are no vampires.

GIN: But if there were--could they?

DAHLIA: I doubt it. They're already dead, right?

GIN: I suppose. (pause) I got detention today because of my razor blade earring. Isn't that lame? Mrs. Gray actually thought it was a real--as in razor sharp--razor blade. I told her they sell them at the mall, but no way. Sends a negative message she just kept blabbering.

DAHLIA: Yeah, well, we're reading Poe in English Lit. I mean, the guy writes about people getting walled-up alive. Nobody goes "ooh" that's sick.

GIN: Heather does.

DAHLIA: That doesn't count. Even scaredy-cat Candy was bragging about her autographed copy of Stephen King's book "Salem's Lot". I wonder if she's actually read it.

GIN: The first day of school she was running around showing everyone a picture of her in front the gate around his house in Maine.

DAHLIA: A sophomore in high school and she still believes in show and tell.

GIN: It is a pretty cool gate though.
DAHLIA: True. (pause) Lately, I feel like at 15, I know everything about the order of this petty little universe.

GIN: That's a pretty negative way to look at the world.

DAHLIA: Not the world, this one.

18c   Blackout

(Mother and Principal on TV)

PRINC: Mrs. Wright, I called you here today to talk with you about Susan. She is being extremely disruptive in her classes.

MRS. W: She is?

PRINC: Yes. Surely you've noticed all the detention time she's been getting?

MRS. W: Dentention? I thought she'd joined the Civil Rights group.

PRINC.: What Civil Rights group?

MRS. W: The one that meets afterschool everyday.

PRINC: Are you aware--well, of course you are--that Susan thinks she's a....

MRS. W: A what?

PRINC: A boy.

MRS: A boy!

PRINC: A **black** boy.

MRS. W: A black boy?

PRINC: Yes.

MRS. W: No, she doesn't.

PRINC: Oh, yes, she does.

MRS W: Doesn't!

PRINC: Does!

(SILENCE)

PRINC: Well, that certainly got us nowhere. Let's try this again. Let's just say that she acts like she **believes** she is a black boy. I mean, you have at least noticed her clothes.

MRS. W: Oh, Yes. She's into that rap, hip-hop thing. Plays the music all the time.

PRINC: And you don't think it's odd for a girl to wear boxer shorts?

MRS. W: It's a fad. Isn't it?

PRINC: None of the other girls are doing it.

MRS. W: Really? I guess Suzy just marches to her own drum.

PRINC: Well, there you're right Mrs. uh-- Wright.

MRS. W: May I go then?

PRINC: No. Well, I mean, of course you can go, but I'd prefer if we came up with a solution to our problem.

MRS. W: What problem?

PRINC: Mrs. Wright, your daughter is jive walking all over this school spouting off about how she's been, and is being, oppressed.

MRS. W: Well, teenagers are sort of oppressed. Aren't they?

PRINC: SHE THINKS SHE IS A BLACK BOY! *(pause)* Why-would-I-make-this-up?

MRS. W: Good point. I just don't understand it.

PRINC: Sometimes, parents are the last to know.

MRS. W: I'll have a talk with her.

PRINC: On behalf of the entire school, I thank you.

MRS. W: It's that bad?

PRINC: *(blurts)* Oh, yes. *(catches herself)* Well, it's very disruptive. Might I suggest you have her evaluated?

MRS. W: By a shrink?

PRINC: Yes.

MRS. W: Don't push!

PRINC: Just a suggestion, Mrs. White--I mean Wright.

MRS. W: I'll **think** about it. (TV off)

(The Garden of Eden. Afterschool hangout))

JOE: I still can't believe you got an A on the History exam. Who did you cheat off?

CANDY: I did not cheat! I'm not a dummy.

JOE: Everyone else thinks you are.

CANDY: Pretty good bluff, huh? Just wait until I get accepted at an Ivy League school. Everyone I hate will like totally drop dead.

JOE: A girl with a plan.

CANDY: Don't leave home without it.

(ENTER GIN & DAHL)

JOE: Here comes the goon squad.

CANDY: They're just a couple of ghouls trying to have a good time. *(snorts when she laughs)*

GIN: A pun. She made a pun. Amazing.

DAHLIA: Candy, there's a fly in your soup.

CANDY: What soup?

DAHLIA: I mean a roach in your hair.

GIN: Must like the smell of bleach.

CANDY: What? A what?

JOE: Calm down. They're just messing with you.

CANDY: *(feeling her hair. Dahlia has put a plastic bug on her head)* A--! I feel---- HELP!!!!!!

DAHLIA: *(takes bug)* It's just a piece of plastic. No need to shatter.

JOE: Beat it.

GIN: Fine. It's always a pleasure leaving you. *(They go sit)*

CANDY: Jerks.
G & D: *(sweetly)* Whatever.

21 ½

(At the Graden of Eden, "coffee shop" and local teen afterschool hang out)

EMMA: (to Darby) I'm curious Darby, what you think of all of us?

DARBY: What do you mean, Em?

EMMA: Like those two. *(nodding over at Gin & Dahl)* And Barbara and me and Sue Z.

DARBY: You seem like a pretty normal bunch of girls to me.

EMMA: So you have loons in Australia too?

DARBY: The place is crawling with them.

EMMA: So you like it here?

DARBY: I think it fantastic. I mean if I were one of you, it might not be so fun. I get to kind of watch it all somewhat removed.

EMMA: Yeah. It's kind of weird right now. We all pretty much grew up together. I remember Gin and Dahl from like forever. It's strange when people start trying to be different.

DARBY: Trying?

EMMA: So you think they **are** different?

DARBY: I think one of the hardest things is letting people you know change.

EMMA: Now that's the truth!

DARBY: What about Tiffany?

EMMA: What about her?

DARBY: Has she always been such a nervous nellie?

EMMA: She moved here two years ago. I don't know what she was like before, but ever since she got here it's like she's been trying to figure out how to fit in.

DARBY: And she never quite makes herself fit?

EMMA: Yeah.

GIN: *(with magazine)* What do you think of this dress?

DAHLIA: I like that. I think we could make one, don't you?

GIN: Yeah.

DAHLIA: Let's go to the discount fabric place this weekend and buy some stuff and do one up.

GIN: Terrorific.

ZOE: I heard Merle is going to finish high school Upstate.

CANDY: I heard she's taking prozac.

(Enter Tiff. She goes to the table where Emma is sitting with Darby)

TIFF: Hi, Emma! Darby. Can I join you guys?

DARBY: Sure.

(Tiff waits for Emma's cue)

EMMA: *(noticing Tiff hovering)* Well, sit down Tiffany. I'm not the Queen.

DARBY: Everybody else thinks you are.

EMMA: Huh?

DARBY: Even Barbara defers to you.

EMMA: Defers to me?

DARBY: She totally admires you.

EMMA: That's kind of scary.

TIFF: But it's true. Everyone likes you. Why is that? I mean how do you do it?

EMMA: I--Everybody does not like me.

23

DARBY: Name someone who doesn't.

EMMA: Ginifire.

TIFF: That doesn't count.

EMMA: Why not?

TIFF: She doesn't like anybody.

DARBY: Hey, Ginifire!

GIN: What?

DARBY: Do you like Emma?

GIN: Sure.

TIFF: Wow.

EMMA: Stop it.

DARBY: Just making a point.

TIFF: What's your secret, Emma? I wish I knew how to get people to like me.

DARBY: Let's see, she's pretty, smart, well-read, hard working, and N-I-C-E.

EMMA: You are really embarrassing me.

TIFF: How do you decide what to wear in the mornings?

EMMA: I just put something on.

DARBY: She does. It's disgusting.

TIFF: But how did you come up with your look?

EMMA: My look? Do I have a look?

D & T: Yeah.

EMMA: Go figure.

24

TIFF: I've tried to, and I can't.

DARBY: Maybe you should give it a rest.

TIFF: Everyone likes you too, Darby.

DARBY: That's because I'm from away. First of all I'm new and different. Second, they know I'm going to leave, so I'm not a threat. Third, I'm coasting on Emma's popularity.

EMMA: Shut up, Darby.

TIFF: You don't even seem to care that you're popular, Emma.

EMMA: I don't.

DARBY: So, you wouldn't care if everyone hated you then?

EMMA: Of course I would care. I don't want people to hate me. But I'm not going to put myself through the wringer to get them to like me either. I just try to get things done. There, Tiff! My secret. Just try to get things done.

DARBY: Remarkable.

TIFF: This isn't funny. You don't know what it's like to be a total nobody.

DARBY: Everybody's somebody, Tiffany.

TIFF: Not me. I'm the invisible girl. I'd give anything to be you, Emma! *(Starts to cry and runs out)*

ZOE: What a loser.

MARTY: A total desperado.

CLOSE CURTAIN

(Enter Tiff still crying)

25

TIFF: I don't believe it. I blew it. Made a total fool out of myself. Total and utter humiliation! I am so stupid! I can't do anything right. I can't even dress myself right. Idiot! Moron! *(pause)* I'm never going back to school! How can I show my face again? Now even Emma thinks I'm a loser. *(pause thinking)* I'll find a way to change myself. I have to break out. Find the real me. The one they'll like. Like they like Emma. *(exits)*

26

(Girls gathered waiting for beginning of school)

CANDY: I heard that Barbara and Heather got suspended from school!

ZOE: They deserved it. Poor Merle's gone to some private school upstate.

CANDY: Brad kept calling her and sent her flowers and she wouldn't even talk to him.

EMMA: I think she just couldn't get herself to believe he wasn't going to dump her. Brad wrote her a great letter and mailed it to her up at school. He let me read it. I hope **she** reads it. I think he's a great guy.

DARBY: Maybe **you** should go out with him.

GINIFIRE: I think those witches should've gotten more than two weeks.

DAHLIA: Hey, it's enough to blow them out of the Honor Society.

GIN: Good!

(Enter Tiff as a wannabe goth. It is a mess. It doesn't "work")

DARBY: Oh, Em, would you look at that.

DAHLIA: Bats outta hell!

CANDY: *(giggling)* She makes you guys look great!

GIN: Oh, gee, thanks!

ZOE: What a total loser. Has she like, totally lost her mind?

(Enter Sue Z)

SUE Z: Whoa! Who beat her up with the ugly stick? Yo, Girl, what happened to you!? Looks like you were kidnapped, beaten and left for dead. A true casualty of fashion!

EMMA: Hey! Would everyone just chill?

SUE Z: I'm cool.

27

TIFF: I--I--- Oh, somebody help me! *(Sways and faints.)*

EMMA: Marty! Go get the school nurse!

BLACKOUT

(Tiffany is gone. *Everyone's waiting to find out how Tiffany is)*

(Enter Emma)

DARBY: Is she going to be all right?

EMMA: I think so. She doesn't have a concussion, at least.

BARB: Of course she'll be all right. No one ever died of a bad makeover.

CANDY: 'Are you sure?

ZOE: Yeah, liposuction can be lethal.

BARB: I'm not talking about plastic surgery. Did she look like she'd had plastic surgery to you?

GIN: Just about. The nerve of a Spice Girlie trying to be a Goth! It's insulting.

HEATHER: I thought **you** were beyond being insulted.

GIN: Oh, dive off a cliff, Heifer.

HEATHER: She called me a cow!

DARBY: If the "moo" fits.

SUE Z: "Old MacDonald had this farm. And on this farm he had these chicks. And the chicks went Ooh! And the chicks went Ah!"

EMMA: Please! Everyone just stop...it.

DARBY: It's a lovely day in the neighborhood isn't it, Em?

Sue Z: I rule this hood!

28

ZOE: She is certifiable.

CANDY: I think we're about to set a record for most students lost to the nut house in one semester

GIN: Job Stress.

ZOE: We're high school students.

DAHLIA: You telling me you don't feel stressed?

SUE Z: "Can you dig it? Dig it, Dig it, Dig it, Dig it?

DAHLIA: WHAT is your problem, Suze?

SUE Z: It's a black thang. You wouldn't understand.

DARBY: What I want to know is, if you are a guy then why is your name Sue?

SUE Z: What you gonna do with a boy named Sue?

GIN: What's she blabbing about now?

ZOE: It's a Johnny Cash song. (people stare at her) My Dad listens to him, I don't!

EMMA: Would everyone at least try to not be a jerk?

(Silence. People start realizing that Barbara & Heather aren't supposed to be there)

DARBY: Hey, Em. (Whispers in her ear)

ZOE: I can't believe it.

DAHLIA: What are you two doing here. I thought you leeches were suspended?

GIRLS: Yeah! Hey! What are you trying to pull? *(etc. pick one)*

GIN: I hope someone throws you in jail.

EMMA: Why are you guys hanging around here?

29

DARBY: Cleaning out your lockers?

HEATHER: Our parents fixed things.

EMMA: How?

BARB: That's confidential.

ZOE: 'Cause her Dad's a hot shot lawyer I bet.

CANDY: What did you parents do, make a deal with Merle's Mom and Dad? Hey, here's X amount of dough so you'll let our little princessess stay on the honor roll?

SUE Z: I think you're all forgetting something.

ALL: What?

SUE Z: Barb's Dad is the Man. The Super man.

EMMA: That's right. You're Dad's the Superintendent of Schools.

SUE Z: The white chicks have been pardoned!

HEATHER: We are still suspended.

EMMA: Then why are you here?

HEATHER: We are doing our time in the principal's office.

DARBY: Or the faculty lounge.

ZOE: So you can still do your school work!

CANDY: And not fall behind academically.

SUE Z: It's a great White wing conspiracy!

BARB: Oh, give me a break.

PANDORA: (speaking for the first time. Her speech is almost halting at first. Through gritted teeth. She has been moved, perhaps against her will, to finally speak out) Why? Why should any of you get a break?

GIRLS: *(various stunned reactions like)* I can't believe it! She can talk!

HEATHER: I thought she was a mute.

EMMA: An elective mute.

PANDORA: Right. And I just elected to start talking again.

(long pause. Everyone starts to think she's not going to say anything else)

PANDORA: When I was five I decided not to talk for reasons I don't see any reason to share with any of you. In the past few weeks I have seen things done which have convinced me even further--and I was already firmly convinced--that people can be swine. You're all so self-absorbed. Each one of you worrying about your makeup and your hair cuts. About zits and boyfriends and whether or not you're too fat or too thin. Is your butt too big? Are your boobs too small? What kind of jeans should you buy: big and baggy, stove pipes or bell bottoms. What color fingernail polish should you wear today? Will you flunk the big history test this Friday? And if you do, will you still be able to get into an Ivy League school? Do people think you're stupid? Do they think you're too smart? Are you parents going to get divorced? Were you dropped on your head at birth. Do people think you're a loser? And, those few of you that think you're perfect worry that you won't--and so you make desperate calculations to-- stay that way. *(pause)* What you two did to Merle McDonald was inhumane. And just today, none--but one--of you had mercy on poor Tiffany Taylor, who's only crime has ever been to want to be liked. Just look at the lengths she went to trying to fit in around here. Even you Emma: great, wonderful, smart, popular Emma, thought she was a loser.

EMMA: No, I didn't.

PANDORA: Not even just a little? Didn't you sort of well, pity her?

EMMA: *(pause, thinking and feeling crummy)* Yeah a little. I-- I just thought she needed more self-confidence.

PANDORA: You all do! *(stalks off)*

CURTAIN OPEN

(ENGLISH CLASS)

VOICE: Now Miss Wright. It's your turn.

(Sue Z does not respond)

GINIFIRE: Hey, fresh princess the teacher is talking to you.

VOICE: Miss Wright!

DAHLIA: (poking her) You're wanted by the man sister.

VOICE: Miss Wright!

SUE Z: (to Dahlia) Your wrong there missy, she's calling on that Wright chick whose never here.

VOICE: Miss Wright!

ZOE: Sue Z! She is talking to you, believe us.

VOICE: MISS WRIGHT!

SUE Z: (Standing) Are you talking to me, teach?

VOICE: Yes, Miss Wright.

SUE Z: Stop with the Miss Wright jive, all right? Whaddaya want?

VOICE: It is your turn to recite a poem.

SUE Z: Oh, okay. Sure. Why not? Here goes:

I'm a lean mean could be fightin' machine
Stones can never break me.
Words are spears to the ears
But I won't let 'em shake me.
I'm steel, real. Touch, I feel.
But I won't let you make me.
I got plans you can't understand
No jake, you cannot fake me.

(applause)

VOICE: Order! (gavel bang. BELL) Class dismissed.

SUE Z: you see how easily we are dismissed!

(Girls leave except Darby)

DARBY: That wasn't bad Sue.

SUE Z: Thanks.

DARBY: Can I ask you a question? I promise I won't tell anyone if you answer it. Well, just Emma.

SUE Z: Hey, honesty. Whoa!

DARBY: Do you really--I mean really--think you're a black guy?

SUE Z : Yeah! What's it to you anyway, girl?

DARBY: Well, I just don't think you really are a nutter. I mean, you're obviously a bright person. And you're also obviously a girl. So, what's up?

SUE Z: Whiteys! Poking around trying to help with one hand and trying to hold us down with the other.

DARBY: Don't you like being a woman?

SUE Z; I'm not a woman. I'm a girl!

DARBY: Didn't you just say you were a boy?

SUE Z: Well, I ain't no woman.

DARBY: But you will be.

SUE Z: Not if I can help it.

DARBY: You planning on having a sex change?

SUE Z: (Pause) Don't mess with my head Australia.

DARBY: This thing you've got going, it's different.

SUE Z: Huh?

33

DARBY: Sure beats an eating disorder.

SUE Z: You are seriously screwed up in the head.

DARBY: Am I? Funny, everyone thinks **you** are.

SUE Z: Well, puff them!

DARBY: It's about power isn't it?

SUE Z: Now there you got it right, sister. Say it loud, I'm black and I'm proud!

DARBY: What about Girl Power?

SUE Z: You mean the Spice Girls?

DARBY: I kind of like the Girl Power part. And in the movie, how they stick with their friend when she's gonna have her baby. When all the of London is waiting for them to come and sing silly pop tunes.

SUE Z: I didn't catch that flick.

DARBY: It's something to think about though, isn't it? Girl Power.

SUE Z: Why?

DARBY: It's who we are. Where our power comes from. Think about it.

BLACKOUT

34

(Enter Barbara & Heather)

HEATHER: Hey, Babs! What's up?

BARBARA: A little of everything.

HEATHER: Brewing up a new scheme?

BARB: Nope. Hey, how did you do on the Chemistry final?

HEATHER: I got an A. How 'bout you?

BARB: A-.

HEATHER: Sorry.

BARB: Don't sweat it.

HEATHER: Listen, Barbara, do you ever, well...

BARB: What?

HEATHER: You know: What we did to Merle. I heard she's on prozac.

BARB: So? We live in the Porzac Nation. I figure we upped her hipness quotient.

HEATHER: I don 't know. What we did was pretty raw.

BARB: That's life, Heather. She'll either toughen up or she won't.

HEATHER: And if she doesn't, "toughen up"?

BARB: Society can only support a certain number of people. Better to weed out the losers early on.

HEATHER: I never thought of her as a loser. Just a sophomore.

BARB: She didn't have run off boo-hoo-hooing Upstate. She could have just come back to school and acted like she didn't care. Then she'd still have Brad. And everyone would think she's really cool. Now, well, she's just a victim.

35

HEATHER: Survival of the socially fittest.

BARB: Right.

HEATHER: But would you want her to still be going out with Brad?

BARB: Hello! Of course not. Brad's taking me to the homecoming dance. I've got to show you my dress.

HEATHER: This is just too weird.

BARB: I was just making a point. Hey, it isn't our fault. Merle had options. She made a choice.

HEATHER: She made a choice. Yeah.

BARB: We are in charge of this corner of the universe.

BOTH: It's the natural order of things. *(exit)*

BLACKOUT

(Zoe & Candy come out. They have tried to visit Tiffany in the hospital. She wouldn't see them)

LIGHTS UP

(Enter Emma and Darby)

EMMA: Hey, guys, what's up? You see Tiffany?

ZOE: She didn't want to see us.

CANDY: Yeah, we came all the way down here to this bug house, let them search us and everything, and she wouldn't even say hi.

DARBY: Well, what do you expect?

ZOE: What's that supposed to mean?

DARBY: She's having a breakdown, isn't she?

ZOE: I guess.

CANDY: Some nurse said she's in some kind of shock. Is that for real?

EMMA: I don't know why she'd lie to you. She's a nurse.

CANDY: Maybe she thought we wouldn't understand the truth.

EMMA: Maybe Tiffany's condition is confidential.

ZOE: Whatever. Come on Candy, let's go.

CANDY: See you guys at school.

EMMA: Yeah, later.

DARBY: Do you think she'll see us?

EMMA: Beats me. *(they exit)*

CURTAIN OPEN

37

(Tiffany is curled up in a chair. Enter Emma & Darby)

DARBY: Are you sure this is a good idea, Em?

EMMA: The nurse said Tiffany talked a lot about us. She seemed to think it was okay. We're in, right?

DARBY: Right.

EMMA: Hi, Tiffany. How're you doing?

TIFF: *(startled. Starts freaking.)* How did you get in? I didn't want to see anyone. Anyone!

DARBY: That nice nurse thought you might like a visit.

TIFF: Traitor!

EMMA: It's all right, Tiffany.

TIFF: No it isn't. I'm not prepared for guests.

DARBY: This is a hospital, love. No one expects you to be prepared for anything.

TIFF: I look awful! I haven't washed my hair in a week.

EMMA: Tiff, that doesn't matter. We're your friends.

TIFF: No you're not. I don't have any friends.

EMMA: Tiffany, stop it.

TIFF: You stop it. Liar! Get out. I have the right to be left alone! I have that at least. So get out. Get out. GET OUT!

DARBY: Em!

EMMA: We're going, Tiff. I hope you feel better.

(they rush out)

TIFF: Liars!

Blackout   38

SUE Z: You see, everything was going fine. I was eleven and doing my thing. I could beat all the best boys at hockey, basketball, whatever and then the puberty thing kicked in. It's like a hostile take-over. I started slowing down. I could still outrun all the girls, but the top guys could beat me. And it burns me. I don't want to be a woman if it means losing my edge. But I don't want to be a big hairy, macho guy either. I want to be something that isn't boy or girl--crackling, icicle lightening! I was listening to that John Lennon song, "Woman is the Nigger of the World" and isn't it the truth? It's a man's world and pretty much a white man's world. At least here. And I am apart from it. They call that alienation, right. Well I am alienated and angry about it. maybe that's why alien gear is so hop right now. *(pause)* You hear angry black man. Angry young man. The Rebel. The Outlaw. And it's always a guy. How come it's all right, sometimes even cool, for guys to get angry? Hey! What's an angry young woman? Starts with a B. Ends with an itch. I'm gonna scratch it.

39

(Zoe and Candy at The Garden)

ZOE: Everyone in our school is going crazy.

CANDY: I know, it's like a total Twilight Zone.

ZOE: By the end of the year we may be the only two sophomores left.

CANDY: Wasn't Sue Z whacked in class today? Do you think she like really does believe she's a guy?

ZOE: You tell me. She should go on Jerry Springer.

CANDY: "I am a black guy trapped in a little white girl's body".

ZOE: Maybe she's like a real sicko. Maybe she's one of those whaddaya call 'ems.

CANDY: A schizo?

ZOE: No, that other thing. Like that movie with Richard Gere. You know, the guy pretends he's got--that's it-- a multiple personality. Maybe there's this black guy living in part of her brain.

CANDY: Ooh, invasion of the body snatchers.

ZOE: I'm serious.

CANDY: Well, let's say she's not nuts. Let's say she thinks she'd be happier if she was a guy. That's she's a transwhatever. So then, does she like boys or girls?

ZOE: Like? Like like how?

CANDY: You know, "like" like.

ZOE: Yuck. Let's like totally drop this line of thought.

(Enter Sue Z in still in rap clothes, but with signs of femininity thrown on)

CANDY: I do not believe it.

40

ZOE: Looks like the wild game's afoot, Sherlock.

(Going to Darby and Emma)

DARBY: Sue Z!

SUE Z: How's it shakin' mama.

DARBY: We are shaken, but as yet unstirred.

EMMA: You look different.

SUE Z: I'm not black anymore.

DARBY: Someone give you the Michael Jackson skin treatment.

EMMA: Are you a guy?

SUE Z: Nope. Say it loud. Say it proud. GIRL POWER!

GIN: Another Spice Girl born each minute. They're cloning them at the mall. Let's see, is she Sporty or Scary?

DAHLIA: You know, I've been having this recurrent nightmare.

GIN: Does it take place in your room? I think those are like the worst ever.

DAHLIA: Yeah, those scare the bat poop outta me.

GIN: So what's the dream?

DAHLIA: Well a lot of basically Alice in Wonderland, funhouse-mirror stuff happens--but here's the creepy part: I'm walking past a mirror and I see all this whiteness. I stop and walk backwards really slow. I look in the mirror and--

GIN: What?

DAHLIA: I've turned into Baby Spice.

GIN: UGHK!

DAHLIA: I know. I've got on this little white baby doll dress and white knee highs, and around my neck I've got on that rhinestone necklace

41

that says "BABY". Then I wake up in a sweat.

GIN: That's bloody awful, Dahl.

DAHL: And I usually like nightmares.

(Sue Z has walked up behind them)

SUE Z: GIRL POWER!

G & D: (jumping up) YEEEEEEE!!!!!!!

BLACKOUT

LIGHTS UP

PANDORA: Imagine this was all a Hollywood movie about a bunch of girls in high school. It kind of feels like that right? Real stagey and all acted out. Well, In high school--or Life in general for that matter--pretty much everyone is acting. Constantly. Of course, by the time you get older you sort of get "fixed" in one character. Most of you. Right?

If this was a Hollywood movie, Barbara and Heather would get what you all probably feel is coming to them. Tiffany and Merle would come back and be all better again. And more sure of themselves.

At the end of the movie all the "good" characters would be together with all their little, big problems pretty much solved or resolved, and the whole thing would ride out on the Big Hit from the movie soundtrack--some peppy alternative rock song.

And all of that would help you feel that life is "fair", which it isn't, and lull you off into a false sense of security that at the end of the day nobody really gets hurt, which of course they do. Some people never have to pay for the cruel things they do to others. So don't expect it.

(Enter Sue Z who passes through singing)

SUE Z: It's your thing, do what you wanna do. Ain't no one gonna tell you who to sock it to!"

42

PANDORA: Anyway, this isn't a movie. It's a play. Time for the grand finale.

(Girls come out and stand in a line.)

GIRLS: If I just had a chance to:

PANDORA: Change people's minds.

GINIFIRE: Get five more piercings in my left ear.

ZOE: Be a pop star.

HEATHER: Get a BMW convertible.

DAHLIA: Design my own line of clothing.

CANDY: Get my parents back together.

DARBY: Climb Mt. Everest.

SUE Z: Help people understand.

BARBARA: Rule the world.

EMMA: Be the first woman President of the United States.

TIFFANY: Start over again.

(Everyone fades back except Tiffany)

TIFFANY: But you can't change the past. No one will let you. It's set and fixed. Concrete boots on the wings of your dreams. It feels that way to me. Nowhere to go but down. *(she takes her mark)*

GIRLS: Might as well jump.

(She runs foward and seems to jump off stage)

BLACKOUT

GIRLS: AHHHHHHHHHHHHHHHHHHHHHHHHHHHHHHHH! *(like falling)*

(no thud is heard)

LIGHTS UP

(TIFFANY is nowhere to be seen)

PANDORA: It just goes to show you **can** push some people too far.

GIRLS: It's the natural order of things.

44

THEATRE of the SILVER DRAGON

Presents:

@@@@@@@@@@@@@@@@@@@@@@@@@@

@@@@@@@@@@**Y2K**@@@@@@@@@@@

@@@@**THE END OF TIME**@@@@@@@

@@@@@@@@@@@@@@@@@@@@@@@@@@

Written & Directed by: Tamela Glenn   1998/1999

At the end of 1999 computers all over the world had to be reset. This turn of the century crisis had programming experts scrambling, while another hysterical group prepared for an end of time apocalypse. And the clock was ticking down....

HAPPY NEW YEAR>CENTURY>MILLENIUM!!!

the last bus leaves............

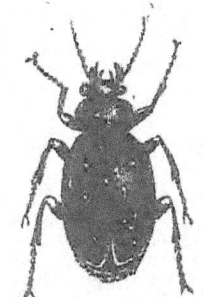

............NOW.

@@@@@@@@@@@@@@@@@@@@@@@@@@@

CAST

MISTER

PALOMA

SURVIVA

ANGIE

TACO

MIAMI

Theatre of
the Silver Dragon
P.O. Box 171
Stillwater, ME 04489-0171

ACT I

(An alarm clock is sitting downstage ticking. It goes off)

(Enter actors in a line downstage)

ALL: *(to audience)* Where will **you** be when the year 2000s?

(BLACKOUT)

MISTER: *(to Pal.)* It's the End of the Era.

PALOMA: *(to Mr.)* But is it the end of the error?

MR.: *(to her)* Don't get them started.

PALOMA: *(to him)* Too late. Sorry.

MIAMI: *(out to audience)* Think you hear the four horsemen approaching?

MR: HERE.

MIAMI: Anyone care to lay odds?

MR. WE GO.

MIAMI: Is the world gonna end?

MR.: AGAIN.

MIAMI: Come on, people! Ante up! It's the end of the century. heck it's the end of the--the--the watchamacallit. *(No takers. So shrugs and exits)*

PALOMA: The Millennium. What a great word. M-i-llinn-i-ummmmmmm. Just roll it around in your mouth. Hold it on the tip of your tongue. It's tasty! Yum-yummy. Millennium-yum-yum. Creamy. Dreamy! Millennium!

MISTER: And counting: 98, 99, 00!

TACO: 00?

ANGIE: That's what it says on my driver's license. Good until 1/1/00.

MR.: Means 2000. Reset. Start a new millennium.

PALOMA: The New Age.

SURVIVA: *(charging in)* Reset? Reset?! We're gonna see about that, aren't we? Those computer hacks messed up big time. Come the year 2000, the computers are gonna fry!

TACO: Why?

SURVIVA: Y2K, man. Head for the hills!

TACO: Y2 what?

MR.: Y2K. It refers to the fact that back in the Dark Ages of cyber technology, computers were designed to read a two digit code. 96, 97,98 99. The year two thousand, therefore, will come up as 00.

TACO: So?

MR.: Well, there is a strong belief that computers will interpret this as **1900.**

ANGIE: Why would they do that?

TACO: Can a computer really "interpret".

PALOMA: No, and I'd say that's the problem.

SURVIVA: It's a problem all right. They're gonna fry! The Stock Market's gonna come crashing down. No planes will be taking off or landing.

PALOMA: *(makes **sound of air dive** and)* CRASH!

SURVIVA: Global corporate meltdown! No more telephoning, telemarketing, investment banking, bingo, lotto or credit card purchases.

MR.: Stop being such an extremist!

SURVIVA: No more pick up the phone and two tickets to Honolulu. No more home shopping network. No more direct deposits. No more paying your bills by phone: "Welcome to the Terrordome"!

MR.: We still have time to finish reprogramming.

TACO: We do?
ANGIE: Do we?

SURVIVA: No more simulated archery. No more Disneyland!

ANGIE: I never liked that place anyway. I prefer Sea World.

SURVIVA: You can forget Shamu, honey.

ANGIE: Never!

TACO: Free Willy!

ANGIE: What?

TACO: I just felt it was about time I had a line.

ANGIE: Oh.

MR.: People are working on this.

TACO: What?

ANGIE: What people?

MR.: Our government. The governments of the world.

PALOMA: And?

MR. And What?

PALOMA: Exactly!

AN & TA: Huh?

MR. They're trying "fixes".

PALOMA: Sounds like they're in a fix.

ANG & TAC: Exactly!

SURVIVA: NO more steak and lobster. NO more Fast Food!

ANGIE: No more McDonald's?

SURVIVA: No more Mickey D's, Burger King, Pizza Hut, Kentucky
Fried, Taco Bell!

TACO: Ouch!

SURVIVA: You'll be eating spam out of the can.

Theatre of
the Silver Dragon
P.O. Box 171
Stillwater, ME 04489-0171

3

TACO: Barfo.

ANGIE: We'll all starve!

PALOMA: It's the Mill-en-ium-um-um diet.

MR.: HEY! People! There is no reason to panic.

SURVIVA: It's past time for panic! Now is the time to horde food, guns, & diapers!

PALOMA: Sound the alarm!

MR.: I assure you, there is no reason to be alarmed.

ANGIE: Why?

TACO: Why not?

SURVIVA: Take your money out of the banks. Buy gold. Precious metals. HARD CURRENCY.

MR.: You're being an alarmist.

SURVIVA: That's the idea, mister.

MR.: You'll start a national stampede of fear.

SURVIVA: Good.

ANGIE: Good?

SURVIVA: You gotta wake up, honey. You all gotta wake up. WAKE UP!

ANGIE: I feel like I'm dreaming.

SURVIVA: Well, it's gonna turn bad. *(exits)*

ANGIE: Did you hear what she said? We're going to be plunged into chaos!

PALOMA: Millennium Mayhem.

TACO: People always get all hooey at the end of a **century** let alone a millennium.

ANGIE: They Do?

4

TACO: Yeah. Everybody gets into astrology and tarot cards and thinks the world's gonna end.

ANGIE: Why?

PALOMA: It's that *fin de siecle* feeling.

TAC & ANG: That **what**?

PALOMA: FIN DE SIECLE. "de siecle": of the century. "Fin": The END. *(She exits)*

MR: How do you say millenium in french? Oh, yes! *(holding up a finger, but doesn't tell us)*

TACO: What if this is Armaggedon, man. The Apocalpyse--Now.

ANGIE: Well, in a couple a years.

TACO: Then now is the time to prepare. Before there is no more time!

ANGIE: You're starting to sound like Miss End of the World as we know it.

TACO: Think about it! Looting. Starvation. Food riots! Cannabalism.

ANGIE: Come off it.

TACO: A nation--the whole world--running wild! I'm gonna buy a tent and move to Montana!

ANGIE: You? You in a tent in Montana on January 1st, 00. What a hoot! You've never been out of the city. You wouldn't even go to Boy Scout Camp.

TACO: "Necessity is the mother of all........what?

MR.: Invention.

TACO: Right.

ANGIE: So you're going to invent a tent in Montana?

TACO: No. I-- Well, what are **you** going to do?

ANGIE: Join a cult.

TACO: How New Age. Can I come with you?

ANGIE: Whatever.

TACO: What kind of cult?

ANGIE: "Any port in a storm". *(They look at each other a beat)* But it won't be solo in a tent in Montana!

MR.: People, please. All this alarm. It's so unnecessary.

TACO: That's your opinion.

ANGIE: Yeah, things are looking pretty grim.

MR.: Since when? Since that off-balance person scared you witless?

TACO: Yeah, basically.

MR.: What's different right now from yesterday? Or this morning?

ANGIE: We're talking about the future! *(Enter Paloma)*

PALOMA: The future is now!

MR.: First of all: You could get hit by a bus and never live until the year 2000.

PALOMA: Now there's a cheery thought.

MR.: Second: Biblically speaking "The Apocalypse" can come at any time. I believe it was worded as a "when you least expect it: expect it" major sort of occurrence.

TACO: Really?

MR.: Yes, really.

TACO: How comforting.

MR.: Further, The world already is in stinking shape. Why suddenly see the light just because some nut-case ran around yelling a spate of relative nonsense?

ANGIE: Are you following him?

TACO: Less and less.

6

SURVIVA: *(off)* WAKE UP!

TACO: I don't know about you, but I'm going her way. At least she's awake.

ANGIE: Awake?

TACO: At least I think she is. *(exits)*

ANGIE: Wait! *(pause)* Oh, terrific. What about me you loser? So much for friendship.

PALOMA: There are no atheists in foxholes.

ANGIE: What? What's that got to do with **anything**?

PALOMA: You need something to believe in. I'm talking about faith in a higher power. Something outside of yourself.

ANGIE: Sounds good. Like what?

PALOMA: Or some...one.

ANGIE: Like who?

PALOMA: Like me.

MR.: She's got to be joking.

ANGIE: Just who are you, and why should I believe in you?

PALOMA: I was only joking.

MR.: Thank Heavens.

ANGIE: Oh. So?

PALOMA: Don't believe **in** me. Follow me, I'll show you a way.

ANGIE: What about THE Way.

PALOMA: That's someone elses's line.

ANGIE: Oh, yeah. Do you think He'll come back before the big meltdown?

MR.: *(finally losing it)* THERE ISN'T GOING TO BE ANY

MELTDOWN!!!!

PALOMA: They also said no one would ever walk on the moon.

ANGIE: And that the world was flat.

PALOMA: Now you're getting the hang of it! Shall we go?

ANGIE: Where?

PALOMA: The last bus leaves...*(sound of TIRES SCREACHING)* Now. Are you coming? *(She holds out a hand which Angie grabs. They run off.)*

CLOSE CURTAIN

(Enter Mr.)
(During speech. Hammering, Dragging materials, etc can be heard).

MR.: "People! People who need people!" Are **not** the luckiest people in the world. "People" are sheep. Oh, yes, once in a while you get that rare, special, unique **individual** . A Ghandi. Or a Hitler. It's a toss of the coin. And they stir everything up. And the Sheep. The Sheep....Follow....Them... like lemmings. To the sea. Off the cliffs of reason. And somehow, someway it all and always and in all ways ends in chaos for the mob of sheep and/or in the death of that unique individual. Though some good and some evil is always left behind. For better or worse. Til death do we all depart. "People"! What will they think of next?

SURVIVA: *(Voice off)* Y2K! "God didn't tell Noah to sit on the top of the hill and let the flood come over his head!" He said build an ark. Take animals. Provisions! Wait for an olive branch.

MR. *(shakes head. Looks at pocket watch)* 97, 98, 99... *(exits.)*

CURTAIN OPEN

Curtain Open

(Surviva and Taco at Tent Camp. Surviva is scurrying around doing stuff. Taco is trying to help, but generally getting in the way.)

SURVIVA: Hey! Outta the way! Go over there and siddown!

TACO: All right, Already! I give up.

SURVIVA: *(alert like a hunting dog)* You w h a t?

TACO: I surrender.

SURVIVA: *(Grabbing him by the neck and throttling him)* No giving up! And never, never, NEVER utter the "word".

TACO: What word? What's wrong with you?

SURVIVA: The "S" word.

TACO: (wracking brain) the S word? oh..."Surrender"!

SURVIVA: NO, No, No, No, No, No, No, No **NO** ! , There is no quitting, only quitters! We! Are survivors.

TACO: That's an "S" word.

SURVIVA: Don't get smart with me .

(**Honking.** Surviva lets go of Taco ,who sinks to the ground. Enter Miami)

SURVIVA: Password!

MIAMI: Supply the demand.

SURVIVA: That's a good one. Okay Miami, whatcha got?

MIAMI: I got survival domes for seven grand.

SURVIVA: We're all set for shelter.

9

MIAMI: *(looking around at the tent camp)* Whatever you say.

SURVIVA: What else you got? Toilet Paper? Candy? Napalm?

MIAMI: Hey! Now, you know I don't do napalm. Grenades okay. Napalm, no way!

SURVIVA: Whatever. I'll take a hundred.

MIAMI: I can drop 'em off next Tuesday.

TACO: What if the world ends before then? What ever happened to carry and get cash?

MIAMI: Listen kiddo, if you think I'm gonna traipse around with a hundred grenades on me, you're crazier than she is. I might accidently pull a pin.

SURVIVA: ANYWAY! The world is not going to end until Y2K and don't forget that. Next Tuesday's fine.

MIAMI: I've also got some really good computer gear.

SURVIVA: What on earth do I want with a computer?

TACO: Uh-Oh.

MIAMI: People all over the globe are searching the Internet for supplies, refuge, e-mail contacts & chatroom pals. Get with it, Surviva. Surfing the net about Y2K is t h e thing to do!

SURVIVA: The thing for who to do--Morons? Get out of here. Scram! Forget the grenades.

Miami: What's your problem?

SURVIVA: Computers! Computers are the root of all the evil in the first place.

MIAMI: Just because some of the computers--

SURVIVA: All! All of the computers are gonna crash!

MIAMI: All right!*(rolls her eyes)* Just because a l l the computers are going to crash in 2000, doesn't mean they're evil. They're computers! How they can be good or bad?

TACO: She's got a point.

SURVIVA: Yeah. Right on top of her head. Scram, Miami, before I have to shoot you. You're a spy!

MIAMI: For who?

SURVIVA: Don't ask me.

TACO: The government?

SURVIVA: Yeah. You're trying to brainwash me!

MIAMI: What?

SURVIVA: Other yopes may be out "surfing" the NET, but they'll all be boo-hoo-hooing come Y2K. No more chatty Kathy's and Kens.

MIAMI: You're losing it.

SURVIVA: Yeah, well, you better get lost!

MIAMI: Fine. I'm going. I can see when I'm not wanted. *(exits, watching her back)*

TACO: Do you really think she's a spy?

SURVIVA: Why take chances?

(ENTER MiSTER)

MR: This is only a test. This is nothing but a test. In the event of an actual disaster you **will be instructed.**

TACO: I certainly hope so.

SURVIVA: Don't speak unless spoken to.

TACO: Why? And don't say because you say so.

SURVIVA: *(looking like she might snap and then calmly)* You have to be careful. The looser the lips, the tighter the noose.

TACO: Yeck.

350 Play 8

SURVIVA: Exactly.

MR: This is only a test. This is nothing but a test. In the event of an actual disaster, you **will be instructed.**

TACO: Why does he keep saying that?

SURVIVA: What?

TACO: That.

SURVIVA: That what? What are you blabbering about?

TACO: Him!

SURVIVA: Oh..... *(looking Mr. up & down)* Well. There's always a **him** around.

TACO: There is?

SURVIVA: You better believe it.

MR: They can't say I haven't warned them. *(exits)*

TACO: That was cryptic.

SURVIVA: We'll all be in the grave soon if we don't watch our steps. Now! Time for our workout.

TACO: Terrific.

SURVIVA: Are you carping again, Taco?

TACO: Hey! I wait all day for this.

SURVIVA: How do you expect to survive if you can't carry the weight?

TACO: What weight?

SURVIVA: The weight of the world. And one, and two, and three and four and one and two and three and four *(etc.)*

(They do "exercises. Jumpging Jacks-Karate lunges-kicks-twizzles, and eventually end up leanng foward standing face to face in a staring contest. Meanwhile, Angie, wanders out the door and talks to the audience)

ANGIE: Where did Paloma go? We got on that dumb bus and rattled what? Fifty miles? Who knows? Who cares! When we finally pulled into the station, she was gone. And so was everyone else. Or was there ever anyone else? *(looks around) There is a chair, rug and a little table with a potted cactus on it)* So now what?

(Enter Paloma up on the stage)

PALOMA: This is your time in the desert. To be tested. To grow strong. Become a prophet!

(Onstage, Surviva and Taco end staring contest with a war cry)

SURV & TAC: YARRRRRRRRR!!!!!!!

ANGIE: What on earth was that?

MR: *(Appearing in the doorway). When he starts speaking, Angie is startled and picks up the chair and holds it out like a lion tamer.)* You are not alone. You are never alone. You are just one person on a planet swarming with humanity. But you can still make a difference.

ANGIE: Is that a riddle? *(puts chair down)* Oh, great. I'm halluncinating. Wait a minute! *(walks towards him)* You're that guy from the beginning. You're Mister.....Mister.... Hey! Who are you?

MR: Just "Mister" is more than enough.

PALOMA: Loose lips. Tight noose.

ANGIE: My guide tells me not to talk to strangers, so maybe you'd better hit the road, "Mister".

MR: Whatever you wish. In the event of an actual emergency, you **will be instructed.** (exits)

ANGIE: Good, That's good to know. Right. *(Silence)* So now I'm totally alone. Okay. Why don't I just sit down and ....sit. *(she sits. A light shines down on her.)*

PALOMA: "In the beginning was the Word"

SURVIVA: YARRRRRRRRRR!

PALOMA: It's that fin de siècle feeling! *(exits out door)*

(Enter Mister, from curtain center. Noise of hammering, etc., under speech)

MR: Every age believes it will be the last. Every person believes their life is unique. No one wants to die. But we thrive on gossip, the misfortunes of others, reports of disasters--as long as we have some semblance of control. Control! So bring out the weather charts, the possible paths of hurricanes, the dectectors of seismic activity and asteroid belts and comets hurtling though space towards Our Town, U.S.A. Ring in the New Age, where every person is a high priestess or priest full of intuition, capable of divination. Protection. Offering "hope"--the last Evil in Pandora's Box. I've been here before, folks. Heard most of this before. Except that this pre-millenium freak out, it's a technological armageddon they're predicting. Y2K. The computers will crash. 00. And TIME...WILL...STOP. *(Noise has stopped behind curtain. Mister clears throat. Exits)*

BLACKOUT

ACT III

(Enter Paloma in door way with a candle)

PALOMA: We are the light bearers. We bring tidings of a New Age! The dawn of a time when harmony shall be restored on planet Earth. But we must do the work! No outside Being is going to help us . We have lost touch with the magic--with the power---inside each one of us. *(pause & shift of tone)* Of course, some of us have more of it than others. *(blows out candle)*

(Spotlight up on Angie)

ANGIE: Paloma? Is that you? Where have you been? Where are you now? *(she walks to stage)*

PALOMA: Your time in the desert is almost over. You have been purified by the sun. You are almost ready.

ANGIE: For what? I feel like I'm going to have a heatstroke. Hey! How about some water? Or a Coke? It's the real thing--which is more than I can positively say about you. *(sits on edge of stage)*

14

PALOMA: It is normal to pass through a period of questioning and restlessness.

ANGIE: I'm gonna die out here!

PALOMA: You are passing through the Valley of Death. *(passing her hand over Angie's head)*

ANGIE: I don't get you. You say every one of us has the power to save ourself, and then you keep spouting this stuff that unless I am mistaken is right out of the Bible.

MR: *(popping out curtain center)*   Beware false prophets.

ANGIE: Oh, great. **He's** back. I'm surrounded. I surrender!

SURVIVA: *(off)*   YARRRRR!

MR: A tree falls in the forest, but I'm not there to see or to hear it. Did it really   fall?

ANGIE: Who cares?!

PALOMA: You said, "A tree falls". So it falls. So it fell.

MR: But did it fall for me? What does it have to do with my Reality?

PALOMA: We're all in this together.

MR: Are we?

ANGIE: I repeat: WHO CARES ??? *(silence)*   I surrender.

SURVIVA: *(off)* YARRR!

PALOMA: What do you surrender?

ANGIE: Huh?

MR: Be careful.

ANGIE: Hey! What is going on around here?

MR: Exactly.

Theatre of
the Silver Dragon
P.O. Box 171
Stillwater, ME 04489-0171

ANGIE: What?

MR: Beware false prophets.

ANGIE: Stop that!

MR: In the event of an actual emergency. This is not a test.

ANGIE: What are you talking about? Are we in a state of emergency? Should I take cover? Is the end at hand? What is going on????

MR: You will be instructed.

ANGIE: Stop saying that!

PALOMA: *(to Mister, commanding)* **LEAVE NOW.** *(suddenly sweet)* Please.

(Mister gives her a disappointed look then exits reluctantly)

PALOMA: Now where were we?

ANGIE: We? There is no we. There is only me here frying in the desert and you there--wherever that is????

PALOMA: There's a map in your pocket. Follow it. You'll find water in one mile. *(she exits curtain center)*

ANGIE: *(finds map. Opens it)* What is going on!?

MR: *(off)* Pawn to Queen Four.

ANGIE: After I get some water, I'm going to figure this thing out. *(Exits out door looking at map)*

((Enter Paloma from curtain center wearing techno boa)

PALOMA: The end is coming. If you make a careful search of the Bibles of the world and know how to read the signs around you, it's obvious : The End is at hand. Mankind has sold its collective soul to technology and put its faith in computer chips. *(tosses a handful of poker chips)*

The Milleniun-um-um-um is coming! The year 2000. Y2K. 00. The End ...of... Time. *(She exits)*

CURTAIN OPEN

(SURVIVA and TACO at Tent Camp. A Flag is now flying. They do Song and dance)

SURVIVA: Okay and:

SUR & TAC: Do Do Do the Apocalpyso! Do it Now!
We'll survive Apocalypso! We know how.

We've been tried and we are true.
Now we're only waiting for you.

Woo Woo Woo Apocalypso! Come right now!
Do Do Do the Apocalypso! We know how.

We are tired, but we're true
And we're only waiting for you!

Y 2 K! Y 2 K! Y? Apocalypso! *(4xs Building to last one)*

(pause)

TACO: What's for lunch?

SURVIVA: Not so fast. First, the manifesto!

TACO: Again?

SURVIVA: Everyday until the end of time.

TACO: Then get it over with. I'm starving.

SURVIVA: Get used to it. When the End comes there will be famines. Mass starvation. Cannabalism. You'll be glad for spam in a can.

TACO: I told you to lay off the Spam.

SURVIVA: One day you'll beg me for Spam.

TACO: Never!

SURVIVA: We'll see and soon.   (Gong *)

MR.: 98, 99..... "Ask not for whom the bell tolls. It tolls for thee."

TACO: He's back.

17

SURVIVA: I told you: There's always a him around. Now!
At the stroke of midnight December 31, 1999, the computers will
advance to OO. Y2K!

TACO: And time will stop.

SURVIVA: AND TIME WILL STOP!

MR: 97, 98, 99....

TACO: Now is that literally? Are you sure it's literally?

SURVIVA: What are you getting at?

TACO: Well, just because some of the computers don't know what
time it is; even if they think it is 1900; that doesn't mean time has
stopped.

SURVIVA: SOME?

TACO: Yeah, I read they've fixed the Y2K bug in most of the
Computers built aftert (looking through magazine) let"s see

SURVIVA: See? You don't see anything. That's propaganda!

TACO: Huh?

SURVIVA: Hogwash that's supposed to lull us all into a false sense of
security and then boom!

TACO: Well,who wants to lull us into "a false sense of security"?

SURVIVA: The Powers that Be.

TACO: And who might they be?

SURVIVA: Open your eyes! Your ears! Y2K is coming, man. And it's
not a bug! It's a plague!

TACO: But that doesn't mean that TIME will STOP.

MR.: OO. Reset.

SURVIVA: TIME WILL STOP!

TACO: How can you be so sure?

SURVIVA: I KNOW IT TO BE TRUE!

TACO: How?

SURVIVA: I feel it in my gut.

TACO: So it's a gut feeling?

SURVIVA: Borne out by a careful study of the times, the signs and the scriptures.

TACO: I see.

PALOMA: Do you?

MR.: **Every** Age has used the scriptures to support its Apocalpyse-Now theories. Every doomsday cult has a list of verses that all add up to **proof**. At least to them.

TACO: Really?

MR.: Really.

TACO: Wow. So how do you know **you're** right, Surviva?

SURVIVA: Because I'm turned on, tuned in, and plugged into the cosmologic rumblings of the universe.

PALOMA: Is that painful?

MR.: Just look at her. It must be.

TACO: Excuse me asking, but just how did you...Let me rephrase, just **when** did you first get this "gut feeling"?

PALOMA: This ought to be good.

MR.: Quiet. I'd like to hear her answer.

SURVIVA: One night I woke up around three a.m. and it hit me right between the eyes: I'm going to die. I mean really. One day. Bang! It'll all just end.

TACO: What did you do?

SURVIVA: I went back to sleep.

TACO: (disappointed) Oh.

Theatre of
the Silver Dragon
P.O Box 171
Stillwater, ME 04489-0171

19

SURVIVA: But, the next day when I woke up, I started to wonder: What if I was wrong. What if there is more to life than life?

TACO: Huh?

SURVIVA: Well, we came here from somewhere, so.....

PALOMA: What?

SURVIVA: Exactly. So what else is there?

MR.: And?

SURVIVA: I turned on. Tuned in.

PALOMA: Dropped out?

MR.: That was Tim Leary.

TACO: How? **Exactly.**

SURVIVA: We're all part of the same game, Taco.

TACO: What game?

SURVIVA: It's all out there to read.

TACO: What?

SURVIVA: What?

TACO: Yeah, WHAT?

SUR & PAL & MR.: The Vibes.

TACO: The Vibes?

SURVIVA: Right. And the vibes spell Doomsday. The End of Time.

MR.: If Time did End, would that be bad?

PALOMA: Would we still have Space?

TACO: Listen: I think I've just had a major revelation.

SURVIVA: Really? What is it!

TACO: With all due respect, you're a loon. I'm leaving.

SURVIVA: Wait! You can't abandon ship mid-voyage. You'll drown. You barely know the ropes.

TACO: It's my neck. Ck! *(Makes hanging gesture and exits)*

SURVIVA: Traitor! TRAITOR! *(silence)* Good help is so hard to find in these last days. Target pratice time! He may have been a spy. I have to be prepared. I am prepared! I have to be ready. For anything. *(She runs in tent to get gun. Sounds of rummaging.)* Now where is my pistol? *(suddenly peering out)* You don't think? Would he? Could he have taken it? TRAITOR! It's got to be in here somewhere! *(more rummaging)*

(Enter Angie from door. She is lost. The map has run out. She studies it and then stuffs it in her pocket.)

ANGIE: And the map leads here. The end of the road. Looks like the place I started out from.

MR.: You learn from your mistakes and in the end all you have are your mistakes.

PALOMA: That certainly is a negative sentiment. Especially from you. Getting tired and pessimistic at the end of another century?

MR.: Don't try to read my mind. It was just a passing thought.

PALOMA: Ooh. The most dangerous kind.

ANGIE: WHAT NOW?

MR.: The Age Old question.

(Enter Miami)

MIAMI: Hey, kiddo. You look lost.

ANGIE: Completely.

MIAMI: Need some supplies?

ANGIE: I'd like a Coke.

MIAMI: *(handing her a can)* Here you go. Now, while I've got your attention: How about some survival gear?

ANGIE: What have you got?

21

MIAMI: Well, you look like you need the Starter Kit.

ANGIE: What's that?

MIAMI: All the Y2K basics. *(Hauls it out)*

ANGIE: Looks big. What's in it?

MIAMI: *(going through bag)* Let's see....Candles and matches. A compass. Some dehydrated food. One of those foil blanket things. And, of course, books.

ANGIE: What kind of books?

MIAMI: All the majors. The Bible: NIV & King James versions; The Qur'an; The Bhagavad-Gita; The Dhammapada; The Heart Sutra, The Dead Sea Scrolls....oh, and a pack of Tarot cards with a book on how to use them; several books on Astrology as well as an Ephemeris with astro-chart forms. Two cans of sardines and some soda crackers. A jar of peanut butter. No jelly, and sorry, but no bread. The collected poems of Emily Dickenson--go figure. And the I Ching complete with coins. Notebook and pen. Hey! A flashlight! and...lessee...Well, that's about it. I can get you a tent if you want one.

ANGIE: Well.....

PALOMA: Give her a gun.

MIAMI: *(reacts)* Uh, I think you'll need this.

ANGIE: A gun?

MIAMI: Yeah. That's all you'll need. Gotta go. Now. *(exits fearfully)*

ANGIE: *(staring at it)* A gun?!

PALOMA: Snakes. You know. The usual dangers of the wasteland.

ANGIE: Oh. *(pause)* Hey! Where are you?!

PALOMA: There's a camp ahead. Shelter. *(Goes to Mr.)*

ANGIE: Thanks. That's what I need. Gimme shelter! *(notices Miami is gone.)* She's gone! Oh, well, what else is new? *(walks to and onto stage.)* Hey! Is anyone here?

SURVIVA: Intruder alert! Intruder alert! *(comes out gun in hand)*

ANGIE: Don't shoot!

SURVIVA: Shoot or be shot! *(raises her gun)*

PALOMA: It's a snake.

ANGIE: Huh?

MR.: Stop that.

SURVIVA: The safety is stuck!

PALOMA: *(in a whispering hiss)* She'll kill you.

ANGIE: She will!?

SURVIVA: Prepare to die! *(She raises her gun. It just clicks. Angie shoots her.)*

(Silence)

ANGIE: What? I--- *(looks at gun)*

PALOMA: It's called self-defense.

MR.: Millennium Mayhem.

ANGIE: How did I get here? This isn't real. I feel like I'm dreaming. *(runs off)*

SURVIVA: And it's gonna get bad. *(She assesses her damage and has a realization)* No. No! It..isn't...supposed...to happen...this way. **Y2K!** man. *(exhausted pause)* I had it all figured out. OO. The End of Time. But--this isn't.... It isn't time yet! I want to be here for Y2K. Gonna miss the whole thing. I WANT MORE TIME!

MR.: Every day until the End of Time.

PALOMA: More time for what?

SURVIVA: I'm a survivor. I should survive. **Y2K!** The End of Time!

PALOMA: Whose time?

MR.: I warned her. *(shakes head, Says kindly as if speaking about a young child)* They make so many plans.

PALOMA: It's touching.

MR.: Tragic.

SURVIVA: *(angry)* Is this some kind of joke?

MR.: You could get hit by a bus before the year 2000.

PALOMA: And the last bus leaves....*(screech)* Now!

SURVIVA: I was tuned in to "the vibes". I was **ready**. I had **a plan**. Which is more than I can say for most of you. *(to audience)* WAKE UP! *(pants, exhausted)*

MR.: They always have a story.

PALOMA: Their version.

MR.: Their plea.

PALOMA: For mercy.

MR.: More time.

PALOMA: To prolong the inevitable.

SURVIVA: To be understood.

MR.: And I've heard them all.

PALOMA: Nevertheless...

MR.: *(tired of it all and wondering)* Nevertheless?

PALOMA: *(firm)* Still.

MR.: *(accepting)* Still.

SURVIVA: *(turns to tent flag)* I pledge allegiance to the flag of the united camp of Surviva and to the republic of which I ...*(she collapses)*...stood. *("dies")*

PALOMA: *(finger up)* "Live by the sword. Die by the sword." *(changes hand gesture to "peace sign" then exits, first hopping over Surviva))*

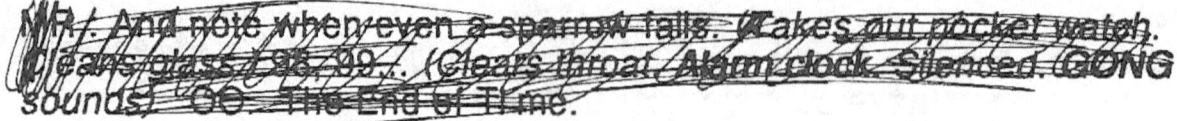

BLACKOUT

24

MR: And note when even a sparrow falls. *(looks at pocket watch)* 97, 98, 99. *(exits)*

(enter Miami)

MIAMI: Surviva? What are you up to now? No! Let me guess. This is one of your drills. Uh--I get it. "Playing dead": To fool the enemy. How clever. *(silence)* All right, already! Yoo hoo! You can get up Surviva. *(nothing)* Very convincing. Bravo! *(claps. pause)* Now get up. *(silence)* Surviva?

(suddenly worried, she kneels down to look her over) Surviva?

CURTAIN CLOSE

(Enter Taco who goes and sits on stage)

TACO: Now, you tell me: Is it better to be alone in the desert, totally without food, water, or shelter; or pretty well-fed and watered, but terrorized by a lunatic? *(silence)* IS THERE ANYONE OUT THERE!

ANGIE: *(off)* TACO!

TACO: Angie? Hey! Angie! Over here!

ANGIE: *(entering)* Taco! I--oh, you aren't going to believe me!

TACO: At this point, I could believe anything. Where have you been anyway?

ANGIE: Where have you been?

TACO: I asked first.

Theatre of
the Silver Dragon
P.O. Box 171
Stillwater, ME 04489-0171

25

Angie: This is a nightmare.

Taco: I'm with you so far.

ANGIE: I killed someone.

TACO: You what?

ANGIE: I killled someone.

TACO: Whoa there. Stop the ponies. You're joking, right?

ANGIE: (whimpering) Noooo.

TACO: Why?

ANGIE: Why?

TACO: Yeah. Why?

ANGIE: Is that all you can think of to say at a time like this?

TACO: Well, excuse me, but I think that "why" is a valid question. Now and always.

ANGIE: Shoot or be shot!

TACO: What?

ANGIE: Heat of the moment. It's a snake! Anyway, those were my instructions.

TACO: Instructions? From who?

ANGIE: Or what?

TACO: Okay, now you're losing me. Did you get brainwashed?

ANGIE: Possibly. Possibly.

TACO: Were you told to kill anyone else?

ANGIE: What? No--You chicken.

TACO: Hey! You can't be to careful in these last days.

ANGIE: "These last days". Are you sure you aren't brainwashed?

TACO: Yeah. My brain is much too gummed up to have been washed.

Angie: Don't joke about this.

TACO: I'm not!

ANGIE: Well, now what?

TACO: Life in prison?

ANGIE: Very funny.

TACO: Let's back this all up.

ANGIE: Okay.

TACO: All right. Who did you kill?

ANGIE: I don't know! She looked familiar, but....

TACO: So, you killed someone of the female persuasion.

ANGIE: Yes.

TACO: You sure about that?

ANGIE: Of course I'm sure!

TACO: Well, you haven't been very sure of anything else.

ANGIE: (a slight growl)

TACO: Are you sure you actually killed her?

ANGIE: Well, I shot her. Several times. Then I ran.

TACO: But she wasn't dead when you left?

ANGIE: No. She was still talking. Shouting actually.

TACO: Then she wasn't and may not be dead. Where's the gun?

ANGIE: That's a good question. It's gone.

TACO: So you threw it away.

ANGIE: No. It just disappeared.

TACO: What?

ANGIE: Well, I was running along and then I had this snake in my hand and I flung it into some cactus. I never looked back.

TACO: Are you trying to tell me the gun turned into a snake?

ANGIE: I never said that!

TACO: Not in so many words, but, well, it's implied.

ANGIE: Only by you!

TACO: Calm down.

ANGIE: Why? I just killed someone.

TACO: Maybe. Take me back to where it happened.

ANGIE: How did I know you were going to say that? *(sigh)* Let's go. *(They exit out door)*

CURTAIN OPEN

SURVIVA: I don't know why I put myself through this. You take them in, try to show them the ropes, and then they turn on you.

MIAMI: But he didn't do anything.

SURVIVA: He left!

MIAMI: And someone came and shot you.

SURVIVA: That friend of his. From the beginning.

MIAMI: But you aren't shot.

SURVIVA: But I was!

MIAMI: In your dreams.

SURVIVA: Don't sass me, Miami!

MIAMI: Hey! I'm not the one with no bullet holes claiming they were shot dead. Maybe you were dreaming.

(Enter Paloma)

Theatre of
the Silver Dragon
P.O. Box 171
Stillwater ME 04489-0171

29

PALOMA: And it turned bad.

SURVIVA: I prefer to think of this as a miracle of these last days.

PALOMA: That's my girl.

(Enter Mr.)

MR: There you are. Haven't you done enough meddling for one millennium?

PALOMA: But this one is almost over. And the end is always the most exciting part. I just want it to go out with a bang!

MR: Very unfunny.

PALOMA: You need to loosen up.

MR: Coming from you, I take that with a grain of salt. *(Takes shaker out of his pocket , pours in hand and swallows).*

SURVIVA: Do you hear something?

MIAMI: The wind in the trees?

SURVIVA: The rumblings of betrayal.

MIAMI: In your dreams.

SURVIVA: I'm indesctuctable.

MIAMI: I'm leaving.

(She starts to go. In run Taco and Angie)

MIAMI: Trust me on this. You're heading the wrong way.

SURVIVA: Traitor! Killer!

ANGIE: She's not dead!

TACO: You shot Surviva?

ANGIE: Who?

TACO: Her!

SURVIVA: Yes, she shot me. You abandonned ship, and she came and shot me. Now what does that say about you, Mr. Loyalty?

TACO: I knew when to get out of a bad relationship?

ANGIE: You know her?

TACO: She's the fruitcake from the beginning.

ANGIE: Oh, yeah.

SURVIVA: And he's the traitor from the middle.

ANGIE: I thought I shot you.

SURVIVA: So did I. Will miracles never cease!

ANGIE: I'm so glad you aren't dead.

SURVIVA: Oh, really?

ANGIE: Yes. Shooting people is totally uncool.

MIAMI: You sure about that? Give youself another five minutes before you make that decision.

Theatre of
the Silver Dragon
P.O. Box 171
Stillwater, ME 04489-0171

31

SURVIVA: Butt out, Miami. Well, then why did you shoot me in the first place!?

ANGIE: I was hearing voices.

SURVIVA: Now tell me who's the fruitcake.

MIAMI: Give her a break Surviva, she's probably been out in the sun too long. Haven't we all?

ANGIE: What happened to my guide?

TACO: Your guide?

ANGIE: She told me to get on that bus --

MIAMI: What bus?

ANGIE: The bus that leads Nowhere.

MIAMI: Oh, that bus.

TACO: What?

SURVIVA: There's something going on here that I don't understand!

MIAMI: What else is new?

SURVIVA: YARRRRRRRR!

TACO: I don't know what you were so worried about Angie, she's too mean to kill.

SURVIVA: I am not "mean". I am a survivor.

Theatre of
the Silver Dragon
P.O. Box 171
Stillwater, ME 04489-0171

MIAMI: But you are pretty wound up about it.

SURVIVA: Y2K man, head for the hills! We're getting distracted! The End of Time is at hand.

MIAMI: She's back in form.

TACO: I'm getting out of here, before she makes us do "the drill".

SURVIVA: First! The manifesto!

TACO: That's my cue. *(exits)*

MIAMI: I'm right behind you. *(exits)*

PALOMA: And the last bus leaves... *(screech)* Now! *(honking)* Shouldn't you be leaving?

ANGIE: No, thanks, I'll walk this time. *(exits)*

PALOMA: Same difference.

MR: I hate that expression. And it is not. She chose her way, not your way.

PALOMA: We have to give them that.

MR: And I keep asking "why". Why do we have to let them make all these mistakes?

PALOMA: They'll never learn anything if you carry them all the way.

MR: But all the meaningless destruction.

PALOMA: And scrapped knees.

MR: Hooked up with you for eternity!

PALOMA: Hey! I keep life interesting.

MR: Yes, and I keep it from coming unglued.

PALOMA: *(in his face)* ORDER!!!

MR: *(back at her)* CHAOS!!!

(They both sigh)

MR: Sorry, I just had to get that out of my system.

PALOMA: I know. Shall we continue.

MR: What else would we do? *(She blows a kiss to the audience and exits)* Every day until the End of Time.

MIAMI: *(off)* Supply the demand!

ANGIE: *(off)* I just want it to be spring 2000 and for all of this to just be over.

TACO: Whatever.

SURVIVA: YARRRRRR!

MR: *(sighs) (Takes out pocket watch and cleans glass.)* 98, 99... *(clears throat.) (Alarm clock, Silence. Gong.)* 00. *(sound of champagne cork popping)*

(Blackout)

✶ FIN ✶

(Light up)

> Enter Cast for a reprise of "The Apocaly

Theatre of
the Silver Dragon
P.O. Box 171
Stillwater, ME 04489-0171

The Theatre of the Silver Dragon

Presents

BORDERLINE
by

Tamela Glenn
1998

A LOOK AT ISSUES ADOLESCENTS MAY EXPERIENCE
-SERIOUS & SYMPATHETIC-

"I created these characters as disorders," says Glenn. "And they have grown into people." Then with a gentle wave of humor: "Now I'd like to rediagnose some of them."

Characters

CHLOE: delusional, fairytale characters
REBOP: Aggresion Disorder
JERSEY: Obsessive Compulsive disorder
VAL: Attempted Suicide (pills)
FRANK: Teenage alcoholic
FERN: Anorexic
LIZ: Seizure Disorder (like Van Gogh)
LULU: Sensitive artist
CLINT: Sociopath
MICHELLE: Multiple Personality Disorder
ROSE: Bi-Polar Disorder (manic depression)
SARA: Schizophrenic
DAN: Delusional, pathological liar.

DOCTOR(s)
NURSE
BLACK FIGURE (s)
WHITE FIGURE
MISS PSYCHOTROPIA 1998
THE LIBERATOR

VOICES

GAME SHOW HOST: ILACK RESPECTKE
CONTESTANTS: CHARLOTTE WEBB
             MIKE MCGUIRE
             JESSICA JONES

TALK SHOW HOST: FRED SNAPPLE
PANEL: DR. JACK DUCHAMP
       DR. ROBERT ST. CLAIR
       DR. WILMA WALKENS
       WIND SANDS

DSM 4: The Diagnostic and Statistical Manual of Mental Disorders, published by the American Psychiatric Association, offers a common language and standard criteria for the classification of mental disorders. (Portions are used in the play)

CROSSING THE BORDERLINE

Theatre of
the Silver Dragon
P.O. Box 171
Stillwater, ME 04489-0171

(Blackout. Curtain Opens on the boxes. Actors are in their boxes. Song: "**LAY YOUR HANDS ON ME**" by Peter Gabriel. Actors slowly come out of boxes --as choreagraphed. Person in bright white lab coat--a doctor enters--as choreaographed. Song ends with actors scurrying back to and into their boxes. Spot on Doctor, which fades.)

CHLOE: (Popping up) " I'm Little Bo Peep, I've lost my sheep! I don't know where to find them!

VOICE : "Leave them alone,and they will come home. Wagging their tails behind them.

CHLOE: Who said that? Oh. Oh no! I'm hearing voices again. (ducks down)

REBOP: (up in box) This place is nowhere, man. I've lived all over. Four foster homes before I was twelve. And this is the worst. Or close to it. The McGillicutty's was pretty horrid. Yeah, I know a few of those hoity-toity words. My fifth grade teacher said I was gifted. She said I had potential. So now, I'm sixteen. Do I still have potential? The doc here says I'm potentially violent. A crime ready to happen. Overly aggressive. Me? I think I suffer from poor primary caregiver syndrome. Let them stuff that one into their big DSM IV manual! (ducks down)

JERSEY: (rises up in box) When I was a little boy, It started. And it's just gotten worse over time. At first, I just had to not step on cracks. Stuff like that. If I stepped on a crack, well, I'd freak. I made up these rituals. It was like magic. I had to undo negative stuff. Doctors used to say it was all about control. Now they say it's in my head. Literally. Something wired wrong in my brain. A chemical or a nerve or something that keeps telling me I have to avoid this and repeat that. And germs. I worry a lot about germs. I wash my hands a lot. A lot. I have to. Sometimes they bleed and that's not good, 'cause more germs could get in. So I have to wash them again. I have to. Now. (ducks down)

VALERIE: (rising) I didn't plan it. They always think you planned it all out. I guess some people do. Well, I didn't. Maybe the ones who succeed do. I'm glad I didn't die. I had been depressed, I guess. I

\

wasn't happy that's for sure. One afternoon, I was walking home from school when I just thought, why not? So, when I got home I went straight to my mother's room and got her valium--she's going through a hard time since Dad left--and I swallowed all the pills in the bottle. I didn't know that Valium is hard to OD on. Calms you down, but won't turn you off completely. That's funny. Getting my stomach pumped was no picnic. I don't remember the actual, well pumping, just waking up and realizing I wasn't dead, but my throat sure hurt. Then they told me I'd have to come here for a while. For observation. I just want to go home. (sitting back down)

POEM

FRANK: (gets up in box stretches. Climbs out and goes downstage.) I don't belong here. Okay, so maybe I broke the law. Sort of. Yeah, sort of. But why put me here?

VOICE 2: Because you were a minor.

VOICE 3: Because we had this option.

FRANK: That's what **they** say. I'd have preferred jail.

VOICE 2: That's what you say now.

VOICE 3: In prison, they wouldn't have helped you with...The Problem.

FRANK: "The Problem", she says. She can't even say it. Drinking.

VOICE 4: You're an alcoholic.

FRANK: No, I'm not.

VOICE 5: Denial is a--

FRANK: Spare me the alcoholic rap sheet.

VOICE 1: Whatever you say, Frank.

FRANK: Yeah, well, that's what I say so you can all shut up. (Silence) (to audience) A person can't say he is what he isn't, right? (pause) My friend Matt is really cool. He's twenty five. I met him at this concert last year, and we started hanging out once in a while. On the weekends. He's building this killer hot rod. It's an old 'vette body with a mega engine. An aluminium 427. Super-charged. 500 Horsepower. Man can that machine sing! Mostly, I'd just hand him tools. Matt's a perfectionist. He Likes to do the work himself. That way it gets done right, he says. He's a way cool guy. Maybe a little edgy. Once in a while. But that's cool. We'd work on the car, go out and open her up on the backroads. Have a bud or two. That's what Matt likes: Budwesier. He says it's the King of Beers. Me, I never drank enough to know whether it was king or not, it just made me feel good.

VOICE: 5: Do you feel good now, Frank?

FRANK: I thought **you** were going to shut up.

VOICE 1: Fine, Frank. You just carry on.

FRANK: So one night, a week ago, major meltdown.

VOICE 2: I didn't raise him up to pull this kind of stunt.

VOICE 3: Arrested! Armed robbery!?

FRANK: That car of Matt's, well, it cost a lot of money to keep her up. So one night Matt asked me to help him out on a little job. That's the way he put it--"a little job". We'd had a few beers.

VOICE 5: How many?

FRANK: Now **you**, I told to shut up!

(Silence)

FRANK: Okay, so, I'm driving the car. Matt's got a gun, and he goes in to hit the register. All I gotta do is drive, right?

VOICE 1: He let you drive his car?

FRANK: What is it with you people! Yes, he let me drive.

VOICE 2: You don't even have a license.

FRANK: Quiet! (pause) Guess he didn't have a choice. He sure wasn't going to give me the gun. Anyway, he got the money. We drove off. A mile or so later, Matt took over the driving. I thought, hey

3

this is cool. $750 bucks. He gave me a C note. We had a couple more beers. Then the cops showed up. They ID'ed the car. Then Matt. Then he ratted me out.

VOICE 5: But the gun wasn't loaded was it?

FRANK: Yes, as a matter of fact, it was. **That** was scary. I mean what if...--?

VOICES: What if? What if? Whattttt????

VOICE 1: Well, **you** certainly were loaded.

FRANK: Lighten up, man. I told you, we'd had a couple of beers.

VOICE 5: And then a couple more. How many in all, **that** night?

FRANK: Who cares!? (silence) Eight. So what?

VOICE 1: And the night before?

FRANK: Just stop it. I don't belong here! (Turns and stalks back to box and gets in it.)

(Enter Fern to Centerstage. Negative self enters stage left. Ideal self enters stage right. They will slowly creep in on her)

FERN: They think I don't know. I do. I'm too thin. So what? I have the right to do what I want with this body. It's mine! I want to starve myself to the bones. To see what remains. I wish I was all spirit. (pause) I hate this thing, my body. It's heavy. It holds me down. (Neg.Self takes her arm) I want to be like that! (She reaches for her ideal self, but can't quite reach it) Perfection! Nothing less! I'll never achieve it. And that is tearing me apart. (Ideal self grabs other arm. They pull her back and forth) It's a struggle. Life and death. I won't be less than perfect! (She breaks their grasps. Realizes she's alone. Panics and flees.)

BLACKOUT

(Four chairs are brought out in blackout)

4

PANEL OF EXPERTS

FRED: Good evening. I'm Fred Snapple and I'd like to welcome you to another episode of "The Mind at Play". Our topic tonight is mental illness. A debate is raging. Is mental illness caused by brain malfuncions or by the environment. Can we cure all mental illnesses with drugs. Recently, shock therapy has made a comeback in the treatment of depression. Everyone has an opinion. Many think they have **the** answer. Joining us tonight are psychiatrist Dr. Jack Duchamp, psychologist Dr. Robert St. Clair, historian Dr. Wilma Walkens and New Age healer Wind Sands. (They enter as called) So in this debate of nature vs. nurture, pills vs. talk therapy, who would like to be first to set someone's teeth on edge!

JACK: I'll be glad to start. As everyone here is aware, I'm a firm believer in the theory that all mental illness is caused by changes in the brain and can be remedied either by drugs or surgery. Talk therapy is a complete waste of time in most cases.

ROBERT: What about the evidence that most cases of Multiple Personality can be traced to severe childhood abuse!

JACK: Yes, well, what makes this person multiply and that one stay united as one.

FRED: Talk for a minute, if you will, Dr. Walkens about the history of mental illness and its treatment.

WILMA: Of course, Fred. In a few sentences, let's see. Mental illness was once thought to be caused by demons which possessed people and caused them to use foul language and do violent things. Exorcisms were performed to get rid of these forces. This wasn't just in Catholics. African tribes, etc., have their own possession cases. Along with the rise of science and fall of religion as the dominate force in our society--though some might argue that science is a kind of religion--came Freud and his theories on hysteria, the id, ego, and superego. While we still hold that a lot of what he said is good thinking, it is hard to deny that the man got a little carried away and tended to blame everything on sex and, well, he was definitely a woman hater.

ROBERT: I beg your pardon!

WILMA: Anyway, for a while It was thought that there was some key to a patient's illness, and that you could find it through talk therapy, psychoanalysis, etc. Then when the patient understood, whatever, they were cured.

ROBERT: That is a gross oversimplification of things!

FRED: Of course it is. We only have an hour here, you know.

WILMA: Now, they think that biology holds the key. Broken brain equals sociopath. Bad childhood leads to chemical changes in the brain that may or may not be reversible. Anyway, it sure is making the drug manufacturers happy.

FRED: Before we open this up to debate, go ahead and throw in your two cents Ms. Sands.

WIND: Mankind is out of harmony with the natural world. Until balance is restored we will see more and more so-called mental illness. It is the soul that is afflicted.

WILMA: So we're back to square one. New Age possession. And like everything modern, it's abstract.

BLACKOUT

(LIGHTS UP. Song "I HAVE THE TOUCH)

BLACKOUT
(boxes back in)

6

LIZ: (up in box) So there I was about to throw in the towel. I'd been called everything from a neurotic to a psychotic and then it turned out I have a seizure disorder. No, I don't drop down and foam at the mouth. see, if your brain gets scarred on one side you hear voices and stuff--like a schizo--and if your brain scarred on the otherside you're more emotionally volatile, prone to anxiety--like me. how does the brain get scarred, I know you're wondering. Lots of ways. A difficult birth. Too long in the birth canal--the brain gets scarrd from lack of oxygen. A blow to the head or too many blows to the head-- this is starting to show up in jockeys and fooball players. Of course, not everyone who gets whacked o the head ends up like me. Why not? Is a good question. It's the Van Gogh thing. Man, that poor guy got tagged everything in the book, too. He's my hero. Of course look how he eneded up. Miserable. Poor. Or was he? Miserable? He saw things like nobody else. Those paintings. They're incredible. All because of a scar on the brain? Well, I don't paint like Van Gogh. What makes one brain-scarred person a genius and another a hopeless mental patient? Of course, he was kind of hopeless. If it hadn't been for his brother, Theo, where would he have been? I take good pictures. When I get out of here, maybe I'll do more. Who knows? (ducks down)

CLINT: (up in box) They'd all like me to say I'm sorry. Okay, everyone, I'm sorry. Not. They shake their heads and seem so concerned. "He has no conscience". I see it this way. I do what I have to for the forward movement of me. Clint. People are weak and easy prey. (ducks back down)

DOCTOR (enters and reads DSM IV definition of sociopath)

CLINT: (in box laughs)

LULU: (up in box) A writer can use experiences. This place is another experience. I hadn't slept more than six hours in three days. I was onto something. I took longs walks. The moon was full. you could see without a flashlight. It was amazing. I thought that if I walked long enough I would get it. What exactly, I had no idea. But it was there, waiting to be had. This insight. This--I can't put it into words! I just kept walking. i was reading this book--and this is embarrassing, but it was "Zen and the Art of Motorcycle Maintenance." And it was great. I

7

always hate it when a super popular book turns out to be great. it seems like greatness is only supposed to be graspable by the great. Well, that's certainly came out elitist, didn't it? Sorry. Well, I came i from this ten mile hike, walked into the bathroom, looked in the mirror above the sink and POW! I got it! (Pause) i feel over backwards and then I blacked out and then I woke up, here. Mom and Dad felt I needed a little observation. Me, i feel like i know something i never know before. And it can't be taken away in here. Or anywhere. (down)

Blackout

(3 chair in)

IN JEOPARDY

(Enter Game Show host)

HOST: Greetings! I'm Ilack Respeckte, and welcome to "In Jeopardy". Let's welcome tonight's contestants.

(Enter three contestants.)

HOST: From Walla Walla, Washington, we have Charlotte Webb. (applause.) Tell us about yourself Charlotte.

CHARLOTTE: Well, Ilack, I'm a schoolteacher and mother of two. I t love horses and watering my gernaniums.

HOST: Great. Wonderful! Nice. And next, from Detroit, Michigan, meet Mike Mcguire. And who are you Mike?

MIKE: I'm Mike. I work on the assembly line of the--can I say the name of the car company?

HOST: No, you may not. We went over that in rehearsal, remember?

MIKE: Just checking. Well, I work on the assembly line of a major car company. I like surf and turf food. I'm single and I'd like to stay that way.

HOST: Ohhh-kay. And finally, meet Jessica Jones from Orlando, Florida. Now who are you, Jessica?

JESSICA: I illustrate children's books. I love sunshine, my Persian cats, Pause and Clause--that's P-A-U-S-E and C-L-A-U-S-E.

HOST: How clever.

JESSICA: And I adore alligator watching.

HOST: Alligator watching?

JESSICA: Yes. They're amazing reptiles. My sister has one living in her backyard, which is--for all intents and purposes, a swamp.

HOST: Nice. Wonderful! Great. Now Charlotte, you won the draw to start first, so pick a category.

CHARLOTTE: Okay. How about Mental Illness for $2oo?

HOST: A mental Illness involving periods of elation followed by periods of despair.

BUZZER

CHARLOTTE: What is manic-depression?

HOST: Close, but no cigar!

BUZZER

JESSICA: What is by bipolar disorder?

HOST: Correct!

CHARLOTTE: But!

HOST: They changed the name, sweatheart. Jessica!

JESSICA: Mental Illness for $500!

HOST: A word that means both a detached mental state and a musical composition.

BUZZER

CHARLOTTE: What is "The Blues"?

HOST: Wrong!

BUZZER

MIKE: What is "Funk"?

HOST: Wrong again!

BUZZER

HOST: Jessica!

JESSICA: What is a fugue?

HOST: Right again, Jessica!

JESSICA: Mental Illness for $1000!

HOST: A condition who's name literally means fear of the marketplace.

BUZZER

CHARLOTTE: What is shopophobia!

HOST: Wrong!

BUZZER

MIKE: What is Arachnaphobia!

HOST: That's fear of spiders! Jessica?

JESSICA: I have no idea.

HOST: Agoraphobia! (They all freeze)

(Joan turns her box over. We can see her, but she doesn't come out.)

DOCTOR: (Enters and reads from DSM IV, definition of agoraphbia)

JOAN: That's easy for him/her to read.

VOICES: (whispering)

JOAN: Sometimes it seems like even the walls are alive. Then I have to go into an even smaller space. One I can control. Now I'm here in this place. Where they control me. At least I'm safe. At least I think I am. Safe. (pause. She creeps out of the box towards the audience) I remember the first time it...well... happened. I was at the circus. All the noise. People talking to each other. Hollering. Babies crying. Some guy trying to get everyone to come into this little tent and see the bearded lady and the frog boy. I didn't go in. Just the thought of what I might see made me feel like throwing up my cotton-candy. Then the show in the big tent. Elephants and Tigers. Women twirling fifty feet up in the air by their teeth. And then...the clowns. All that face paint and.. well, I started to feel like I was choking. Everyone was laughing and laughing and they looked so strange--like images in a funhouse mirror. And the clowns! Killer clowns. I got up and started forcing my way out. People looked at me like I was nuts. I thought I was going to die. I stepped on some kid's foot and he started yowling. I didn't care. I had to get out of there. I ran all the way to the car. It was locked. I couldn't find the keys. I sat down on the ground and waited to have a heart attack and die. But I didn't. In a while, I felt more like my normal self. I went home... (Pause as she crawls back to box and stands it up) Then it started happening in stores--the marketplace. Then in restuarants. Then at my friends' houses. Finally, my own house wasn't safe. I couldn't keep it--the fear--out. (She jumps in box.)

BLACKOUT

(The game show people exit.)

(Chairs for Group get set during blackout)

VOICE: Please report to Group, now.

LIGHTS UP

(Eight people are seated in chairs)

SARA: Intestinal protein sandwich dinner.

CLINT: Someone's medication isn't working.

SARA: You Squib!

CLINT: She speaks sheer poetry. Squib. How imaginative.

SARA: The imagination is the key to the soul of the universe. My soul coughs blood. I'm going nowhere fast.

REBOP: If you don't shut up they'll haul you back to your room.

SARA: What?(listening to internal voice) Really? They're all insect robots? So I should run? (listens) Oh, okay. I won't move a muscle. (She becomes catatonic--frozen).

CHLOE: Me? (As if reacting to a therapist's question) I'm just fine. It's these drawves--I can't do a thing with them. Me? I'm Snow White, of course. Don't you recognize me? You don't? Well, I think that as the wicked queen, you should. The drawves? Yyou should know that too! Humor you? Well.....all right. That's Grumpy. Sneezy. Flopsy, Mopsy, Sleepy, Creepy and Dopey. What happend to who? To Doc? You made that up. There never was a Doc. No creepy? I should know the drawves names--I live with them! (Sits down and Silence)

ROSE: I'm terrible, how do you think I am? This medicine makes me feel like a slug. (listens) No, It's not better than being out of control. It's the same thing, only backwards. I'm numb, that's what I am. So pick on someone else for a while.

REBOP: Me? I'm fine. Anyway, I came here, what more do you want? (Listens) Like I said, I came here and that's better than half the losers in this joint. So move on to the next victim..

FERN: Me? I'm doing fine. I want to go home. There's nothing wrong with me. (Quieter and confidentially) These people are nuts.

REBOP: Who are you calling nuts, bone-bag! (Listening) What? Would I like to talk about my anger? What anger! She called me nuts. (listening) Oh, really? Well, tra-la-la to you Doc. Huh? (listens) No, I don't got nuthin' ta say right now, thank you very much.

CLINT: No, I have nothing to say, either. (listening) No, I haven't been thinking about any of that. I've been planning what I'm going to do when I get out of here. (Listens) Guilt? Remorse? I don't know what you're talking about.

JERSEY: Well, Doc, I think the new medication is working. A little. I don't think I'm... Listen, do I really have to talk in front of these people? (Listens) Then I don't want to. It would be different if they had ...well, if they had the same problem.

JOAN: I second that motion. Huh? (listens) No, I don't want to talk about anything. I think I just made that clear!

REBOP: Yeah, like let's outta here. Isn't it time for lunch yet?

VAL: I seriously question how being made to sit down with a bunch of hostile and depressed and generally messed up people is going to help me!

BUZZER

(They stand up to leave)

BLACKOUT

(Two empty chairs. Enter Clint who sits in one)

CLINT: How am I today?() I am fine just like yesterday. () Guilt about the fire? No, I can't say that I have any feelings about that at all. It was a necessary action. () I beg your pardon? () No, I didn't get any kind of enjoyment out of it. I'm not a pyromaniac if that's what you're getting at. () I told you it was a necessity.() My parents? () No, I don't care if they are upset or disappointed or whatever. Things happened. Can't we stop harping about the past? () Conscience? () Of course I know what that is. What are you getting at? () Why develop something I don't need? I have plans. A Conscience and guilt-- whatever that is--are things I don't need. They're your problems, not mine. (He exits)

(Enter Jersey)

JERSEY: I'm sorry, but I just didn't feel like talking about it in group today. All those weirdos. They'd just laugh. And that guy, Rebop. What a supercreep. () Okay, that's what you think. Listen, if you put me in a group of other people with OCD, I'll talk. Okay? () Yes, I did say I thought the new med was working. Sorry, I lied. I just didn't want all those people judging me like I judge them. At least I want to get better. That's more than I can say for half the people in here. (exits)

(Enter Michelle with personality of Beth active)

MICH: I really don't see why we have to be here? () Yeah, tell me about it. How would you like to live in a body with ten other people? () No, I will not let Michelle out to talk to you. She couldn't handle this. () Me? I'm Beth, remember me? I'm the one who plays hardball. () Tell you about the others? Why? () Don't make me laugh. I've got the situation under control. () Oh, please. () You want to talk to someone more reasonable. Forget it. Listen, I run the joint, got it? () Good. Hypnosis? Don't threaten me. We're not going to let you get your hands on Michelle, so forget it! () Why am I angry? () I've been guarding the fort forever. () I'm the oldest. I'm the one who got Michelle through high school, and I'm the one who'll get her through

College. () You want to talk to who? () (Peggy comes out. She is quiet and not hostile) Hello. () Yes, It me, Peggy. () No, I'm afraid I can't let Michelle come out. Beth would kill me. () I think you underestimate Beth. She just told me she'd break my legs if I don't let her come out ()(Beth comes back) Oh, shut up! () Yes, it's me again. Now I'm taking us all out of here. (exit)

(Enter Chloe)

CHLOE: You decided what? () You're diagnosing me with borderline personality disorder? () How dare you! () Yes, I'm angry! You know you aren't supposed to use that for adolescents. We're **supposed** to be trying to figure out who we are! () Oh, please. How come they always tag that on women. Typical. "She's a woman. She can't make up her little mind." How scientific! Listen to this Doc: you're a neo freudian loser! (exit)

(Enter LuLu)

LULU: How am I feeling?() Angry at my parents a little. I could be out in the sun and wind, walking. But everything is an experience, right? () I'm keeping a journal.() Therapeutic? () I never thought of it that way. I write to remember and to reflect. How about you?() Sorry.() Right. I'm the patient, you're the doctor. Got it.() The bathroom? () Yeah, that was something! () No, I'm sorry. I can't talk about that. () No, I'm not being hostile. It's not translatable. That's all. (exits)

(Enter Dan)

DAN: Why do we always have to talk about lying? () And the checks. If you intend to charge me with a crime do it, officer. If not, then let me go! () Okay, I'll indulge you. My parents took me off their credit cards. I needed money. () Tickets to Hawaii, of course () For the Ironman Triathalon. () No. To compete. The latest in my series of physical challenges. I'm a world class athlete, you know. () What do you mean do I really believe that? Look at me! () I'm what? () Oh, really? Well, you know what I think? () **You're** delusional! (exits)

(Enter Liz)

LIZ: So after two years of being told I had post traumatic stress disorder, now I have Temporal Lobe epilepsy. The right seizure control drug and I'm a new person. () Angry? No, I'm more relieved I

15

guess. A little afraid I'll wake up tomorrow and get called something else.() I guess you're right. Not a new person. Me again. Or almost. (exits)

FERN: Yes, I understand why I'm here. My parents were worried about me. () Yes, I know why. () Because they think I'm too thin. () Am I ? () Will I get out of here any faster if I say yes? () Of course I won't mean it. Anyway, this is my body. I have rights! () Well, what about when I'm over eighteen? () Why don't you people do something that means something! () I thought you were the Doctor? () Why shouldn't I be hostile, I'm a hostage. Notice the similairty in those words? Hostile. Hostage. And you're the host. H-O-S-T. () Yeah, I got it. If I want out I've got to gain 15 pounds. What a joke! You just handed me a life sentence. (exits)

(Enter Val)

VAL: Why? Everyone always asks, why? Why did she do it? I say, why not? When you think about it, Doc, it's amazing more people don't try to leap of the planet. () Whatever. The way I look at it now, I don't know what happens after death--I mean I figure something does, because we came from somewhere so...() Oh, I was just going to say that I figure I'll stick it out. () My life. This may be the only time I get to be here, so I'll just go along for the ride. Until the next stage of whatever this is all about. (Exits)

(Enter Rose)

ROSE: No, I don't like my new medication. I want to get out of here and go home and paint! () Yes, I understand why my parents thought I needed to come here.() No, I don't agree with them. () Okay, so I was "out-of-control" By **your** definition. I felt great. () This is what? () Functional! You call this functional? I feel like a zombie. () Like I believe that! (exits)

VOICE: Your body will adjust to the new medication.

VOICE 2: Time for your meds!

(A line forms. A Nurse hands out a pill and a cup, and checks all patients--They go "Ah")

16

(Enter Miss Psychotropia 1998.)

VOICE: And now, please welcome Miss Psychotropia1998!

APPLAUSE

Miss Psych: I'm the new pill. The new thrill. Forget prosac! I make it obsolete. I go boldly where no pill has gone before. I'm good for all afflications. I can cure multiple personality disorder **and** cancer at a single pound.

VOICE 2: Cancer?

MISS PSYCH: One of my many many many side effects is delusional thinking!

VOICE 3: Oh.

MISS PSYCh: Oh! Indeed. Now just open up and say AH!

VOICES: AHHHHHHHHHHHHHHHHHHHH.

BLACKOUT

(Chairs are removed during blackout. Boxes are pulled back into position.)

ROSE: (standing up in her box. Climbs out and moves downstage during monologue) One night I was painting. I'd been at it for hours. Days maybe. I didn't sleep. I didn't eat. I felt connected to everything. But mostly to my painting. Suddenly out of the blue I got this idea. Why not paint my room? I don't mean like change the color. I decided to paint a reproduction of Leonardo Da Vinci's "Last Supper" on one wall and Michelangelo's " The Creation of Man" on the ceiling. When that was done. Days. Weeks--I don't remember--I decided to paint the outside of my parents' house. I decided to do it like Jackson Pollack. Abstract action painting. It was glorious. The paint. Flying and drippig. Then, eventually, I maxed out my parents' account at the hardware store on paint. That's when they.....stopped me.

VOICE: Were straight-jackets involved?

VOICE 2: Who needs straight-jackets when you have tranqs?

(Miss Psychotropia whirls through) They come with me oh so willingly!

ROSE: They say I'm bi-polar, which is a fancy name for good old manic depression. Can you see Jimi Hendrix writing a song about that? It sounds like some kind of science project about magnets. Right now I feel just depressed. I miss the thrill. I want to feel the way I used to. I can't create this way.

VOICE: Your body will adjust to the drug.

ROSE: (going and getting back in her box) That's what **you** say.

(ENTER DOCTOR. Reads from DSM IV about bipolar disorder)

(Chloe rises)

CHLOE: I don't know how much longer I can take it. My ugly stepsisters are unbearable. Where's a handsome prince with a glass slipper when you need him?

VOICE: So now you're Cinderella?

CHLOE: Of course I'm Cinderella.

VOICE: But last night, you were Little Red Riding Hood.

CHLOE: You must be joking!

VOICE: So is she multiple?

DOCTOR: (reads definition of Multiple Personality Disorder from the DSM-IV and then exits)

CHLOE: If he doesn't come soon, I'll turn into--

VOICE: Sleeping Beauty?

CHLOE: Now, there's a thought! (goes down)

DAN: (up in box) I came here voluntarily.

VOICES: Liar!

DAN: Well, I did. I needed a rest. Life can be so exhausting. Last year I climbed Mount Everest. I was the only one in my team that made it. This year I represented our country in the Summer Olympics. I won not only the gold medal in the marathon, but three different swimming events. I just signed an exclusive deal with Nike to represent their company. I'm filming my first comercial for them next week and I have to shoot print ads which will run in every magazine from Spin to Sports Illustrated!

VOICE: What about the checks?

DAN: Well, the amount of money I'll be paid is staggering!

VOICE 2: Not those. The ones you forged.

DAN: What? What are you suggesting?

VOICE 3: That you are a liar. A pathological one.

DAN: I am not. It's just amplification. Reality is so boring. It's like the business of advertising. Making things seem more appealing. I say what should be. What I want to be.

VOICE: And the checks?

DAN: There were things needed. It was a tactical necessity.

VOICE 2: We warned him.

VOICE 3: It was jail or...

VOICES: This place.

DAN: I really have no idea what you're talking about. (gets back in box)

19

THE WARD--Living Large

(Lulu is sitting by herself writing in a journal. She makes note of things that interest her. Other characters can attempt to talk to her.)

REBOP: Why don't you just blow it out your nose!

VOICE : Are you talking to me, Rebop?

REBOP: I'm talking to the whole lot of youse!

VOICE : You sound hostile? Are you upset?

REBOP: Of course I'm "upset"! I'm in here aren't I! I'm sixteen years old and I'm stuck in looney toons! (Stalks off and around. Improv. by actor in character. Muttering to self, etc.

CHLOE: (walking cautiously, watching Rebop) My, my, I'm glad he's gone. Big Bad Wolf-boy! Now if I can only get this bag of goodies to Grandma's, everything will be all right.

VOICE: Are you going somewhere, Chloe?

CHLOE: Yes. No!

VOICE: She thinks she's Little Red Riding Hood, again.

VOICE 2: Do you really think she does?

CHLOE: They think they're so smart. How hard was that to figure out? I'm wearing a red cape with a hood!

VOICE: You are?

CHLOE: (Feeling her head. looking at her arms.) I was! I was! You stole it! Help! I've been robbed! (runs and rocks in a corner)

ReBOP: Help me! I've fallen and I can't get up! Blah! Blah! Blah!
                              (menacing her)
               Little Miss Muffet. Sat on her tuffet.
               Eating her curds and Whey.
               Along came a spider and sat down beside her.
               And said What a good boy am I! (he sits by her)

CHLOE: (jumps up) That's not right. You mixed that, messed that up!

REBOP: So what? Scaredy cat.

CHLOE: It didn't even rhyme, you moron!

REBOP: oooh.

FRANK: Listen you bonehead, why don't you leave her alone?

REBOP: Why should I?

FRANK: First 'cause she's nuts and even firster because she's an easy target. And more important, 'cause I said so.

REBOP: Who died and made you boss?

FRANK: Only a chump picks on the weak.

REBOP: Okay, so how's about I wail on you, you putz!

FRANK: Let's get down to it, moron. (They square off)

BUZZER

VOICE : Security to the Ward. Security to the Ward.

FRANK: Terrific. Here comes the tranq squad..

REBOP: Hey, we was only having some fun. Look (puts up hands) I'm clean.

VOICE: Security cancelled. Frank report to therapy.

REBOP: I hope you get electroshock, you cretin.

FRANK: He called me a cretin. I'm crushed. That's a pretty big word for you, you weenie. (exits)

(Enter Rose, manic)

ROSE: First we start in the lobby. We knock out the south wall and build a solarium. Then add sky lights in here. (she reaches up for imagined light. Basks in it.) That would...Yeah! Yeah! That would be exquisite. I want to paint this whole ward with murals in the style of Henri Rousseau Thick green jungle. Thick! Thick! Green! (She runs about wildly)

VOICE: Someone is certainly manic today.

VOICE: How do you feel, Rose?

ROSE: Fine. Great! Wonderful! Like myself. The self I like to be. Free! Wild! Free!

VOICES: In here?

ROSE: You can't take me away from me!

JERSEY: (who has entered) They can with the right medication.

ROSE: Kill-joy! (She darts about as if planning her renovations.)

VOICE: How are you doing, Jersey?

JERSEY: Well, personally, I think I would be a lot better off at home at this point. This place gives me the creeps. (Walks off examining hands for germs)

(Enter Joan)

VOICE: Joan. It's nice to see you on the ward.

JOAN: Ah! (startled) Why do you do that?

VOICE: Because we care about you. It's been weeks since you felt able to come out into the Free Room. We're pleased.

JOAN: Well, goody for you. Keep up the disembodied voice-thing and I'll be right back in my room.

VOICE: We can follow you there, too.

JOAN: Are you threatening me?

VOICE: Of course not. Just making a point.

JOAN: Listen, I'm not crazy.

VOICE: No one ever said you were.

VOICE 2: Are you afraid you're crazy?

JOAN: Yes! (She retreats into corner)

MICH: How? Where am I? Oh, my--This is a psych ward! (Beth comes out) Peggy, that's what I get letting you go to sleep in command. Feel asleep on the job again! Well, Two strikes and you're out! No, not three. Not in **my** game. Two! Michelle can't handle this place. That's what we're for. So let's do our job. Rachel, think you can handle it for a while? Good. (R. comes out) Beth gets way too wound up about these things.

VOICE: How are you feeling Michelle?

MICH: Never better. (very pleasantly. Calmy strolls about the Ward.)

SARA: (enters followed by figure in black) Stop following me!

VOICE: She's paranoid again.

SARA: They're soooo smart.

*****
VOICE 2: They're poisoning the food.

VOICE 3: They're releasing poison gas into the rooms at night.

VOICE 4: Everyone here is an alien. They're planning to take oer the entire United States, one block at a time.
*****
(Repeat ****** loop three times.

VOICE: I think she's hearing voices, again.

SARA: Everyone in here hears voices. You! Stop following me!!!! (black figure disappears) I wish the whole lot of you alienoids would get off my back. When the end comes--and it will-- I'll escape in a chariot of fire!

VOICE: She's delusional, again.

SARA: I'm not listening to **you** anymore! Poison or no poison I'm going to live. I see what you don't see. Light! I know what you don't

23

know. Light! In everyone. Everyone! There's a little spark of light. Untouched by chaos, sickness, decay, torture, robots, rayguns, chaos, torture, rabies, decay. And this light. This light! Inside everyone. Ev-er-ry ONE! Defeats Oblivion!

LuLu: (looks up from her journal) That's profound. (She writes.)

SARA: This spark--which can neither be created nor detroyed-- defeats oblivion! So none of you can touch me. Inside. And I can't touch you! This spark! Defeats Oblivion! This spark in this dark-- defeats oblivion. Conquers the darkness. I'm moving in light!

BLACKOUT
(Boxes are brought on during blackout)

(Song: "**WALLFLOWER**". Characters will slowly get out of their bloxes and be liberated. Two black figures and The Liberator are involved. Actors make a human chain which will go offstage, down stairs and out doors at the back of the House. left onstage will be the defeated(prone black-clad figures and The Liberator who in kneeling in light. BLACKOUT. Actors will come up fire escape and enter building for curtain call.)

24

ACTING ON THE BORDERLINE

In this original production, written and directed by Tamela Glenn, a theatrical group of Orono, Maine teens, tackled mental illness issues and the changing identities of adolescence.

Tamela, director and founder of *THE THEATRE OF THE SILVER DRAGON*, often conferred with her actors about what part they would like to play in an upcoming performance, and then she would go home and write the play. In this instance, they said they would like to play crazies. "Do you want to play wacky or insane?" They answered, "Insane."

The resulting production covers mental disorders, the people who have them and the doctors who treat them. The play is episodic and in the style of modern drama. In writing the play, Glenn drew on her own interests, extensive readings on mental illness, and experiences as a teen. The play is very pro-patient, but there is some criticism of mental health professionals who use definitions of mental illness too neatly and narrowly to account for the whole person behind the disorder.

-excerpted from an article in *STYLE : ORONO AREA TEEN ACTORS TACKLE MENTAL ILLNESS IN "BORDERLINE"*.

DIAGNOSTIC AND STATISTICAL MANUAL OF MENTAL DISORDERS

FOURTH EDITION

DSM-IV™

American Psychiatric Association

Epilogue

In addition to her work with the *Theatre of the Silver Dragon*, Tamela performed in the *Penobscot Theatre* and *Ten Bucks* production companies, including *Amadeus* in 1995, *Sweeney Todd* in 1996, *A Flea in Her Ear* in 1997, and *Our Town* in 1998. For the *Ten Bucks* production company, she acted in *The Bald Soprano* in 2002 and *Rumors* in 2003, as well as writing and directing several plays for the theater group.

While Tamela performed in serious plays such as *Marat/Sade*, she also had roles in perennial favorites like *Peter Pan, The Music Man and The Fantasticks*.

ALL'S WELL THAT ENDS

The pages of this book were scanned and organized in book form at www.Lulu.com by Jerry Farlow, former Professor of Mathematics at the University of Maine and friend of Betty Glenn, Tamela Glenn's mother. One observation, parenthetical notes on several pages, such as page numbers at the bottom of the pages and other notes penciled in script, are Tamela's own writing, added while working on the plays

THE END